HIGHLIGHTS
* OF THE *
OFF-SEASON

by Peter J. Smith

SIMON AND SCHUSTER * NEW YORK

Copyright © 1986 by Peter J. Smith
All rights reserved
including the right of reproduction
in whole or in part in any form
Published by Simon and Schuster
A Division of Simon & Schuster, Inc.
Simon & Schuster Building
Rockefeller Center
1230 Avenue of the Americas
New York, New York 10020
SIMON AND SCHUSTER and colophon are registered trademarks of Simon & Schuster, Inc.
Manufactured in the United States of America

10 9 8 7 6 5 4 3 2 1

Library of Congress Cataloging-in-Publication Data
Smith, Peter J.
    Highlights of the off-season.
    I. Title.
PS3569.M537912H5   1986   813'.54   86-10196
ISBN: 0-671-62503-9

The author gratefully acknowledges permission to reprint the following:

Lyrics from "Psycho Killer" by David Byrne, Chris Frantz, and Martina Weymouth. Copyright © 1977 Bleu Disque Music & Index Music. All rights reserved. Used by permission.
Lyrics from "Cities" by David Byrne. Copyright © 1979 Bleu Disque Music & Index Music. All rights reserved. Used by permission.
Lyrics from "What A Day That Was" by David Byrne. Copyright © 1981 Bleu Disque Music & Index Music. All rights reserved. Used by permission.
Lyrics from "Sweet Baby James" by James Taylor. Copyright © 1970 Country Road Music Inc. & Blackwood Music Inc. All rights controlled and administered by Blackwood Music Inc. All rights reserved. International Copyright secured. Used by permission.

For A. O. S., A. K. S., K. A. S.

* Chapter 1 *

BEFORE Christmas, I was living with my sister Lucy and going to this private school in North Hollywood, California. It was called the Lane School for Boys. It's a fairly famous place actually, a row of low pink buildings packed along the side of a very steep, quiet, winding road with a Spanish name that no one out there pronounces with anything resembling a Spanish accent. You take the trouble to pronounce a city or a street the right way, rolling your *r*, taking the tap off your *t* and sounding it *d* and people out there stare at you as though you've fallen from the moon or something. The people out there have the worst Spanish accents in the world. There are millions of clay-faced Mexicans in L.A., brawny hearts for faces on the men and long thin beautiful purple arms under white sleeves on the women and you know they say the street names right at home at night in these obscure private ceremonies lit by stubby white votary candles or something, but during the day at least not even the Mexicans seemed to give a damn about sounding authentic. It really annoyed me. Also, just about the only people who went to Lane were the sons of astronauts and second-rate comedians. Just about every astronaut who ever went up into

7

space enrolled his son at Lane. At one point, in May I think it was, the sons of the entire Apollo Twelve mission were on the Lane speech team, opening their mouths so wide and with such care you wanted to stuff something inside, pieces of worn newspaper, vegetables, whatever you were holding. Plus, there was this phalanx of comedians' sons who went around not talking to you. I admit that may have impressed me once, being friends with comedians' sons. Coming out of the East that impresses you even though the kids at Lane weren't even the sons of good comedians, comedians you liked. Marty Kellogg's son was there, to give you an idea of the poor quality of the comedians involved here, so was Sandy Bergman's kid Benjy. Real laugh riots both those guys, I'm spelling that l-a-f-f too. Talk about the losers of yesteryear. They're the kind of comedian who goes on TV and says they're about to play Lake Tahoe, wherever that is, or Las Vegas or you know, the Kahala Hilton in Honolulu, the sorts of places you win trips to rather than ever actually want to go to. If you're lucky you can make it through your life without ever visiting those places. These guys sit there on talk show couches and say things like, You're all very special human beings and isn't that what it's all about, blah, blah, blah, well, I've given up the booze, ha ha ha, one day at a time, ha ha ha, give credit to the man upstairs, ha ha ha, all the comedy is in Washington these days, ha ha ha, hope you'll come up to Tahoe and see me, as though they hadn't set the whole thing up in the first place, and then the audience starts clapping and whistling and stomping. The sons were junior versions of their fathers. I called it the Lane School for Assholes.

Lane was a progressive school, which, in case you don't know the lingo of prep schools, meant you could pretty much do what you wanted so long as no one caught you. It was started up in the late eighteen-hundreds by this bearded guy Jed Lane, who had a whole lot of lime and lemon money and free time, and since he hadn't made it past second grade himself he started this school. He set up the curriculum so that if you got up one morning and you didn't feel particularly like going to class you could go for a swim or shoot baskets in the parking lot or ride horses along the beach, anything you wanted. Supposedly you could do whatever your mood dictated. Even though they were giving you this incredible choice, though, they still expected you to go to classes. It was some psychologically sophisticated system that had been proved on a bunch of blackboards and it seemed to work for most people but it wasn't working all that well for me.

The point is, I wasn't doing extraordinarily well at Lane. For one thing I had stopped going to classes in about mid-November, right before Thanksgiving. I was spending a lot of time perfecting my skyhook at this playground in Santa Monica and since it was one of my worst shots I didn't feel all that guilty devoting time to it. Practically everybody said my getting kicked out of Lane was the start of the disastrous couple of months I had, but I think it was sort of a crazed season for me generally. Everything I did around that time seemed to make me sad for some reason. I would hear about some baby being born and rather than think, Another Life, I'd think, another unprincipled little jerk who'll grow up spray painting the name *Donna* on some highway rocks. Around that time, late December and January, getting born sounded to me like just about the height of opportunism on the kid's part.

One thing was I missed the East a lot. I'm from the East originally, from New York. When I wasn't practicing my skyhook I was at my sister's house on the beach listening to these old Laurie Benoit albums I brought with me from the East. I'd drag the speakers out onto the porch and take off all my clothes and turn on the volume full-blast. In case you've never heard of Laurie Benoit, she's this dead musical comedy star of the thirties and forties. She had a pretty disastrous life. Nobody listens to her at all these days. You go into a record store and look under Benoit and all they have is one

Greatest Hits album for about thirty cents which they've filed under The Dead or Nostalgia or something. There was this one particular live record of Laurie's I kept playing over and over, this concert she recorded when she was making a comeback in the early sixties. She was trying to beat gin and pills so she checked into this gorgeous drying-out hospital in western Massachusetts for some rest and relaxation. It really was an idyllic place to check into, a big white peeling colonial with dark shutters and columns in the front, all gracious and southern-looking and slightly removed from all the action. I went past the place once and there were all these locust pods on the front lawn, hard brown curling things with pounded skin and small loud loose seeds inside them. They looked a little bit like snakes and given the nature of the place I thought it was an incredibly bad idea on someone's part not to rake them up, if only so poor old Laurie wouldn't think baby serpents or something were after her. Otherwise it was a pretty sterling place. Laurie spent about nine months there with all these private-school kids with their brown guitars and their lousy voices and these straw-haired women whose Augusts in Maine or Sagaponack had just about done them in, and then she went out on a sixty-city tour and just about slaughtered everybody.

I was living with Lucy out in Malibu, which is this ritzy, lit-up hunch of beach and brush just north of L.A. My sister's pretty famous, at least she is in the U.S. She has a television show on Tuesday nights from ten to eleven in which she plays this outspoken nun detective, Sister Kate, which is also the name of the show. It's a terrible show but it's in its sixth season and it's popular as hell. My sister's good in it but that's the only reason you'd ever want to watch it. In case you've never been up there, Malibu runs along the coast about a hundred yards up from the waves, under swingsets and steel saguaros painted yellow and light blue, past psychic parlors and surfboard shops and bars and one-bedroom bungalows with paint flaking off their windows and slim gardens down in front, charred dirt all slit up with broken green glass and weeds and pink flowers. There are cement benches all over the place and a huge spinning sign on top of Pacifica Pancakes that says, Los Angeles, Dynamic Empire of the West. Down on the beach you get smells the wind's tried to chase across the water looping back at you: gas, tortillas, fish frying, abalone, horse leather, suntan lotion, flan, smoke and mussels. When the red sun goes down behind rough smoking clouds early in the winter you can see the soft cotton strings of a hundred volleyball nets up and down the beach and the palm trees with their bright dirty leaves fencing with TV antennas for space. My sister lives in a fairly snobbish part of Malibu, though, about three miles north of the nearest volleyball net, where it's all fences and garages and wire. Her house is even on the Malibu Movie Stars Homes map. I mean, if you have one in front of you she's number thirty-two, at the end of Zumirez Road. She doesn't live there anymore though.

I guess what started everything was my father coming out to Los Angeles unexpectedly on Awards Day, which was held on the last Saturday before the Christmas break. I decided to go to the ceremony even though I knew I wouldn't be coming back in January. They had asked me in a pretty civil way that I not return to Lane after the New Year. The headmaster let me know that if I came back there would be so many restrictions on me that I wouldn't be able to make a move without someone marking it down in a tablet, so I was feeling depressed about that. Also I wasn't exactly thrilled out of my mind to be spending Christmas in California. The sun was hot and dry and white and the mayor of Los Angeles had hung all these ugly green-and-red wreaths on just about every palm tree and lamppost in the city. Then somebody had dragged this nine-hundred-pound sequined snowflake out of his garage and slung it across the intersection of Sunset and Fairfax. I mean, that snowflake had sat in the corner of some clammy garage getting rancid for eleven months and people had thrown their coats and their sticky old waders over it, and then some guy had brought it out and hung it in a nest of gold wires so it sagged over your car like some monster minnow out of hell. Plus, in all the stores they were playing Christmas carols over the speakers but they were these California Christmas carols. They were all written in the early 1970s by some coked-out couple slumped on a hot beach somewhere and they had this tireless beat behind them and their lyrics were all incredibly snide and knowing. They were sung by people like Mel Tormé, Ella Fitzgerald, people like that. I like Ella Fitzgerald fine but not when she starts scat-singing Christmas carols, I just can't listen. Even Laurie Benoit cut a Christmas album a couple of years before she died. I think it was called *Me, Alone, with No Friends or Family, on Christmas Eve, Alone,* or something fairly downbeat like that. I admit it was a depressing album in a lot of ways but at least it was halfways traditional, which is more than I can say for *Come Swing with Ella* or whatever. Laurie sang "Ave Maria" and "O Come All Ye Faithful" and "I've Gotta Right to Sing the Blues" and then she ended up with "I'm Nobody's Baby" with all these high crystalline bells shaking like crazy in the background. When you come right down to it, Laurie was a pretty joyless woman. I don't know why I enjoyed listening to her so much. The strange part was I didn't care for Laurie's earlier stuff at all, when she was young and in the movies and exuberant and fresh-faced and all. I liked her when she was older—by forty she was through like an athlete or a horse or something—when she was always leading the audience in these raspy singalongs of her old movie hits. As soon as she'd get everyone in the audience going she'd quit singing herself and slip behind the curtain. I always thought that was fairly shrewd of her, the singalong idea.

The Lane Awards ceremony was held about a half-mile away from the varsity soccer field, on a wide bright green patch of lawn in back of the gymnasium. In the spirit of

Christmas the school had draped a greasy string of colored lights along the railing of the gymnasium steps, and a huge sign that said, A Joyous Noel to You and Yours. Boy, when you saw that sign you really wanted to kill yourself. You wanted to commit a little suicide on the spot. I think *to you and yours* is one of the worst expressions in existence. It's even worse than *Noel,* which is saying a lot. *Joyous* is a pretty terrible word too but it's not half as awful as *Noel* and *to you and yours.* Both of them compete for the disaster prize with *X-mas* but at least *X-mas* wasn't anywhere in evidence that day, thank God. It wouldn't have been out of place is my point here but they spared you *X-mas* that morning even though you knew the Lane administration would spring it on you sometime just when you were starting to feel good about yourself.

I was sitting with the other guys in my class on these hard olive-colored folding chairs, watching a plane fly overhead, cutting down the center of the sky. It was very hot that day. Across the city you could see brown mountains and the ratty grey letters of the Hollywood sign with its slump in the middle before the second syllable. The headmaster, David Skully, was standing on the podium about a hundred feet away and going on and on about how close the voting had been this year and how everybody should feel like a winner even if he loses. You know, all that sanctimonious jazz they feed you every year that no one believes for a second. It's like the speech they give out at the beginning of the Academy Awards year after year about how the recognition of your colleagues should be satisfaction enough and that getting nominated in the first place is a victory in itself and so forth. Then the camera pans out over the nominees' faces and you see, Winning is everything, Winning is the only thing. Nothing else matters.

David started reading the prizes that Lane awarded for character and leadership and things like that. It was a pretty long process but luckily the winners weren't allowed to make speeches. All the character prizes were voted in by your classmates so they were supposed to mean a lot more than the scholastic prizes or the awards the school was pretty much obliged to hand over, like the brass torch in the bed of ivy that they gave to the president of the class. I was looking up at the sky, trying to read what it said. There was writing, you couldn't tell how far up, thick, grey, faint letters. It was a pitch for one of the Hollywood law offices. The letters spelled: Personal Injuries. I stared at those letters for a long time. As the plane added fresh loops the old letters would start to drip and then you couldn't tell them from clouds. We Are the Accident People, the airplane said. Finally only three words, The Accident People, hung over our heads. I got tired of reading the same words after a while and I was looking over at the parking lot when I saw this old broken-down station wagon come through the gates and roll to a stop beside a brown Mercedes.

I didn't think it was Bob at first. My father lives in New York and he never comes out to California. I hadn't seen him in about a year or something. The last time I saw him was Thanksgiving in New York and we went to Café des Artistes because it was easier. I looked over at my sister Lucy. She was sitting next to this crew-cutted astronaut with a chin like a goddamn shovel but I couldn't tell whether she'd seen my father or not. She was wearing a dirty old Red Sox cap and these enormous black sunglasses and she looked tanned as hell. My sister's just about the brownest white person I know. She had a bandage on her left wrist, or rather two small bandages laid out in a cross shape, from where a spider bit her when she was taking a shower.

My father took a seat in the back row. He was wearing pretty much what he always does, this dark baggy suit and a white shirt that strained over his stomach and his black glasses. My father's worn those glasses for as long as I can remember. They fit him so perfectly that his lashes are always rubbing up against the lenses, the bottoms of the lashes catch before pulling away and down, and the glass gets swept clean of dust. He keeps about twelve pairs of them in his sock drawer at home, along with these old pieces of flat leather, wallets he doesn't use anymore, chipped belts and watch-straps and gas cards of companies that aren't in business anymore. I think he keeps all those glasses around so he can provide us with a kind of consistency, you know, so that if he breaks a pair neither Lucy or I will think that if some out-of-control express train or something were heading toward us Bob wouldn't be able to see it in time and we'd all die. In the same spirit of consistency he gets his short, stone-colored hair cut every two weeks so it never gets noticeably longer or shorter. It sits there on his head, square and sensible like a hymnal. My father's hair fascinates a lot of people and not just kids.

David started to announce the Freddie Bennett award, which is just about the saddest award in the world. Freddie Bennett was a thin, blond, quiet kid who drowned in the breakers off Zuma Beach. He'd been surfing, paddling around like a tern or something, and while he was thinking of girls or cities or what he was going to have for dinner that night, some guy in a cream-colored speedboat ran over him. It was pretty grisly. I remembered where I was when I heard about it for the longest time and then I forgot the place. His parents and the school called it an accidental drowning and I suppose if Freddie had been my kid I would have called it a drowning too. I didn't like Freddie that much—I won't say that, I just didn't have an opinion about him one way or an-other—but I knew he wouldn't be best man at my wedding or my psychic twin or anything. You hear about these psy-chic twins, one of them gets slapped in Motown and the other one screams in Sacramento, but Freddie and I weren't like that. The sad thing was that Freddie was just about the last guy in the world you would ever have expected to go surfing. You knew the only reason he went in was because he wanted people to like him. After he died I felt kind of bad for a while. I started feeling guilty that I hadn't been nicer to him, invited him out to dinner or given him lots of money or something, but I told myself I was handicapped by not knowing he was going to die. His parents had endowed a memorial prize in Freddie's memory. They weren't rich or anything but they had taken all the money they ordinarily would have spent on a trip to Finland or on some refrigerators and given the money to Lane, which I thought was pretty decent of them.

David put on his glasses and read: For the boy who regardless of ability exemplifies the spirit of enthusiasm and willingness embodied by your late classmate Freddie Bennett, I'm pleased to announce the award goes this year to Samuel Grace.

Well, everybody started clapping. My sister practically knocked the astronaut's chair over. She took off her Red Sox cap and her dark glasses and began pounding, really pounding, the lenses with her free hand. I was as shocked as she was. I sat there in my seat until someone pushed me from behind. People were whistling, thin ones and those long loud curling ones I've never been able to do that you use to get your stupid Labrador out of the bushes when he's chewing up some rats or something. All the astronauts and comedians were clapping, which I thought was pretty mature of them considering I had out-cooperated their slick sons and all. I looked over at my father but his face hadn't really changed and then I made my way up to the stage and David handed me a package that must have weighed ninety pounds and we shook hands and I managed to get back to my seat before the clapping stopped. I always get embarrassed when I'm watching a talk show on television and the guest is introduced and the audience starts applauding but the guest moves so slowly, as if he's in a dream, that by the time he reaches the couch the whole place is like a morgue. You hear the cushions squeak. Usually I have to shut the sound off I get so embarrassed for the guy.

I tore open the package. It was three books, bound in black vellum and boxed and the box had my initials on one side in

gold. They had gotten my middle initial wrong. They had
carved a gold *P* instead of *R*. The books were *The Decline and
Fall of the Roman Empire* by Edward Gibbon, volumes one
through three. People were staring at me so I opened up the
third volume and pretended to look entranced by its wisdom
or whatever. I think I knew right away I'd never read the
damn thing in a million years. I knew I'd probably end up
donating it to a hospital for the criminally insane or giving it
to the wives of some firemen to raffle off for hose money. I
didn't even know why the school would want to give me
something like that. I was mystified, frankly. It was pretty
odd to expel someone and then give him a door prize on the
way out. I thought that was a fairly mixed signal to give
someone. I thought that could maybe be the definition of a
mixed signal in fact, you know, for kids who didn't know
what one was yet. You'd look up *mixed signal* in the Random
House dictionary and there would be a little sketch of me sitting on a hard fold-up chair with these three books on my lap
and everyone but me would have a diploma.

I slid the books back inside their box and then I put them
under my chair. I tried not to think about them for the rest of
the ceremony. The presentations went on for another twenty
minutes and at the end all the parents stood up and sang
hymn sixty-one, which was all about giving praise to some
birds or something. I didn't bother to sing with everybody. I
just moved my lips around, which I guess didn't look that
convincing since the words I was making with my lips were
the ones everybody else had just finished singing. It was kind
of a brilliant echo effect on my part. I don't think anybody
noticed though. Sometimes you think people are looking at
you when they just don't care what you're doing. When the
hymn was over I made my way across the lawn to where my
father was. I don't think he had moved once during the
entire ceremony. Everyone else was moving around and my
father was standing there stiffly looking at the green-and-
white-striped tent where they were serving lunch.

The first thing I said to him was, "What are you doing out

here?'' which I guess wasn't the friendliest thing to say to someone, especially if you haven't seen them in a while.

My father shook my hand loosely. "Merry Christmas," he said.

I told him Merry Christmas. I couldn't believe Bob had traveled three thousand miles to wish me a Merry Christmas and I told him that and he acted as though he hadn't heard me.

"Not so very wintry here is it?'' He glanced around him. "I don't know how these California people do it. These trees, all this unnatural green grass."

"How they do what?"

My father looked straight at me. "Get up the energy, Sam. For Christmas. Get up any enthusiasm at all. Was that Mr. Skully? The man up there on stage?"

"David," I said. "Everybody calls him David. He's a very informal headmaster. You can call him David."

"I don't think I want to," my father said. "I take it he's in charge of things. I received I believe it was from the same informal guy a pretty sober formal-sounding letter about your performance here."

"Oh." I nodded my head. "Yeah, I was going to write you about all that."

My father shifted his heels. "First of all, congratulations, Sam. On this thing here. This personality jazz, this award nonsense. I see I made it for that in time. I don't know whether there's all that much else to congratulate you about just now but so you know." He looked down at the books I was holding. "So what have you got there anyhow?"

I handed him the box and he read the spine aloud. Both of us stood there for a minute blinking in the sun. I heard a car siren go off in the parking lot. It was a hot high whine that lasted less than a minute. My father handed the box back and finally he spoke. "For Christ's sake, Sam. I mean, congratulations and all that but Jesus, this is school number two. Isn't it? Winning these honorifics is just dandy, friend, but where's it going to get you into college? Where's it going to get you a year from now? Nowhere if you keep on getting the boot wherever you go. What the hell's going on with you?"

"Nothing is," I said. I was staring at the top leaves of this enormous gold-green palm tree on one side of the Lane parking lot and trying not to cry. The fronds looked like dreadlocks. The letters that spelled The Accident People were becoming the clouds and on the other side of the sky, over the water and the surfers, the airplane was trying another approach. Slip and Fall? the letters, all grey and thick and vague, wanted to know. Slip and Fall? My father's hands were deep in the pockets of his pants and when I looked at a point that wasn't the ground or his face I could make out the shapes of his ten knuckles, flexing, relaxing, flexing again.

Bob said, "This isn't the easiest thing in the world for me, Sam. You know that? Do you think all this Dad jazz is easy? Doing this I mean? Coming out here on a mission like this? Well it's not." He shook his head, a little wildly I thought. "Of course I don't mind it, Sam, the coming out here, that is. That's not the point really. Sometimes you have to do things you don't want to do. The last thing you feel like doing sometimes is the thing you do first, that's just the way it goes, that's being an adult. But Jesus, I hate it out here." He stared for a minute at the chapel, which stood up the hill from the gym. "Now what the hell goes on inside there?"

I told him it was the chapel. "People go in there and they get their knees dirty and then they pray like crazy."

My father kept staring at the chapel doors. They were made of glass and cedar and they had rose-colored knobs. He turned to me. "You're kidding, aren't you?"

"No."

"You're not kidding?"

"No."

"That's just about the ugliest piece of architecture I've ever seen. Would you agree with me that's ugly?"

I nodded my head.

"Yes?" my father said, wanting to hear me say it.

"Yes," I said. "Ugly."

"You ever go in there for any reason?"

"No."

"Maybe you should," Bob said after a minute. "Maybe you should. Maybe that's what's, uh, not on your mind. That ought to be on your mind but isn't." He made a small heavy gesture with his hand. "You guys are both really out there, aren't you?"

I didn't understand. "Out where?"

"Out there. What do I mean by that exactly. You're in a different zone, Sam, than me. Your being out here in Los Angeles for instance with this unattractive-looking church as one of your influences. You don't know your influences until it's much too late to do anything about them either. Do you remember St. Stephen's in the Pines, out on the island? Now that's a handsome church, can we agree on that? Do you remember it? It looks like a church, for one thing." My father took a couple of steps backward and then he looked up at the sky and shook his head. "I can't tell you how long it's been since I was out here last. Yes, I can actually. The last time I was out here was in August of 1947."

"How in the world do you remember that?" I said.

"You do. One does or at least I do. It's the way my mind works, months and numbers. Months, numbers and dates of things and occasionally faces. San Olera Air Force Base, right up the coast there. Pretty seedy place then and probably still is a seedy place. I had one hell of a time by the way making it out here. Speaking of airplanes. And traffic jams. I had to rent a car."

I stared over at the battered station wagon. "I see you chose an excellent model."

"It runs very well," my father said without any irony. "It's a good little car. It's impossible to get a taxi at that airport of yours."

"It's not really my airport," I said.

"Well, for argument's sake, Sam, it is your airport. For this time of your life it is. I didn't mean it was yours personally. You don't have to take everything I say so personally. I meant your airport as La Guardia and Kennedy are my airports. As Newark is sometimes my airport. Meaning I take a little responsibility for them."

I said, "That's one of the problems with New York. I mean, something goes wrong there and everybody turns around and they start taking it so personally." I didn't really know what I was talking about. All I wanted to do was change the subject, badly. "You have a houseguest or something and if there's a fire five miles away from your apartment or if a bomb that has nothing to do with you goes off in the basement of some bank you consider it some kind of stain on your hospitality. You start apologizing to your houseguest as though you're the one who put the bomb there. It's sick. Only because no one in New York has any room to move around. They start thinking of New York as one long, incredibly complicated wing of their apartment. So they start blaming themselves if something goes badly in their stupid, dirty, ugly wing."

My father didn't seem to be all that interested in what I was saying. "You haven't visited New York with any regularity since you were fifteen," he said pleasantly. "How can you make any kind of case for what New York is or isn't?"

I used to visit my father in New York on weekends sometimes when I was going to this private school in Massachusetts, Briar Hall. It was about a four-and-a-half-hour train ride from Briar to New York and you got to travel past the water and the submarines, so it wasn't a bad ride at all. Briar Hall was the first school I got kicked out of. It was this huge old campus outside of Boston overrun by all these golden retrievers. I don't think I've ever seen so many dogs in one place in my entire life. On weekends the place was like a kennel, you know, these packs of damp aging yellow dogs stumbling around with their purple mouths barking like mad or sleeping in the shade of a tree or else trying to hump the knee of some faculty member's four-year-old kid or something. I mean, the golden retrievers at Briar weren't what I'd call heroic animals. They spent half their lives swimming in this brown shallow pond next to the running track and when they came out their flanks would be all forky with mud and white foam and sometimes they'd be trussed up with miles of oily brown cassette tape or lengths of colored yarn that people had thrown into the pond. The worst part was you got the feeling that those old dogs enjoyed getting trussed up, you know, that they kept returning to that pond for a reason. When you patted their heads or their stomachs, not that you did that much, your fingers smelled for about six months afterwards.

I remember I was sitting on the steps of the chapel on a Sunday morning right before the start of summer listening to the bells ringing. The chapel at Briar Hall was pretty much the focal point of the campus. It was a big gloomy building overlooking the commons and it had all these colored flags blowing off it. It was warm out and lilacs were hanging all over the place and yellow sprinklers shucked off water and I could hear a saw cutting into a tree and somewhere the sound of light regular hammering. About a mile from campus there was a parade going down the town's main avenue. I can't remember what the parade was for but I could hear bagpipes screaming and drums and after a while I saw a float that looked like a giant tambourine moving past the dormitories. In back of the float these formations of little orange-faced girls in green dresses were marching down the middle of the street, chewing grey gum and throwing batons up into the air. Massachusetts likes to think of itself as a fairly dignified place but there's this whole dark side to New England that no one ever talks about much. It consists of copper-faced majorettes between the ages of six and twelve trudging in depressing parades to the beat of canned bagpipe music. You never hear about any of that parade stuff but you're aware of it more than you're aware of the Walden Pond stuff.

I was sitting there listening to these chapel bells and behind me some guy who worked for the school and who wore thick black glasses was scrubbing the whitewashed rocks that lined the chapel steps. He had a white rag twisted up and a pan of grey-yellow suds and he was crouched down and the stones were gleaming. They had just mowed all the lawns and the smell of cut grass was strong and sweaty. The blades of the mower had seized a bright blue potato chip bag and cut it up and flung it out the other side along with the spat-out fragments of a Styrofoam cup. This raucous curtain of sprinkler water kept veering over and coating the Styrofoam and the blue plastic and the green chopped grass with water so the lawn was turning into a kind of gruel. I kept imagining those majorettes marching along and seeing a scrap of the blue plastic and thinking they'd spotted an emerald soaking in the grass that some queen or someone had dropped, not that there were any queens at Briar except for the usual suspects, old guys with grey chest hair who wore red tank tops and watched team practice from their cars and suffered like hell, and if they were asked said they were married to teaching or administrative work or whatever. I kept imagining all these poor old orange-faced girls rushing up convinced they'd found an emerald and that they'd get some massive award from the owner and be able to retire to the Left Bank or someplace and then they'd lean down and see all it was was a fragment of mowed-over potato chip bag.

All these guys were standing around on the commons playing lacrosse, throwing baseballs and Frisbees back and forth to each other. The golden retrievers sat in the shade underneath trees in twos waiting for some underage kid to pass by alone. One of the guys playing lacrosse, this blond guy named Arkie Cowan, kept overthrowing the ball and it would go sailing over his friend's head. His friend kept coming over near where I was sitting to hunt for the ball in the bushes.

At one point Arkie stuck his stick back and threw the ball so far it went flying over my head and banged up against the chapel door. The ball rolled back down the six stairs, under the bar of the railing, behind the bath of yellow suds and down three more stairs until it came to a rest where the bottom of my spine met the jut of the grey stone. Both Arkie and his friend came dancing over with their sticks nodding and waving and started poking around in the lilac bushes. They were taking the heads off all the dandelions in the process. I could feel the ball pressing up against my spine but I didn't say anything, I just leaned back into it. I wasn't feeling all that anxious to be helpful. After about fifteen minutes of digging around killing lilacs Arkie straightened up and called over to me, "Hey, man, you see where the ball went to?"

I can't tell you why Arkie Cowan annoyed me so much but he did. Everybody else in the school loved the guy, which I suppose was good enough reason right there not to be able to stand him. He was the captain of the lacrosse team and the hockey team and the student body president so the school waived all these requirements for him. His real name was Arthur but everybody, even people whose formality you liked, called him Arkie. He was tall and hipless and his hair was so blond it was almost white and his chin was square as one of the vaults in an egg carton and he had this slow, slightly bow-legged way of walking across fields. There were a couple of habits of his that drove you up a wall. One was shaking hands with you whenever he saw you and the other was the fact he said "howdy." I can't stand "howdy." You knew Arkie wanted everybody to think he was some kind of rangy westerner, you know, born of salmon in some grubby stream in Montana or somewhere, all easygoing and laconic, some guy who drank beer all the time and ate steerburgers and whooped whenever he got good news, even though Arkie's father was the president of Boston or something and the only time Arkie ever went west was to go skiing in Vail with his perfect family, his mother, whose name was actually Calliope—I'm serious—and his lookalike perfect younger brother. All of them had their names twisted around, you know, to be a member of that family you had to have an embarrassing nickname. I mean, Arkie was about as far removed from being the son of a couple of slimy salmon as you could get.

I said, "How's that?"

"Ball. You know. Little white round thing. Ball."

He started waving his stick around in the air, twisting its huge clownish netted head, pumping his hairless brown wrists side to side. I think lacrosse is just about the most pointless game ever invented in the history of the world. Once you leave high school you never hear a single thing about it again. You ask yourself, was lacrosse just a dream, and it might as well have been for all the play it gets during the rest of your life. Actually, that's not quite true, I heard about it once when I was visiting Bob one weekend and it was about two in the morning and I was flipping through the cable channels and somehow I turned on the Argentina versus Hungary lacrosse finals. It was the last two minutes of the game and all these stumpy fans with facial hair were flooding the field, trying to kill each other with wooden chairs. It was pretty disturbing, you know, fans can get pretty truculent sometimes. The only reason I ever stay to the end of any game, hockey or basketball or football or anything, is so I can see all the sentimental stuff at the end when all the players shake hands and hug each other and cry and say, Good Game and so forth. I have a real weakness for that kind of heroic sentimental bullshit.

"I'll tell you if you're hot or cold," I told him.

He stared at me. "Do you know where it is or don't you?"

"Yes," I said, "I know where your little ball is."

"Asshole." He started poking around in the bushes again. He kept throwing his stick out ahead of him and then pulling it back, like a clammer.

"Listen," I said, "do you suppose you could spare some of

the grass? Maybe a dandelion or two? Just until the winter maybe, please?"

He didn't answer. The head of his stick kept scraping away at the ground, uprooting things. I started staring at Arkie's underwear and getting annoyed. The guy was wearing boxer shorts, the kind that swim around your knees and which look pleated when in fact they're just too big for you. These boxer shorts he had on were climbing up the sides of his grey corduroy pants, bagging up and creating all these wide foolish smiles up and down his legs like the smiles a lot of religious fanatics have. You know those smiles people get sometimes when they're lit by something off the wall and inner. That used to happen to me in New York quite a lot. I'd be sitting around talking to someone, having a normal conversation and then all of a sudden the person I was talking to would start smiling in a deranged way and say something like, "Why, that reminds me, there's a little group that meets at my house on Tuesdays and Thursdays at seven-thirty, maybe you'd be interested," you know, very low-key and all, and the person pretends it's a sort of general discussion symposium for concerned people under thirty in order to analyze contemporary issues like the bomb and gypsy moths but then in the end the person can't stand it anymore and he bursts out with the name of some insane reverend or another. By that time you're a hundred miles away from them. The point here is that you knew the only reason Arkie wore boxer shorts is because his father did. Bob wears those old long limp boxers too, but it's not to show off his maturity or anything. He even told me once that he was issued those languid old boxers in the service and the habit stuck, that was all.

For some reason as I watched Arkie's boxer shorts climb up the sides of his pants I began getting really angry. I can't explain why exactly. I just abhorred the guy's motives for wearing those shorts. There was something about those boxer shorts that made Arkie look as though he'd stepped out of another generation, as though all his blondness and athleticism were some sort of timeless thing. You could see him frozen in time. I started thinking that when I was ninety or something I'd be walking down the street and I'd see a blond guy who looked like Arkie and I'd call out his name and then I'd realize it wasn't Arkie at all, it was just his type. Arkie didn't really exist when you came right down to it, you know, he was just filling out a role that called for a blond good-looking guy. Someone who looked just like him had probably played on that same lawn when the grass was fifty years younger and in another fifty years someone else, probably Arkie's grandson, some kid with perfect teeth who was nick-named Kippy or something, would be playing the same rough, graceful, pointless game, using Arkie's old lucky patched-up stick with its black-and-yellow head tape. I got an ache in my upper stomach just thinking about this sequence of privileged blond guys wearing their fathers' boxer shorts on the Briar Hall commons.

Arkie came over to where I was sitting. He held his stick across his hips like a guitar. He looked like a folk singer, you know, Pete Seeger or someone. "You gonna tell me where our ball is, man?" He sounded very tired.

"Who's Carla the Unstoppable?" I screamed.

He squinted at me. "Who?"

I screamed it again. What I was referring to was Arkie's yearbook page. The Briar Hall yearbooks had come out that morning and that year they were bright orange with brown stripes and everyone was rushing around getting inscriptions from each other. Arkie's yearbook page had a couple of things on it that made you want to commit suicide right there on the spot, you know, while the print was still warm. The first thing was this long quotation from some Bruce Springsteen song about traveling or rambling in some burnt-out little town, one of those *-ing* words that makes you think of the slow grey road. Maybe it was trucking, I can't really remember. You knew Arkie probably thought of himself as the kind of guy who just rambled on and on and on, he couldn't help it, blah, blah, blah, he'd try and go faster but his legs and knees would automatically lock in the rambling mode, and so forth. You also knew Arkie probably thought Bruce Springsteen was the finest writer of our time, that Arkie was one of those people who referred to Springsteen as a poet, you know, right alongside Shakespeare and Eliot and Wallace Stevens, and that Bruce spoke uniquely to Arkie's condition with all his songs about downhill skiing in Vail and prep schools and especially that album Bruce did about lacrosse, Jesus, that was a great album. If you'd asked Arkie who his favorite poets were he'd probably say Springsteen, Dylan, Paul McCartney or another one of those the sky is blue/so are you sorts of nonpeople, you know Shakespeare can just go to hell, Shakespeare can just die. What really got on my nerves the most was that right under Arkie's picture was this compendium of his high school experiences set out in kind of a montage form. It was something like: Here you be, Mama . . . LKD and Scooter . . . Carla the Unstoppable . . . Molson dawns and the St. Pauli sisters . . . Swallow it, it's good for you . . . Thanks, PG and RRD and Boris the Rat, and so on. I think you know what I'm talking about. All these arcane references to the people he'd slept with or gotten drunk with or who had waived science requirements for him so he could graduate, all of them restrained by those stupid black dots so you didn't know what Arkie was referring to but you felt excluded all the same.

"None of your business," he said but I could tell he was pretty flattered I'd asked. He brought his stick up into the air and when he did his shirt lifted up a couple of inches and the muscles in his stomach tugged upwards. He was a pretty brown guy, not as brown as Lucy but still brown. Arkie was always running off to Eleuthera or St. Kitts with Calliope and the father and running up incredible drink tabs from poolsides and then coming back to school in the middle of February and pretending his tan was accidental, you know, the result of stacking logs in the sun or something. He didn't want anybody to think for a minute that he'd actually stretched out on an actual chair and tried to get a tan. I could see the white puckered elastic of those boxer shorts running at a slant across his stomach and a scrap of the fabric: red and black squares. About that time I reached around behind me and brought out the lacrosse ball.

He saw it in my hand. He lowered his stick and closed his eyes. "Give it over," he said, very softly.

He was standing about five feet from me. His legs were slightly bent and he was twisting the head of the stick. The ball was hard and fairly grubby. There were blades of green-and-brown grass clinging to it. In the sun it looked blue. I got a grip on it and then I wiped my fingertips against my pants and I stood up. I had the ball between my index finger and my thumb. I was planning to hand it over leisurely—I really was—but then I saw the boxer shorts again, the strap of which was like a bridge to a whole generation I'd missed, and something in me hurt like hell and I threw the ball just as hard as I could at him.

Arkie just stared at me. He looked amazed and disappointed. He stood there with his long tanned fingers wrapped around the grip of that stupid stick as though he thought he might be able to coax a song out of it and then the stick suddenly had a life: the taped-up head ducked down, it twisted out the tuck of Arkie's sunburned fingers and spilled onto the grass and one of the brown knotted squares of the head dropped precisely over the exposed head of a yellow dandelion, sparing its life. The chances of that ever happening were so remote that all I could do was look on in wonder. The head wasn't even grazed. A small low sound came from his mouth. It was a pretty heartbreaking sound actually, and then he fell backwards.

What happened immediately after that I can't remember too well. Arkie's friend came over and started yelling at me to go away, to just get the hell away. The majorettes had rounded the driveway and were marching across the commons. The guy cleaning the rocks rested the rag across his knee and started smiling and ten seconds later he was wiping down the gravel, the individual stones I mean. I think there might have been something wrong with the guy's brain, actually. Arkie had blood in a crooked halo shape under his bangs and all these dandelions were sticking out around the sides of his joints like kids with their hands up in a classroom or something. He looked as though he were doing one of those angels in the snow except it was seventy degrees out and the clouds were white and beefy and it was about to be summer again for about the millionth year in a row. The lacrosse ball was lying in the damp cut grass looking blue and sort of luminous and I picked it up and started walking across the commons. At one point several golden retrievers began following me. There were maybe five of them in a ring around me, sons who had never left home, a couple of mothers, maybe a father, this solid wave of hot gold fur and I thought, they all want to sleep with me now that I've shown someone I'm dangerous. Everybody likes dangerous, look at the cult around the dead young actors. I had an idea that those dogs would become my personal cult. I thought, I'll be the first person ever to have a cult consisting entirely of golden retrievers. I imagined those dogs sending out pictures of me signed Forever, Sam; keychains, T-shirts, a newsletter, the whole treatment. I broke into a run but the dogs, even the very weary ones, kept pace with me and I didn't manage to shake them until I got inside my dormitory, Harkness House, and somehow got myself up six flights of stairs and onto the roof. Harkness House was a big new dormitory that overlooked the squash courts and the rink. The rink had a heavy blue roof with a rusted skylight running down the middle of it. Through the opening I could see the duffers preparing the ice for the figure skaters and the kids who were allowed to use the rink three times a week. I watched the heavy black Zamboni coursing in a smooth circle around the ice, the circles getting smaller and smaller until there was just a plank-sized patch of unsoaked ice in front of the visitor's goal. The Zamboni had a couple of ways it could have handled that patch and in the end it just backed up over it.

You could see all the way to Boston from the roof of Harkness. You could see dirty yellow marshes and the Prudential and the routes of dark creeks and little rivers that led up to the strip of grey expressway and all these ancient brick mills that had once manufactured combs or chocolate or pens and which now stood above waterfalls unused and empty. The windows were shattered and the water in the waterfalls looked like beer and there were white pie boxes in the weeds. That morning the air was clear and salty. I stared all the way to Boston and I wasn't moved at all by its history, or by anything. Through the skylight the first figure skaters skimmed across the wet ice and canned music started playing over the rink speakers. You felt if you bent down and licked that ice you'd get back lemon on your tongue. The Zamboni bowed back inside its cave. Poor old Karen Carpenter was singing "We've Only Just Begun." Two skaters fell, holding hands. Then everybody was whirling.

For some reason I had a copy of *The New Yorker* magazine in my left hand. When I was going past the Harkness mailboxes I had dropped the lacrosse ball and grabbed the mail out of my hutch and when I reached the roof I forgot I still had it. I sat on this warm black sheet of tar on top of Harkness reading *The New Yorker*, high over the golden retrievers and the parade and the figure skaters. The chapel bells stopped ringing. In case you've never read *The New Yorker* there's this section at the end of all the long articles where they drag out excerpts from rural newspapers and then make some kind of snide comment about them. It's one of my favorite parts of the magazine actually. I was reading this paragraph they'd taken from a newspaper in North Dakota that said something like, "Barbara Easton, archivist for the Audubon Society, asked about the future of the blue heron, said, 'There are perhaps five left in the state and if I calculate right in five more years there could be plenty. If we play our cards right.' " Then whoever it was at *The New Yorker* had answered in bold type underneath that: "Keep your powder dry, Barbara."

I didn't understand that. I kept reading that line, "Keep your powder dry, Barbara" over and over again but I couldn't understand any of it. I didn't understand what was so funny or ungrammatical or erroneous or what. I stared uncomprehendingly at that page for thirty minutes. I didn't understand what herons had to do with powder or drying or archives or fertility or anything. Nothing seemed to have to do with anything else. Usually I can figure these things out but with that one I tried and tried and I just couldn't get it. I stared at the word *heron* for so long it left the English language. It didn't look like a word I knew anymore, or it looked like a word from a foreign language. None of its letters seemed to fit in a coordinated word with each other. Below me I could hear the drums and the screams of the bagpipes and when I got up onto my feet I saw the little girls marching under the white goalposts on the Jayvee football field. All of a sudden I couldn't stop crying. I was crying in the dull sun of the millionth or so summer and the tar under my winter black shoes was beginning to flop and all these terrible girls with bright faces and green skirts were sending batons spinning end over end under their elbows and over their heads and working their tough red jaws like mad. You would have hated to be bitten by one of those girls. I watched them file past the forty-yard line. It felt as though the campus were under attack. The rink was playing "Benny and the Jets" but the parade was louder. My eyes were soaking the pages of *The New Yorker* all because I couldn't understand the connection between herons and powder. Finally this English teacher from Missouri I liked got me down off the roof but by then I had twisted the magazine so badly it was unreadable—you couldn't have given it to a library with the lowest standards in the world.

The point here is I nearly killed Arkie but I didn't. I gave him a subdural hematoma, whatever that is. The doctor who treated him figured out some infinitesimal fraction of an inch, one thirty-fifth or something, by which I'd missed some crucial spot in his brain. Arkie ended up with a long greasy scar right where his face met his hair, all pink and curling like some awful beach community in Florida or someplace, you know, some ruined old coastal town crowded with old gay playwrights and blue-haired women artists and thin soft white sand that's like the color of mortality itself, all packed with cigarette butts and plaid cardboard hot dog holders and everyone on the beach has seen better days and you notice there's an incredible weight problem in the U.S. that no one gives a damn about—he could have concealed all that if he'd just let his bangs grow long and stiff but instead he kept them wet and pushed back. A couple of people told me that Arkie had told a bunch of girls at a party that he'd had an accident with a fishing line in some bay off Bar Harbor, Maine, if you can believe it. I suppose his parents, Wilson and Calliope, could have sued me and the school for millions but somehow the headmaster and my father convinced them not to, that is, on the condition I go see a shrink in New York about five times a day all summer. I couldn't stay on at Briar Hall either. After that I came out to Los Angeles and moved in with Lucy. That was a couple of years ago.

My father looked down at his watch. He has one of those black diver's watches with red and green arrows all over the dial. I don't think my father's ever gone diving. "Well," he said, "do you think they have anything edible under that green-and-white tent over there? I didn't eat anything on the plane except for some very very sweet peanuts."

"Oh," I said, feeling discouraged all of a sudden, "some junk or another. Rare roast beef, you know, the school doesn't want to mislead you or anything." On Awards Day Lane had a big production for all the parents and the alumni so they would see how well-fed we all were and give the school more money. The school served food you never once laid eyes on during the rest of the year, rare roast beef and cornish game hens and tiny shrimp and parsley potatoes and goose liver pâté and so forth, everything in very frail portions, sliced thinly as hell. I don't know whether the parents fell for it but I had a feeling they did.

Just then my sister came over. She looked pretty shocked to see my father but she gave him a big hug anyway. "Why didn't you tell us you were coming?" she said to him.

"I didn't want to get in you guys' way," my father said. "And I did try, sweetie, a couple of times. I left a message with that southern woman who answers your phone sometimes. Both my children move away from home and they install phone machines, southern women. These are obstacles, I can never reach either of you guys."

My father told Lucy he wanted to drive up the coast and visit his old air force base. I could tell my sister wasn't wild about the idea but she said she would go along anyway. I stood there holding my books. "You want to come with us?" my father said, turning to me. "See where your old flyboy dad hung out in his twenties?"

I told him I was supposed to go to a party later and that I was going to stay around campus until it started.

"Aren't I enough of a party for you?" my father said to me.

"I'm not going to see the people here for a while," I said.

"Oh." He blinked. "I thought you didn't like any of the people here."

"I don't," I said. "Really."

I watched them both get into my father's dirty old station wagon and when they were gone I went over under the tent and stood in back of Marty Kellogg and his wife and his son and tried to pretend I was a member of a comedian's family. Marty wore a lot of jewelry on his fingers. He was smoking and gesturing and whenever he laughed it made him cough and then choke. I couldn't imagine what it would be like to have a father who wore a Sagittarius medallion around his neck. There were a couple of hundred people milling around, talking and drinking and eating folds of roast beef and ham off paper plates, and all these old grey-haired women were stumbling around the lawn carrying black trays and looking dazed. On Awards Day the school imported old Irish women with brogues to serve the food and the sherry. It was one of those ballsy coups Lane was always pulling off to your astonishment. I think it was because being in Hollywood and all they treated everything as a casting problem that could be solved with imagination and a little money. I don't know where they found those old women, Boston or someplace semielegant like that. I guess they were supposed to lend a little elegance to the joint, old-world elegance I think you call it. It was stiflingly hot underneath the tent and they were all wearing thin blue sweaters with enormous white buttons down the front. They looked like they were going to collapse and die any second. When one of them passed by me I reached out and grabbed a plastic glass off her tray. I don't like sherry all that much but I drank my glass down fairly rapidly. It tasted oily and sweet. You weren't supposed to drink at Lane, or in California for that matter, but I didn't really think it mattered that much in my case. They couldn't do anything to me at that point anyway. I was feeling so daring I lit a cigarette and then I set my glass down on the edge of one of the brown folding tables. I saw another glass someone had left on the seat of a chair and when no one was looking I drank that one down too.

I wandered out into the parking lot after a while. The sun felt hot on my neck and my hair. I smoked three more cigarettes but the third didn't taste like anything. I really didn't feel much like talking to anybody because I knew they would all ask me what I was going to do with myself next and I didn't know. People are always asking you that the first thing. They ask you that practically before they say hello. They want to know what you're doing now and what you're planning to do next, for money. Otherwise they're at a loss.

They have nothing to talk about then except how there are no good movies around or else some boring dream they had which involved getting chased by some guy with no features on his face, no nose, no mouth. In the spread of orange driveway sand I could see all these silver bottlecaps with riddles on their stomachs and edges dented from someone's teeth and cheap wood barrettes bucked off by anonymous girls and a lot of old foil wrappers balling up gum or just the tinny sheet stamped flat and dusted with white powder, like snow on a shop's window. Everywhere I looked I saw spit.

You knew that the spit, saliva, whatever, had to have come out of the comedian fathers' mouths. That was something those dads probably did all the time, spit like crazy when they thought you were looking at the sky and not at them. They spat on words started with *s* and *f* and then they spat in general. Some of it was white, still new I guess, and some was clear and still, busy soaking into the sand. I thought that spit was some of the most plaintive stuff I'd seen in a long time. I walked around it lightly as though I were some sort of lone soldier on a field rigged with mines. In retrospect I guess I must have been in a fairly low state of mind if I could let saliva affect me so powerfully. It just looked so forlorn there sleeping on the grit, here and there, getting trampled or else dissolving on its own time. In a couple of hours there would be no record of it ever having landed. Short-lived things can bum me out for days.

I was still wandering around the parking lot when I saw David Skully, the headmaster, walking in my direction. He had a woman with him I'd never seen before. She was holding onto his arm and as soon as they left the shade of the tent she reached into her purse and pulled out a pair of dark glasses and put them on. I heard David calling me. "Samuel, please hold on for a minute," he said. "Hold on there, please."

I was at the gate and I stopped and turned around. Nobody calls me Samuel, I don't allow it. I was holding a cigarette and I put it out against the heel of my hand. If you do it quickly enough it doesn't hurt. David and the woman came over to where I was standing and David put his arm around my shoulder. "We've been looking all over for you." David had a very soft high voice. You always expected a much deeper voice to come out of him and when it didn't you had a tendency to stare at David as though he were crazy. He put his other arm around the woman's shoulder. "This is Freddie Bennett's mother. Sam Grace, Sandy Bennett."

I almost ran into the road. The mother was just about the last person in the world I ever wanted to meet. I said, like a metronome adjusted to slow even strokes, Thank you for the books and I shook her hand and she said, How do you do, Sam, and then she smiled. She had a small dry palm. She was about the same size as Freddie and her hair was pushed back with some kind of strange bright pin in the shape of a road runner and she was wearing a white Mexican shirt that showed off all this dark tremendous skin on her arms. She had fantastic veins running down her arms and into her fingers. It looked like some kind of irrigation system, you know, like the pipes that water little African villages and bring relief and so forth. I realize that's probably a stupid thing to say, that if I said it in front of some scientist he'd say something back like, Well, you're not that far off the mark, veins are in fact very much the irrigation system of the human body, as it were, you know, that flat, stiff, colorless way scientific guys explain things, but the mother's veins were blue and glassed-over like evenings way back in the East when your backyard is in shadow and the air is mild and soft and a little wet. Mrs. Bennett was also quite pretty. The fact her son was dead and she was pretty made me fairly uncomfortable actually. It seemed disrespectful or something. I don't know.

"I wanted you to meet Mrs. Bennett before she had to leave." David tightened the hold he had on my shoulder. "Sam's from New York. You gotta be careful around these easterners, don't you, Sam? Never know what they'll do next, do you?"

I nodded my head a couple of times like some idiot. Then I

adjusted the three books in my hands since my arms felt suddenly weak.

"Unfortunately Sam won't be at Lane next year." The heels of David's shoes shifted and the dust that rose burned the inside of my nose and put me into a kind of temporary stupor.

"Oh," the mother said to me. She laughed. "Don't tell me you're one of those hotshots who gets to graduate in the middle of the year."

I said, "No," and when I said that she looked concerned.

"Well, I hope there's no one sick in your family, no illnesses—"

David said, "Well—"

"No, no, everything's under control," I said to her.

"This is a big thinking time for everybody," David said and then he smiled a maniacal, brotherly smile. I felt like hitting him in the mouth.

"That is a shame," Mrs. Bennett said. "That you have to leave all this, I mean." There was a row of cut-up fruit, strawberries, lemons, kiwis and some kind of drooping fat red berry sewn into the fabric of her shirt. "Someone at the hotel was telling me you drive seventy miles and all of a sudden there are skiing slopes and you come back here and you can get a tan on your face and swim in the ocean and then you take another trip and there's your desert and you don't see another person for days." She pointed to the playing fields in back of the gymnasium. "Are those tennis courts down there? Those green fences?"

"Eighteen of them," David said. "Two of them grass and sixteen clay. With lights overhead so the boys can play at night. We were southern California champs the year before last. And one of our boys was in the state finals."

"He lost." I turned to her. "Badly. Boy was massacred. Some ten-year-old kid beat him."

"Oh, not just any ten-year-old kid, Sam. We should probably give away to Mrs. Bennett that the ten-year-old kid just happened to be state champion twelve-and-under at the time."

I said, "He's still a ten-year-old kid. A brat. Our guy still lost badly." I was really in a terrible mood that day. I think it was the combination of seeing my father and the heat and the wind that kept pulling up dust from the ground and blowing it into my eyes and up my nose. "I don't see what having to go to Lane has to do with being any good at tennis."

"Well, it doesn't necessarily, of course," David said. He was laughing but I could tell he was nervous.

Mrs. Bennett said to me, "It's my first time out here. In California. Never been, always wanted to come."

"We just love it out here," David said. "I can't speak for Sam but I know for myself I wouldn't dream of living anyplace else. At this point. I went to school back east of course but I got tired of shoveling snow. Winter seems a long way away from here."

"Freddie really loved that stuff." Mrs. Bennett nodded at the books I had in my arms. "Those books. That kind of writing. It seems a funny choice. Compared to nowadays, the things people are reading these days. It's not something you take with you to the beach certainly. Not that the beach should have to do with anybody's decision making." She brought her hand up to her hair and smoothed back a blond bang that had slipped out from behind the barrette. She had long lovely hands, really lovely, and when she brought them up all the blood went out of her fingers. The skin around the tips of her fingers was all pink and groggy, like some kid's ratty old chewed-up bunny. "When Freddie liked something a lot he would do it over and over again. I'm a little like that too I think." She laughed. "He did that with books. Or records. He'd go out and buy a record and bring it home and once he got it home he'd play it over and over. You know, so you wanted to say to him, stop, stop, stop playing that, go play something else. Then after a few days you'd never hear it again. You missed it quite frankly. You'd be asking him where he put it." She was quiet. "I suppose that's a common thing what I'm describing."

David said, "I think you'd be surprised. That sounds a lot like Freddie's M.O. The Freddie I remember. That concentration, the complete undivided concentration and then the mastery of the subject and then boom, no need for old information anymore, he was flying." The guy was such an asshole you wanted to kill yourself.

"I just hope the books stand up," she said to me. "I'm not just saying that."

"Well, we'll miss him here you know," David said.

I waved my hand and said, "Oh, I've had a pretty good time here."

I realized too late he was talking about Freddie so I screamed, "I'll miss him too," something fast and insane like that, I can't remember what words I said, and then the three books fell from my arms onto the orange sand and one of them spilled from the box and opened up halfway, trapping a page underneath it like a wing. I bent down before anyone else could and tried lifting it and I nearly lost my balance— that book must have weighed about a thousand pounds. I got it up as high as my belt but I couldn't really get a grip on it and I kept apologizing to no one in particular. David took the book from me and started brushing sand off the cover in rapid downward pats. Mrs. Bennett leaned down and picked up the box with the other two books inside it. I could see her glance at the inscription, the stuff about enthusiasm, and then pretend to me she hadn't. All of a sudden I couldn't even remember what her son looked like. I remembered he was small and blond and thin but I couldn't remember any details of his face. All I could think of was this picture of him in the Lane bulletin, which is the recruitment rag they casually leave around the admissions office under the plant or something as though it's fallen from the ceiling. Inside there are all these pictures of students supposedly caught in action learning, you know, violently learning, learning so much it hurts, their faces tipped over books, pictures of the slimmest, best-looking teachers, the guys with mustaches who are photographed low and from the back as they're writing on the blackboard so their white oxford cloth shirts pull out from the waist of their pants. I mean, they want you to think that there's so much excitement going on in the Lane classrooms that it causes teachers' shirts to rip out of their pants in a frenzy as they whip their bodies toward the blackboard or something, I don't know. In the class pictures all the Lane boys look tanned and good-looking in a kind of combative way and then there's a picture of the losing soccer team and one of the sunrise as you see it from Pepperdine University and under the science section there's a picture of Freddie that was taken a long time ago but which has been in the Lane bulletin for about ten years running. In the picture he's sitting with another guy and both of them are wearing dark green raincoats with belts hanging off them and they're smoking and there's this giant black eucalyptus tree rising up like a hand behind them. Freddie is trying to look as though he's really savoring this cigarette so when he shows off the Lane bulletin to his kids so they'll know what a cool guy he was. It was all kind of heartbreaking actually. Not only did Freddie not smoke ever, he was one of those non-smokers who carried around a little battery-operated fan in his pocket so he could blow your smoke back into your face and make you cough. He was really a terrific guy in that respect, very consistent, going around with his miniature fan whirring and then you turn and there he is smoking a cigarette for the benefit of the Lane admissions bulletin. The only way I could remember Freddie was from that photograph. Sometimes you picture photographs of people when you can't imagine them otherwise, you know, in action, with no cameras around.

When the books were back in the box I said, "I can remember once when a whole bunch of us—including your

son I mean—were out driving back from a picnic. We were
in this Jeep, someone's black Jeep. Someone had borrowed
that Jeep from someone else and we were all coming back
from this disastrous picnic. And Freddie—" whenever I
mentioned Freddie I looked at Mrs. Bennett "—was sitting
in the backseat. And I remember there was sand all over the
place. It hadn't really been a beautiful day, that's why the
picnic was a disaster, but the sand was everywhere. It was all
over the floor, you know, the short rugs Jeeps have, in your
pockets, in your hair, your ears. It was like having a sixth passenger. We were the one through the five and the sand was
six there was so much of it. We were driving back to Lane
and all of a sudden we saw this deer spilled out in the middle
of the road. You know, someone had hit it and then taken
off."

I stopped. The mother looked fascinated. "When was
this?" she said politely.

"Last year sometime. Approximately one year and two
months ago." I don't know where in the world I came up
with that figure. "Huge antlers." I showed them the width
with one of my hands. I used the books as the other border.
"Like someone carrying a couple of sculptures on their head.
And so we passed this deer by. And whoever it was who was
driving honked. Honked, you know, let's be derisive as hell
about the deer, let's mock dead deers, ha ha ha, scorn the
dead deer. Amusing, right?" David made a move with his
shoulder that was probably a shrug and Mrs. Bennett nodded
a couple of times. "But even though it was a shame and
tragic and a loss there was nothing anyone could really do.
Then Freddie, who was sitting in the back with all that sand,
Freddie said, in this very deep, powerful, commanding voice:
We must stop this minute." I looked at Mrs. Bennett. "None
of us had ever even heard this voice before."

I had both of them entranced. You can pretty much tell by
people's faces when they're entranced. Mrs. Bennett took off
her dark glasses for a minute. She had large brown eyes and

the skin around them was lighter and redder than the rest of her skin.

"Anyway," I went on, "we tried arguing Freddie out of it. Saying it was too late on in the day, we were due back here, the sand was a sixth passenger, you know, don't stop. But Freddie wouldn't have any of it. And you kind of had to obey Freddie or else you didn't know what would happen to you. I'm talking here about retaliation. I'm not talking about small retaliations spaced out over a period of time, say, six months either." I thought of Freddie and his hand holding the fresh borrowed cigarette and the other unpopular boy, the one who fixed radios so quickly, sitting beside him and the tall black eucalyptus behind them. "I'm sorry," I said to Mrs. Bennett, "but you should probably know that Freddie had a very rough, exacting, bullying side to him, I mean, this Marseilles striped-jersey aspect that surfaced when you didn't expect it. He had one of those voices that just split through your protests. It was like a lighthouse beam. It was one of the great voices. It was like the sickle of some immigrant worker, you know, slicing at lettuce roots or something. I mean, I think Freddie might have turned out to be some terrifically powerful orator if he'd been given the chance. So we turned around. We had to make an illegal *U*-turn to do it but Freddie said in that incredibly stentorian boom of his, Let me worry about the law. You fellas do the driving, so we were more or less helpless. We were pinned to our seats just about." I looked at David. "He called us 'fellas,' which you probably recognize as not being what you call other people these days. The point here is that Freddie dared to be uncool." I faced the mother. "Your boy dared to be uncool. And when we got back to the deer Freddie scaled the side of the Jeep—he was always scaling things, cars, tennis nets, hurdles—and went over and knelt down beside it. All these other cars were going by honking, yelling, and then Freddie picked up this deer, just hoisted it up over his shoulders as though he'd been lugging game around half his life, then he walked that dead

deer over to the bushes by the side of the road and laid it
down gently so no cars would hit it. He covered it with
branches." I paused, wishing I'd never begun the story. "I
don't think I've ever forgotten that."

When I finished no one said anything for a minute. Both of
them looked pretty moved. David finally said, "That's a heck
of a story, Sam."

"I know," I said. "I know what it is."

"Boy," said the mother, shaking her head. She looked like
she was about to say something else but she just kept shaking her head.

"What I find remarkable is how Fred could have lifted up
something as heavy as a full-grown deer. That's dead weight
pretty much. If the antlers were as big as you said the rest of
the deer must have been colossal." David glanced at the
mother. "Freddie wasn't a physically large person."

"No he wasn't," Mrs. Bennett said.

I said, "That amazed me too. I mean, I've given it a lot of
thought. I think it's like one of those cases you read about in
those supermarket magazines, the *Sun*, the *Moon*, the *Star*,
one of those night magazines. You know, ninety-year-old
women who are able to lift up entire tractor-trailers with one
hand in a spunky way or else rescue fat boys who've sunk
through the ice because they didn't see the sign. Or babies
who are born singing Christmas carols. Certain people just
get this surge of energy when they see other people in trouble. In this case it was this deer. I think Freddie was probably
one of those people, spunky, plucky, whatever."

David said, "I didn't even know there were deer around
here."

"Oh, sure." I said it as though everyone knew about the
deer. "Oh, sure. In L.A. tons of deer. Deer all over the place,
on the beach, in the woods. Deer love it out here."

"Well, I didn't know anything about any of this," David
said to the mother. "I like to think I know pretty much
everything that goes on in this school but I just don't. I don't

think one can. That's a heck of a story, Sam," he said again.

"Yes, thank you, Sam, for telling me." For the first time Freddie's mother sounded tired. "There are whole sections of Freddie's life I don't know anything about. You hear about it, you know you have to wait to hear about it. You can't go around asking people."

David excused himself after a while to go say good-bye to someone and when he was gone Mrs. Bennett and I started talking about Lane. I could tell she thought it was a really fantastic school and everything. She asked me why I wasn't coming back in January and I almost told her but then I decided not to. I didn't think she would be exactly thrilled out of her mind that the Freddie Bennett Award for Willingness or whatever had gone to someone who had just gotten kicked out of his second school so I told her I would be doing an independent school project at home. That seemed to make her happy. At least she didn't ask me anything more about it. She asked me why I didn't like Los Angeles and I told her there was going to be an earthquake sometime and that I didn't want to be around when it happened.

She laughed. "Oh, they've been saying that for years. Years and years and years. I don't think you have to worry about that. Really I don't. You can't live your life that way, Sam. You can't go around thinking that any minute there's going to be an earthquake and you're going to be caught in the middle of it."

I said, "Yes, I can."

"Well, of course you can. But I wouldn't think you'd want to. Things are difficult enough without going around thinking that."

I said to her, "I don't really want to go around thinking that but I do anyway. I can't help it. It's not that I want to. It's not that I go out of my way every morning to think that. The only reason I'm out here in the first place is because my sister's here."

"What does she do? Your sister?"

"Actress."

Her face changed. "Is that so? You know, I used to do a little acting myself. Once upon a long long time ago. Regional things mostly. Musicals, a whole bunch of ladies my age kicking their legs in a chorus line. I did do Mrs. Alving in *Ghosts*, though, the Ibsen play. I still remember that. That was my favorite. Oh, I think I could have gone on playing Mrs. Alving forever. What's your sister's name? Would I know her?"

I said, "Lucy."

"Lucy what? Lucy Grace, of course." She was quiet. "That's your sister?"

I said yes and then I took a couple of steps backward, wishing I hadn't said anything.

Mrs. Bennett said, "Oh." Then she said, "Is that really your sister? Are we talking about the same one? The one who's on television?"

"Yes."

"The nun? Sister Kate? The nun on the scooter?"

She couldn't believe it. She sounded totally elated. I nodded and then I tried acting bored. I actually kind of enjoyed it when people found out.

"You know, I always wished I could have a television show," the mother said after a minute. "All my own. My very own television show. An actual show built around what I could do well. And I could choose who it was I wanted to have appear with me every week. Only the people I liked. But it would stay my own show. I would keep artistic control, isn't that the expression? And it would spotlight what I could do well." She smiled apologetically. "Whatever little talents I have. I'm pretty talented with people I guess." She shrugged. "Some people tell me."

She looked at me in this admiring way and then she reached down into the center of her purse and started fumbling around inside it. She kept talking. "I'm sure you'll be all right out here, Sam. In Los Angeles I mean. Really all right. And if you're back in the East ever I want you to come look us up. Seriously. Come visit us. I don't make that offer to everyone I meet either. We—I mean I—have a huge house, lots of room. There's even a hidden staircase off the dining room. I'll give you the keys to the car and you can take off and be free as a bird. I'm serious. You don't even have to eat with me. You can eat when the mood strikes you. I'll just give you the Duster and you can disappear off into the sunset."

That sounded pretty nice when she said that, disappearing into a sunset. She really was quite a decent person. She had a blue wallet in her hands now and she unzipped one side of it and then she took out five twenties and counted them off. She had pretty old-looking bills, all white and soft and beaten-up. The wind blew one of them down to the ground and it clung to Mrs. Bennett's ankle like some lost kid.

"This is for you." She pushed the bills down into my shirt pocket. "I don't even know if you and my son were friendly but you can consider this a present from us both."

I could feel the five twenties jammed against my chest. They felt warm. Mrs. Bennett put her wallet back inside her purse. She wasn't looking at me. "Buy something you really want. I wanted to give cash to whoever won but my husband, former husband rather, insisted on the Gibbon. I find Gibbon a great big bore myself. I tried reading it after Freddie died but I never made it through. I was pretty deranged then anyway, reading his books, listening to his records, trying to figure out what you do with someone's clothes. But I was clear enough to know I couldn't make it through the Gibbon." She gave a little shrug. "So I'm happier if you just had the money."

I thanked her and she kissed me on the forehead. I noticed she had all these thin little lines around her mouth that appeared when she kissed. "You were good to tell me that story," was the last thing she said and then she walked away. In a minute she was lost in the crowd milling beneath the green-and-white-striped tent. I stood in the driveway for a little while and then I wandered back over to where the tables were lined up. At the end of one of them I saw a tray of sherry glasses that one of the old Irish women had set down and I grabbed it and balanced it on top of the Gibbon books. I didn't take just one sherry glass, I took the entire tray, eight full glasses worth, and then I turned around and started walking in the direction of the soccer field. I could hear someone calling my name but I didn't stop.

To get down to the soccer field you have to cut through a tall green hedge. I laid the books and the sherry tray down on the dirt and climbed through the opening until I was on the other side of the hedge. When my body was through I got down on my hands and knees and pulled the tray and the books along the ground behind me. All these little curly green leaves fell into the sherry glasses and the sherry was so oily they didn't sink, they just started floating around. For some reason it made the sherry look festive. I'm crazy for drinks that have things floating in them. Anyway, I managed to drag the books and the glasses through the opening without spilling any sherry and then I reloaded the tray on top of the Gibbon and walked down a slope of short hard pavement in back of the library and crossed a private driveway that belonged to some foreign movie director, I can't remember his name exactly, and finally I was on the soccer field.

I started walking up the sidelines. I was holding out the books and the sherry tray like a waiter and trying to walk one yard at a time, which is pretty difficult if you've never tried it. The thick grey stripes on the field were pulpy from the rain that had come down the night before. The rain had taken everyone by surprise. It drove the smog out over the ocean. No one in Los Angeles knows what to do when it starts raining. You see all this panic rush like mad into their eyes and then you don't see them for about a week. The rain had messed up the field pretty badly. There were all these things lying around in the dirt, an old cracked blue shoelace and a couple of black and copper-colored batteries and a small heavy rusted pinball and someone's soggy theme tablet. I walked along past the team benches and the stone water fountain. The fountain was dribbling and the grass below the faucet was gleaming. I went around behind one of the soccer goalposts. The soccer nets were blue and they bagged in back of the frames. To my right was a long line of palms and on the other side of the field were these old green bleachers.

Back east a lot of people's houses and barns and pumphouses are that color: fir green and disintegrating all over the place. I crossed the field on about the sixty-five-yard line and when I got to the bleachers I started climbing them. The stairs made a lot of noise as I climbed, you know, you got the feeling the whole thing was about to cave in. All these sprays of wood were standing up and the grain was splintering and there were oval salty-looking puddles from where the sun had dried the planks. I sat down on the top bleacher and rested the Gibbon and the sherry tray beside me and then I drank a glass. I drank four glasses in a row, one after another, fast, barely tasting them. I don't want you to think I'm a lush or anything, I was just feeling slightly off my game that day, that was all. I stretched out my legs and I started thinking about Freddie Bennett.

I was flattered and all to get the books—I don't want you to think I wasn't grateful or anything—but it was the third award for a dead boy in a row that I'd won and that started to depress me a little bit. For one thing it sounded pretty ominous. I won an award at camp when I was twelve or something and then at Briar Hall I won another one. I never knew either of the guys the awards were named for but both of them were history before their eighteenth birthdays. The first guy was watching this television show, "Community Showcase," in the bathtub and he got himself electrocuted. In case you've never watched it, it's kind of a local talent competition and whoever's watching at home is supposed to send in a postcard with the number of the act they think is best on it and then the cards are tallied up by the show's producers and they name a winner, usually a little girl. The problem is that all the acts are usually terrible so it's a question here of choosing the one that's most bearable. There are about ten acts in all, mostly four-year-old kids wearing bells and straw hats and tap shoes and singing songs you know from the radio, using the same phrasing and inflections the original singers use and then smiling unhappily when they've finished. You know the mothers spent about three years in front of a mirror teaching these brats how you smile in a believable way and then when the time comes and it's worth something the kids flub it. Right before the show goes to commercial the cameras pan over the audience and you can see all these mothers sitting in the good seats, huge white gentle arms resting on their laps like the arms of mothers in family-owned businesses, you know, the ones who sit in chairs outside the store getting dive-bombed by bees or something. Sometimes middle-aged men in madras jackets come on and play ragtime or "Für Elise" and they stomp the pedals with this lifetime of accumulated rage. I mean, the show is embarrassing to watch. You have to make yourself watch it because otherwise you wouldn't. Anyway, the guy had a black-and-white set balanced on his wet raised knees and his hand was casing the bottom of the tub for some soap and he received this massive jolt of electricity and died.

That was one guy. I won the award named after him, which was a statuette of an eight-inch guy serving a tennis ball. The other guy was on one of those outdoor leadership programs Bob used to try and send me on, you know, where they cast you out into northern Montana or the Yukon or some other god-awful abandoned place like that and then tell you not to call them. This program was supposed to teach you self-reliance and responsibility and so forth but the guy ended up freezing to death so even if he succeeded in learning all those things they were kind of lost in the general freeze, if you get my point. They gave the guy a chocolate bar and a pack of wet matches and some fly-fishing lures and then they told him not to show his face for two weeks so the poor guy wandered around Montana or wherever it was for three weeks admiring all the clear lakes and the mountains, you know, the stark awesome beauty and so forth, and then he sat down on this grey rock and froze to death. His parents sued the hell out of the wilderness program and won about five million dollars. It was in all the papers, at least it was in all the Massachusetts papers.

I didn't know what winning these things meant. I didn't know if that meant I had the qualities of those guys right before they died or what. The sherry was making me pretty morbid and I decided that winning probably meant I was about to die too. I got the feeling someone was trying to tell me something, you know, giving me those three awards. It made me want to plan my funeral at once. I finished off all but one of the sherries and swallowed a couple of hedge leaves, which were still crisp, and then I started thinking I wanted to be one of those people who leave a lot of money with instructions that it be used to give a big party. Everyone would drink juleps and smoke More cigarettes, those long brown ones, and there would be dancing and things would fall and break. I leaned back against the bleacher frame. There were all these miniature spiderwebs up there, frail and ghostly looking, covered with a light cinnamon dust that I realized I had all over my fingertips. It was pretty dirty up there on that top bleacher. There's this whole universe of dirtiness high up that most people aren't even aware of since they can't see that far. It's on ceilings, handrails, pipes, light bulbs and along the rims of picture frames. It's just about the most unpublicized stuff in the world.

After a while with all that sherry and dust around me I kind of lost track of the time. Even though I'd had about seven glasses of sherry I couldn't manage to get myself drunk. It was pretty frustrating. One of the hedge leaves was caught in the back of my throat, at a point where my tongue couldn't get to it, and I tried swallowing it down but it wouldn't move. The only thing the sherry did for me was to put me in this elegiac kind of mood. From the top of the bleachers I could see most of the city spread out in front of me, sunny and dirty, brown and yellow, surrounded on all sides by blunt mountains. About three-quarters of a mile away, on the other side of a highway, I could see the North Hollywood Drive-In and above it a weather helicopter dropping and then swinging back up into the hot white sky. There were a couple of trucks in the drive-in parking lot and a guy who looked like a weight lifter was hosing down the screen. He had his fingers over the spout so the spray came out fast and a clear grey color. It curled off the screen in slow runs. The guy was so muscular he looked helpless.

I looked at the back lawns, at each dormitory, at the movie director's high fence, at the soccer goalposts and the tennis courts and I tried to commit each of them to memory. I figured it would be the last time I'd see any of those things for a while. I mean, I wasn't coming back to Lane and then I was going to die. I started wondering whether my father would establish some kind of annual award in my name. I couldn't decide what the award would be for but I knew it wouldn't be a good thing to win. Boys would have to be dragged up to the stage to accept it. I stared hard at each building and gritted my teeth until I could hear them, until it felt as though my ears were inside my cheeks and my jaw was going to break and then I said to myself, as sternly as I could take it, You will remember that building, the color of it and what its windows looked like from here, You will remember the tennis court, the way its net is hanging, the way its clay is all scuffed up. There was one more glass of sherry on the black tray and I grabbed it by the stem and stood up with it and almost fell. I started toasting out loud all the campus buildings I could think of. I toasted the library as though it were some great old show business friend I'd worked with in the early days, vaudeville or something: To a beautiful library, I screamed into the hot L.A. day, no, to a beauteous library, thanks, babe for being so special, even during the dark times. I toasted the science building: To a beautiful science building, I screamed this time more softly, you're the chief babe, you're it, big guy, it couldn't work the way it does without you. You know, toasts like that, empassioned and everything but basically empty.

I must have fallen asleep after all that toasting because the next thing I remember my neck felt stiff and the sky was grey and pink on one side of the city and purple on the other and the air had a soft dirty smell. I looked at my watch and it said five-fifteen. The party I was planning to go to had started at three and it was supposed to go on all night if it was good but I didn't feel much like driving up there anymore. Across the highways the first yellow and silver lights were coming on in the hills. From where I was sitting the entire city, curving up and away from me toward the brown, bulb-speckled mountains, seemed to be made up of small lights arranged in tired exact lines that extended forever, up the sides of the foothills, past the cold blue gel of swimming pools, over the buzzing wires of the canyons, the steep roads and back down to the beaches.

Just then the streetlights in the parking lot came on. I mean, they lit up right as I was looking at them and for a minute I didn't know what had happened exactly, only that something was different. The pavement under the bulbs changed color but I thought it was my mood that had changed. It was strange and kind of depressing seeing streetlights come on like that. I guess it was such a mature thing to have to witness, you know, the precise moment when it happened. I didn't particularly want to be around at that moment. I'd rather it took place when I wasn't anywhere around. It tended to ruin the mystery of the thing. I think if I were someone's parent I'd cover my kid's eyes if he happened to be in the vicinity of streetlamps between five and five-thirty at night, just so the kid wouldn't have to watch the actual moment when the lights turn on. I wouldn't want to let him know the whole thing was rigged.

I kept shrugging my shoulders and moving my neck

around in little circles, then bigger ones, to get out the sore-
ness. For some reason the streetlights coming on reminded
me of this night a couple of months earlier when I was walking down Melrose at about two in the morning. The only people on the street were these sudden bunches of kids in
black-and-white jackets. I remember I'd just read someplace
that Jennifer was the most popular name in California for the
seventh straight year in a row or something dynastic like that
and I remember thinking that I didn't know anybody named
Jennifer. I knew one Jennifer but she was old and pretty
neutral and the naming of her had taken place a while ago
but I didn't know any of the new ones. I was feeling sure I
would run into a couple that night and I was wondering if
there was anything distinctive about them, any way to know
them when I saw them. I was walking not on the sidewalk
and not on the street and I remember passing a boy and a girl
who were playing badminton in the middle of the street. The
yellow stripe down the center of the pavement acted as their
net. The guy had a stripe of hair taken off his head the thin
brown hair, slanting on his skull like a very light rain, was
just starting to grow in because he kept reaching up to drag
his fingernails along the stripe. The girl, who was Mexican
and plump, had her hair cut short and dyed part orange but
her bangs stayed black and they fell stiffly across her forehead. Her eyes looked puffy and one of them was yellow and
almost closed. No one else was out there on the street except
for these odd bunches of kids watching the game and the two
players. Both players had long wood rackets and it was dark
and warm and light came both from a moon and from the red
neon script in the windows of the bars and the nostalgia
clothing stores and somehow the two of them kept the dog-
nosed white bird aloft, even when an occasional car passed
under their net. The shuttlecock spun back and forth, quiet
and silken, and neither of the players spoke a word to each
other.

I was supposed to meet my sister at this bar called Jorges,

which everyone pronounced Whore-Gays and then they'd laugh afterwards. I was early so I hung around outside this old strawberry-colored theatre about a block away from the bar. The theatre was in pretty terrible condition. On the dark slippery glass of the box office someone had drawn a woman's lips and eyes and nostrils with a red crayon and coal for outlining, the lips swelled like two red balloons touching and the eyes huge and suspicious with sunflowers for the pupils. Across the street were people in long cars waiting outside the grey wire fence that wrapped around the park. In the backseats you could sometimes see the shoulders of old rich grey-haired gold-skinned guys or maybe you couldn't even make out the shoulders, just the brake lights and the hat of the hired driver and then after a while you heard a door open and slam shut and you could see these small blond figures disappearing through the soft rips in the grey wire and vanishing into the black park. Otherwise the street was silent except for the far-off swat of the bird and then after a while a tall thin man with one arm came out of Jorges with a plateful of marachino cherry stems with long curling tails and bits of old dark frayed cherry on the throats. He dumped them into the gutter outside the bar.

I was standing under the marquee when these three huge guys came out of the theatre carrying tall ladders. The last one out had beer cans clutched to his stomach. One of the guys propped his ladder up against the bottom shelf of the marquee and a second guy rested his ladder against the other side and then both of them started climbing into the night. When they were both at the top the guy who was still on the ground laid the beers down on the cement. He dragged a couple of cardboard boxes out from the shadows of the theatre entrance. He handed each guy on the ladder a box. He put on a hard hat and then he slit open one of the beers and took a long swallow. The ears of the boxes were worn and they looked as though someone had rubbed grease on them. Both guys on the ladders started taking the black letters down off the marquee and putting them in the cartons. Someone from inside the theatre turned on the marquee lights and the whole board was flooded with light. I thought I'd never seen a brighter light. In the new light the men on the ladders worked much faster, stopping only to drink the beers the man on the ground handed up to them. In fifteen minutes or so they had swept all the hard letters back into the carton and replaced them with the letters of another show. There were a couple of letters repeated, you know, an *a* and some *t*'s. The tall thin man came out of Jorges again, this time dragging a long green plastic sack behind him and across the quiet street I saw some movement under a steep shining slide and more kids were getting into cars and bending down or else getting wrung from backseats and then ducking through the wild rips in the fence wire and then the black cars drove away under the arc of the slow white bird.

There was nothing at all wrong with those workmen being up there, you know, I'm not saying there was. I'm not saying there's anything wrong with people doing their jobs and so forth but it was just something I didn't want to see. It was just so furtive, the fact they were changing the letters in the middle of the night with no one around. What you wanted to say to them was, Don't let me see that. What you really wanted was to come down in the morning and see that there was a new show and think the marquee had changed itself. I probably shouldn't have gotten so worked up about it, I realize, it was just the transition that bothered me so much. I remember walking away from the theatre and going inside Jorges and my sister being late and finally arriving but then we left almost right away. It had started to rain a little bit and we were almost at Lucy's car and we passed by a group of young boys with spiked blond hair squatting inside the doorway of a beautician's, trying to keep dry but not being spectacularly successful at it. Behind them, chalked against the soft brick, was an enormous cream-colored clock with no hands. It was just a clock with a bare face, a stopwatch maybe. The rain was coming down these kids' faces and all their mascara was crumbling, leaving twiglike shadows beneath their eyes. All of them looked like the same person, a blond boy with bright hair and blue eyes and the same caked black color on his cheeks. My sister offered them a ride somewhere, that is if they were headed anyplace in particular, and it turned out they were all going to some old guy's house up on Doheny, another party. I mean, first they told her she wouldn't want to go anywhere near where they were going and then I know they recognized her and they all got in the car and spent the ride trembling and telling jokes.

I was thinking about all that for some reason and then I got down off the bleachers. I had to hold onto the rail practically the whole way down. When my feet touched the field I managed somehow to swallow the shrub leaf that was still in my throat and I almost gagged on it but then it was in my stomach. I was feeling pretty dizzy and if you'd asked me something I think my voice would have come out soft—I'd have had to say it twice. Across the fields the dormitories were dark and still. There were a few lights on here and there but most people had already left for Christmas vacation. Everyone had either gone back east or gone south or gone to the beach or just plain gone home. When I pushed back through the hedge I could see the green-and-white-striped tent lying on its sides in thick ballooning folds. Close up you saw the white was actually this well-washed grey and the green stripe closest to me had a series of small razor nicks across it. In one corner of the lawn the old Irish women were silently stacking olive chairs onto a dark metal dolly. An old man was sweeping the grass with a yellow broom. The guy must have been about ninety or something. I knew him a little bit, you know, enough to nod to and to know that if I said hi to him he would never say it back. Once after some exam or another I gave him a light and when I did he held my hands tightly even though we weren't in a wind or anything. As he swept he left long yellow bristles on the grass and the transistor radio that hung from his belt swung back and forth. The reception was wavy as though the songs were coming from underwater. The old Irish women were upsetting the long tables and folding back the legs. The old man saw me walking across the lawn toward the parking lot and he stopped sweeping. "Hello, Richie," he called. He sounded pretty cheerful. "Beautiful night, isn't it?" He held his dustpan up against his chest as though he were using it to take an oath. The left side of it had come too close to flames and it was all mangled, swollen with old dried bubbles. "You don't get them prettier than this."

The thing is, it wasn't all that terrific a night. Almost every night in L.A. was exactly like that night. I just kept walking.

"Sweeping up here," the old man said, leaning into his broom. "People give out a heck of a lot of mess these days. Maybe it's imagination but it seems they're giving out more than what's plain habit. Still it's a privilege working here, Richie, every year the same privilege. Remind me though not to take a second job again."

He tossed his dustpan into the orange garbage can. The sides of the can were sticky from misaimed sherries and the stickiness had hardened in the wind. Five or six striped wasps were flying around the stacks of empty glasses. A couple of the wasps were sitting on the bottom of the top glass, up to their ankles in sherry, not moving. They looked as though they were praying.

"They can do that, Richie," the old man said, staring at the garbage can. He seemed suddenly glum. "The stars can throw away entire dustpans when they're dirty, the way I just did. Not empty it but throw it away and buy a new one. I did that just then to see what it felt like." He was quiet for a minute and then he went over to the can and fished out the dustpan. He held it in both hands. "I didn't like the feeling of that," he said.

The wasps were buzzing at the bottom of the sherry glass. The glass had tipped over in the wind so the half inch or so of sherry at the bottom was beginning to close over the wasps' heads. The plastic was cloudy. I wondered without interest whether wasps had breath. I wondered why the old man was calling me Richie, who he thought I was.

He stared at me. "Having two jobs is not very good for the energy level," he said after a while. "It starts to wear you down right about this time of night."

"Yeah it must," I said.

The old man sighed loudly. He started sweeping again.

"Okay," I said, "what's your second job."

He stood absolutely still. Even his radio stopped swaying. I could hear the vibrations of the wasp in the plastic glass. Then he said, "I'm an actor."

"You too." Sometimes it seems as though everybody in the state of California is an actor or else wants to be. There's something a little bit depressing about everybody wanting to be an actor all the time.

"Are you, Richie? Is acting your particular calling too?"

"No," I said pretty stiffly. "It's not my calling."

"Oh, don't be sorry. An overcrowded field now as it stands. More opportunities for me then, you see. Yes, I'm a little bit of a bit actor is what I like to call myself, Richie. You don't mind me calling you Richie, do you? Or do people call you Richard?"

I said, "Either."

"A supernumerary," he went on. "Still do a lot of extra-man's work today but you don't make much of a living at it. So I supplement." He was gripping his broom. "You graduate, Richie? Folks here today?"

"My father was," I said. "And my sister was."

"Mom couldn't make it, eh?"

"She's dead," I said.

"Ah, so's mine," he said. A moment later he said, "I miss her, my mother."

We didn't say much after that. I started wandering around the lawn and I stepped on a long piece of plastic and it cracked under my heel and the crack made me jump. The old man turned on his radio and a song came on that they had played a lot during the Olympics a couple of years ago. It was the unofficial theme song of the little girl who won the balance beam competition. I mean, most people associated the song with this flat little braided kid in plum-colored tights. She actually came in third or fourth in the competition but the song got to be number one on the radio so people got confused and started thinking that this American kid had won the gold medal, which she hadn't. In any case the song was ruined forever. The old man turned down the volume. He looked at me and shook his head. "I hate the junk they play all the time," he whined. "You ever heard any Ray Noble? Bandleader?" I shook my head. "How about a guy name of Al Bowlly? Are they listening to a guy named Al Bowlly anymore?" I kept shaking my head. It felt good, shaking my head. I could have shaken my head for about a month. "High clear voice. The Boswells? Boswell girls?"

"Nope." I started walking toward the parking lot again.

"Nothing was sweeter than those three Boswells, Richie," he called after me.

I was thinking about that wispy little American kid circling the hard polished bar and in the audience her father the surgical instruments salesman waving a small striped flag on a stick that looked like an emery board. I thought about her springy walk and her proud, narrow ribs and how she threw herself backward into space and onto the rubber mat that was hard and soft at the same time. You expected her to crack her skull or something but she landed on her feet, spreading her arms like a dictator.

When I was almost at the parking lot I heard the old man calling Richie's name again. "What are you going to do during Christmas hiatus? Stay here?"

All of a sudden I realized I had left the three Gibbon books and the box they came in on top of the bleachers. My arms and fingers still felt the weight from carrying them but it was only the past impression of weight, weight from three or four hours earlier. The books themselves were back across the soccer field, sixteen stairs up from the grass and the mud. I debated going back for them but instead I went into my pocket for my car keys. Somehow during the day I had gotten white paint on my fingers. I called back to the old man, "Go west." I pinched the key that started the car. Then I shouted, "It's Sam, it's not Richie."

"Go west," he echoed back when I was half inside my car. "You'll be in water then. You can't get more west than the water now. And it's sharktown U.S.A. out there." When I looked back he was sweeping again and the radio was yelling and the hot plastic of the car wheel was burning my hands.

* Chapter 2 *

No one was at my sister's when I got there. The house was quiet and there was a scrap of blue paper taped to the glass doors facing the ocean telling me to meet Lucy and my father at eight at some restaurant called Billy's-on-the-Dock, which meant I had about an hour. I went out onto the porch and unclenched one of the tall thin windows and a gust of warm salt air blew into my face and shook my lashes and then I turned on the VCR and sat down in this incredibly ancient dark green lounge chair that my family's had for about as long as I can remember. It's a pretty terrible chair, actually. All the buttons are chipped or missing and these hard springs jab at your skin and the foam is pale and it's uncomfortable as hell but for some reason I like sitting there. I sat for about twenty minutes listening to the waves and I watched the sky turn a strange green color like pickle water and then I realized the record player was on and the needle was splashing up against the end of the album and that was the sound I'd thought was waves.

There was an old cassette of Lucy's show in the VCR and the show opened to a shot of Sister Kate's convent, which is this huge brown stately building overlooking a vineyard.

There was tape of my sister in her nun outfit sitting on a narrow bed looking dejected. A white bird was poised on the windowsill and Lucy was saying, "Oh, bird, you're the only creature I can confide in," and five minutes later she was still bitching to this bird. Outside the convent window the sun was bright and the clouds were in sort of a heaven formation, all puffy and layered, the way you imagine heaven to look like when you're about four years old, and Lucy was slowly taking off her veil, releasing her hair from behind the tight elastic and letting it spill down her back. Then she took off the blue triangular glasses they make her wear on the show and put them on the bedside table.

I swear, they had that same shot every week, not the bird but the undressing. I think it was meant to show that beneath her habit and her beliefs and all Sister Kate was a woman and so forth, with needs and urges, etcetera, with all that entails and that if she'd only take her hair down once in a while she'd be, you know, a more relaxed person, or at least a more well-rounded nun. It's a pretty offensive concept actually. A lot of women in the Midwest make up signs and stomp around in circles in front of the affiliates whenever the show comes on. You see them on the late news all the time, these short stocky dark-haired women with their daughters trailing behind them, miserable little kids already named Doris or Leonore carrying placards with their mothers' black handwriting on them and looking bored out of their minds. Part of the tension of the show is whether Sister Kate will come to terms with her womanhood or whatever or whether she'll stay on at the convent solving crimes no one else can solve. My sister says the producers want her to do both and that they also want the white bird to become a permanent member of the cast and maybe sing on some future shows. Anyway, the result of all this tension is that Kate is constantly having to renew her vows in front of everybody, all the other sisters and the mother superior, even Chato, the convent gardener. It's pretty embarrassing. I mean, it's embarrassing as a viewer to have to watch. She has to renew her vows at the end of every show practically and on this one show she had to renew them four times. "Sister Kate" is only an hour show too, remember. Lucy keeps saying it'll be her absolutely last season but the show is so popular and they pay her so much money I think she'll probably do it for a little while longer.

There were all these polished holly bushes out on the porch, small slippery leaves and red berries and sprays of wheat-colored wood tied at the bottom with red felt string and jammed into glass vases. All this stuff was supposed to be holidaylike and all but the only thing it did to me was make me think of the East. It was Christmas and it was hot and I felt like going to bed and putting the covers over my face and smothering myself or something. Down the beach someone was drilling so all the time I was out there on the porch the holly leaves were trembling and the glass was chattering and I started thinking of earthquakes and of strangers jumping the high walls and coming down onto the beach and then I drove out to the restaurant because I couldn't stand being alone in the house anymore. It was about a twenty-minute drive and the restaurant was at the end of a long brown pier. My sister and my father were sitting in a booth by the window. Lucy was wearing baggy purple shorts and pink socks and dark green glasses with white frames and her Red Sox cap.

I sat down in the chair next to my father. He moved his chair closer to the window. "Have enough room," he said. It was somewhere between a question and an instruction.

"Boy, that's a really smashing disguise you have there," I said to Lucy. "Really, no one in a million years would ever guess it was you."

"You can't see my face, can you?"

I said, "I can't see your face but your clothes—I mean, no normal person would wear those clothes. No normal person would bother to conceal themselves up that much."

"Oh come on, leave me alone," Lucy said. She said it kah-mann and she kept her dark glasses on. "Kah-mann. I'd rather look like a clown or a juggler than, I mean, the alternative doesn't really reach out and grab me."

"Conspicuous anonymity," my father said. "That's what that is." On either side of us were huge clear windows and along the thin spine of dock fishermen in red slickers were fishing for garibaldis. He looked across the table at Lucy. "I never knew you were such a Sox fan."

"Well sure." My sister shrugged. "They lose all the time, why not be. And they always do it in a dignified kind of regal way so it reverberates in you. So after a while it's an inevitable thing. It's like watching a Greek drama. It's a march of losing. You say to yourself, Of course they lost and I look the way that I do and my car's where I left it. It becomes part of the composition of your life, their losing. Just like the way you look. Driving home: Of course they lost." Her voice rose. "Of course. What did I expect them to do, win one? Win a couple? I think winning might throw them, us, everything into a chaos, Bob, come on."

I asked my father how his afternoon had gone.

"We were creamed," Lucy said.

My father shook his head. "Terrible."

"Why?"

"Disaster," Lucy said. "We had an afternoon of minidisasters."

"What happened?"

"It was very disappointing," my father said to me.

Lucy said, "We drove up the coast, about an hour up. Or I drove. I did all the driving so Bob could look out and see the water and that was very terrific of me. It was halfways up the state practically. It made my wrists ache." She spun them and then she started pulling at the tips of her fingers.

My father said, "Oh, I offered to drive."

"Yes, you did but you only go twenty miles an hour in fourth. He does," she said to me. "In fourth gear he's just pushing twenty, eighteen, nineteen. Here the car's agonizing underneath you, it's saying, This is not right, this is not the way I like it."

"Not true," Bob said to me.

"Yes, it is. Anyway," Lucy went on, "we went into a mall to ask directions and at this place where we asked directions, this Ronnie's Pet Chalet, we asked Ronnie or Ronnie's brother, some male in charge, where we could find the air force track and he took us back outside until we were almost back at the car and he pointed to a dog track about a half-mile away and he turned to Bob and said, There's your air force base right there, Major, and he started laughing. He couldn't stop laughing. I think there might have been something wrong with him actually. He wouldn't stop."

Bob looked at me. "It was a dog-racing kind of operation, Sam. If you can believe that. They'd bulldozed the base and half a neighborhood to make a track for those greyhound dogs."

"And rabbits too." Lucy took off her dark glasses. The waiter came and we ordered. "Big mangy rabbits in the straw," she said after he'd gone. "I think it was a farm for rabbits of some kind. So we went down to the track to see if anything was salvageable, like the trip for one. No, I mean like one dormitory or an airplane wing but the only thing we saw were these tense ugly dogs. No hair on them. Like swimmers in the Olympics. They looked like knuckles. Just disgusting. Just revolting. And the stadium was filled with big white people clapping. And just as we were leaving some woman came up to me, I think she was a maniac." My sister rubbed her eyes. "Bob, don't you think she was a maniac of some kind? She said, Sister, Sister, I have a problem and I need you to solve it and she started rubbing my back. I screamed. I mean, it would have felt good if it weren't so weird, right? I told her if she was asking for advice on any subject she was, what was the word I used, misdirected. At least," she said to my father, "we saw a little bit of your L.A."

"Lucy, at least we saw a little bit of my L.A.," Bob repeated.

"Well, all this is too bad," I said.

"Well, yes, Sam, sure it's too bad," my father said. "Like a lot of things, nothing you can do about them, or it."

On the dock one of the fishermen pulled up a garibaldi and slung it across the wood. He knelt down over it and pulled the hook from its lip. In case you've never been out to California garibaldis are the state fish or something like that. They're orange and it's supposedly against the law to catch them but people come around at night and fish for them anyway. If you catch one during the course of a normal fishing expedition you're supposed to throw it back, but what usually happens is that people throw back the fish that aren't garibaldis. A whole bunch of people get together and drink a lot of beer and drop their lines and when they catch one they drop it in a tub of dark warm water and watch as the tail slaps the sides. Then they take it out and stun it with a shingle or something. When they're finished with it they stand high over the greasy marina water and watch as the orange figure twists twenty feet until it punches the water and drifts back-first to the bottom of the harbor and you can't see it anymore.

My father asked the waiter for a wine list and after a while he ordered a bottle of red wine. Lucy began drawing on the tablecloth. They had a dirty drinking glass full of crayons of long and short lengths and you were supposed to draw on the table while you waited for your food. My sister drew some huge eyes with long lashes and my father held a red crayon between his fingers but he didn't draw anything and I just smoked and looked out the window. A fisherman with orange cheeks and eyelids was opening up a baitbox. The baitbox was green and it had shelves that came out on short plastic arms and the shelves had shallow drawers in them and the drawers were soaked with chew and dark blood, whittled skin, dewy flecks of bait and long-soaked feathered flies. On the rails of the dock grey enormous gulls were perched and the wind was blowing their mouths open and closed and on the beach thin black smoke poured out of barbecues standing on spider legs in front of the crooked boardwalk houses. Grunions were peeling around the sand. Some of the houses had writing on their porches and glass doors and chairs, filmy red-and-green circles and arrows wildly drawn.

When the wine arrived my father poured three glasses. "Well, here's to all of us," he said, looking at Lucy and then at me. "I've never won a thing in my life, Sam, congratulations."

"That's not true," Lucy said. She was drawing a girl's nostrils in pink and black and a color the crayon called peach melba. She looked up and drank half her wine in a hurry. "What about that junky bowl in the bathroom? In New York?"

"Oh, they were giving those things away," my father said. "All that year they were giving those awful things away. You're right, junky. All you had to do was get in a line. It's worth about a buck fifty." Bob was silent for a moment and then I guess he decided he hadn't made clear just how unimportant the bowl was because he added, "Everybody got a bowl that year, even the people who didn't play. The people with sprained ankles got one."

It was hard for me to picture my father as an athlete. In New York I was used to seeing him come out of the shower and then he'd walk down the hallway dripping water on everything, you know, his stomach all stretched and austere, and then I remembered once I was digging through some old drawers in the kitchen and I found his posture picture. In case you've never seen a posture picture that's when a guy has to stand on some kind of strange dais totally naked except for a jockstrap. The guy is supposed to hold back his shoulders and squeeze in his ass and then the coach or someone like that snaps his picture. It's pretty embarrassing. Anyway, in this posture picture my father must have been about twenty-two and his hair was smooth and short and brown and the skin on his arms was flat and his stomach was hard. I remember being pretty shocked you could change in looks that much during your life.

I started thinking about the summer after I was kicked out of Briar when the school made me go to some shrink on Ninety-sixth Street. I was living at my father's apartment and I remember this shrink I went to was always after me to get some exercise and he suggested I try running. The guy even offered to go with me but I told him I ran better alone, which was just a guess. After that I started jogging through Central Park in the heat about three times a week. I never ran that far, maybe four miles or something, but this route I followed always took me past an incredibly old, scuffed-up baseball diamond that no one played baseball on anymore. I mean, occasionally these bad actors from soap operas played there for charity and little kids in loose blue sweatpants played pickle and ran dashes with one of them squeezing a watch, but otherwise it was just another ruined thing no one used anymore. All the bases were gone so you had to use your sweater or your sneaker if you wanted to play an actual game. You could just imagine some guy from Columbia or N.Y.U. sneaking into the park some midnight and tearing up the bases from the dirt and thinking they'd made his room look deeply sporty and that girls would think he was this interesting gritty guy but then he'd get back to his room and find out the bases just made his room ugly.

The batting cage had holes from where the wire was torn and on either side of home plate there were all these terrifically old people sitting on reddish wood benches, kind of watching a game that wasn't taking place. You could tell it wasn't all that good a game since most of them had their faces tilted up toward the sky. The first time I ran past that diamond and saw all those old people I slowed down until I was skipping and then I reduced my skip to a walk. I suddenly started feeling guilty that I was able to run and they weren't. I was in the area between third base and home and I turned around and went into the outfield so they couldn't see me running and start feeling like hell that they couldn't. One very old guy with wire glasses actually smiled at me when he saw my sneakers and that just made me feel worse, you know, that he was being mature enough to condone my running. After that I kept seeing all these people who for some reason or another couldn't run: old people, babies, fat people, bums, and since I didn't want to make them feel bad I refused to go faster than a walk when I was around them. I'd only start running when their backs were turned and then a couple of weeks went by and I noticed I wasn't getting any exercise at all anymore so I quit running and started riding this old red bike I found in the basement of my father's building.

The next thing that happened is what I remember when I think of my father coming out to L.A. and it happened right after the waiter brought our food and my father was asking us what we wanted for Christmas. All of a sudden I noticed this couple staring at Lucy. The man was tall and his hair was grey and pretty long and he had a pair of crutches under his arms. There were rings of dirty white tape around the wood leg, above the pink rubber tips and securing the bridges where your hands wrap. The woman was small and her hair was short. She stared hard at my sister. I'd seen people look that way at Lucy before. It's one-third filled with desire and the middle third is helplessness and the last third looks like hatred. They were standing about five feet away from us and then the woman softly called out Lucy's name and my sister paused in the middle of what she was saying and looked up. "Lucy," the woman said, "would you sign your autograph for my husband Ben, please?"

Bob looked at Lucy and then he touched his hand to the stem of his wineglass. He looked amused.

Lucy said, "Sure. Sure of course."

The man's crutches came forward slightly. "Do you have paper on you?" my sister said to the woman. "Or pencil?" She asked the woman what name she should write.

The woman said, "What do you mean what name?" She

came closer but the man stayed where he was. "We watch you every week, dear, what name should I write, we love you. We love watching the show, Lucy. Ben is the name you should write. That name is not my name, that's my husband's name. My name is Sally, very pleased to make your acquaintance." She put out her hand and my sister took it and then let it go. The woman smiled at my father and touched him on the shoulder. "We're sorry to interrupt your meal, dear. Hello," she said to me. "Nice meeting all of you." She looked at the bandage on Lucy's wrist and she touched her own wrist. "What did you do to yourself, dear, were you in the dumps?"

Lucy acted as though she hadn't heard her. "Is it just plain to Ben? Or sincerely?"

"Ben would like you to sign his cast," the woman said. "Something for which we have a special marker. A thick dark one. Thank you, Ben, for watching my show week after week, very best wishes, followed by your name, Lucy." She started again. "Thank you, Ben, for watching my show week after week and then you add, As time goes by. Very best wishes from Lucy Grace." She held out a black magic marker. "Or put down whatever the muse inspires you.".

Lucy looked confused. "I'm signing a cast? Is that what I'm supposed to sign?"

"That's right. Ben had an accident at his brother's farm. In Lake Geneva, Wisconsin. Four hundred spectacular acres, Lucy, if you're ever in Lake Geneva for any reason you must stay at the fantastic property owned by Ben's brother Donald. Four hundred acres and Ben happened to be standing on the acre with the funny mower on it. Before you know it he has a cast on one of his legs and for six months he can't walk like a normal man."

Ben smiled a little weakly. He was standing next to Sally now. He said in a low voice, "Oh, it's not so bad, Sal," and then he nodded at Lucy and shifted his weight on the crutches. Outside through the glass I watched as a boy in a yellow beret spread out a black rug and began stacking paperback books and records. All the records were by folk singers from the sixties. The women had octagonal faces and long thin hair and the men had pockmarks and most of their songs had to do with transportation. Finally the boy took four bottles of orange salad dressing out of a leather bag and stood one bottle on each corner of the rug.

"You know, I might wait until we're all finished dinner," my sister said. "If that's all right. Under the table I could feel her foot looking for mine.

"Well, Ben and I are leaving the restaurant this very minute," the woman said, "so that wouldn't be altogether convenient for us." She was smiling but her lips were hard.

"I'm pretty starving," my sister said. "I haven't eaten anything yet and we're all trying to have dinner—" She gestured and looked at my father.

"Lucy," the woman said, as though they were these two terrifically old good friends from high school or something, "what's eating you dear? What's the big bug? Is it the fast-lane life that's making you so snappish? Every time I see your face now in the magazines it's walking out of this or that nightlife palace, this or that location that's fashion, dancing and drinking until 5:00 A.M. in the morning. Other people are home to bed but Lucy Grace stays out and she dances and she takes a lot of drugs probably is what the sources say." The woman leaned down. "If you want my opinion, Lucy, you should never have left Mr. Bel Air hotshot big-budget producer cocaine man. You should have gotten married. That's just my opinion, Lucy, take it with a grain of salt. It's not a problem for him anymore—"

"Just a minute," my father said.

"It's not an ugly or time-consuming thing I'm asking, Lucy. The cast is smooth, here, feel, it's no different from touching wood that hasn't been sanded. Here, dear, feel the wood." She made a move for Lucy's hand but my sister's hand flew up.

"Don't you touch me." The skin around my sister's mouth was trembling like crazy. She said, "Please."

"Don't you touch me," the woman repeated the same way only higher. "Don't you touch me, oh, I'm a delicate flower, don't touch me. That's marvelous, Lucy. May I quote you on that nice talk? The bigger the star the better-mannered the star and of course I'm being sarcastic now. The Bob Hopes, the Carole Lombards, the really big ones, the supernova stars, can be civil and afford to be. In Mr. Hope's situation here is a man with the energy of maybe five men traveling the world over performing class acts as America's premier entertainer of people. A man who's made more people the world over happier than any other performer. It's the television such as yourself, the too-much-too-sooners I call you people, who are the boors."

My father said, "Excuse me but we're trying to have a little dinner here. We're trying to have a conversation. We haven't see each other for at least a year, her brother here—" He pointed at me "—and my son. I'm her father."

"Don't tell her how we're related for Christ's sakes." My sister's voice was getting louder. "It's none of her goddamn business what we are to each other."

"Is it because of Ben's condition?" Sal was holding out the magic marker and the cap was off now and I could smell the tip. She was jabbing it at Lucy. "Is it because Ben is a physically challenged individual? Or is it because you're arrogant?"

My father stood up and he hit the woman across the mouth with the side of his hand. It was soft, the way he did it. It sounded like a chunk of snow falling off the roof. I think he changed his mind right before he made contact but by then it was too late to take back his hand. Immediately he said, "I'm sorry. I'm very sorry that that just had to happen. Will you please accept my apologies for having done that."

The woman was bent over as though Bob had hit her in the stomach. "How could you have?" she kept saying. "We never ever hurt you."

"I'm sorry," my father said. None of us moved. Then Bob said, "Oh, Jesus," as the couple started walking toward the door and I looked out the window for the boy in the yellow beret. My sister said, "I can't believe my life involves this." The four bottles of salad dressing shook in the wind. One of the fishermen had a bite and his line was jumping softly. I watched Ben and Sally walking down the dock close to the rails and my sister's face was dark and then she started drawing some sort of large animal on the tablecloth. My father and I just sat there watching her draw. The woman had left the magic marker cap on the table and Lucy's strokes went around it. She drew stripes on the animal's coat and she colored in the tail and put arches inside the ears. She did too much, she ruined it. The fisherman with the bite pulled in a garibaldi. You could see patches of black inside its stomach and the head and the tail were covered with little blue spots, which meant that it was a juvenile. It was struggling like crazy, biting at the air. My father's hand was wrapped around the handle of his fork and the fork looked bright and sad. When the waiter came he ordered another drink. "You know, I can't get over those dogs," he said when his drink came and then he laughed.

"Dogs?" I said.

"At that track." He stared at me. "I only wish you'd seen them, Sam. Right over the place where I used to take my meals. Fifty dog bowls lined up in the dirt. I can't get over that, how far it was we had to drive for those dogs. How far it was you drove rather," he said to Lucy.

"When were you there?" she said.

"Oh, 'fifty-three, 'fifty-four." My father sounded a little sad. "And maybe some of nineteen fifty-five. You know, I used to go to a lot of concerts when I was out here. Believe it or not. I don't know why this place reminds me of that but it does for some reason. Classical music is something your mother attempted to introduce me to. She loved it a lot. She thought it was just about the height you could get to. A human being, I mean, not only a musician."

"Ah." Lucy nodded.

"Do you like classical music?" I said to him.

My father looked surprised. "Oh," he said. He shook his head and drank some of his drink. "Well, nowadays, Sam, no, not particularly much. Not much anymore. I find it depressing for the most part. Too moody. Too sad really." He laughed again.

God, I didn't want to think of my father sitting around getting sad. Neither did my sister, I could tell. A little while later when we were drinking coffee Bob touched Lucy and me on the hand at the same time and said, "Well, I think this is just great, being here with you guys," and I thought that was pretty sad as well. Everything Bob said that night had this faint taste of sadness to it, maybe not enough to mention but just enough to make you pretty depressed. My father stared down at his hand. "You know, I don't think I've ever done that before. Hit someone. I don't think I've ever done anything like that." He looked at Lucy. "Have you? Ever hit someone?"

"Thank you, by the way," Lucy said. "I mean that." It was the first time the subject had come up since it happened. "And yes. I've delivered some shots in my life."

"Who?"

She was vague. "Oh, I don't know. I just remember there was a time, some time I seemed to be hitting someone for one reason or another every two weeks or so. Or more. It probably wasn't that way at all though. And I guess a few were retaliative."

"Someone hit you?"

There was a silence.

"Oh sure," Lucy said after a minute. She pulled a blue crayon out of the glass.

Bob turned his spoon over. "Like who?"

"Who?"

"Who. Hit you. Who did you need to be retaliated with, at? Jay?" Jay was some producer my sister went out with.

"Probably it was Jay," she said.

My father said, "Why didn't you say anything?"

"What are you talking about?" she said. "It didn't occur to me. Just Jay wasn't all that crazy about breaking off. After it happened he offered to make me up all these tapes, you know, to show there were no hard feelings. He has a huge collection of old jazz records, about four walls' worth, old seventy-eights and a victrola. He made up these tapes and then he pretended it was this general archival selection, the best of, and when I played it I noticed all the songs were things like 'You're Mean to Me' and 'No Moon at All' and 'Don't Worry about Me' and 'Nobody Knows You When You're Down and Out.' And so forth. You get the picture. As if anybody could possibly miss it."

"But he hit you," my father said.

"Don't look like that, Bob. I shouldn't have mentioned it. Forget I said anything about it. Who else is some guy going to hit? There's no third sex waiting around and women who beat up each other, well, that's usually over some oboist they both like or in prison bitch movies or something. Who else was he going to hit?"

My father looked at me. "Sam, has anybody ever hit you?"

Automatically I shook my head.

"But you've hit a few people."

"You slugged that lacrosse player," Lucy said. "That was a major hit."

"A few people," I said.

"Jesus, I remember that," my father said. He looked back at Lucy. "That's it, Jay, then?"

"Can't think."

"How about Ted?" I said to her.

"Nope."

"Lorne?"

She said, "Why are you asking me this?"

"Who's Ted?" my father said to Lucy. "Did I ever meet Ted and Lorne?"

"A couple of deadbeats," Lucy said.

"Santo?" I said.

"Why have I never heard of any of these people?" Bob said. "Where did this Santo come from? Originally I mean? When was all this? And what was I doing?"

"Just the tip of the iceberg, Bob," my sister said. She laughed.

My father was quiet. Then he said, "I don't like the idea of you two getting hit."

"Well, we don't desire to get hit," Lucy said. "It's not as though we tell these people to hurry up, hit us. Usually we defend ourselves. We don't want it particularly."

The bill came and my sister took it off the tray.

My father held out his hand. "Please," he said.

"It's mine."

"I want you to save your money."

"I'm loaded," she said.

"You should save it."

"For what?"

"I don't know. Christmas is coming up."

Lucy was searching through her handbag. "Oh, shit," she said after a minute. "I must have left my wallet in my other pants."

Bob took the bill from her and started studying it. He took his glasses off and put them on the table. I looked through one of the lenses and it made the saltshaker look as though it were a million miles away. My father paid with a credit card and as we were getting up to leave one of the waiters came over and asked Lucy if she would sign the tablecloth. Bob watched over her shoulder as she wrote "Lucy Grace" under the animal she'd drawn and wrecked and when she finished he stared at her signature. "It's like mine a little bit, you know that? The way it's turned out. Look at that." He sounded pleased. "You do your *g*'s the same way as mine. I'll bet you cross your sevens too."

"Always," and I wondered why she said that because I knew it wasn't true. We went outside. It had gotten even hotter while we were inside the restaurant. The thin white masts in the harbor were rocking and the water looked warm and grey. There were kids climbing on the rocks. I told my father and my sister that I'd meet them by the car and then I went to find a bathroom. I found one in a pump house at the end of the next dock over. It was half on the beach and half over the water. The door was made of purple slats and there was a poster stuck to it. The poster was losing its glue and there were about thirty tackholes in each corner and in two of the corners the streak of thumbtacks had slit the paper so you could see colored wood underneath. The poster showed pictures of four children. There was one child's face in each corner. The children must have been about seven or eight. There was a long-faced girl with braces named Adana. Then there was some kid in the top left-hand corner named Bobby Maker who was blond with a long thin neck. He looked like a pretty nice kid. The other children were named Andrea and Alfred. Alfred had black eyebrows that touched in the middle. Across the top of the poster was written in big broad letters, Have You Seen These Children? and under that someone had written in light green ink, slanting, Maybe We Have. Either the same person or another person had marked up all the kids' faces so that even if you spotted them you wouldn't know it was the same kid. The girl named Adana had one black sharp tooth to every white one and her eyes had been singed with a cigarette end. Bobby Maker had a mustache and the start of a goatee before the artist had gotten bored and quit shading in the hair. Alfred was wearing one of those soft white high collars as though his throat had been shattered.

The bathroom was just beyond a small changing room and it smelled like ammonia and pot smoke and old fish. On the wall someone had painted, L.A. Was the Place in black. There was this fat bearded guy standing in front of the only urinal with his back to me. He had a huge stomach like a sheriff and he wore a grey cap. When I came in he looked once over his shoulder and then he looked back down. I

waited by the sink for him to finish. There were wet pieces of
paper towel clinging to the green crossed metal of the drain. I
would have gone into the stall but I could see two sets of legs
and shoes in there. The stall didn't have a door, just a set of
flapping hinges that had been painted white, and a blue
overcoat slung across the space where the door used to be.
There was no mirror above the sink either, just the screws
and wall holes and dust where it had been removed. The
paint was very white above the sink but everywhere else it
was pale.

"I'm gonna be here a while," the fat bearded man called
behind him. He didn't turn. "Melting the ice. Use the fucking sink." He looked over at the shoes under the stall. "Good
buddies over here to our left. To our left are some especially
good buddies. Guess they couldn't wait."

I ended up using the sink, which jutted out at waist level.
There was dried green toothpaste on the spokes of the faucets and patches of white paint inside the sink that were so
close to the color of marble you almost didn't notice them.
The fat man turned around and looked at me. I stared ahead
into one of the empty screwholes. On the wall someone had
written, Get Girls through Hypnosis and then circled it. Underneath the circle was a name, Nick, and a telephone number that was mostly threes. I mean, out of seven digits four of
them were threes.

The fat man started laughing. He hadn't zipped up his
pants. "You're all right, man," he said, still looking at me.
"You're actually really doing it. You're all right."

I finished and moved away from the sink.

"What's your name, man?"

I turned around slowly. I didn't even have to think about
it. "Nick."

"Nick, you got a car?"

"Yes."

"Alone."

I didn't understand. "Alone?"

"You seeing the great state of Californicate by yourself, man? You from here?" He looked me up and down. "You don't look like a Californicator to me."

I said, again, "Alone?"

"How many times do I have to say it once, man?"

"Yes," I said finally. I had forgotten what I was saying yes to.

He spread his legs slightly. I wished he would close his pants. "So you wanna take me along with you? Name is Jack so you know. You want a little company come with you? Point out to you what you need to know?"

"Where are you going?" I said. To tell you the truth, what I actually said was "Where are you goin'?" with the *g* at the end of "going" snapped off. I do that a lot around other guys. Sometimes I call them man right back but my mouth twists up and freezes afterwards.

He waved his hand. "Carmel. Upstate. See my woman."

"Your woman." I couldn't imagine her.

He laughed. "I had this woman a couple of weeks ago, she goes and tells me now she has something for me and she can't wait any longer. But see I don't have a way to get up there."

"You had a woman," I repeated. God, I thought that was just about the worst expression in the world. I don't think I'd ever heard anybody actually say it though so I just stared at the guy. "You had her," I said again.

"Hey parrot-ass, so you want me as a come-along passenger, don't you?"

"Sorry," I said to him. "I'm going in the other direction. Sorry. I'm driving away to Guatemala. Check out Guatemala." Behind the overcoat two shoes shifted, turning sand under the heels. I could hear someone laughing very lightly and I saw blond hair and parts of a white face so flushed it looked black. I put my hand on the door. "Wrong direction."

The fat guy said, "Hey, Nick, I'll come with you to Guatemala. Mexico, Guatemala, Central America, whatever you say, man. You're the driver, correctamundo?" He bent down and then he did this little half-spring off his toes and pulled up his zipper. There were gold diamond patterns across the tops of his black boots. The zipper must have been pretty rusty because it made this incredibly loud noise when he pulled on it, so loud the legs in the stall suddenly hardened. "Do whatever the chauffeur says, right, man?"

I thought for a second. "I have about seven other passengers, Jack," I said finally. "All children. All mine. We're a detective team too. And it's a Saab. That's the car I have. That's what I'm driving. It's not a van or anything."

He looked disappointed. "I thought you said you were alone."

I backed out of the door as quickly as I could. "We'll be in touch," I said. "I think I have your number written down somewhere and I'll call you and we'll do something. We'll do models. I'll call you."

I got out of there and started walking toward the parking lot. The fat guy stood at the bathroom door and yelled, "Hey." I walked faster. Then the guy yelled, "Hey, sink pisser," which was embarrassing but I still didn't turn around. When I reached Lucy's car my father and my sister were standing around talking and my father said for a joke, "Who's your friend back there, Sam?" The car next to my sister's MG was a yellow Mercedes and it wore two bumper stickers that said, I Ate the Worm at Hussongs and Welcome to L.A., Now Go Home. I told them I'd meet them back at Lucy's and I walked over to my car and got in and put the key in the ignition but it wouldn't start. I turned it about ten times but the motor wouldn't catch. Nothing happened. My windows were rolled up but I shouted, "Hold on," to my father and my sister. "Hold on," I kept shouting. "Don't go without me." I looked back and the fat man had reached the end of the dock and I got in my sister's car, the backseat. We drove back along the Pacific Coast Highway. My sister turned on K-Rock. We drove in the left lane until gradually it slanted toward the middle lane and disappeared under sand and dirt and four lanes turned into three. It was hot as hell, and windy. I felt like taking off my shirt it was so hot. "This is very unlike," Lucy kept saying to my father. "Heat this time of year." We drove over patches of sand and whenever we did you could hear the dry crystals sprinkling into the chassis and it felt as if it were settling into your body. It made you want to scratch. I could feel the wind pushing against the car and trying to force it over the road. At every lookout point there were large bunches of kids drinking wine and twisting bug-faced steel telescopes around on their stands so they could see each other close up.

At the entrance to the freeway boys were selling bags of oranges and long-stemmed red roses but Lucy drove past them and squeezed onto the highway. I looked across the divider and about two miles away on the right I could see the North Hollywood Drive-In. The entrance to Lane peeled off in another half-mile, another dark green sign. You could always see the drive-in screen from the highway, you were always passing it. I once spent a whole day trying to find the exit that led to it and no one I asked could tell me where it was or how you got there. I'm pretty much convinced you can't get there. My sister was going about seventy but it was the screen that looked as though it were in transit and we were sitting still. The sky was a dark dark pink. The screen was propped up at the base of a canyon and surrounded by bushes and branches. A couple of years back the arms of a tree cut through the middle of the screen and for two weeks at the end of the summer you could see the shadows of leaves sticking out of the actors and the streets and furniture the actors moved around in. As we went past the screen there was a close-up of a huge male face. Its lashes were tightly curled and the eyes were facing the water. The mouth was moving rapidly but you couldn't hear what it was saying. Whenever the screen lit up you could see sudden stabs of white on the hills, briefly lighting the slopes of chaparral and mustard and the little glass houses. I closed my window. In the front seat my sister was telling my father she had read someplace that people weren't supposed to live in California. "It just wasn't built for anybody," she said. "Humans." The car seemed to be climbing and at one point my ears locked. The wind was rattling the car like crazy. I stared at the top of my father's head and the white face stared us home and until we reached Lucy's street and I saw some things I more or less recognized and the freeway was blocked by a hill I knew was fairly substantial I kept my window shut.

When we got home my sister started making a fire in the living room. For some reason Lucy likes to keep a fire burning all winter long, no matter what the temperature is outside. A lot of people in L.A. do that, I think it reminds them of back home. She knelt down on the brick and began twisting up pages of the Lifestyle section of some newspaper and as soon as the paper landed in the fireplace it opened up so you could see the creases made by her fingers. She lit the paper right under a photo of a social worker accepting a big bowl for volunteer work and when the flames were tearing through the bowl she sat back on her legs. Lucy has pretty amazing legs, long and brown and hard. They remind me of the legs of women golfers, you know, those tanned women named Kathi or Toni who stride around the course with pom-poms shaking out of their sneakers. My father watched the fire burning for a while and then he disappeared into the kitchen. When he came back ten minutes later he was dragging my sister's yellow wastebasket behind him. He crouched down in front of the fireplace and stared at the logs.

Lucy looked at me and then at him. "What are you doing?" she said. "What's that for? Are you going to dehair some corn or something?"

My father moved the screen to one side. "No, sweetie, I just thought I'd get rid of some things that are burnable, that's all. Save you a trip to the garbage dump." He pulled a couple of sheets of paper towel from the top of the garbage and threw them on top of the logs and they caught and then he pulled out an empty grey carton of eggs which he stuck underneath the andirons. After that he brought out a magazine and about fifty pages of a screenplay and three dried pink grapefruit shells squeezed sideways. He molded the sides until the grapefuits were round. "These should burn like crazy," he said, tossing them into the back of the fire. "Sure you want to throw away that manuscript, it looks important."

By now the flames were going wild. None of the logs had caught yet but the burning screenplay gave you the impression that the fire was very hot. My father started throwing things on faster. The fire made his wrists orange and his fingers looked fat like the fingers of a kid. He threw on some dead yellow flowers and half a soft cucumber and a rind of cheese. The things that wouldn't burn, like a coffee can and glass and tin foil, he lined up on the brick.

My sister stood up. "I don't understand why you're burning my garbage."

My father was watching an empty Triscuit box smoke. "Gives you room," he said, "that's all. Saves you an extra trip. To the dump, if you guys even have garbage dumps out here. I don't know what you have here, you probably just keep building over what's already there. You throw your garbage in back of a hill and then build more houses over it." He picked out an orange juice carton and added it to the fire and then he moved back a little and put his hands together. "Getting warm." He nodded at the orange juice carton, which was burning at the spout. "I think that's the brand they found the woman's hair in," he said. "I'd be careful with that brand if I were you."

"What woman?" Lucy said.

Bob was still looking at the carton. "I think it was that brand. Either that one or one that sounds like it. One of them." He took a wet newspaper from the wastebasket and stared down at the headline. "One of them had hair in them. I remember reading that. Some little boy or his sister was pouring juice in the morning and woman's hair, curls, came out instead. All over the table. Or could be it was a rumor started up by a rival. They do that sometimes. Those boys play pretty rough with each other sometimes."

Next he brought out a smooth paper towel tube and he waved it over the flame until the cardboard started to tan. Lucy was shaking her head. "I still don't understand why you're doing this."

My father looked up. "Sweetie, if you don't want me to I won't. I just want you to put me to work. I want to be of some use. While I'm out here. I'm just not out here that much. I want to be useful to you guys."

"It's really all right," my sister started to say but Bob was holding up a small black velvet box. "Probably be a good idea to hold onto this, Lucy. In case you move. Or in case you want to take it back to the store. For repacking. I hope you've held on to the sales slip." He patted the velvet top. "The coffee ought to come right off this."

"The package my watch came in."

"Watch might break down." Bob laid the box next to the coffee can and the glass and the foil. "Mine did. Right in the middle of the opera. No warning whatever. Anyway, you make up your own mind, Lucy, you're old enough. I'm just giving you the option." He was almost at the bottom of the wastebasket and his arm was in very deep, almost to the shoulder and when he brought his hand back up it was empty. He started putting the things that wouldn't burn back into the wastebasket. He held up the coffee can. "You don't want to keep this to put grease in?"

"No," my sister said.

"Sure?" He left the watch box on the brick. "There. Now you have a great deal more space in the basket. And you won't have to make a trip to the dump for at least a couple of weeks." He went back into the kitchen with the can.

"What was that all about?" Lucy said when he was gone. She picked up the box her watch had come in and then she hurled it into the flames. "Burn, fucker," she said.

"I don't know."

"You know," she said after a minute, "he wants to take you back to New York. You know that's what this is all about? That's what we were talking about earlier. You knew that, didn't you?"

I didn't. "No."

"Well, it wouldn't be the worst thing in the world. Maybe." She turned toward the monitor that was hooked up to the ceiling. "I think maybe he thinks I've corrupted you or something. I haven't, have I?" She sounded anxious. "I mean, you're in pretty all right shape, aren't you?"

"Fine," I said.

"It wouldn't be the worst thing," she said again. "Would it? Being back east? You could have the winter again, all the snow."

I said, "Snow's pretty good."

"Besides he's always saying you should get to know each other better or something. Better than now I mean."

She started rubbing a streak on the screen of the monitor. Lucy had that screen put in when she came home about seven months ago and found three girls sitting on her living room floor passing around a jug of red wine and smoking her cigarettes. They were all naked and they were wearing pieces of her jewelry around their necks and wrists, a gold beetle on one of them, dancers on a chain hanging off another girl. They were playing the record player loud and when Lucy came in they had this old Troggs song on, "Wild Thing." I think "Wild Thing" is the only song the Troggs ever recorded. Lucy has an album of their songs but that's the only one I've ever heard anybody play. I think the rest of the album is blank. Anyway, these three girls were sitting around listening to "Wild Thing" and cutting pictures of my sister out of magazines she had lying around the house. In one picture they scissored off her ears and in another they cut up her waist and her legs. When my sister came in they were all holding up the scissors and roaring the chorus.

My father came back into the room then and he looked down at the fire, which was smoking. Then he looked at me. "Well," he said.

"Well what," Lucy said. "Well what."

"Well, Sam," my father said.

I looked up at him.

"What do you have to say?"

I shook my head. "Not so much."

"I suppose I have something I want to propose to you." My father took a sip of his drink and then he put his glass on the mantel. He turned to me. He was looking about two inches away from my eyes. "What I was going to suggest is that when I return to New York you think maybe of doing the same."

I stood there, smiling brightly. After five seconds I could feel my teeth drying. My father kept talking. I felt like the winner of the Miss Congeniality Award, you know, during the Miss America pageant. That's the one that's supposed to mean more to the girls than the big one since it's for qualities you showed when you didn't know you were being observed: backstage between the talent and the gown segments when your cruelty to all the other girls could go unchecked. I know the girl who takes Miss Congeniality is supposed to keep smiling no matter what but after my teeth dried out and my father wouldn't stop talking I shut my mouth.

"An official offer here," Bob was saying. "With a witness and everything. Enough Los Angeles or L.A. as you guys call it. Come back to New York, N.Y., you can call it and we'll see if we can't get you into a decent school back there. Come back to N.Y. You can always live with me as you know."

"Someplace like Briar?" I said. "You mean someplace like that? You're going to make me put on green corduroy pants all over again?"

"No, not like Briar. Briar was a mistake, my mistake. It was my fault sending you to the school I went to."

I knew there was no way in the world I could live with my father in New York. Bob lives in this enormous top-floor apartment on Fifth Avenue, right across the street from the Metropolitan Museum, not that he ever goes there or anything. I don't know if you've ever been up in that area, walking your little dog or going to see the Etruscan footwear or some other irrelevant thing like that but if you're on Eighty-second Street and you look up and see a straight row of dark new green-tinted windows with their white stickers still attached to them you're probably looking at my father's apartment.

Anyway, Penthouse C, which is what it's called, has about five hundred rooms but that's about all it has. I think it's just about the least cozy place I've ever been in. Even though my father has all these rooms to play around in he pretty much stays in his bedroom or else he's out in Southampton playing tennis with all the media types. He pays for this South American maid, Esperanza, to come in a couple of times a week to clean but all she really has to do is dust since my father lives out of his bedroom. Esperanza means "hope" or "the wait" in Spanish even though when her parents named her I think they were thinking of the first one. Esperanza can't stand me for some reason. She really loathes me. Once when I was home from school she left a note propped up on my pillow saying, "You are big pig and your room is pen," which I thought was a fairly presumptuous thing for someone I hardly knew to communicate to me. I think she was probably just annoyed that she had to work for a change, you know, do something more strenuous than flick dust off the goddamn highboys all day. Anyway, where Esperanza's from they use wedges of fresh lime instead of deodorant so she's always leaving these seeds all over the place, drab yellow hard things that jam in the skin of your feet if you walk around barefoot. At the end of the day she goes around collecting them in this little brown pouch, which is disgusting but at least it gives her something to do. There's a certain innocence to walking around barefoot that I sort of used to enjoy but ever since my father hired Esperanza I have to wear shoes all the time. She kind of killed my childhood that way.

Mainly, though, I couldn't live with Bob because I just can't stand the women he goes out with. My father has amazingly bad taste in women. All of them look like needles with faces and they've all been divorced about seventy-five times apiece and they have custody of these pretentious New York children. The little girls are always named Pandora or Tyasha or something and they wear long hippie dresses to cocktail parties and the little boys are named Archer or Nils, which makes you want to call all of them John. You feel like saying, "Hey, John" to the little girls too, just to see how they like it, to let them know you hate their pretentious names. You want to kill those kids or at least you want to line them up and plead with them to be real children, Johns, be real children. Sometimes I just want to call everybody John, that's my reaction to certain extreme events. The worst thing is that these children are included in everything their needle-mothers do, which is mainly sitting around my father's dining room table saying things like, "Oh, Bob, ha ha ha, how typical of you to say that," or "Bob is Bob and England is England and thank God for that," as though my father is some kind of goddamn institution, you know, known to all people in all lands or something.

"Or I have another possibility for you," my father said to me. "You might want to think about going abroad for a semester. The reason I say that is that I got a letter from a very old classmate of mine who runs a boys' school in London. Boys' college, I should say, school to us, college to them." He looked straight at me. "If Sam would be interested."

"Gosh, Dad, maybe we could ask Sam when he gets home from the 4-H Club," Lucy said.

My father looked embarrassed. "I'm sorry. Of course you're right here, Sam. You have a standing invitation though. To go to London for as long as you'd like. The school has an excellent reputation too. Or, you could come back to New York with me and we could try and fit you into something there. I'll be honest with you, I don't honestly know how this is going to affect your standing with the colleges, I almost don't dare find out. I suppose you should plan on going to summer school."

"Well, those are two options," Lucy said. She stretched. "Or you could stay on here with me. Guard me. Guard me from the two-bit hustlers. Who I kind of like," she added.

"Oh, I don't think that's such a good idea, Lucy," my father said. "I don't really think it's all that healthy to be out here. I wish you'd think about coming back east yourself. We could all leave this place together."

"That school in London," my sister said. "It's not reciprocal is it? There won't be some English boy over here, will there?"

The reason she asked is because in my junior year at Briar I went to Paris for about three months. I was living with this authentic French family in some arrondissement or other and going to this ratty old lycée during the day. Every night I'd come home to French parents, an older sister whose name was Nathalie and who was a nurse, and these two *jumeaux*, which is French for "twins." These twins were named Hugo and Georges and each of them weighed in at about a thousand pounds apiece. They were pretty much inseparable, too. They rode their bikes to school, they ate the same breakfast and they wore these blue sweatshirts all the time that said University of Oklahoma, which I guess both of them thought was the leading college in America or something. Anyway, when I came back to the U.S. these twins came back to New York with me and I had to entertain them for three months. That was part of the bargain. Those *jumeaux* were so frightened of New York that all they did was follow me around all day. They couldn't do anything by themselves. They were scared of the subways and of anybody taller than five ten and both of them had gone to a terrifically strict Catholic school before going to the lycée so they refused to ride any buses because the white flaps reminded them of the sisters, or something off the wall like that, I can't remember. Anyway, I tried to enter those *jumeaux* in all these tennis tournaments out on Long Island, you know, just so I could get some time alone away from them, but both twins were so out of shape that they always got eliminated in the first round and then they'd come and find me again. Those *jumeaux* destroyed my summer. I don't think I've ever had a worse summer in my life. I felt like suing both of them.

"Twins," Lucy said. "As far as I'm concerned they should give us money."

"Oh, the twins were all right," Bob said. "I liked the twins all right." He looked at me. "Have you ever heard anything from those two? If you're over in England it might be worth it knowing their address, looking them up. They owe you quite a lot."

"Money," my sister said. "They owe him money."

I said, "I'd sooner kill myself than go visit those twins." I went over to the ledge next to the fireplace and sat and lit a cigarette.

"You don't have to make a decision this second," my father said to me.

"Of course you don't," Lucy said.

"But it would be polite maybe to let the school in London know if you plan to accept the invitation. Let the headmaster know. I think it might be the thing for you actually."

"Okay," I said. I didn't mean to say it so loudly. "I'll know and then you'll know."

Everyone was quiet after that. Then Lucy said, "Well, I think it's just fantastic about the prize anyway. What was it for again? Enthusiasm?"

"Enthusiasm," I said. I coughed on some smoke.

"There was another thing."

"Willingness."

"Wasn't there something else?"

I had so much smoke in my throat I couldn't talk. I just shook my head. Sitting there I had one of those sensations that I mentioned earlier, when it seems as though everything in the world is conspiring to depress you at the same time, at the exact same moment. "Those two," I said when I could talk, "that's all," but Lucy was talking about going abroad and my father was telling her that she was economically a boy and that was a quote from Scottie Fitzgerald and Lucy asked him if he would want someone to call him Bobby. I looked at Lucy's hand spread against the orange pillow on the couch and I thought about the skin getting old. Then for some reason I started imagining Lucy with blonde hair almost white touring the Berkshires in *Bell, Book and Candle* or some crummy show like that that everybody pretends is pre-Broadway but which you know will probably close down in Boston. "It's the kids in the show I feel the worst for," she'd tell the Boston newspapers. "Those great energetic kids who gave and gave of themselves," and then the reporter would ask her what she planned to do herself and she'd laugh and say, "Oh, I have a myriad of projects lined up," and she'd go home and hit the Boodles and tonic for about three years. I looked at my father, his worn, boyish-looking thumbs and his shabby chin with the unshaved hairs like the light blue tips of nails and he looked so old at that minute I wanted to cry or something.

For a long time after he went upstairs that night I sat out on the porch drinking beer. The beer made me feel a little better but not that much. I stared across the water and there was a hill, far away, that looked as though it were on fire. My sister came out after a while and told me to move over and when I didn't she sat down on my legs. The phone rang but she let the service answer it. I started making this sound with my mouth that I make when I'm nervous. It's four sounds actually: tongue and teeth together, then just teeth, then a smacking with your lips, then a single click with your tongue. My sister told me to stop it. She lit a sparkler. The wind blew the sparks over the railing but the sparks didn't do all that much for me. The sparkler smelled bad. There were ten days to go before Christmas and I didn't know what the hell I was doing with myself and I was on some beach in the middle of nowhere in the world and my nun detective sister was holding out a sparkler that didn't do a thing for me. I felt like discussing all this with somebody but I couldn't think of anybody I wanted to talk to. Sometimes you feel like talking to someone who isn't male and who isn't female, who doesn't have the prejudices of those two. In L.A., though, all the smart people were out of their minds or trying to escape them and all the dumb people were just dumb. You were better off not saying anything.

When the flame had burned halfway down the wire my sister tried to pound the sparkler out on the railing. It wouldn't stop sizzling. The phone started ringing again. "Help, this sparkler's crazy," Lucy said. She dropped it onto the sand, twelve feet below the railing. I came over and stood beside her and looked down. The sparkler had landed in some beachgrass but the sparks kept shooting off onto the sand. The phone was still ringing. "Who is calling here?" Lucy said. "Who wants us?" I was hanging onto the railing and I touched the underside of the wood with my index finger and since I had done it with one finger of one hand I thought I owed it to the index finger on the other hand to do the same. While I was doing that I grazed the edge of the railing with my thumb so then I grazed the other thumb. I like to keep myself in balance, I like keeping both sides even. I suddenly got this crazy idea that the terrace was going to go out under me, you know, that everything was going to give way. I could picture it all pretty clearly. The sparkler was still spitting onto the sand and when I put my hand up to my mouth I realized the wind was the same temperature as my breath. The wind caught on me the way a lump snags on the nail in your throat. Lucy put her hand down over mine. "You're shaking," she said. "Are you cold? It's boiling out here. How could you be cold? You want me to get you a sweater? You want me to answer the phone?"

I don't know whether you're aware of this but there are rats in the palm trees in Los Angeles. I think they're German rats, roof rats, and they build these meaty nests right where the leaves start curling out. When the leaves pull and snap the rats sail down into your drains. In an earthquake they'd be all over you. In an earthquake a million actors and actresses would end up in the water. Everybody in show business would have to swim a little. They would all be treading water and spitting out mouthfuls of salt and mud and they would be forced to get along. Then a tidal wave would kill all of them. Whenever I think of earthquakes I think, no more movies.

* Chapter 3 *

Y last week in L.A. I went to the beach and I went
Christmas shopping and I went to the movies a lot.
My father flew back to New York a couple of days
after the awards ceremony and then he went up to Boston to
have Christmas with his mother. He called us at about eight
o'clock on Christmas Eve. He sounded pretty drunk but I
guess it wasn't all that much fun to be fifty-five or whatever
and having Christmas with your mother. I had a pretty dismal Christmas too. I mean, to give you a good idea of my
Christmas, at three in the afternoon I was sitting on this ratty
old cranberry towel on some beach out in Malibu and this kid
with bright red eyelashes who I'd never seen before was
pouring sand on my legs. I don't think it had any parents, at
least its parents weren't anywhere around. The waves were
dark and freezing and there were all these seagulls washing
ashore, grey and tousled like wigs and on the boardwalk a
guy with a ponytail held in a green rubber band was holding
his palm up in front of his face and screaming the same word
over and over at it. There were a lot of blond kids in black and
pink rubber suits surfing or else running around in that stiff
way surfers move when they have to get someplace with their

legs. "Under the Boardwalk": I kept singing that old song, the couple of versions I knew, or else hearing it, all because I was facing an actual boardwalk that went on for miles, for as far as I could see. Even when I shut my eyes tight that old song still drove all the carols from my mind. That night some ex-boyfriend of my sister's offered to drive me back cross-country but I really didn't want to see the U.S. at that point so I told him no. I mean, I'm happiest smacking to the sides. I get pretty paranoid when I'm in the middle with all those brown empty states surrounding me. You can't escape by water for one thing.

I flew back to New York the day before New Year's and Bob picked me up at the airport in his old yellow Maverick. On the highway I turned on the radio. I pressed the fourth button from the left so I could get this one New York station I'd missed while I was in California but when I pressed it all this violin music started pouring into the car. I pushed the button next to it, which I knew played only jazz but in its place was some twenty-four-hour news station, you know, with all these typewriters clacking away in the background, terrifically urgent and on top of it all and so forth. My father watched as I pressed all the buttons but each one brought in something unfamiliar. "While you guys were out there I reassigned the system," was all my father said, which sounded ominous as hell. We ended up listening to this sports call-in show and then when the car was stalled at a toll booth Bob pulled out a telegram he'd gotten from his headmaster friend in England, which said something like Looking Forward to Meeting Lad.

I guess somewhere along the line it had been decided I was going to England. I mean, I really didn't have all that much choice in the matter. My father found out that it was too late for me to do anything else that term. None of the private schools in New York wanted to take someone for just four months and I couldn't stay out in California, so Bob had gone ahead and made reservations for me to leave New York

on New Year's Day and fly into London. That meant I'd be in
New York on New Year's Eve, which didn't exactly thrill the
hell out of me. I never know what to do on New Year's Eve
anyway and whatever it is I end up doing never seems to be
the right thing and then New Year's Eve is over. Usually I sit
around in a stupor drinking one vodka tonic after another
and at some point I turn on the TV even though Guy Lombardo is dead. The problem was I didn't know anybody in
New York except for these old actor and comedian friends of
my sister's. I knew quite a few people from Briar Hall but I
wasn't really in the mood to look them up. I knew that old
Arkie Cowan lived somewhere along East End Avenue in the
Eighties with his boring old parents but I wasn't about to
take some breezy stroll up there and invite myself in for a
glass of eggnog or whatever, some foamy pointless excuse for
a drink like that. I thought that would be fairly inappropriate
behavior on my part, frankly. I could just imagine how delighted old Wilson and Calliope would be to see me on their
doorstep with all that fishy wind off the East River blowing
my hair around like crazy. The last time I'd seen the Cowans
was in the driveway of the headmaster's house at Briar when
I had to apologize to Arkie in front of what seemed like everybody in the whole world and Mrs. Cowan, Calliope, who had
been a psychology major at Rollins or some college like that,
kept her eyes on me the whole time. Later I heard her telling
my father that I wasn't bad, I was sick. I mean, whatever.
These days according to some people everything you do is a
goddamn disease.

Anyway, on New Year's Eve Bob had made plans to spend
the evening with this journalist he knows, Susan Dennis.
Susan is pretty well known, actually. She had gone to Borneo
or someplace like that when she was eighteen to live with
this incredibly hostile tribe and then she came back to New
York and her husband ran off with another woman and her
children burst into flame for no reason and so she wrote this
book, all about her tragedies, sort of hooked them all together

and called it *Laughter in the Sky*, whatever that means. I've never been able to figure out what that means and I'm too embarrassed to ask her. I don't understand who's supposed to be laughing at who. Is it the children who are supposed to be laughing at her or are they all laughing at the husband, or are all three of them, the husband and the two children, laughing at Susan—I have no idea. I mean, you can read Susan's book a hundred million times and still not have any idea what the title means. Anyway, Susan's terrifically tall and she has this soft white face like an old doll and her hands are large and not very strong. Bob kept telling me he was going to cancel his date with her and spend New Year's Eve with me but I told him not to bother. Then he invited me to come with them. He told me they were going out to dinner on board some old Danish yacht moored off Thirty-eighth Street and afterwards they were going dancing. Boy, I declined that one in a hurry. I could really picture that happening, me being a third to my father and old blunted Susan on some white old boat's floor with all this herring around me, dancing like mad to some slick guy like Lester Lanin playing "Just in Time" or "I Loves You, Porgy" or something. Actually, I don't even think Lester Lanin's in circulation anymore but Lester's son or his grandson is doing it now. I'm not really sure how the Lanins divide all that stuff up. I don't really care all that much either.

My father left the apartment at around six-thirty. He was wearing a tuxedo that was a couple of sizes too large for him and he had this salmon-colored cummerbund strapped around his waist and bright red socks. His glasses were shining like mad. I don't think I'd ever seen the glass so clear. "You're sure you're going to be all right here alone?" he kept saying. I told him I'd be fine and he told me to turn out all the lights if I went out and then he left. In a couple of minutes I went out onto the terrace and looked down Fifth Avenue and I could see Bob's shoulders and his hair emerge from underneath the dark green canopy and then the red taxi light lit up. It was dark as hell out already. I had forgotten about the short dark cold days in the East. Below me I could see the water frozen inside the reservoir, bridle paths, pale lanterns with black stems, a low green gate, joggers in hoods, thin dark trees. When the trees shook the lanterns seemed to move side to side. For some reason I started getting melancholy as hell out there so I went back into the living room and sat down on the end of the couch. After a while I got up and started going from room to room. Bob has about twenty rooms in his apartment so it took me about half an hour. I went into his bathroom and swung open the medicine cabinet. I wanted to see if he was taking anything interesting in the way of drugs or prescription pills, you know, for anxiety or fear, but there was nothing in there but small Band-Aids and dust and this moth that had gotten in there and suffocated. There was brown powder on the shelves and when I pinched the moth on its scruff it collapsed. The only things I found that were remotely interesting were all these ancient shaving tools, these old straightback razors and brushes to spread the lather onto your cheeks and about fifty jars of some kind of incredibly expensive pink shaving cream that you can only get in India or someplace like that. My father likes to buy things in bulk so there's usually fifty of everything: soap, shampoo, Ajax, coffee. Next to the jars of shaving cream was this old bottle of Bay Rum, brown flakes around the green cap, which smelled fermented. Then I went into my father's bedroom. Bob keeps a little refrigerator next to his dresser but it was empty except for a couple of trays of ice cubes. The cubes started me thinking of food, which made me hungry so I retraced my steps until I was back in the kitchen. I opened up the refrigerator. On the top shelf, casting an enormous shadow, I saw this brown wicker basket with a red bow knotted to one of its handles. A piece of paper was taped to the side. I lifted it off and read: Happy New Year's, Sam! This is in case you want to have a friend over! Please remember to lock doors and extinguish lights if you go out.

There was a white linen napkin covering the basket and I

took it off and underneath it was one of those enormous spurious French picnics that you're supposed to take with you on your private jet or something. It was called "Le Pique-Nique," if you can stand it. I never saw anybody in France eat any of the stuff they had in this basket. There was smoked mozzarella cheese in the shape of an adult pig, I mean, with hooves and everything, and a slab of duck liver pâté and something called "Macedoine of fresh fruit" and then beneath that was a "country sandwich," whatever the hell that is. I'd never heard of anybody in France or anywhere else eating a country sandwich. Anyhow, all this stuff was wrapped in shrink plastic and they even had a red-and-white-checked tablecloth you were supposed to spread underneath everything.

God, that note from my father really depressed me. I stood there for a while letting the cold grey steam float out into the kitchen. It went into my sleeves and made the skin on my arms and chest tighten. I walked the Scotch tape from finger to finger until it got to my thumb and then I removed it with the other hand. It stuck to that thumb so I pressed it against the hard braid and waited and after a minute I pulled my hand back and the tape stayed. My father's note depressed me for a number of reasons but it was mainly because of the exclamation marks, particularly the one after Happy New Year's. I found that exclamation mark incredibly sad. It was so sad I didn't even want to think about it all that much. I forced myself to think about other things: big boats, old churches. I started thinking that only four days earlier, the day after Christmas, Lucy and I were on her next-door neighbor's motorcycle in the hills above the Pacific Coast Highway. She was driving and I was behind her with the cold metal arch pushing into my back and I was wearing about a hundred sweaters and my sister's hair was snapping at my lips so after a while I just rolled them up shut. I had my hands around her waist, very lightly, not touching, but when we'd go around curves or up a straight hill my hands always found each other and I'd dig my fingers into Lucy's guts and

I think once I had her heart directly under my hand. I could feel her breathing, high, light, and my hand rose and then it'd fall. The water was on our left and it was sunny where we were but across the ocean was a chute of rain and muddy air and the sky surrounding it was blue-white. The hills were scorched black and hairy from the fires and the sun was coming in through Lucy's ears and they were glowing almost orange and I remember thinking what it would be like to sit through an entire sunset reflected through somebody's ears, that it would probably be dramatic and intriguing but also fairly frustrating. When we were about a half-mile from the house it started raining like mad through the sunlight and the drops were hissing like grease against the haunches of the bike. We got inside the garage and Lucy cut the motor and I took my hands away finally and I had no feeling in them for some reason, not even a prickle, nothing.

I just can't stand exclamation marks. They're just so intrinsically pathetic they make me want to kill myself or something, anything just so I don't have to think about them. I think they're just about the most pathetic punctuation in the world. Nothing even comes close to challenging them in the pathetic department. The problem with exclamation marks is that they have this joyful, exuberant quality to them that's just so damn inappropriate. There's really nothing all that joyful going on. They're like this skinny little kid with a cowlick jumping up onto your lap in the middle of a funeral service for your parents or some stupid dog's wagging tail knocking over a tray of crystal champagne glasses in the middle of a wake or something. You can always imagine exclamation marks on little party invitations right after the words "We're having a celebration and we want you to come!" but then the party turns out to be a total disaster and the food is terrible and no one shows up, and the people who do come arrive too early and leave after about four minutes. That kind of party. Exclamation marks always make me think of people's failed attempts at having a good time.

I left the basket in the refrigerator and went back into the living room with a couple of beers and then I smoked half a joint and opened up one of the beers and then I started reading this enormous coffee-table book of Bob's about Paris in the twenties, you know, everybody boxing like mad with each other and drinking too much and diving fully dressed into fountains, and while I was reading the downstairs buzzer rang. I was pretty surprised. I didn't do anything at first because I assumed the doorman had made a mistake and pressed the wrong buzzer. Plus, I was pretty much settled in for the night even though it was only seven-thirty or whatever. I didn't want anybody to see that my New Year's Eve was practically over and it was only seven-thirty. The buzzer rang again and I got up and went over to the monitor that hangs in the pantry and turned it on and my two godfathers were standing there with the doorman between them.

I hadn't seen either of them since I was kicked out of Briar Hall. Uncle Frank stared straight up into the camera. He was wearing a grey tweed cap pulled over his black eyes and Uncle Louis was wearing a raccoon coat and blinking. I told the doorman to send them up and I was in the foyer when the elevator door opened. "Happy New Year's, fella," Louis said to me. He turned to the elevator man. "You're dismissed," he said. "You're fired. Thanks for nothing. Pushing a button, hope it didn't wear you out." Then he laughed. "That's a joke, my friend," he said as the elevator door closed. He turned back to me. "Your pa anyplace in the vicinity or just you?"

"Just me." I held open the door.

"Happy New Year's, boy," Frank said. He held out his hand and I shook it.

"Well, he missed a goddamn near-perfect reunion is about all I'm going to say on that particular subject." Louis pushed past me into the living room and after a minute Frank followed him inside. Frank looked thin and his skin was pale. Something happened to him during the war, I'm not sure what exactly. He was in some command or another and they lost their oxygen supply and there weren't enough shots of clean air to go around and ever since then he's had a full-time companion.

"It's cold as hell in here, Sammy." Louis stood in the middle of the room and then he started going from room to room, shutting windows. "What are you fella, part penguin?" He shut the terrace door and locked it. Then he came over and stood next to me. He looked at me sadly and pretended to shiver. "Can't you feel it, Sammy? The difference? Or don't you know hot from freezing anymore?"

He went over to the liquor cabinet and started fixing himself a drink. The backside of his raccoon coat was matted and the fur was a thick dark blond. While he was cracking the ice tray he asked whether I had eaten yet and I told him I hadn't.

When he had his drink and he was sitting on the couch Louis said, "I'd forgotten about the view from up here, Sammy, the sights. Your pa's certainly got one of the great ones here. I'll give your father that much. But not much more, right? We don't get views like this one in Cambridge, Massachusetts, I'll tell you that much."

Frank was over at the terrace door, staring out over the city. He was still wearing his grey. cap. Finally he turned around. He looked at me and then he looked at Louis. He said, very slowly and quietly, "This city is a disaster. We are helpless—" he gestured out the window.

Louis said, "Oh, don't be so Swedish, Frank, it's New Year's Eve." He slapped one of the cushions on the couch. "Frank," he went on in a loud voice, "this is a young man's town. Here we have a town that tires out all but the great young men."

"Aren't you hot in that coat?"

Louis put his hands on his knees and leaned forward. "It's freezing in here, Sam, for your information." He looked at me. "Are you with us, Son?" He shook his head and plucked at one of the black buttons on his coat. "I'm crazy for this item," he said. "You're not going to meet many people in this lifetime be able to say they own a coat like this one. Take it off a second, someone'll grab it. Now where's your pa at?"

"He's with Susan," I said.

"Which one is that?"

"She the bubbly gal?" Frank said suddenly. He always spoke suddenly.

I shook my head.

Louis said, "Is she the blonde long-haired I met? Always touching you with her hands?"

"She's not the bubbly gal?" Frank sounded disappointed. He put his hand through his black hair and the hair pushed up around his fingers.

"Everyone missed your pa." Louis put his drink on the floor. "He usually shows up at these things, which is why I was surprised not to see him. That's why we stopped by, thought he might have hit his head. Tomorrow's the thirty-fifth reunion dinner dance. Small drinks thing earlier on tonight at some Asian library. Where we learned all about Charlie Fields."

I asked who that was. "Classmate of all of ours. Best-looking guy you've ever seen practically. Had the girls all over him. Married to the daughter of the man who invented rug shampoo or mints or some damn inessential thing, made him a fortune. Money coming in from all directions. At any rate, Sam, Charlie threw himself off the roof garden of the building where he worked. Last month sometime. Found this all out tonight. Charlie's wife was walking around in a daze. She'd had a little too much to drink, poor thing, she was walking around staring into the eyes of everyone there. Said she wanted to find out who had the same eyes Charlie had the morning he jumped down. Said she had to warn the wives but one problem here is of course Charlie gave no one any clue what he was planning. So she ended up confronting all the normal eyes and letting the owners know they were on the brink of doing something catastrophic, suicidal. The real crazies, the seventy-eight rpm eyes, she left alone."

Frank looked at us. "You got anything to eat here? Any nuts?"

"You got plans for later on, Sammy?" Louis said. "Meet some little girls downtown in a cul-de-sac someplace? Have some drugs with 'em then take their limp bodies dancing, they pay?"

"No."

"Well, what were you planning for tonight, Sam? I hope not sit around like a lump."

I said, "I really hadn't made any plans," and I probably shouldn't have said that because twenty minutes later I was sitting in between Louis and Frank in the backseat of Frank's blue Lincoln and the radio was playing "Blue Bayou" and Joey, Frank's driver and companion, was offering me some brown crackers with brie on them. I took one and stretched out my legs. There was a black telephone and a bar and a television set in the backseat and the car smelled of leather and licorice and cigarette smoke. Louis had brought his drink along with him and he rested it on the seat between his knees while Frank leaned forward and told Joey to drive down Fifth Avenue in a leisurely way until we made up our minds where we were going to eat. Louis put more Scotch into his glass. "One for the road," he said to no one in particular. He raised his glass in the dark as the car moved slowly down the street. "One for my road baby. One for my roadie. That's slang." He was silent and then he looked at me. "Someone once asked me right out what kitsch was, Sam, and I started humming a few bars of that one. Set 'em up Joe." He rapped on the partition glass. "You hear that? Set 'em up, Joey. One for the avenue, one for Fifth effing Avenue. Dullest effing avenue in the city. Even duller than Park, which is the dullest of the dull avenues. Only avenue I know the color of a husky. Ever owned a husky, Sam?"

When I shook my head he said, "Meanest effing dog in the world. Effing alien animals sooner nip your legs off than look at you." He patted me on the knee. "We're going to have a ball tonight, Sam. A chic old time. Christ, this is good fun."

Frank looked at me. His eyes were blank. "Sam, where are we going?"

"We'll do whatever you want, Sam," Louis said. "It's your night. It's your New Year's Eve after all. Last night in the country before they deport you, put you in a uniform, take away your rights. What do you say?"

I had no idea where to go. All of a sudden I couldn't remember the names of any restaurants in New York. The only place I could think of was this old cheeseburger palace up some bright orange steps on Lexington Avenue that I used to go to a lot when I was a kid. Then for some reason I thought of this French restaurant near Lincoln Center where I'd gone once after hearing this blind pianist so Frank turned on the little black lamp behind my head and Louis started turning the pages of the phone book. When he found the restaurant he pulled the phone toward him and dialed. "Good evening," he said after a minute. "I'd like to reserve a table for three. Right now, if you could take us. Oh, for Christ's sakes." He put his palm over the receiver and looked at me. "Only tables they have are at twelve-thirty. That's four hours from now. If you ask me all the action is over by then." He took his hand off the receiver. "Who the hell eats anything at twelve-thirty? Where do you think we are, Spain? Italy?"

He hung up the receiver and I said after a little while, "I guess we're not going there." I was in kind of an understated mood that night.

"Damn right we're not. How'd you ever hear of that hole anyway?"

I said, "That's the only place just about that I can remember."

"I thought you grew up here."

"I've been away for a long time," I said.

"And your brain's shot to hell from living in California. Can't even remember your name, I'll bet you. What is it, Michael, Paul, bet you don't know. Lose a vocabulary word a day by living out there. One day you wake up and there's another word missing you could have sworn you knew the day before yesterday. Should have stayed put here in town, Sam. My advice and my advice to your sister Lucy too. Might have gotten some idea of what's going on, of what the hell time it is in the world."

"Leave him alone," Frank said. He was staring out the window.

"I will not leave Sam alone. Sammy is my godson. I am the officer in charge of his effing continuing moral education, am I right, Sam?"

"Right," I said. I was too tired to argue.

"Right, Sam said," Louis said to Frank. "Did you hear him? Now, there are fifty million second-rate restaurants in this town, one of them should be able to take us in."

He licked two fingers and reached for the yellow pages and opened them to the page that said "Restaurants." Joey made the turn at Sixty-fifth Street over to Madison Avenue and he went up Madison for a little ways and then he crossed back over to Fifth and stopped at a red light in front of the Plaza Hotel. Something was going on at the Plaza. There were a whole bunch of girls in long white dresses standing on the red steps leading into the lobby, shivering like crazy. Most of them had orchids pinned to them and the petals were ruffling and the wide colored flags over the girl's heads were snapping and all these hard silvery pieces of snow were crumbling suddenly in the eaves and spraying down and the girls were dodging the heavier lumps. All these yellow cabs and black limousines were lined up outside the hotel and everybody was honking and shouting and there was steam in the air and all the girls' dates were leaning around in their tuxes very casually, talking to the chauffeurs and the porters, you know, man-to-man, not employees to spoiled rich assholes, which you knew was the real story. None of the girls on the steps was particularly beautiful but all of them were pretty in a way that was definitely heartbreaking. I don't

know, maybe you would have had to go to a terrible prep
school like Briar to know what I mean exactly. You just kind
of knew from looking at these girls that they were all named
Nina or Heather or Christie or something and that they were
all amazing skiiers and that their boyfriends were always trying to get them alone at the lodge. All of them had these incredibly small upturned noses—I mean, you were shocked
they got any air inside them—and about four freckles and
you knew all of them had taken dance in their senior years
with this sad, beautiful, long-faced intelligent female dance
teacher they all idolized and thought was tragic since she
had mashed up her toe when she was a little older than they
were and had to give up dancing in favor of teaching and so
on, and then all the girls came to New York and they never
danced again. They got married instead or they went into
business, they quit dancing altogether. The sad thing about
going by the Plaza was that you could see these girls before
they got married, while they were still running a fever under
their furs and their asshole boyfriends were discussing baseball or kick boxing with the limousine drivers. You wanted to
look at those girls forever, maybe scream at them Don't Do It.

"We could go back up to the apartment," I said. I was remembering the pique-nique in the refrigerator.

Louis was still looking down the restaurant columns in the
yellow pages. "Zero enthusiasm for that idea, Sam," he said,
not looking up. "For God's sakes man, we're not in the
Southwest, we're in New York City. You have any idea what
they're doing with themselves back home in Cambridge,
Massachusetts, this minute? They're rereading a book. Not
even reading it for the first time around but rereading it.
Their doors are locked and their lights are off with the exception of one and they're rereading some book that probably
wasn't much good in the first place. Now if that's not a por-
trait in fear, well, I don't know what is anymore. We're in the
Big frigging Apple, Sammy, and we're going to have fun if it
takes us all night." He dialed another number. "Good eve-

ning, we're in the market for a table that fits three. Three, yes. I'm calling you from the backseat of an automobile, that's why the connection is so hopeless." He held the receiver against the lap of the raccoon. "All they say they have at this point are tables in their Emerald Room. Larry Jefferson and the Brooklyn Bridge is the name of the band. You ever heard of them, Sam?"

I shook my head.

"Well, they sound like pretty doubtful types to me," Louis said. "We'll go for the table, though, Sam, if you say so. Come on, Son, I'm waiting for the word."

I said, "I've never heard of them."

Louis spoke into the phone. "The boy who's with us who knows bands says he's never heard of your particular combo. And he would know, Jesus, he knows the bands. So don't count on seeing this table of three anywhere near your Emerald Room tonight or tomorrow night or any night." He held the receiver out and smiled but no sounds came from it and a moment later he brought it back up to his ear. "The shit hung up on me."

He started turning pages. He was looking at restaurants that began with the letter L. "Never go anyplace, Sam, that has a Le or a La prefix. French don't know what the hell they're doing. French are out of control." He dialed another number but there was no answer. "Oh that's just great," he said after he hung up. "No answer on New Year's Eve. Very professional establishment. Very together establishment as the kids say." He tried another number and the woman on the other end told him they didn't take reservations. Louis said in a loud voice, "Well, if you don't take reservations then we have serious reservations about your restaurant, ha ha ha," and then he hung up. He called two other restaurants but both were booked for the night. "Jesus, I should have thought of all this sooner," he said, sitting back in his seat. "Back in November. Of course these places are reserved up to their eyeballs. People planning their lives two months in

advance, refusing to go with the spirit. Just so they could be
sure they won't be left behind tonight. In New York City you
go with the spirit else you get trampled. Right, Sam? Come
on, Son, wake up." He poked me. "I thought you were a live
wire."

I thought, *Don't touch me I'm a real live wire.* Frank
leaned forward and gave Joey the name of an Italian restaurant down in Little Italy, on Carmine Street.

"Where the hell is Carmine Street?" Louis said as Joey
started driving west. "All of a sudden you get down low in
this city and you get stranded in streets out of some kid's
small-town fantasy that life goes on forever. Maple Street,
Willow Street, life's not going to last. Last time I was here,
Sammy, I found myself doing business on Greene Street.
Somewhere below Fourteenth Street there was a Greene
Street. Now what the hell is Greene Street doing in New
York City? If you ask me you come here to get away from
places called Greene Street."

To the west was black shining water and the shore of New
Jersey, steep rock cliffs and yellow lights and cranes on dark
beaches. Joey pulled the Lincoln into the left lane as Louis
opened his window an inch. A cold thin wind blew into the
backseat. "New Jersey looks just fine from this side, doesn't
it?" Louis said to me. "It almost looks romantic. You could
almost take your bride there, couldn't you." He unrolled his
window and put his head out and then he drew his head back
inside and shut the window. "This is the real thing, Sam," he
said, hitting me on the knee. He had a huge fond smile on his
face. "You don't get it any more real than this. This is the real
New York." He looked at Frank. "We don't get a ride like this
every day in Cambridge, Massachusetts, I'll tell you that,
Frank."

"No, sir, we don't." Frank shut his eyes and put his head
against the seat.

"It's all right, we'll be eating before you know it." Louis
sipped his drink and then he added more Scotch. "This

England thing by the way is just the thing for the transcript. We're dealing here with a credentially oriented society and foreign travel is something the boys in admissions like to see. It sharpens a fellow's reflexes, having to thrash around a foreign culture for a little while. My friend Wheatie Enright, who's over at the Harvard College admissions, says they like it just fine when the applicant, whoever he is—Sam, I'm not saying it's you—has spent some time abroad. Not too much time but some. And not Paris either. Everyone your age worth his salt has wasted a little time in Paris talking English a hell of a lot and drinking wine, taking pills, dancing their dances. In fact, I daresay you'll probably discover someday that most of the people you choose to call close friends will have in common the fact they once spent a semester or two in Paris. These'll be people you've met before, even though many of them may be strangers. I say that, Sam, in the most reassuring way. But this England thing buries Paris vis-à-vis the transcript. Might even serve to erase the bad taste of that Cowan kid affair. What was Cowan's first name, Sam? Unusual first name. You ever hear from Cowan?"

We were racing down the West Side Highway now, passing rows of dark piers and long flat wood berths, past bars whose windows were strewn with red-and-green Christmas lights and swirls of hard powdered white frost. Outside the bars on the sidewalks men were standing around with their hands in their pockets laughing and their breath when they breathed out was long and grey and trembling. We passed old meat warehouses where trucks were herded, past a parking lot where pieces of glass hung in the empty windows of the old Mustangs and the school buses. Under a brown bridge on Thirteenth Street men in muskrat furs and high black heels were leaning against the heavy stanchions. Their shadows were cast onto the dirty stone wall that rose behind them. When a car went by shining its front lights the pale stone lit up and the shadows of the men got narrow and sloping as if the shadows were stepping down a sharp hill. On the wall, pretty high, someone had sprayed in thick pale green paint, 100% of All Orange Juice Drinkers Die. I thought about that for a while but since it wasn't true I got mad at myself after a while for wasting any time believing it. Whenever a car came to the red light closest to the bridge one or two of the men would approach the driver's window, teetering like glass, say something, step back. Frank, who was watching them, made a comment on poor women being out in the cold but I didn't say anything.

Louis lit a cigarette and opened his window. The smoke blew into the backseat as we got close to the exit the car slowed suddenly and the hard glass knocked the tip of Louis's cigarette onto the sleeve of his coat. He dropped the rest of it out the window and started slapping at his sleeve.

"Did I get it all, do you think?" he kept saying. Finally when we turned onto the ramp he told me he thought it was out. "I once knew a guy, Tom Something-or-other, nice guy, decent guy, was smoking in his bed and did what I just did. Got it in time though, before it went through, I mean. But he was planning on going out in a little while and he wanted to be absolutely sure so he stripped the sheets and poured a pot of cold coffee, what he hadn't drunk that morning, onto the bed. Then he carried on, ate, theatre, got back three hours later and no mattress. Even with the cold coffee. No place to sleep, just a wet hole in the floor." Louis laughed loudly.

At that point I was pretty famished. In fact I was getting depressed I was so hungry. I started imagining my father and Susan dancing aboard the Danish boat, surrounded by tables of food. Lester Lanin or Lester's son would be playing "That Old Black Magic" or "I Concentrate on You" or something and Bob and Susan would be glancing at each other in this delighted way that makes you want to shoot yourself and my father would be lifting his knees too high off the ground and singing along with Lester. It was an image that disturbed me.

"Sam, you should go get yourself a coat like this," Louis

said. He settled back into his seat. "It's a real showstopper. People, strangers, say to you all the time, where can we get a coat like the one you're wearing? And I tell 'em, Friend, if you haven't inherited one yet, well, it's not coming. Be a good item to have in a city like New York, to help a guy make his friends. Only problem is a lot of the time women give you crucifying stares. They remember all the foolish good-natured raccoons and garden pests from books they read out loud to their kids, where the effing west wind is the protagonist. Imagine reading *Hamlet*, Sam, but having the damn west wind be prince, prince of the whole thing. Unbelievable." He shook his head for a long time. "Damn women think I tormented the animals personally."

We weren't on the West Side Highway and we entered a grid of small short streets. The buildings on either side of us were low and all the Christmas decorations were still in place in the windows of the stores. There were red Santas that blinked and sleighs made out of tricked-up bulbs that made the knees of the reindeer look as though they were bending forward and snowflakes that went from white to blue to red and then back to white. We drove past signs in Chinese, grocery stores, souvenir shops, open-air markets, restaurants, weapons stores. "Chinese are a very shrewd race," Louis said, pouring himself another Scotch. "Have their New Year's later on in the year, when no one gives a shit."

Inside the restaurant the maitre d' told us the wait would be about fifteen minutes and he offered to take the raccoon coat but Louis waved him off and went over to the bar and ordered a drink. Frank sat down on one of the red barstools and started eating popcorn from a blue bowl. It was a pretty gloomy-looking restaurant. The walls were made of plastic salmon brick and each table had a white candle standing on a red dish. Next to the cigarette machine was a big blue aquarium. There were a couple of green-faced fish swimming around in still yellow water. Neither of the fish seemed to realize the other one was in there. On the radiators in back of

the cash register green plants were growing from out of cut
red milk cartons. A sign was sticking out from the dull green
leaves of the largest plant and it said, Please Keep Us Clean
and Crisp. Behind the cash register the walls were covered
over with black-and-white photographs. There must have
been about two hundred of them, I'm not kidding. The name
of the person was printed at the bottom of each picture and
all the people were either actors or boxers. I don't think there
was a free inch of wall that wasn't totally plastered with
someone's face and neck.

I leaned over the cash register and started squinting like
mad. I was trying to see if I could recognize anybody. In case
I haven't mentioned it I'm pretty blind but I don't wear
glasses so you see me squinting a lot of the time or else pulling the ends of my eyes. Sometimes if you squint you see
things more clearly than if you were looking at something
round-eyed. Anyway, even though I was squinting I still
didn't recognize anybody on that wall. Usually I'm pretty
good about these things too, actor trivia, what with my sister
and all, but I wasn't having any luck. The only thing I could
be sure of was that everybody who had his or her picture up
on the wall had obviously eaten at the restaurant at least
once since most of the inscriptions mentioned food or good
service or something. A lot of people had posed with this big
heavy guy with a long dark jaw who looked like the kind of
guy who would own an Italian restaurant. It was pretty obvious that they had put up all these pictures so you would admire the place and feel thrilled to be a part of its food service
history or whatever but since I didn't recognize anyone on
the wall the display kind of passed me by. It went right over
my head. You would have had to spend most of your life at
Golden Gloves tournaments or at Off-Broadway auditions to
know who any of those people were. All the actors and actresses looked so confident and glitzy, too, they started to
make me feel guilty for not knowing who they were. The
guys were theatrical-looking in a way I've always found a lit-

tle bit offensive. You knew they were the sorts of forlorn people whose agents described them as Triple Threats even when they weren't very good at anything—they tap-danced and they sang and they acted and they had that kind of trouper mentality that makes you want to kill yourself. I mean, if the theatre was in flames and their parents had just gone down in a Cessna and there was a nuclear war these guys would still bound up onstage and start cracking jokes about the difference between New York and L.A. or something.

After a while Louis came over to where I was standing. "You still here, Sam?" He shook my hand and then he let it go. He was pretty drunk by then, I think. His wrists were red and damp and he seemed to be sweating under the weight of his raccoon coat. He looked over past the bar to the tables where people were eating. "Sounds like there are a lot of Italians here."

I'd always heard that was a pretty good sign, Italians eating in Italian restaurants, Chinese people eating in Chinese restaurants, and when I told him that he looked at me disgustedly. "That logic is totally full of shit, Sam," he said. "Only reason Chinese people go to Chinese restaurants is so they can order off the menu, feel superior as hell to you. You have your whatever, your beef and pea pods, your chicken and water chestnuts and the Chinese table has the fucking horseshoe crab. You try and order the horseshoe crab yourself and the waiter proceeds not to understand you." Louis was breathing heavily now. "You mainly got fat white sons-of-bitch Protestants eating at McDonald's, does that mean the food's any good at McDonald's?"

I thought. "No."

"That's right, Sam. Negative. Use your head." He started picking at the honey-colored Scotch tape coating the twenty-dollar bill that hung to the side of the cash register. He gestured at the wall. "You ever heard of any of these people?"

I shook my head. "No."

"Not friends of your sister's? Lucy's friends? I thought all those show-business types knew each other."

Boy, if any of those people were friends with Lucy I'd probably commit suicide. "I don't think so."

"Take a look at the resemblance between this guy here—" He touched the bottom of a picture of a man shaking hands with a woman in a sequined dress "—and that guy serving pie over there, in front of the cart. Pretty extraordinary. Pretty extraordinary resemblance."

The maitre d' came over and told him please not to touch the photographs, they were fragile. Behind the counter the bartender started polishing the bottoms of shot glasses.

"Mind your own business, little fella," Louis said. He turned back to the wall and pressed his palm against a photograph of a boxer, Tommy Palomino. "Hey, Tommy," Louis said in a loud voice. "Hey Tommy, you're a big bum."

"Please," the maitre d' said.

Louis looked at him and then he looked at me. He said, very slowly, "Little men make me sick, Sam, have I ever told you that?" He started speaking in a loud whisper. "You know what the little men of this world are all about, Sam? You want the clear picture? Ever had a Chinese meal and you've looked down and there were little pieces of corn in there all stirred up and floating around. Kind of look like they've spent their whole life in a jar? They're not even slivers from a big cob, they're fully formed. That's what little men are, Sam. Like those pieces of Chinese corn. Chinese corn with cowboy boots on for a lift."

The maitre d' asked Louis to please keep his voice down but he kept talking in his exaggerated whisper. I was getting pretty embarrassed. "Not even dark glasses," Louis went on, "make the little man a cool man." Then he started gesturing wildly at the wall. "These people are hoaxes. Somebody call the *Times*. Somebody call the AP. Call the UPI. Get the wire services going. These people are frauds." He pulled a picture down off the wall so it tore across one corner, leaving a triangle under a thumbtack. It was a photograph of a woman with long dark red hair and a wide necktie. She was singing something and her mouth was open wide. An inscription at the bottom said, "To Tony and Shelley. Great ziti. You guys are magnifico. Fondly, Monica Beck."

My godfather waved the picture in front of the maitre d's face. "Who is this person?"

"It says so there, sir." The maitre d' looked pretty upset. I felt a little sorry for the guy. He was joined by the bartender, who had slipped underneath the counter. Most of the people in the room had stopped eating and were looking over at us.

"Sam, you ever heard of Monica Beck?" Louis said. I told him I hadn't. The maitre d' started to say something and Louis said, "Just a minute, little corn. Why don't you climb back inside a Chinese meal and start enhancing the effing thing? Start enhancing the taste." He shook his head and looked at me. "Problem with these little guys is all they're able to do is widen. Since you don't see 'em getting any taller they have to grow out. That's why you see them struggling to lift weights. Frank," he called and Frank, who was still sitting at the red stool eating popcorn, looked up. "Frank, you ever heard of Monica Beck?"

Frank said, "Doesn't mean anything to me."

Louis looked as though he'd won something. "The woman's a joke," he announced. "Belongs right there in the carnival with the tripod rabbit."

I said to him, softly, "What's that?"

"What's what?"

I repeated it.

"Oh." Louis waved his hand. "Some poor son-of-a-bitch bunny in a carnival up in Portland, Maine, I once walked into by mistake. Bunny lost a leg, so they called it that."

The maitre d' told us there weren't any tables and that we should leave.

"Right," Louis said. "We'll gladly take leave of this pantheon of the mediocre. Get your coat, Sam." He put his arm

around me and pushed me in the direction of the door.
"We'll happily depart this galaxy of the shoddy and the second-rate." Right before we reached the door, in front of the
basket of tiny green-and-white mints, he stumbled a little. He
took a carton of matches from a basket and then he turned
and stared hard at the maitre d'. "I couldn't have stood having all that trash staring at me while I ate anyway."

Outside on the sidewalk, we waited for Joey to bring the
car around. It was cold and my teeth started clicking like
crazy. "Come under my coat," Louis said to me. He lifted up
one of the raccoon flaps and sort of steered the coat around
me. The fur smelled like peppermint and sweat. Then Louis
lifted up the other raccoon flap and found Frank's shoulders.
"Life in sweet old New York," he crooned. "That's o-l-d-e,
Sammy. What's more evocative than those old spellings, I
don't know. O-l-d-e. What a difference one letter can make.
Oh, I'm getting sad here." He pulled the coat tighter around
me. "What a great town this was once. It's pretty dreary now,
isn't it. Nobody can take a joke anymore. Oh, it makes me
sad." He was silent and then he said, "Sammy, you must be
ravenous. You must be ready to chew on the air. There's a
pack of Lifesavers in the pocket on that side if you want to
break them open."

Back inside the car Louis said, "Now, I've just gotten this
terrific idea. Really splendid. Why don't we head up to the
Harvard Club, I'm sure they're still serving something."

"Now?" Frank said. It was about eleven-fifteen.

"I don't see why the hell not now. We went to the joint. I
give 'em half a million bucks every year. Which they don't
even use."

Joey pulled away from the curb and we came to a red light.
While we were stopped this little kid ran out of a shadow up
to the car. He must have been about seven or eight. He was
wearing black pants and a black sweatshirt with a hood. The
hood closed up around his face and knotted under the chin.
Another kid came up to the other side of the car. He was the

same size as the first kid and he was holding a squeegee and a spray bottle. He lifted up one of the wipers and sprayed the windshield underneath it while the first kid positioned himself in front of the car with his legs spread apart, staring at us. Even though the light had turned green Joey couldn't go ahead without ramming him. The kid with the squeegee finished spraying the glass on the passenger side and he began dragging the hard black rubber across the glass. The rubber against the glass made a sound like someone screaming.

Louis rolled his window down an inch. "No," he called out, as though he were talking to an animal. "Go away. This car is clean enough." He rolled his window down farther. *"C'est pas nécessaire mais merci tout de même. Allez-vous en."*

I said to him, "I don't think they're from France."

Louis leaned back inside. "Sure they're from France, Sam, look at them. *Disapparez maintenant,"* he called back out the window. "They wash your windows," he said, turning to me, "and then they expect to be paid. If you don't deliver you feel like a shit. Sure they're French," he said again.

Another kid came out of the doorway of a building. "Christ," Louis said. He rolled up his window. "A real pack of gamins."

On the sidewalk I noticed an older man who was watching the kids with his arms crossed. I think he was probably their father. By now the car was surrounded by kids holding spray bottles and squeegees. Two of them scraped the rubber arm across my window, down and up. The glass screamed. All the windows were screaming. Frank put his hands over his ears. Joey yelled something out the window and then he turned back to us and said, "They can't hear me, they're all wearing Walkmans." He put both hands down on the horn and kept them there. The windows were soaked with water and soap and the horn was going and the glass was screaming and then Joey put the car into reverse. It jumped backward and stalled. He started it again and put his foot on the gas and the kid standing in front of the car dived onto the pavement and we nearly clipped the leg of another kid and Joey ran two red lights in a row. When I looked back the kids were standing there at the intersection shouting at us. As we drove up Third Avenue with the wipers crying Louis said, "Sam, is there a French Quarter down here?"

"No," I said. Then I said, as earnestly as I could, "They weren't French."

"How do you know what they were or what they weren't, Sam? You don't even live here anymore."

"I just know."

He wouldn't believe me. "That was the real thing, I think," he said softly. In the dark of the backseat I heard him humming.

By that time I was starting to get a headache. When we were on Thirty-seventh Street I told Frank and Louis that I was falling asleep and I asked them whether they could just drop me off at my father's apartment. Louis looked a little offended. "Well, if you want to quit on us at this point, Sam, I suppose it's your prerogative." He was quiet and then as we turned onto Park Avenue, away from the Times Square traffic, he said, "Tell you what, Son, stay with us and we'll take you down to one of those sex clubs I'm always reading articles about. Would you like that? For your last night I mean? Frank and I could stay in the car and we'll take care of whatever admissions charges there might be and you can go inside and do the drugs and the—" He hesitated "—the other empty gestures you kids like to do with yourselves and then you could join us back here in the car. With a friend if you'd like. We'll even stake you to a friend. How does that sound?"

"I think I'll just go home," I said.

"In that case you sure you won't come to the H-Club? We three?"

I shook my head. "I think I'll just go home."

"Party pooper, Sam. You're no fun at all. I thought you had more life than this. I think I must have had you confused with someone else." Louis poured two glasses of humid Scotch in the dark. He handed me one and when I was holding it he proposed a toast to Harvard College. I was too tired not to drink. "To Sam Grace being the, what are we up to, the sixth Grace to go onto Cambridge, Massachusetts." He drank and watched me drink. "You'll fall in love with the place, Sammy. Has all the advantages of a city plus the intimacy of a small town. Harvard Coop's the best department store in the world."

"Maybe Sam doesn't want to go to Harvard." It was the first thing Frank had said in about two hours.

"Of course he does. Where else is he going to go? Princeton? Come out all blond and mean-spirited and promiscuous? Yale? Come out bright as hell but snide and friendless? Columbia? Come out totally lacking charm? Men without tans attend Columbia, white men, plus you have to live in this dreary town. Of course Sam wants Harvard. Only decent education left over in the country."

"New York is a young man's town," Frank said. He sounded depressed. "Maybe a school out west is the answer."

I bit down on the empty glass I was holding. It tasted hard and warm and I thought I could taste fleetingly the remnants of someone's lipstick from a long time ago. "Since when has the West been the answer to anything?" Louis said after a moment. "What's out there that you can't get in here? Besides, Sam's already done the West. The West is old hat. He can't go back there."

At Eighty-second Street Louis stood on the curb outside my father's apartment and we shook hands. "We'll have to do it again sometime," he said.

"Good-bye, Sam," Frank called from the inside of the car.

"Give your pa our regards," Louis said and he started toward the car.

It had started to rain very slightly, cold thin drops. I was almost inside the lobby when I heard Louis's voice. "Hold it.

Jesus Christ, Sam, hold on." I turned around and I saw that
Louis was trying to walk and take off his raccoon coat at the
same time. Finally he managed to get his arms out of the
sleeves. He cradled the coat in his arms. "Here." He was
standing two feet away from me and he practically threw it in
my face. "Take it away. I'm sick to death of the damn thing.
And England's damp as hell this time of year. That coat's
seen most of the things there are to see in this life. Take care
of you when you think no one gives a shit. Only problem is its
chief asset, it's too goddamn hot."

I stood under the green awning, trying to gather up the
heavy hairy arms and the tails. "Go on," Louis said. "Get the
damn thing out of my sight. You're doing me a favor. It'll
come in handy when you get back too. In Cambridge, I
mean. Everybody'll want one. People'll be following you
down the street."

He walked back to the car and got in and shut the door.
Without the coat he looked much smaller. Joey hit the horn a
couple of times and they drove off. I went straight into the
lobby with the coat slung over my shoulders. The tall thin
strange doorman was on duty. I think he was born in the
Basque country. There was a television set on one of the
lobby benches and the network kept going back and forth
from a live report in Times Square to some late movie with
Patty Duke Astin as the mother. I wished the doorman a
Happy New Year and he said it back. His lips smelled of
champagne and chicken livers. The elevator man took me up
to twenty-two but before I could get my keys out of my pocket
Mrs. Thornton, who lives in the other penthouse, opened her
door and came out into the hallway. I hadn't seen Mrs.
Thornton in about three years. She was wearing this gold
beaded top and a navy blue Mets cap and black shoes and she
had made a braid of her long white hair. It hung over her left
shoulder like a canvas strap. I could hear noise and music
coming from the Thorntons' apartment. She started making
a big deal about not having seen me for ages and then she in-

vited me in for a drink. "Leave your baby bear behind though," she said. "It might panic the piano player."

Whatever that means, I thought. I wadded up the raccoon coat as compactly as I could and laid it down in front of my father's door. I didn't know what else to do with it. It looked like a tranquilized animal and I looked at it for a while, forgetting where I was, and then I followed Mrs. Thornton into her apartment. She moved ahead with the long delicate definite moves of a fencer. I think she was drunk as hell by then but she was making a pretty heroic effort not to show it. In the hallway she held me tightly around the waist and said in this husky voice I didn't exactly remember her having, "Let me get you a glass of Piper, my love."

She disappeared into the living room, leaving me standing in front of all these men's and women's coats piled up high on a long couch. There were bowls of white scented flowers all over the place and the rugs had been tripped up so often you could see the green puffy mats underneath. A huge mobile was hanging down off the entrance to the kitchen, blue-and-white stone dolphins suspended from clear silk threads. I guess when the wind blew those stone dolphins were supposed to jostle the hell out of each other but they sure weren't doing it that night. All they were doing was turning around in kind of an indifferent way, silky strings twisting. Through the strings I could see a lot of people standing around holding drinks and a lot of platters of cheese and in one corner of the room this enormous woman in a red-and-white kimono was playing the piano and singing "Poor Butterfly." A couple of skinny effete-looking guys were leaning against the piano kind of mumbling along to the song. Effete-looking guys are mad for songs like "Poor Butterfly." I can't really tell you why. It's a pretty sad melody, actually. I don't blame them for liking it so long as they don't get all melodramatic about it and try and pretend it sums up their life or anything.

While Mrs. Thornton was getting me champagne I started

eating these red pistachio nuts from a little bowl on the hallway table. I was pretty ravenous. I couldn't get the shells
open fast enough. I was stuffing those nuts down my throat
and piling the shells in an ashtray and the tips of my fingers
and under my nails were burning and while I was eating all
the Thorntons' pistachios I started getting riveted as hell by
these two old prints that were hanging on the wall above the
bathroom light switch. One of them was called "The Life and
Ages of Man" and the other one was called "The Life and
Ages of Woman." The first one showed this arrangement of
about twelve or so guys standing around in a semicircle.
Each guy had a number over his head, telling you his age,
ten, twenty, thirty, and so on. The print with the women on it
was pretty much the same setup. Ten was a guy in a sailor
suit and all those gold ringlets and a girl in a long dress and
twenty was this jerky-looking guy in a black hat and a girl
who looked like a nursing student and thirty was a soldier
and a woman holding a mean-looking baby. Forty was a cor-
poral and a matron. At the end were the hundreds, these two
old bent people with canes. I stared at those two pictures for
the longest time. I mean, I was interested in them artistically
and all, but also parties make me feel pretty anxious so
I wanted to look as though I was occupied in some big way
too.

In a couple of minutes Mrs. Thornton came back with two
glasses of champagne. "In case you gulp the first, love," she
said. When she handed me the glasses her fingers touched
my hand. Her fingers were incredibly chilly and her ring was
even colder. There was no sign of Mr. Thornton anywhere
but that didn't really surprise me. Mr. Thornton was always
off traveling in Syria or Yemen or someplace like that, at least
that was the official version of the story. When you thought of
the Thorntons you always thought of her. "Now," Mrs.
Thornton said to me, "where's the divine father tonight?"

"He's out on the town," I said.

"And the marvelous sister?"

"Oh, she's still in L.A." I said.

"And doing some fabulous things I understand from Dad."

"Fabulous," I said. I always use the word *fabulous* around Mrs. Thornton. I don't know why, I guess because she does. I never use it anytime else. I don't even think she notices.

"Oh, Bob, I mean, Sam, isn't the divine father always out on the town with one of his *girls*? Honestly, that man should be locked up in his room and denied dessert until he promises to behave himself and stop being such a tomcat. He tells me you're off to England, now, isn't that fabulous."

"It's fabulous," I said. "Really. Really fabulous."

She had caught sight of herself in the long hallway mirror and her eyes were sneaking off to see how the braid was hanging even though before the party you would have thought she probably had spent enough hours looking at herself. "Princess Molly is somewhere in that imbroglio," Mrs. Thornton said, gesturing toward the living room. "That jungle of revelers. She's the queen's second cousin. They even look alike, same tiny features and the skin, somehow the skin is the same. You might want to tap her on the shoulder and introduce yourself and tell her your situation." She smiled bleakly at me. "It's good to know people in London always. It's hermetic. You wouldn't think so but it is. Get yourself invited to a palace halloo, that would certainly be something."

Someone across the room called her and Mrs. Thornton said to me in a low voice, "Lovely to see you, Bob. Sam. Bob Sam Bob Sam," she practically yelled and then she touched my cheek in apology and broke away. I watched her move chaotically across the room in the direction of the voice, which called her name again. Then she was hugging someone.

The second she was gone I strongly considered leaving the party. I had absolutely no interest in meeting Princess Molly or whatever her name was or going to anybody's palace. I drank the second glass of champagne and put the glass on top of the highboy and then I decided to make a single trip into the living room, just to say that I had, not that anybody was going to quiz me about it later or anything. The Thorntons' apartment looked a lot like Bob's except it faced north-west and it had furniture in it. A bar was set up in one corner of the room and there was a blond perfect-looking guy in a white linen jacket smiling and pouring drinks for the guests so I went over and got in line. The guy's face looked as though it had been sanded and his hands and fingers were brown. His fingernails were white like teeth. I was pretty sure he was from California, you know, friendly as hell be-cause he didn't know any better. He looked like that type. When it was my turn and the blond guy was staring at me I mouthed "No drinks for me, Skip" and turned around and headed toward the door. Behind me I could hear Mrs. Thorn-ton telling someone that nice girls went to heaven but naughty girls got to go everywhere and then the fat woman in the kimono started playing "Miss Otis Regrets," which seemed to me a pretty strange thing to be playing at a New Year's Eve party.

Before I reached the hallway, though, all the lights went off in the room. I heard Mrs. Thornton's voice saying, "Come on, my darlings, we're not going to be around forever." Someone began clapping and in a minute everyone was clap-ping and the piano stopped. "Everybody," Mrs. Thornton called. "Everybody, it's Happy New Year's. It's Happy New Year's, everybody."

I was feeling pretty trapped. I couldn't see a damn thing and I didn't know anybody at the party and the apartment was all black except for the outline of yellow light around the kitchen door. In the park a tremor of green-and-yellow fire-works lit the sky and then fell back in drops. It was raining heavily by then. I started moving sideways toward the door and I had taken about four steps when someone grabbed me from behind, hard, and I was so surprised I nearly fell backward. I couldn't tell who it was. I couldn't even tell if it was a man or a woman or what. It smelled like it could be either one. Whoever it was was holding me by the shoulders and then he or she came around in front of me and started forcing my mouth open with their fingers. The fingers tasted of goat cheese and they were thin and strong. Then when my mouth had been pried open I got kissed. I mean, it wasn't this informal New Year's Eve kiss either. I was breathing like crazy through my nose and the person was biting my lips and tongue and our teeth were smashing and after a while my tongue just kind of quit the fight and lay there. I didn't bother struggling anymore. Everytime I tried to close my mouth the person would put two index fingers on either side of my lips and pull my mouth into a smile and then it would start again. After a while that kiss started to be my center of balance. I could have stood on one leg and not fallen.

The rain was really coming down hard then, braids of it, ricocheting off the ribs of the Thorntons' grille. I heard Mrs. Thornton say, "Oh, Mr. Lights, where are you?" and then the person stopped kissing me and I turned toward the door and when I got to it I stepped out into the hallway that separates my father's apartment from the Thorntons'. I was dizzy. I tasted blood in my mouth, as though I'd been sucking on the blade of a knife or a dime. The hallway stank of smoke and there was a thick greasy gas in the air. I did some flexes with my mouth and lips to get the copper out of my mouth and I swallowed some blood, which was hot and thin. The smell started me coughing like crazy and I thought someone must be burning something in the Thorntons' kitchen but then when I went up to Bob's door and looked down I saw there was practically nothing left of Louis's raccoon coat. I mean, there were a couple of pieces of charred sleeve but most of the fur was black and sticky and all I could make out was a little white tag which gave the name of some men's store on Newbury Street in Boston where his, Louis's, father had bought the thing and some fairly detailed cleaning instructions. I guess Louis had been on fire the whole night, the raccoon had been consuming itself. The rubber mat outside my father's door was black and wet and there were clumps of blond-brown hair across it. I tried lifting the mat but the rubber sucked on my finger and when I pulled my hand away some skin stayed.

Somehow I got myself into my father's apartment. I went into the bathroom and in the mirror my lips were all torn up. There were all these punctures in my top lip as though some goddamn dog had pressed his mouth to mine. My tongue was still bleeding and I started to cry and then I got sick. I remember wrapping this big white quilt around my shoulders and going into the living room and turning on the television. The quilt covered pretty much all of me but my ass and my long feet. I have fairly large feet for someone my size. Bob's always told Lucy and me that large feet and long second toes and bumpy noses are aristocratic but he'll say that about any part of your body that's warped or misshapen. I was sweating like crazy so I got up and opened all the windows and looked out over the city and it was still lit up. There was a race in the middle of Central Park and a lot of people were wearing white togas. The cold air poured in and I sat on the couch with this big quilt foaming over my neck and shoulders and the next thing I remember I woke up and it was about four in the morning, New Year's Day. I didn't know where I was and this blue-and-white light was flashing off the furniture, off the huge book about Paris, off my legs, lighting up every corner of the room. A high buzz came from the television. I tried to swallow but I couldn't, which made me a little hysterical. I crashed into the kitchen and jammed my mouth up into the cold faucet and drank and then I came back into the living room and changed the channel to a station that had videos on it and I started thinking that if Guy Lombardo had lived none of this would be happening. I would have watched Guy Lombardo and his special guests and been in by one-thirty at the latest. Finally I found a station that was just leaving the air and I left it on. An announcer was giving a lot of details about the station that couldn't have interested anyone except the stockholders and then the station switched to a clip of some handsome black guy in a blue pin-striped suit and about three thousand boxy white teeth. He started to sing the national anthem and then there was a clip of some soldiers dumping a flag-wrapped coffin off the side of a ship, letting it twist sixty feet into the cold grey water and then they switched back to the black guy's hard white wet mouth just as he was singing "of the free." He held "free" for so long I was just about ready to shoot the guy.

* Chapter 4 *

My father drove me out to the airport at about eleven the next morning. He told me the roads would probably be all jammed up since it was New Year's Day and that it would take some time to get his car started, but the car worked on the first turn and there were only about seven cars on the whole highway. Bob is one of those people who likes to get to airports about a week in advance so he'll be sure not to miss his flight. I think if he had his way he'd sleep at the airport motel until the plane left. That way he wouldn't have to deal with traffic or a cold car. When we left New York the streets were slick with drying rain and the trees looked moist and brittle. At one point Bob pointed to an exit and said there had been a six-car pileup off the ramp a couple of weeks earlier and that it was becoming dangerous to own a second home and then he laughed. After a while I turned on the radio.

"You have everything?" my father kept saying. He had this litany of things that people going abroad ought to have. "You have your passport? Your driver's license? You have keys?"

I said, "Keys?"

My father looked confused. I think he'd forgotten I didn't own any keys. I had nothing to lock or unlock. "I guess that's right," he said, looking over at me. "What good would keys do you? That's right." Then he said, "You should probably have keys to my place if you don't already. There's a set in the glove compartment. You're welcome to have them."

I hesitated. When I didn't move he looked over. He looked tired. "It'd be a nice thing," he said, "if you had a spare. That way if I ever locked myself out, God forbid that ever happening, I could call you or wait for you and you could let me in." He was silent and then he said, "Do you not want the extra weight of keys, is that it? I could understand that if that's the deal here. You might lose them, maybe I'm better off keeping them."

I didn't really know what I was going to do with a set of Bob's keys but I opened the glove compartment and took them out anyway. My father looked relieved. I put them in my coat pocket.

"Let me see, now, you have keys, passport, how about bags? How about your bags, you got them?"

I could see my bags in the backseat without having to move my head. "Yes."

"Both bags? Do they have your name on them?"

I told him they did.

"Do you have money?"

"Yes."

"Enough money?"

I said, "What do you mean by enough?"

"What do I mean by enough money." Bob thought, or pretended to think, for a minute. "I mean enough to have a good time—"

"But not a memorable time really," I said.

"No, go have yourself a memorable time. Just not a ruinously good time. Enough so you have a cushion. Enough to have a good time but not so you pay for everybody else's good time at the same time is I guess what I meant." He looked at me. "If you get my point."

"I have enough," I told him. I was actually feeling pretty loaded.

"Well, you can always call or write or wire me if you need more. It's not that much fun being abroad and running out of money. I mean maybe it sounds romantic as hell, Sam, but it's just about the opposite of romantic. I spent a year in Germany once like that. That was the year I gave up smoking simply because I couldn't afford the damn things. Still the best way I know to give them up, is not be able to pay for them. My father paid my way over and back but that was it. I think he wanted to teach me a lesson."

"Your father," I repeated, just for the hell of it. I wanted to see how it sounded. Bob's father had been dead for about three hundred years.

"How we doing on time?"

"It's eleven thirty-five," I said. We were almost at the airport. "So we have four and a half hours before the plane takes off."

"You got your traveler's checks? How about those keys? Did you get them out of the glove compartment just now?"

The traffic got even sparser as we got near the terminals. The houses outside the airport were small and dark and most of them had paths leading up to the door. Through the open glass of the front windows color television was on, cartoons and wrestling since it was Saturday morning. My father dropped me off in front of the terminal and then he went off to find a parking space. I waited for him inside and he joined me about fifteen minutes later and suggested that we get something to eat. I wasn't really all that hungry but I told him I'd have coffee with him. There was a coffee shop on the second floor and since the escalator wasn't working we found a staircase and started climbing it. When we were about halfway up Bob stopped and rested his hand on the white railing. He was breathing pretty heavily and he lowered his head just like a bull and put up his other hand so the soft skin of his palm was facing me. He breathed in and out for about thirty seconds without saying anything. People were moving on the ground far below us, dragging luggage on wheels, getting in lines, crossing each other's paths, while my father stood there with his neck dropped. I was five or six stairs ahead of him and he looked up at me. He looked surprised and guilty. "I'll catch up to you," he called up. "You keep going."

I didn't move. I waited and a minute passed and then my father slowly started climbing until finally we were on different sides of the same stair. "I can't go as fast," he said to me. "Too late a night last night." He drew back his elbows as if to climb some more and I said, "Wait a minute," and then I went through this whole business of pretending that I'd lost my wallet somewhere even though I could feel the dull weight in my hip pocket. "This is why I asked you earlier whether you have everything," Bob kept saying and I kept saying, "I know, I'm aware of that," just like a person would, and I went through each pocket, knowing which one I'd end up with. People were pushing past us, their bags slapped against the railing. When Bob had caught his breath I found my wallet and he shook his head and when we started up the stairs again I let him go first.

The L'Age d'Or Coffee Shop was kind of a depressing place. There were about thirty lemon-colored tables with foil ashtrays sunken into their centers and to get food you had to slide a red tray along three thick silver bars and pay a cashier and then you took your red tray to one of the tables. It was all pretty impersonal. I guess the management wasn't all that interested in forming any kind of intimate relationship with you since they figured you were about to fly away someplace and forget about them, or that you'd just come in from another city, or you were between two flights. Everybody in that place was impermanent as hell, which started making me feel a little bit disembodied. I mean, when Bob and I sat down with our trays at one of the tables I felt I wasn't even there, that I was already traveling somewhere, that eating at the L'Age d'Or was a part of being up there in flight. You looked at people's faces, their teeth and fingers, their mouths chewing food, their throats swallowing, their cigarettes going and smoke drifting up and you sort of knew you'd never see any of them again. It was like looking at a bunch of ghosts eating. I didn't even see all that much point in being nice to the cashier if I wasn't ever going to have to deal with her again. I'm not saying I insulted her or kicked her body or anything, in fact I was pretty decent with her, even when she put the change on the counter when I was holding out my hand, but the thought did cross my mind that I could do something pretty shocking in front of her and it wouldn't really matter much in the long run. I'm not saying I did anything, I just thought about it.

Bob poured a tub of milk into his coffee and took a sip. Then he put his hands down on the table. "Well, Sam, this is exciting stuff, isn't it? You want to remember this moment."

"I don't understand," I said.

"This moment. Now. Here. It's not going to happen again. Not this way anyway. You'll never be the age you are now and going abroad, going away to London. You'll never be in an airport under the same circumstances again. You won't ever be quite so on the verge if you get my point."

"What am I supposed to do?"

"Do?"

"Do," I repeated. "With this moment. With the moment that's going on." I shut my eyes. I didn't know what I was supposed to be doing.

"Just enjoy it. Just appreciate it. You don't *do* anything. That's all you can do."

I opened my eyes. I said, "Are you trying to make me really depressed?"

"Why would I want to do that?" He looked worried. "No, not at all."

I shook my head. "Tired," my father said. His thumb traced along the top of his cup and the steam turned the pad red. "Susan's a pretty lively dancer, you know. Or why should you know that. She used to do it professionally. For a living."

"Do what professionally?" I said.

"Dance," he said. He blew on his coffee and it wrinkled. "Before Susan was married she was a very decent dancer. So we danced it turned out. Dancing is very tiring, you forget. What do you think of her, incidentally? Susan I mean."

"You mean you and Susan?" I said.

He was surprised. "Well, you can leave me out of it."

I told him I thought Susan was all right. That was all I said. I really didn't feel like going into it at that particular moment. I wasn't all that mad for Susan but then again I'm not all that mad for most people. I'm pretty unfriendly where other people are concerned. I thought Susan was good company for Bob and so forth and she was certainly better than some of the others and the nights are cold and all, but I still thought she was basically a nightmare. Then I said, "Why, are you going to marry her or something?"

"Oh, I think that's fairly doubtful," my father said.

We were silent for a little while. Both our Styrofoam cups had little sharp triangle patterns on their sides. Bob took off his glasses and began polishing them with this old yellow napkin that looked as though it had been sitting in his pocket for about two hundred years. I mean, I couldn't even look at that napkin, it made me so sick. "What are you thinking about?" my father said.

I told him I wasn't thinking about anything. I thought, I'm thinking about that disgusting napkin you're holding.

"It's actually none of my business," Bob said quickly. "What you're thinking about. You don't have to tell me." He sipped his coffee suddenly and put his shoulders back. "This is a very good find," he said, meaning the coffee shop.

God, I don't know why my father says depressing things like that. Sometimes I think he should go into deep psychoanalysis to find the roots of why he says things like that. The L'Age d'Or Coffee Shop was just that: a loud, horrible airport cafeteria with a fake French name and no service. It just wasn't the sort of place you go out of your way to compliment. My father was acting as though it was the kind of place where you give the maitre d' some bucks to make sure you get the same table next time. I just nodded at Bob and looked away. I didn't even want to meet his eyes after he would say something like that.

My father wasn't looking at me either. "It's all right," he said after a minute.

"What is?" I said.

"To be quiet." He replaced the glasses on his nose. "It's all right. It's hard. You get my point?"

"No," I said.

"You don't?"

I didn't know what the hell he was talking about. "Not at all."

"Oh, you know." He waved his hand and nearly hit a woman who was walking past with her tray. "I was thinking, when was it, a couple of weeks ago, whenever it was, all of us sitting around Lucy's place. That funny white place of hers on the water. Probably tip over any minute." He looked at me. "Lucy's place out in L.A. I mean."

"Well, yes," I said. "I lived there. I mean, I recognized it from your description. There are only three of us anyhow."

My father stared. "That's what I meant, Sam. What did you think I meant?"

"I didn't." I started to shake my head. I could feel myself starting to get sarcastic so I just kept shaking my head until it passed.

"It got me thinking. I wasn't really thinking thinking but I was thinking and I suddenly could imagine a Peeping Tom outside all our windows. Someone on the beach, some spy of some kind. There was a point there, all of us were doing different things. Naturally I mean, it wasn't some sort of strange thing. I was reading that *L.A. Times* Lucy gets and Lucy was fooling with her fire and you were doing something, I can't remember what. Anyway—" Bob lowered his voice "—I started to think about this spy looking in on us, seeing us. Maybe thinking maybe, these people haven't seen each other for a year, two years—"

"Year and a third," I said.

"—Year and a third, whatever it's been. It's actually been a little less than that I think. And they're not saying a damn thing to each other. Isn't there something more they could be doing?"

He looked at me. "You get my point? You see what I'm saying?" I lit a cigarette. "I wish you didn't do that, Sam," my father said. "Smoke I mean, it's so bad for you." I lifted my shoulders. "At any rate," my father went on, "then I thought—" He stopped.

I put my cigarette under the table so the smoke wouldn't go into his face. "What?" I said.

"Well, I was thinking. Well, now I've completely lost my train of thought."

"You were thinking," I said. "California spies. On the beach. Lucy's fire."

"Oh right," Bob said. "Oh, just that that's simply our *way*. It's nothing necessarily bad. See, I'm not even sure if it's your sister's way, or, say, if it's your way necessarily, but when we first all get back together like that it's somebody's way, certainly. Initially at least. But it's not a bad thing, certainly."

I said, "Whoever said it was?"

"Oh." My father took off his glasses again and held them in his hand. "Well, that's a very good point. No one I suppose. But my point here is that even though all this self-revelation, uh, crap, excuse the expression, is all over the place these days that we don't go along with it all the time." He smiled suddenly. "Am I making sense to you? I mean, who needs all that crap anyway, right? We're all smart people. We're all good guessers. Lucy's a bright girl. We can all guess all that information, what we need to know when we

need to know it. So in a way we're going against the self-revelation crap current. Which if you ask me is a pretty healthy
sign of something. Bucking the current, isn't that the expression? May I get you some more coffee?"

I shook my head. "It's all on me if you want more." I shook
my head some more and said no with my lips. "Or if you want
to change your mind about that eating a little something.
Honestly, Sam, I'm sorry about getting you out here so early.
I really did think the traffic would be worse than it was.
Clogged today, people having to get places."

"It's okay," I said. "Queens is fine." I stubbed out my cigarette in the bottom of my coffee and it sank a hole in the
Styrofoam. "Queens is an underrated borough," I went on,
not knowing what the hell I was talking about. I looked down
at my watch and it was about a quarter to one. The plane left
at four-thirty. Bob said again, "Sure I can't convince you to
have something to eat? What did you have for breakfast?"

"Air," I said. "Air and smoke."

"That's no good." He shook his head. "You should at least
have a little something."

"I had some seeds," I said, just to be annoying.

Bob didn't seem to have heard me. "I wonder," he said,
"why it is I'm telling you all this, Sam, right before it is you
have to take off."

"Well," I said, ignoring that, "I'm sure I don't want anything more than those seeds I had."

He stared at me. "You just want to sit here and smoke your
cigarettes, right?"

I didn't answer him. My father picked up his empty coffee
cup and held it against the window so he could see what light
going through Styrofoam looked like. Then he looked up at
the ceiling of the coffee shop, which was bright blue. "Do
you suppose," he said after a minute, "that anyone could
ever get fooled by that ceiling? Do you suppose anyone would
ever look up and think they were somehow on the outside? I
don't think." He looked at me and he seemed to be making

up his mind about something. He was quiet for a long time and then he said, abruptly, "I'm sorry about John Lennon, Sam."

I was completely disoriented. "What about John Lennon?"

"Well, that, uh, that he died," my father said as though he were in a terrific hurry to say it. "He was shot. Outside the place where he lived."

I said, "Why are you saying sorry to me?"

"Well," my father said, "I just was." He looked confused and unhappy.

I said, "What the hell did I have to do with it? I wasn't even in New York at the time. I mean, why the hell are you saying that to me? What do I have to do with the fact that John Lennon is dead?" I was getting pretty revved up for some reason.

"Because you were off at school when it happened," Bob said. He looked even more confused. "I meant to call and tell you and Lucy I was sorry. But I didn't. I think the circuits were all fouled up that night and then you guys never brought it up. You never talked about it. You know, we had Glenn Miller." He looked at me. "I doubt whether you've ever heard much Glenn Miller, Sam, but we had Glenn Miller. There was a movie made of his life, maybe you've seen the movie. June Allyson and who played Miller, I think it was Jimmy Stewart did Miller. If it's any consolation Miller was our guy who went down. I don't suppose it's the same thing but we thought Miller was just great. So I just wanted to let you guys know that it must not have been a very fun week. Even the *Times* had a thing about it. When all that happened. That's all I meant." He pinched his empty milk tub and milk jumped up onto his fingers. He looked at me anxiously. "I hope they catch the guy."

I said, "What guy?"

"The guy who did it."

"They caught him," I heard myself saying.

"Well, that's a good thing."

"No, I mean that night they caught him," I said.

"Oh." My father wiped his fingers on a napkin. "I always liked them, you know. The Beatles. I think their music really stands up. Even though I could never tell which one was which the way you and Lucy could. I was always impressed how you and Lucy could keep all those guys straight." He stood up and dropped his napkin on the table. "You want to take a walk, what do you want to do?"

I was staring at my father as though he were crazy. "You mean walk around the terminal?"

"You bet," my father said. "Go around to the gates, see who's flying what size craft to where exactly. Kennedy's a whale of a place, you know, the turnover here is pretty fantastic. The planes are a heck of a lot rangier than they were when I was up there. We could probably walk around here for a couple of hours and not even leave the terminal." He looked at me. "So are you up for it? Get you some exercise before boarding?"

I thought that was just about the worst idea I'd ever heard and I said so. He looked disappointed and I started feeling terrible so I told him I'd walk around the terminal with him if he really wanted to. "Only if you feel like it," Bob said so we ended up not doing it. Instead we went back downstairs and into a little magazine store next to the rent-a-car booths. "You have plenty to read?" Bob asked me, pointing to a wall filled with books and magazines and newspapers. "Have you read all these? I'll treat you if you'd like. Look, they have the Philadelphia paper, *Wall Street Journal, Post, Voice,* I guess they're out of the *Times.* You ever do crosswords?"

"Not ever," I said.

"None of the magazines here grab you?"

"No, thank you." That didn't sound appreciative enough so I said, "No, thank you very much, no."

"Are you positive?" My father sounded deflated. "Jesus, whatever you want tell me, Sam, I'm not going to be around forever, you might as well ask me now when I can give it to you. Books, magazines, chocolate." He turned a circle in place. "Anything but cigarettes. You buy your own cigarettes, though of course the point here is don't buy any. You want to kill yourself you do it at your own expense. How about some Chiclets instead of cigarettes? Or Trident. How about Trident green?"

"No thanks," I said.

"Cashews?"

"Nope." I said no to his offer of greeting cards and playing cards and T-shirts that said New York City on them, to bottles of ginger ale and pens and maps of the subway and bus systems. While Bob was looking through a copy of *Life* I told him I was going to check on my gate number. I went over to one of the desks and a woman there told me my flight was delayed for at least two hours, which meant it wouldn't be leaving until six-thirty. I went back into the magazine shop and when I saw my father he was holding a brown paper bag in his hands. He shoved it at me. "Here."

I looked inside. It was two cartons of Newports, which I sometimes smoke when I'm not smoking Tareytons. I'm the only person I know who smokes Tareytons.

"This doesn't mean I condone it," my father said. "But if I remember right the cigarettes over there are pretty nasty. You've got kids rolling their own over there, the homegrown jazz is so poor."

"Well, thanks a lot," I said. "Really." I didn't really know what to say. I unzipped my duffel and laid the package across my clothes and then rezipped it. I stayed bent over. I guess I was hoping the zip sounded conclusive.

"Now," Bob said, "if there's nothing more I can do for you—"

I straightened up. "You should probably get going. Don't wait for me. It's only a couple more hours. I'll just go over to the gate and wait there."

"We could watch some of the TV if you'd like. One of the bowl games starts in about half an hour, forty-five minutes

and I'll bet you anything they have a pretty fair pregame. In-
terviews with some of those big southern boys and the cheer-
leaders and so forth."

"No," I said, "let's not do that."

Bob reached into his coat pocket and brought out a handful of change, which he dropped into my pocket. "That's just
if you decide to change your mind later on. I think it's a quarter for every thirty minutes you watch. That's less than a
cent a minute." He squinted. "In fact it's, what would it be,
what's thirty into twenty-five?"

"I don't know," I said.

"You're not even trying," my father said. "It's point eight
something. It's a bargain whatever it is. Point eight three
something."

"I think I may just go ahead on to the gate," I said.

"You sure? I'd be glad to watch a little of the football with
you. In fact I made a bet on one of them, now I can't remember which one."

"You'd better be taking off," I said. "Traffic's probably a
bitch by now."

He glanced at his watch. "You might be right on that." He
looked at me. "You're sure, Sam? You sure you're all right
here? I don't want to just abandon you here, for you to be
stuck here."

"I won't be," I said. "There's lots to do." I started wondering what the hell I could do for five hours.

My father laughed. "Well, it's seven bucks an hour for
parking if I can get myself back to the car before two. Otherwise it's another four bucks. I'll stay though if you want me
to."

"You shouldn't do that," I said, soft as I could.

"Well," he said, "fair enough. Maybe you want to be by
yourself. You got everything now?"

"Everything."

"Passport, wallet?"

"Both those things," I said.

"Well, all right." People were passing in back of my father and I felt like a photographer trying to take a still picture but people kept going by, blurring the final shot. Soft music was coming out of speakers hidden in the ceiling of the terminal. I hoisted my duffel strap up between my throat and shoulder.

"Be good," my father said. He put out his hand. He already had car keys in the other hand. I put out my hand and behind his glasses my father blinked. He took my hand and then he put the car key hand on the shoulder that didn't have the strap on it and we sort of rocked there for a minute. The way we were holding each other made me think of one of those self-defense moves you set up without actually making contact with the other person. Rocking there with the tips of the keys in my shoulder I could tell I was stronger than Bob was. Sometimes you can tell that just from shaking hands with someone. You're holding onto their hand but you can feel a kind of assurance in your stomach. It's sad as hell, especially if your father is the other person involved.

We stopped shaking hands. "Take advantage of things," my father said, taking a step back. "When you return we'll go ahead on this Harvard thing. I'll let you know if I hear anything from the colleges we've applied to. And call when you get there if you feel like it."

I started backing away from him. I guess I was waiting for him to walk away but he just stood there. I mean, one or the other of us had to walk away first and the other one would be left watching but since my father wasn't moving I said quickly, "Okay," and then I turned around and started walking in the opposite direction. I didn't know where I was going, I was just walking opposite. "Reverse the charges," my father called to my back. I didn't turn around, I put my free arm straight up in the air and kept it high until I was far enough away, until there were whole families between us, and then I let it come down. One of the terminal doors was open and I walked outside into a sort of driveway. I stood behind a low blue wire fence and watched as a little white plane with red numbers on its tail chased down the runway. Its propeller was spinning like mad, whipping the front of my hair, and all these grey-green moths growing in the eaves of the terminal were scattering like buds. After a while a guy in black overalls told me I wasn't supposed to be out there, so I went back inside the magazine store and bought a stash of about twelve magazines. I didn't really select them all that carefully, I just reached up and pulled a bunch of them down. I bought an aerobics magazine and a couple of news magazines and a weight-lifting magazine and then I bought about four of those supermarket magazines that are always picking on my sister. I got so happy having all those magazines that I gave the blond girl behind the counter a huge tip. What happened was that the magazines came to twenty-six dollars and ten cents and I gave the girl thirty and told her in this casual way that she could keep the change and when I started to walk away the girl said, loudly, Sir, sir, excuse me, sir. I turned around and this girl was staring at me as though I were crazy and then she said she was terribly sorry, she couldn't accept more than the price of the magazines. She was obviously very serious about her job. "Take it anyway," I told her but she kind of slapped the money onto the glass counter, ninety cents rolled up inside the shabby ones like some sort of hors d'oeuvre you'd never want to eat. It made a loud clink against the glass and the girl shook her head in this very unaccommodating way and said, I'm not supposed to, sir, I'm not supposed to. She was a pretty tough, horrible girl. She reminded me of one of those big mean grey gulls in front of my sister's house in L.A. She kept calling me sir but she'd say it with her eyes half-closed and she'd spit it so it sounded like a dirty word, *fuck* or something. While she was helping someone else and refusing to look me in the face I pretended to examine the money as though I were some sort of famous scientist of cash and then I threw the money down onto the counter and the change sprayed all over her and I ran out of the store. It wasn't all that mature of me, I admit, but I didn't care. I didn't even look back until I was about half a mile away. It would have been inappropriate to look back any sooner. At that point I wouldn't have taken the money back for anything.

I went over to a phone booth and tried calling up Lucy but her line was busy. I called the number a couple of times more but I still couldn't get through and then I realized I was dialing someone else's number. For some reason I had completely forgotten my sister's number. I called up L.A. information and asked for the number, which is listed under another name, and I got a recording and then I dialed it. The woman on the recording was the same woman who records all the numbers on the East Coast. I think she does the time, too, and numbers that have been changed. She's the one who tells you to check the number, and dial again. She does a lot of things, actually, she's like Peter Ustinov that way. It was pretty great hearing her voice again, in the middle of a strange airport. Out in L.A. there's another more chipper operator who does the time and the numbers that have been changed and I don't think she's anywhere near as good as the East Coast operator. I once read this three-part article about the East Coast operator and I remember being impressed by the fact she actually exists and all, that she lives in a yellow house with a yard somewhere in the Midwest and she has a husband and kids running around and so forth. The phone company makes her sit in this airless glass booth all day long for about three months recording different series of numbers and then a computer puts the numbers together. It must be the most boring job in the world. Anyway, in this article they quoted her as saying she'd never leave her job, she enjoyed the stardom too much. I couldn't get over that: she enjoyed the stardom. That was a pretty wild thing for the East Coast operator to come out and say. After I read that article I started imagining what it would be like to be that East Coast operator's kid. First of all you'd be walking around this glass booth in circles screaming, but she wouldn't be able to hear you, she wouldn't look out, she'd be saying, Please

Hang up and Dial Again, or Please Make a Note of It. She couldn't hear you through the glass and wood, she'd be staring ahead and you couldn't get through to her. Plus, say if you were in a station wagon with her heading upstate and you asked her what time it was, or what the temperature was on the road, or what seven times nine was, anything that required an answer with numbers in it, you'd hear this voice coming out of her mouth that you'd heard a million times on phone company recordings. You'd probably break down after a while, at least I would. People can't take pressure like that and not break down just a little.

After four rings Lucy's service picked up the phone and I left a message that I'd call her sometime later and Happy New Year and so forth. I'm not really the sort of person who goes around saying Happy New Year to other people but it gave me an excuse to call her and say good-bye at least. I suddenly had an impulse to say good-bye to people who didn't even know I was leaving but I killed it since I couldn't think of anybody I wanted to call. I got my magazines and my bags and I started walking down this long hallway and when I had walked about thirty miles it felt like I finally saw a bunch of guards standing around the metal detector. They were laughing but they looked pretty bored, you could tell. On one side of the hallway, right before you got to the passengers-only area, there was this enormous lounge that was completely filled up with babies. Everywhere you looked you saw babies rocking on people's knees like seahorses, taking up space, playing, crying, screaming. There was this one small blond baby—I couldn't tell whether it was a girl or boy—that was screaming fairly regularly. It was screaming so regularly it sounded professional, like a tape of a baby screaming, the way those artificial pink plastic-skinned babies scream in a lot of Broadway shows, you know, screams coming out of speakers. Some of the babies were sleeping, all hushed and wrapped up or what's that Moses word, swaddled, and I started thinking all of a sudden about all the people who had ever wanted to go abroad, these laborers and their wives who had saved up all their money all their lives for one chance to go someplace, you know, three days of vacation in twenty years at the mine or something, and then they had been denied tickets all because the planes were jammed with babies. You knew the babies wouldn't even remember the trip when they got older but in the meantime they were keeping laborers away from new experiences. I started glaring at those babies. I really started to resent them like crazy even though I knew it was really none of my business and that I should just worry about myself and not about a bunch of laborers that I'd never even met. Whenever one of those babies looked up at me in a friendly way I stared back as meanly as I could so its feelings would get hurt, and it would learn a little something about unselfishness, but most of those babies were so callow I don't even think it registered.

I lined up behind a huge family, parents and three boys and a girl in a yellow dress, and they were going through the doorway one by one. You had to step up to this table and put your suitcase on it and then you went under this metal-sensitive doorway while your suitcase slid from sight and reappeared on the other side of the table. A grey-haired woman was standing behind the table looking at the X rays and waving passengers through the doorway. I put my bags down on the table and she waved me through and when I was directly below the frame I heard a siren and the red bulb flashed.

"Go through again, sir," the grey-haired woman said to me. She sounded as though she was pretty used to this happening. I backed up a couple of steps and tried again. I could see my suitcase and duffel bag at the other end of the table. I mean, they had made it through just fine. The second time I walked under the siren sounded again.

The grey-haired woman was looking at me fairly carefully now. She said, "Are you wearing a set of house keys maybe? Maybe a radio or a portable cassette recorder?"

There were a couple of executive-looking types standing

behind me and both of them looked annoyed that I was taking so long so I stepped aside and let them go through. I
could tell the grey-haired woman didn't really care if they
were terrorists or not, she was too busy keeping her eyes on
me. I sort of self-consciously started going through each of
my pockets for metal things. I took out the keys to my father's apartment and all my quarters and dimes. When I
couldn't find anything else metal I started getting pretty
panicky. I stood up and asked the grey-haired woman
whether I could have my suitcase and my duffel back. I was
stuttering my s-words, which always happens to me when I
get upset.

"You'll only have to put them through again, sir." I could
tell she didn't want to give them up. "I'm sure if you look
more closely through your pockets you'll find out what's
making the machine react."

I went around behind her and grabbed both bags off the
end of the table and said to her, "Yeah, just a second, we'll be
in touch, absolutely," or something inane like that. I don't
know why I say things like that. I mumble stuff without
really thinking and most of the time I don't even mean it.
That's a habit I picked up out in California. I may even have
told her that I would call her. I mean, she would be somebody
I'd never call in a million years, two million years. Even if I
were hosting a party for guards and at a quarter of seven or
something I found myself one grey-haired woman short I
wouldn't call her, not that I'd ever give a party like that.

I scooped up all my change and keys from the floor and
started walking in the direction of the lounge. Behind me I
heard the grey-haired woman say, sir, in this stern voice and
I turned around. She was pointing at the floor. "You left a
quarter," she said.

I backed away from her. I said, "That's yours. That's for
you. That's your quarter and thank you," and when I
reached the lounge I felt so relieved I just leaned up against
the wall next to a water fountain for fifteen minutes, taking

breaths that lasted about five seconds each. I couldn't sit anywhere in the lounge since all the seats were occupied by
babies so I sort of slid down the side of the wall until I was
hunched up on the brown rug. I suddenly started thinking I
had some drugs on me or something, you know, that I had
sewed into the lining of my coat a long time ago and completely forgotten about. It was pretty doubtful, I wasn't the
sort of person who sewed drugs into coats, but all the same I
was feeling pretty paranoid. The grey-haired guard was waving other people through the doorway but every so often she
would glance over at me and I'd start pulling lint off the rug
like one of those insane birds that sit on the backs of animals
picking off the bugs and the other crap. After a couple of minutes I lit a cigarette while above me a mother lifted up her
baby to the spout of water. The baby put its lips into a kind of
whistle formation but I don't think it knew a damn thing
about swallowing so most of the water disappeared in clear
curls down the drain. That made me resentful too. In fact, I
was starting off the New Year pretty poisonously. Not only
did I resent the fact babies were taking airplane seats away
from laborers and their wives but I also got annoyed that they
were wasting water all over the place. I imagined this laborer
trudging home from the mine in Montana or someplace, you
know, all smudged and dying of thirst and his wife would
greet him at the door and say, I'm sorry, some baby in New
York just drank the last glass, and she'd tell him to go sip the
moisture eating away at the floorboards, that that was the
only liquid around. The whole situation pissed me off.

I sat on the rug for a couple of hours. A young black guy
with glasses took the place of the grey-haired woman at the
baggage check counter. I heard the flight announcer tell all
the passengers on the London flight to proceed to gate
twenty-seven, where they would be issued boarding passes.
When I heard that I lit another cigarette off the tip of the first
and watched the mothers and babies pack up and leave the
lounge. It was pretty obvious that all the babies were going to

be on the same airplane as me, which made me want to kill myself. I watched them line up behind the metal detector and then I gathered up all my butts from the rug and put them in my pockets where they danced around with my quarters and dimes. There were black plug-shaped burns on the rug from where I'd stubbed out my cigarettes and I camouflaged each burn with a blanket of lint.

It actually wasn't really an idea I had next, it was more a kind of resolution. I think it probably started with me not feeling like moving when I heard the flight announcement. Basically I was pretty comfortable down where I was. My knees were in an Alp-formation, touching my chin, and I was pretty warm and I could see people's waists, hips, calves and shoes, the waist was the top limit of my entire world and I didn't feel like changing that. From not feeling much like moving I started thinking all of a sudden that I really didn't care all that much for England. I've just never been all that enthusiastic about the place. I went over there a couple of times as a kid and I remember there was never anything to do at night. The stores closed down early so you'd try and go to a pub and then the pub would turn off its lights at around ten so you'd go home and watch TV but then the TV would go off the air at ten twenty-seven or some jagged senseless time and after that there was nothing to do except scream. Plus, all the men had these strange squared-off bangs and the women had that pink color in their cheeks, which I know is supposed to be attractive and lusty and all but which always makes me think of rashes. In addition to all that I already knew what England would be like in some ways. I guess I had already taken the trip in my mind a couple of hundred times. I knew I'd board the plane and get to London and someone would pick me up and I'd go to school for five months and wear a uniform and sometime in April I'd find out whether I had or hadn't gotten into any colleges and then in June I'd come back to the U.S. in time for summer school. It was all pretty straightforward and predictable enough to make you want to sleep for about a million years. My point here is that since I knew all this stuff, my entire itinerary for the next five months just about, I didn't have to take the trip really. The trip would almost be superfluous.

I was saying all this to myself as I heard another flight announcement that was a repeat of the first one. Then I began thinking that there were no coincidences and the fact I wasn't able to pass through the metal detector obviously meant something big. I didn't know exactly what it meant but I was reasonably sure the siren was trying to wail me away from something, for example, my flight. I believe in things like that, I really do. I make up these equations for myself sometimes, like if I can make it home before eleven the phone will ring, things like that. If they don't work out nobody knows about it and you can pretend to yourself it's all a lie anyway. I was pretty sure, though, that I'd read in the paper the next morning that the plane had crashed, killing everybody aboard.

The more I thought about all this the more I made up my mind I wasn't going. I heard another announcement but the only thing I did was to pull my knees up more tightly against my chest. Five minutes later when they made the final boarding announcement I started feeling guilty for even entertaining the idea of not going to England, you know, when my ticket was all prepaid and the school was expecting me and so on. I stood up as though I were going back over to the baggage check but then I pictured all those babies being aboard and how I'd probably have to sit between two of them and pretend I was filled with admiration when they cried, and the prospect of that filled me up with dread.

Instead I went into the men's room. I shut myself into the stall farthest away from the world and started leafing through my magazines. I arranged them in the order in which I planned to read them and then I arranged them again by weight. The light cheap ones with bad paper went on top. The advantage to being in the men's room was that you couldn't hear any flight announcers. You couldn't hear much of anything except the bathroom door opening and closing, paper towels torn off a roll and one guy humming. You didn't have to think all that much. I didn't want to voluntarily *not* go to England, if you see what I'm saying, but I told myself it was all right if I missed my flight because I hadn't heard the announcement. I think that happens to people all the time.

I stayed in the bathroom for about twenty minutes, reading this article about my sister and I got perfume all over my fingers from the scented insert inside the aerobics magazine. It was one of those articles that I know drives Lucy crazy. Sometimes I wish they'd stop harassing my sister and leave her alone but for some reason they like to pick on her. The article said that Lucy was getting worried about turning thirty and had taken up with an actor who was about twenty, Kip something or other. I'd never even heard of the guy. It quoted a close friend of the couple as saying my sister is "very much in love" and that Kip and my sister had been seen at a restaurant "kissing and holding hands and carrying on like two teenagers." The magazine quoted Lucy: "I have never been so impressed by a young man as I am with Kip. His wisdom and warmth transcend mere age. My concerns about the natural aging process have vanished."

I don't know how they get away with saying things like that. That didn't sound like anything my sister would ever say. Nobody I know talks in sentences like that. Plus, I think that if my sister had been going out with a twenty-year-old person named Kip I would probably know it. I would have heard them. The magazine had a color picture of Lucy leaving a screening and she had her hands up in front of her face and she looked like some kind of dead woman.

I went back out into the lounge after a while and looked up at the arrivals and departures board. Next to my gate number the word *London* was flashing. "Think of London," I said out loud. "A small city. Dark. Dark in the daytime." Some man was looking at me so I shut my lips up quickly but it was too late and I couldn't stop thinking of that song. Since it was a pretty fast song it made me move around the airport much faster than I would ordinarily. I moved around that empty lounge for a while trying to formulate some kind of master plan for myself. "People sleep. Sleep in the daytime," I said to the huge lounge windows. I didn't like being without a plan of some sort, or at least an outline. You might hear me say sometimes that I'm a pretty spontaneous person who rolls out of bed and makes it up as he goes along but the truth is I'm not really all that comfortable with spontaneity. I like to have a plan for myself usually. The problem was I really couldn't think of anybody in the East who I could stay with. I used to know a lot of people but I lost touch with them when I went out to Los Angeles. I knew a lot of my sister's friends, actors, screenwriters, people like that, but I wasn't sure whether they'd like me without her around. I also knew a lot of Bob's old girlfriends but I thought it would be pretty awkward if I asked to stay with one of them.

Then I had this dazzling idea. This one came down to me right out of the air. I suddenly thought of this aunt I have, or used to have, who lives up in Massachusetts, right at the tip of Cape Cod. She's my mother's older sister and her name is Ellis. She's been married about five times so you never really know what her last name is or where she's living exactly but as far as I knew she was currently unmarried and living year-round on Cape Cod, in Provincetown. My aunt is a terrifically dramatic person, very loud, and she uses her hands to make points that are unacceptable to you and I guess my mother and she weren't exactly passionate for each other because I practically never see her anymore. I think maybe the problem is that none of us is sure whether she's our aunt anymore. She keeps in touch, though, you know, every Christmas she sends us something like twenty pounds of macadamia nuts or two cases of pink grapefruit or maple syrup, expensive and bulky and all but not really what you'd call personal. Then she always writes in her Christmas cards that we must all get together sometime for a reunion at her place but that kind of stuff never works out. Leaving it up to my family is always a big mistake. We just won't come. You're not even sure whether my aunt means it anyway. You get the feeling about Aunt Ellis that she's sent this kind of silencing, all-purpose present to a bunch of people she likes well enough to send a present to in the first place but who she really isn't aching to see all that much.

The last time I saw her was when I was going to Briar Hall. She showed up one afternoon when I was about to go to soccer practice and she had all these old black-and-white photographs with her that she must have kept in some drawer beside the ocean. They were all curled up and yellowing and they smelled like dirt and cardboard and the sky inside them was overcast. They were all pictures of my mother. They mostly showed her in this succession of strange villas in Italy, sitting at tables with thin men and women wearing large hats, or else pictures of her with my father when Bob had a firmer, more closely shaved look to him. Then there was this whole series of pictures of my mother playing with a black Labrador. My mother looks as though she's about seventeen or so and this black dog has an uncomprehending expression on its mouth and my mother's wearing a flannel shirt, one of those faded plaid things girls are always ripping off from their brothers, and her mouth looks pretty tense and beautiful. I don't know who owns that dog or whether it's still alive or it had a litter or anything, but that's how I remember my mother if I'm asked to think her up all of a sudden, you know, screwing around with some idiot black dog on a strip of beach somewhere.

My flight left. The boarding sign stopped flashing and the second flight from the top of the board, which was going to Zurich, rolled up in its place. That made me feel pretty relieved. It cleared the way for this plan I had. I told myself I could take a bus up to Cape Cod to visit this aunt of mine, and maybe spend the winter up there if I liked it well enough. I'd always heard it was quiet up there in the off-season, and beautiful too. A lot of artists go up there to paint quail and marshes and the light and so on, plus there are buses you can take that go directly to Hyannis, which is the largest town up there I think. I don't even think you have to stop in Boston first. Also, I started thinking that this aunt of mine would probably have a lot of things for me to do, like repaint the trim on all her windows or alphabetize her shelves by author or else subject, if that's what she wanted. If she wasn't married there were probably a lot of things that maybe she couldn't lift by herself, cardboard boxes and ladders and wood for instance. My aunt likes to organize things quite a bit. I remember when I was twelve or something I went to visit her when she was renting a house in Montauk and she had the whole week mapped out for me. I had no time at all for myself. She had arranged tennis lessons for me at nine in the morning, then I had to go sailing from ten-thirty to one, then she let me have lunch. In the afternoons I had to play golf, then go to a barbecue on the beach with some kids I couldn't stand, ending up at the yacht club at night with some more unbearable twelve-year-olds she knew. This aunt of mine wouldn't let me alone for a second. But I was sort of looking forward to being around someone like that. Sometimes you need people like that around you even if they tire you out after a while.

I traded in my airplane ticket and got seven hundred dollars in twenties and tens. I added it to my traveler's checks and the cash I already had so all in all I was worth about two thousand dollars. I'm not saying that's an incredible fortune or anything but it could at least get me through the winter, that is if I didn't go dancing every night or play the ponies, but I didn't like to do either of those things anyway. Before I put the money in my pocket I arranged all the bills so the twenties were with the twenties and the tens were all tensed up together and the ones were touching. It was more harmonious that way. Then I waved the whole wad around in the air. I know you're not supposed to do that, people say you'll be robbed on the spot, but I just wanted to see what it felt like, waving lots of money around in a crowd. Nobody stole it from me, though, and it didn't feel either good or bad. I don't even think anybody saw me. My hand still stank from the magazine perfume so all the money started smelling like a girl's money. I expected all that waving to feel fairly liberating but when nothing happened to me and I didn't become changed I just put the money in my wallet and my wallet back inside my coat pocket. It was pretty disappointing.

There was a bus going back to New York in thirty minutes so I bought a ticket and then I unzipped my duffel and got out this huge Icelandic sweater that my sister made for me a couple of Christmases ago that's about eighty times too big for me and which actually makes me colder when I put it on. I pulled it over my head but it kept slipping down my back and strangling me so after a while I took it off and knotted the arms around my neck the way people at Briar used to wear their sweaters. I was in a pretty jovial mood by then. They were trying out a new bus imported from Japan or someplace and it was quite opulent I thought. The windows were thick and silent and tinted blue and when I boarded an attendant gave me these white rubber headphones in a sterile baggie so I could listen to music on the ride into Manhattan. You plugged the headphones into a socket in the arm of your seat and there were ten different channels you could choose from. There was classical and old jazz and new jazz and movie music and then there was something called "Easy Does It," which was all these string versions of old Prince and Aretha Franklin songs with harps and violas instead of guitars. I really hate that stuff but I could tell "Easy Does It" was pretty much the channel of choice aboard the bus that night. I guess a lot of people like that kind of music for whatever reason. They wouldn't play it all over the country if it weren't popular with this certain big undesirable segment of the population. I can't listen to that music without imagining all sorts of terrible things happening to people, though, kids getting murdered in elevators or knifed in dentists' chairs while this music just keeps playing on and on. You can't shut that kind of music off. It'll go on forever if you allow it to. Whenever I hear string versions of "Penny Lane" or "Not Fade Away" I always imagine kids getting slashed or chased or killed.

Next to "Easy Does It" was something called "The Soulful Guy," which was all songs by Chaka Khan and Nona Hendryx and Marvin Gaye, people like that. I decided "The Soulful Guy" was the closest to what I wanted for myself so I put my head back and lit a cigarette and lifted my duffel up onto the seat beside mine so no one could sit there and then I turned up "The Soulful Guy" loud. I came in right in the middle of some song where the singer was doing a sort of recitation. Sometimes in these soulful songs the singers will quit singing for a minute and start in about the moon and the stars, you know, addressing the woman they're supposedly singing the song to, calling her Baby or My Lady or something, and then they sing the chorus one last time and the song ends. I don't know why they do that, it's distracting as hell. I think anybody who calls his girlfriend My Lady ought to be put to sleep, too. It's like something a pimp would call you in the middle of the night. I listened to "The Soulful Guy" straight through until we got into Port Authority and as the bus pulled into the parking space the side began to repeat itself.

In the station I gave the attendant back the headphones and she asked me whether I had enjoyed the music. I told her yes and I tried to look soothed and sort of boneless even though "The Soulful Guy" had made me feel a little bit jumpy. I don't know what she was planning to do with my used headphones, resterilize them maybe or burn them or something. The bus made such a huge deal over their being sterile and packed in fresh baggies maybe the only thing to do was to make a fire of them and scatter the ashes over an ocean, I don't know. Anyway, I'd had the radio jacked up so loud that the attendant's voice sounded distant as the sea or something. I had gotten so used to having back-up singers in my ears that I all of a sudden began wishing I had some back-up singers of my own. I imagined there would be three of them, black girls in bright red dresses that came down to right above the knee. They'd be a unit but each girl would have a distinct cohesion-shattering personality and they'd always be dancing and smiling, showing their teeth and looking beautiful, following me wherever I went, getting their microphone cords tangled up, covering for me. I could make all sorts of mistakes and the girls would be there nodding and singing over me, blanketing my flubs with their voices. I'd never not have company since I could always pull them by the wrists out of the shadows where they'd be keeping up a high steady "Da Bum Bum" or "Uh Huh, Uh Huh." They'd get a group rate whenever they traveled with me, too, so it wouldn't be all that expensive getting around. Because they'd be on key I'd always be on key.

After fifteen minutes of wandering around the terminal I found the floor where all the buses to Massachusetts left from. There was one more bus leaving for Hyannis that night in about an hour and a half so I waited around Port Authority drinking orange juice and listening to the other bus announcements until it was time to line up at the gate. I got pretty hypnotized listening to those announcements, in fact I was in such a stupor I almost missed the bus. What the bus announcer would do was mention the destination first, say, Florida, and then he'd start listing off the hundred or so small towns in between Florida and New York where the bus made stops. The sound of those hundred small towns coming down in a soft male voice from the ceiling of the terminal was just about the most romantic thing I'd ever heard. None of the towns sounded familiar but practically all of them sounded better than the places I knew.

The bus to Cape Cod was pretty shabby-looking. It looked as though it hadn't been swept out in about two hundred years or something. The floors had thin black streaks on them and every time the driver hoisted another suitcase inside the baggage compartment the bus would make this grunt and beer and ginger ale cans started rolling back and forth in the aisles. Under your feet were cigarette butts standing up like cold posts from where they had been stubbed out hard, sometimes in gum. I wouldn't have been surprised if that bus had rats living in it, or rabbits or geese. That's all I'll say: I wouldn't have been surprised if something with wings flew into my head or if something soft started eating my sneakers. It just wouldn't take me by surprise.

I walked all the way back and sat down in this wedge of four seats right beside the bathroom. The upholstery on the seats was blue and speckled. I sat in the seat closest to the window and pressed my left cheek against it so my skin began to burn but I kept my cheek there until we were in Connecticut and only after we passed a mustard-colored jai alai stadium did I peel it off and then my face felt like a freezing mask. There weren't many people at all on board and most of them had shut off their reading lights and aimed the grey cones so they would gasp down air onto the backs of their necks, and had fallen asleep. There was this one beautiful little blonde girl in black tights who fell asleep while we were stopped in New Haven and woke up right outside Providence. It was a pretty intimate thing to see, somebody's eyes shut and the shadow of their lashes against their skin, even if it was a stranger. I had the opportunity to talk to her a couple of times before she fell asleep, once when she was trying to stow her red suitcase on the rack and again when her book fell off the seat and went sliding along the floor but both times I didn't. I'm a fairly antisocial person, I may have mentioned. It's just too depressing usually, talking to people you travel with. You get talking with them and maybe you like them, or at least you don't hate them, and you write down their name and address and phone number on one of those pieces of paper you tear off the corner of this envelope or magazine you're carrying with you and you say you'll look them up, call them. I don't know why you say that, I guess so you can talk about what a smooth ride it was or how the driver made a skillful left turn when you were in Mystic or something. I don't know what you talk about. I guess if you end up marrying the person you can talk about fate and how it brought you two together that day but if you don't marry them you have to talk about, I don't know, the bus industry, traffic, dull things like that.

We were passing dark harbors and coves without boats in them and I started to see patches of dark greasy ice on the sides of the road, old snow dusting the rims of the garbage cans in the rest areas and then I started thinking of this line from an old James Taylor song I used to overhear a lot when I was younger. I can't really remember the name of it but I know he rhymes cattle and saddle and sings about how the turnpike from Stockbridge to Boston is blanketed with snow early on in December and it's quiet and the Berkshires look strange and white. The turnpike from Stockbridge to Boston: that line kept going through my head as if the whole song consisted of that line repeated over and over. It made me so nostalgic I felt like I wanted to cry for about a hundred years. My eyes felt warm so I touched the window and then I touched my eyes to make them cold. I was nostalgic but I didn't know what I was nostalgic for. I couldn't even tell you the year I wanted back. Maybe there wasn't a year, maybe I was nostalgic for nothing at all. Sometimes you get nostalgic for places you've never seen, you want to return there but you've never even been once so you can't go back. I wasn't even sure whether I liked the line in the song because I'd overheard it a lot during a good period or because I liked it for myself. James Taylor wasn't even my singer; he was my sister's singer and all the records of his we owned had her wild black signature on the top right-hand corner. Most of the songs that make me nostalgic are songs I've overheard somewhere. I've been in the bedroom and the music's come out of the living room. They've been somebody else's records. I don't have any singers of my own, you know, singers who sum up years for you, the years you're in right then and there I mean. There aren't any singers or actors or poets or anyone I could say are mine.

All these wisps of fog were drifting across the headlights as we got near the grey bridge that connected Cape Cod to the rest of Massachusetts. The bus stopped in the parking lot of a diner and a couple of people got off and a guy wearing huge white mittens and holding a guitar by the neck got on. As we rode up the side of the bridge the cans rolled toward me and I put out my sneaker to slow one of them and the can went up over the toe and splashed my sock with warm beer. I took it off and twisted the water out of it and put it in my pocket. At the top of the bridge hung a huge white sign that said, "Depressed? Anxious?" and it gave you a couple of phone numbers to call if you were. There was high grey webbing on both sides of the bridge above the two walkways, overlooking the canal below. I guess that was to keep people from jumping.

I was the only person in the waiting room at the Hyannis bus station. I mean, I know it was late and all but it would have been nice to see somebody else in there. The station smelled of hamburger and bacon and sweat. The floors were dirty yellow and they had forgotten to turn down the volume of the answering machine because the phone rang while I was standing there and I heard static and then a woman's voice behind the ticket desk saying, You have reached the Hyannis bus terminal. The station is closed for the night, there will be no more buses running tonight. It was about one in the morning by then and I hadn't had anything to eat except for that orange juice in Port Authority so I was pretty famished. There was one of those shabby old light blue vending machines from the fifties pushed up against the wall and on the front of it was a picture of a woman with yellow plump fifties hair who was wearing a bib of some kind and a guy in a

short wet black crewcut and both of them were drinking
these white cups of steaming coffee and beaming like crazy
at each other. Both of them were acting as though this coffee
were the key to their marriage or something. The vending
machine had all these objects, chocolate bars, cookies, potato
chips and so forth, clenched in these metal claws and you put
your money in and the thing you wanted fell from the claw so
by the time you slid open the plastic hatch and fished it out it
was in two hundred pieces. It was a pretty sheer drop. If the
thing you wanted had been, say, a hiker, he would have died
for sure. Nothing in the machine looked all that appetizing
but I went ahead and bought a ham-and-cheese sandwich
and a Coke and a little red-and-gold bag of Doritos and I used
up all the change I had left. I threw the bread away and ate
the sandwich. It looked pretty ancient and the orange cheese
was stiff around the edges but it wasn't bad and then I finished off the Doritos. It was a pretty pathetic meal but it
made me feel better. There was one other person in the waiting room with me by then, a woman with puffy black hair
who looked like a country-western singer. I think it was the
hair that made me think that, and the swollen skin under her
eyes. She was smoking Gitanes or Gauloises and staring out
the glass doors and not looking at me and then this jazzy little
red car pulled up outside and for the first time the woman
looked at me and smiled. She looked less like a country-western singer smiling. Some guy got out of the car, her father or
her old boyfriend or something, and she went outside and
he took her bag from her and she got in and they drove
away.

I decided it would probably be a good idea to find a motel
before it got any later than it was. I had started thinking of
that on the bus, that I'd need someplace to stay for a while
while I traced my aunt. I don't know why I hadn't thought of
that before but I can be pretty vague sometimes and I guess
I'd been thinking of a lot of other things. I took the steps the
country-western singer had just taken and I dropped my bag

down outside on the sidewalk the way she had. I could smell exhaust from the red car in the air, a thin sweet smell. I guess I was half-hoping that if I did what she did a little red car would come for me too but I wasn't really counting on it. After a while I walked down a slope of pavement onto the street. There were brown bushes on the side of the road and the cold air seemed to enter my nose and shoot right up into my brain. That cold air was like a high sound, something that made holes in you. It was very dark out too, and quiet as hell. There was a large moon in the sky and about a million stars. They weren't blotches either, they actually looked star-shaped, you know, the way you draw stars in pencil, with five arms, like starfish. The air smelled of wood burning and I kept skidding on sand crystals that were spilled on the sidewalk. As I walked I switched hands every two hundred yards so that each hand could have a chance to grip my suitcase. It wasn't that my suitcase was too heavy for me or anything, it was just that my knuckles were getting cold so I'd switch hands and drop the hand that was freezing into my pocket and then I'd take it out and switch all over again. I did that nine or ten times.

I must have walked for about a mile or so. I seemed to be on some kind of main thoroughfare. I started seeing bunches of little motels with gravel paths splitting up their lawns. The motels were white or light blue or shell pink and all of them said Vacancy in the same red neon scribble you see lighting up words you like better, *bar, beer, girl, all night,* words like that. In the empty courtyards were one or two cars and swimming pools the management had probably drained sometime back in September. The pools had tarpaulins stretched from one end to the other, held down in the corners by heavy petaled stakes. I could see blue-green slides contorted in the dark and white diving boards and pine needles in the folds of the tarpaulins. I walked past a bowling alley and an antique store and a movie triplex and an airport with a low cinnamon-colored fence around it and a lot of small dark-tipped planes sleeping on the runway. About half the places I passed had the word *Kennedy* or *Presidential* or *Congressional* in front of them. I mean, I saw Presidential Dry Cleaners and submarine sandwiches and deli and Kennedy Video and boatyards and piers and power tools. Everything seemed to be closed down, too, either for the night or for the season. I turned down a dark street and went past Lobster Larry's and Neptune's Nook and Davy Jones's Burger Locker and Jack-O's Palace of Plenty. None of them were open but they kept dim lights on behind the counters and spotlights above the doors, big white moon-faced bulbs staring out over the parking lots. In the shut-up gas station at the intersection I could see faint light low in the back room, rows of antifreeze in colored cans and thick stacks of folded maps, a desk, a wooden chair, a cigarette machine and oil soaked into the concrete around the pumps.

I didn't know where the hell I was but I kept on walking and about a half-mile past the gas station I finally found a motel that looked halfways awake. At that point I didn't really care where in the world I stayed as long as there was a bed, you know, and maybe a shower. This motel was pink and there was a light on in one of the windows and in front of the lawn on a wooden post a sign read The Tern Inn, Singles and Doubles. Below that was another sign that listed what the place had to offer: color TV, cable, air conditioning, indoor swimming pool and Magic Fingers and since we were on Cape Cod there was this pathetic little wood sculpture of a bird with an orange beak and grey wings. The wood bird was just hanging there in the thin quiet air, suspended by cold loops of brown wire. I think it might have been a tern actually. I mean, some people bring back things like that from their trips around the world and put them in their living rooms where at least you can't see them from the road but the Tern Inn had their bird right on the lawn so everybody passing by couldn't help looking at it. It was supposed to be the archetypal tern or something but it looked pretty unfriendly to me. In fact it looked insane. It had a sort of sneering expression on its face and small green greedy eyes and its wings were outstretched wide as though it wanted to clap them across your face until you screamed and died. I couldn't look at it that long.

There was this tall pink-faced man sitting behind the desk when I went inside. He was reading one of those fright paperbacks, you know, with a raised cleaver on the front cover and listening to classical music off a radio. I think he was pretty surprised to see someone that time of night. Inside a squat silver bell on the desk I saw my face and neck and ears upside down.

I dropped my suitcase on the floor and told him I wanted a room. He stared at me for a while. "Well," he said, "it's lucky you come in when you do, isn't it?" He waited for me to say something and when I didn't he closed his book and slid a bookmark in the margin. He moved a black ledger up from underneath the desk. "Have a reservation, do you?"

I told him I didn't think I needed one and the pink-faced man said, "Oh, we're busier than we might look here, young man, I promise you. It's lucky you come in when you do and there are rooms open. I wouldn't be up even but that I'm waiting for my daughter and her husband to come in from Boston tonight. They should be here any minute. There'll be a crowd here any minute."

I didn't say anything. I didn't really believe the guy, that's why I kept quiet. He started flipping through the ledger and I looked down at the cover of his book. The cleaver was being held by someone with green hands and no little finger. The man looked up at me. "How long will you be a guest?"

A guest, I loved that. A guest of the Tern Inn. "Oh, I don't know," I said as airily as I could. "A couple of days, maybe three days." I figured that was all the time I needed to locate my aunt and call her up and arrange things and also have enough time to scout around Hyannis. It occurred to me all of a sudden that I really wasn't in much of a hurry to get anywhere. I didn't have to do anything immediately, that was the good thing.

The pink-faced man did something with his mouth. "Well, you're lucky," he said, closing the ledger. "We have a room available on the second floor. And that particular room goes for forty-five dollars a night. There's a view." I had a feeling he was about to tell me about a couple of other rooms but I broke in and told him the forty-five-dollar room sounded just fine. I don't know why he was going through all the trouble of checking to see what rooms were available. I mean, the parking lot was deserted and there were no lights on in any of the rooms and I had a pretty strong feeling that all the rooms were available and that I was the only person in the motel. I didn't say that to him, though, I was too tired. All I wanted to do at that point was go lie down somewhere. The man told me to write down my address and I gave him Lucy's and he glanced down at it and then back up at me. "You're a pretty long ways away from home, aren't you?"

When I nodded he said, "What brings you up to Cape Cod? Surely there's not a great deal for a young man to do up here this time of year."

"Yeah, well." I explained to him that I wasn't all that mad for people anyway. I told him that I liked to be alone and when I said that the man looked at me as though I'd said something unpatriotic. Something must have clicked in his mind because all of a sudden he asked me if I had any identification and then he mentioned again that his daughter and son-in-law were due to arrive any minute. "ID's not for me," he said quickly. "It's the policy of the motel. We get a lot of wanderers coming through in the winter. Not that I'm suggesting you're a wanderer." I mean, I guess the guy had suddenly remembered reading that murderers and fugitives, people like that, are always being recalled by their ex-wives and neighbors as loners. You read one of those articles about serial killers out in L.A. and they always interview the ex-wife and the neighbors. The ex-wife has usually moved to Florida or New Mexico but she always says something like, Tex kept to himself and the neighbors say, Nice guy but never came to the pot-luck suppers held in 7A and the landlord says, Paid his rent on time, never gave me any trouble. If you ask me I think murderers give loners a bad name.

I handed the guy my California driver's license that has a picture of me when I had fairly long hair. It was taken a couple of years ago when I had just moved out there. I look like a little Chinese baby in the picture except for the hair since Chinese kids have black silky hair, I think, and mine was just unruly. Plus, these thin wrists of mine got twisted up in the picture somehow and they're sticking out all over the place. I have the thinnest wrists of practically anybody I know, they're like thread. The rest of me is pretty much in proportion with the exception of my long feet and these two thread wrists of mine.

The man held out my license in his palm and squinted at it and brought it up close to his nose and didn't say anything and then he handed it back to me and said, "Can't argue with the resemblance any. In the face anyway. You're who you say you are." He sounded disappointed.

Five minutes later I was standing on a cold balcony in front of my room trying to get the door open. The room key hung off a dull gold plastic diamond and whenever I'd try and turn the key the diamond would rise up and cut into my fingers. The door opened on about the fifth try and the first thing that happened was that this very old striped cat ran out of the room past me. It scared the hell out of me. This cat must have been about two thousand years old at least. It was huge and slow and it had a big square face and double paws and eyes like stones on wedding rings; they shone and first they made you blind and then you looked right through them almost into the cat's head. I had no idea what that cat was doing in my room, or how long it had been there or whether there were a bunch of other cats in there with it. The cat looked back once and then it went behind the ice machine. The ice machine stood ten feet from my door at the end of the

balcony and the cat ducked under the fat black cable so it
was somewhere in the shadows between the machine and
the wall. An enormous rusted ladle hung off a chain made up
of triangles and crashing noises came from inside the machine. Even when I got inside the room and turned on the
overhead light with my sleeve and elbow and shut the door
with the top of my shoulder I could hear the cubes splitting,
exploding in the dark.

It was a terrible-looking room and I hated it. It was all done
in green and it smelled of mustard and wine and the cat. The
bedspread was green and the pleated curtains were green
and the rug was green. Also, it must have been about nine
hundred degrees in there. I looked up and down the walls for
a thermostat but there didn't seem to be one. I considered
going back downstairs and asking the pink-faced man where
it was but I wasn't really in the mood to deal with him anymore so I decided I'd just open up the sliding doors. I pulled
back the curtains and stepped out onto a little stone balcony.
The balcony had a yellow canvas lawn chair on it that cradled
about an inch and a half of frozen water. All these slivers of
bark and leaves were trapped under the ice. They looked like
seeds. The balcony overlooked a parking lot. That was the
view the man downstairs had mentioned. The parking lot
was empty except for this big white bloodmobile parked
across two spaces right underneath my window. Since it was
a bloodmobile it had dark red writing on its sides. I turned to
leave and I almost stepped on this old dead bird that was
lying next to the chair. I guess the bird had crashed into the
glass or something because it was still pretty intact. I don't
think it had been dead for all that long. Its stomach was
plump and its feathers were long and blue and straight. All of
a sudden I started thinking of this friend of Lucy's, this girl
Carol, who was taking an aerobics class in New York somewhere in Chelsea. The class was held in this old brown building and the walls were mostly glass and people walking along
the street below would look up to see where the music was
coming from and see all these girls in leotards pumping their

heads and arms like crazy. This girl Carol was dancing around and I guess she got too close to the glass because one of the panes shattered and she fell through it, three stories down. She was wearing a yellow-and-blue one-piece bathing suit and tights and she landed on top of a newsstand and the newsstand owner, who was blind and gave you back your coins by touch, came out but there was nothing anybody could do. It was a Saturday night in the summer and the sons of the owner were out assembling the Sunday *New York Times* on the sidewalk in front of the church and there was so much white paper around it looked as though a huge snowstorm had leveled the city. Carol landed on a bunch of stacked paper, want ads and real estate, and that softened her fall just a little but really not enough to make a crucial difference. I guess the glass and the bird made me think of her. As far as I could tell the bird had assumed the glass was open air and streaked through and not made it. Anybody could make the same mistake, really.

I picked up the bird and brought it inside the room and then I went over to the bedside table and got out the blue Cape Cod phone book. I tore out some of the G pages and the beginning of HA but before I wrapped the bird I kind of stared at it for a little while. I didn't kiss it or caress it or anything, I just looked on at it. It was a very good-looking bird, actually, soft and whole with a nice face. I wasn't sure what kind of bird it was, I don't know things like that, you know, the real names of birds or flowers or planets or roots or trees. I used to think knowing all that was important but I don't anymore. I finally wrapped up the bird in phone book paper, which was sheer and blue-white like skim milk, and when I pressed the pages down against the wings the moisture on the feathers soaked through so I could see the names and numbers on the other side of the paper: Hamilton, William, Hamilton, Wilma, Hamilton, Zita, and one guy named Hammock, Ted Hammock, I think it was. When the bird was all covered I laid it outside on the chair in the center of the

woody frozen puddle and then I came back inside and un-
packed.

It was the first time I'd opened up my suitcase since I'd
left L.A. and I started noticing that a lot of the zippers on my
pants were sticky and that my socks were all wet and caked
and then I got to the bottom of my suitcase and I came across
this old crumbling pecan pie wedged between two white
shirts. I'd never seen that pie before in my life. I mean, I
hadn't packed it. Under the pie, or what was left of it, was
this porno magazine I hadn't seen before either. It was the
long flat grey kind you get out of blue-and-yellow vending
machines on L.A. streetcorners. They don't have those machines in New York I don't think, it's a California thing.
There was a note attached to the cover but it was covered
with molasses and crust and pecans and I couldn't read it but
at the bottom my sister had signed her name. The cover
showed this huge red-haired girl with gigantic breasts leaning down over a little purple wind-up penguin. I guess the
penguin hopped around or did flips once it was wound up,
I'm not sure. The girl's face was all snapped brown pecans
and flakes of crust. I think Lucy had assumed I'd unpack in
New York but in the meantime this pie had collapsed over
practically everything I owned. The pages were so sticky that
when I pulled the magazine open it split down the middle of
the page. The print started flaking off onto my fingers, leaving silver marks on the joints that weren't already soaked
with syrup and bird, and for some reason I started to cry.

It was stupid, crying. It made me feel as though I were
about four years old or something. Usually I cry only at special occasions like at your funeral if I liked you, and that's
only if I see other people crying. I'm mainly a sympathetic
crier that way. Other people crying makes me feel terrible. A
lot of those Christmas specials that come on TV in December,
cartoons and so on, make me cry too. I cried for a while, not
all that long, ten minutes, and then I went into the bathroom.
The cat had pissed and thrown up all over the inside of the

tub so I cleaned that up and took a long shower and washed the bird and the pecans and the newspaper print off my hands. I came out in a stringy white towel and turned on the TV set and switched the stations around for a while but there was nothing on I wanted to watch so I went out onto the balcony again. The phone book paper was pretty well saturated by then and the head and the throat of the bird had slipped out of the roll. The beak had cut through the ice.

God, I felt so sorry for that poor stupid unlucky bird. I picked it up by the shoulders as though it were this kid who'd misbehaved and I said to it, "Think of London, a small city," and I made it fly a little and then I held it out in front of me in sort of a lecturing position and said, "People sleep, sleep in the daytime." I don't know why I did that to the bird. It's embarrassing to remember. Suddenly I got scared that it would come alive in my hand and say something like, Put me down, you know, start screaming at me and pecking so before it had a chance to do that I threw it as far as I could in the direction of the parking lot. It landed in a yellow marsh.

I went back inside and lay down on the bed. I stretched out my legs and stared at myself for a long time. I could see the whole room reflected in the dark green of the television screen, the lamp, the two pillows, the phone book, my knees. There was a Magic Fingers by the bedside, a grey square box that looked like a safe. For twenty-five cents you could get your bed to shake for ten minutes and then it stopped. I found a quarter in my coat pocket and put it in but nothing happened. I shook the machine but it didn't do any good, my quarter was gone. To add to it all I just wasn't feeling all that exultant that night, looking at myself I mean. Sometimes your body can be diverting if you're all alone with not that much to do and time but for some reason I wasn't feeling erotic in the least. I didn't even have an erection or anything, which I was kind of wishing I would. I couldn't think myself into having one either. I thought it might be fun and all to masturbate since I'm always reading that it's supposed to relax you but I just couldn't. After a while I got up and fished the porno magazine out of the garbage can where I'd thrown it. I brought it back over with me to the bed. The only picture that wasn't totally destroyed with syrup and pecans was an advertisement that showed a Mexican woman inserting a soft contact lens into her eye. I stared at her for a long time hoping she'd trigger some interesting fantasy but I guess I was too scared or disoriented or tired or something because all I could think of was how bad I was at bartering and how in Mexico they expect you to barter for things all the time. They set up these long tables on hillsides and the tables are covered with rings and scarves and hats and piggy banks. The vendors quote you a price and you're supposed to get them down, pick at them, reach a compromise, break it up and then reach another one. I'n not very good at that. Usually I end up paying full price while everybody around me is making out like crazy.

I started to read my mystery but after about a minute I laid it across my chest. My watch said two-thirty. It was seventhirty in London and the sky was probably dark and people were going to work. Schools were starting. The fan above me was turning in a slow windless circle. I was kind of hoping it would have this hypnotic effect on me and put me to sleep but instead it just made me bored and restless. I went over to the duffel and got out this black felt-tipped pen and I lay back down on the bed and started drawing words on myself, my body, whatever. I brought my right leg up until the knee was almost touching my chin and I wrote my name about five times across my calf and I thought, that's how I'll sign it later for little girls. The point was moist and since I don't have all that much hair on my legs and the hairs I have are light it was a pretty relaxed job and the pen moved easily. I started signing the names of famous people, actors, actresses, singers, presidents of countries in Asia and so forth. I wrote their names the way I imagined they would, with lots of egotistical loops and crosses. Right where my ribs meet, right where they arch by your heart, I wrote in caps, You Are Here. Then I remembered words on a sign in Boston in front of some apartment building off Storrow Drive. You see it when you're on the road and tired, so it gets you when you're vulnerable. I wrote that on my stomach too: If You Lived Here You'd Be Home Now. I think that's a pretty clever sign. It's been there for as long as I can remember.

All of a sudden I became aware of this gigantic black fly skimming off the walls of my room. It was about the size of a little bull. It was an incredibly well-built, muscular fly. It flew off as the ice came crashing down outside my door, glanced off the rim of the lampshade and whenever it landed it made a strange bobbing motion with its head, like a fighter trying to shake off a punch. Then its wings would shiver. A *frisson* is what they call that in France. One of the *jumeaux* left me with that word: this fly would make a *frisson*, a *petit* one. For some reason flies seem to move around a lot less enthusiastically at night than they do during the daytime and in a little while it dropped down onto my pillow next to my ear. I decided to let it live. I'm not one of those bearded young naturalist types with orange hair on their wrists who spare the life of everything they see oozing around in the mud, but I was feeling too tired to torture it so I let it play on my pillow. Outside the cubes came down heavily again and I heard a sound that was probably the cat and I tried to sleep.

* Chapter 5 *

I got up the next morning at around eleven-thirty. All this bright yellow sun was flashing through the curtains, across the bottom where the fabric was bunched and for a while I thought I was back in L.A. The sun shone off the grey curtain hooks and pinned the area of the rug where my sneakers were lying untied and turned them this astonishingly white color so they looked like bones. I lay in bed for a while watching my laces burn and the slow weaving of dust and I noticed that the rug on the floor seemed to soak up every sharp movement I made. It seemed to bring everything I did back to a point of absolute stillness. I don't know why motel rugs do that to you but they do, they blunt you somehow. I managed to get out of bed and turn on the TV loud and then I took a shower and when I came back out I shook my hair at the set so the screen got covered with little beads of water. The contestant in the middle won a case of Turtle Wax and a recliner, this ugly, plum-colored thing that tipped back and when it did, a little footrest swung up out of it. The contestant, who was this schoolteacher from Alameda, jumped up and down and her whole family rushed out of the studio audience and onto the stage and took turns reclining

177

in the recliner. At the end of the show it began to snow on everybody, on the players, on the emcee and on the girls who point and smile at the prizes, models they were calling them. It was that time of year I guess. The snow kept falling down as the credits rolled up but since the snow was made of white paper it didn't melt, it just clung to the hairs on your sweater. Game shows always do festive things like that for the holidays. It can be cheery sometimes but that morning it just made me feel dark for some reason and after a while I turned off the set and went downstairs.

The Tern Inn Coffee Shop was situated in the part of the motel that faced the street and it had all these old ship prints on its walls. There were a couple of families there with children and you could tell it was kind of a big-deal excursion for them, you know, taking the kids out for a meal at the Tern Inn, that it broke up the day pretty effectively or something. I hunched over one of the tables and a waitress in a soft white skullcap came over and gave me a tall menu. All the waitresses in the coffee shop had to wear skullcaps and brown skirts and tags over their hearts that said Hi! followed by their names. I think they had to pretend they were muffin maids or something like that. I felt pretty embarrassed for them. The tag on my waitress said Denise but there was no way I was about to address her by name, you know, say, for example, Excuse me, Denise, bring that coffee over here before I count to three, or Denise, I have this problem that only you can solve, blah, blah, blah, anything like that. Some people might do that, get all chummy with their waitresses during the course of the meal but not me. I get embarrassed in front of anybody who's forced to wear a uniform. Whenever you're on an airplane and you see one of those stewardesses, hostesses, whatever they call themselves, pretending to suck on hoses and strapping on air seat belts you feel like dying a couple of times, once for all of them, once alone. Those girls must live a life of total humiliation. This girl Denise was friendly too, which is more than I think I would have been if

I had to pretend it was 1904 and I was a muffin maid. She said good morning and then she wished me a Happy New Year and she asked how I was feeling today and what she could get me today. She was a very today-oriented person.

I ordered something called the Cape Cod Whaler Special but before she wrote it down Denise said, "You can't order that, sir, you have to charter it!" and she shook with laughter. That was the only time I felt like calling her by her name, you know, Denise, enough, Denise, go away, but I didn't. The Cape Cod Whaler Special turned out to be these scrambled eggs trapped inside a replica of an old schooner that the kitchen had made out of three pieces of burnt toast and a couple of toothpicks. When it came I just stared at it. The hull was made up of two pieces of toast torn in half and then the crusts were bent together to form a bow and there were toothpicks for the mast and the boom and I guess the eggs were supposed to be panicked passengers wearing yellow slickers and raincoats because you could see them inside the toast cabin looking out at you in sort of an anguished way, the way zoo animals sometimes look. I tried to eat the thing but I couldn't really deal with it. The concept blew away my appetite. I pushed away my plate after a while and the boat tipped over and some of the passengers slipped out and finally I just spread my napkin over the whole thing.

The drowned egg passengers made me think of my flight to England and when I saw a little kid passing by on a blue girl's bike selling newspapers I bought one from him and read it while I was drinking my coffee. Just about the only news they had was local, you know, zoning controversies and articles about polluted ponds and new malls and mallards. There were lots of obituaries, in fact the obituary section took up about half the entire newspaper. It seemed about fifty people had died just while I was on the bus getting up there.

I read the paper from cover to cover and there was no mention of my plane crashing over the ocean or in Dover or Folkstone or any of those places and when I realized it had probably landed safely in London I decided to go down to the Western Union office. I found out from Denise there was one about a mile down the street, next to a marina, and I took sort of an indirect route getting there. I could have walked straight down the main street but instead I took a road one block north of it and then I cut across someone's front lawn and the parking lot of a bank and when I reached the back of the marina I crossed back over to the main street. I guess I was feeling pretty paranoid that I would run into someone I knew. A lot of people from Briar Hall had houses on the Cape, or their parents did, and Bob had friends who lived there year round and who would probably recognize me, and I wasn't really all that anxious to run into any of those people. In New York you're always running into people you don't want to have anything to do with. You were under the impression that you'd never see those people again and even when you hear from a third party that they've moved to New York you figure New York is so big the chances of ever running into them are pretty remote. Anyway, it happens all the time. You see these people lurching toward you on the sidewalk and you try and hide but it's too late for that and you're too big and you wish you could turn into a paper airplane and fly right over their heads but you have to stop and talk to them about getting together for lunch sometime. It never works out, you never have lunch. If you see them again they say they lost their address book at Mardi Gras or something, which sounds like a lie. Whenever I see someone coming toward me in New York I usually dive down and pretend to be tying my shoelace or else I duck into a restaurant or a drug park or an alleyway, any place to avoid a meeting where lunch will be proposed. It's a lot less trying that way. For some reason I couldn't shake this feeling I had that I'd meet somebody I knew or else some old friend of Bob's or Lucy's. When I read that the flight to London hadn't crashed I started to feel fairly flawed as a psychic but when I actually ended up running into somebody that morning it restored

me a little bit. I got my cool back. New England's a pretty
tight place so maybe it wasn't all that amazing a thing and
I'm not claiming to be the foremost psychic of my age or anything but I was pretty impressed with myself.

It happened at the Western Union office. I went in there
and the woman behind the counter told me she could deliver
a message of any length anywhere practically immediately. It
cost twenty-five cents a word and there was also some sort of
surcharge for taxes and customs and so forth but I thought
all that sounded reasonable. The office still had all their
Christmas and New Year's decorations up, red and gold and
silver festoons, cardboard bells and smoking champagne bottles, a huge wreath with pine cones and berries and oily
acorns glued to it and a couple of ears of purple Indian corn
that slapped the door whenever the wind blew. I took one of
those little pencils, the ones about as long as your finger, and
sat down at a table and thought for a while and then I wrote,
"Sam Grace killed in freak L.A. snowstorm and will thus be
unable to attend classes in U.K. This makes us very sad!" but
then I thought the headmaster would probably send my father some pathetic bright red flowers or something in com-
miseration so I crossed that out. Instead I wrote, "Sam Grace
ill in Houston hospice. Doctors insist brave young Sam keep
feet elevated so will be unable to traverse England. Best, Robert Grace." Traverse, I thought that was a pretty good word. I
thought my father might have used that word just to see
what he could do with his quarter. I crossed that message out
too and got another sheet of paper. I didn't want to create a
situation where the headmaster might reply to my father
even to confirm that he'd gotten his telex, over and out. I
didn't want any condolences, I just wanted mute acceptance.
I had no control over the guy calling my father up on the
phone of course but at least I could control the telex situation. Finally I wrote, "Sam Grace continuing on in L.A.
school. Expulsion a misunderstanding all of us shared a big
diploma-sized laugh over. Everything is under control. Please

do not contact me since I will be unavailable from now on. Fondly, Robert Grace." I hesitated before sending it. I went over every word and I think I must have folded and unfolded the paper about fifty times just so I could experience what it would be like to open and read it for the first time. I decided "from now on" was a little too strong—it made me think of the end of the world, you know, earthquakes and comets and death and all—and while I was crossing it out I heard this voice behind me say, "Well, who's this good-looking guy?" and when I turned around I saw this girl Sarah who I used to know a little bit at Briar Hall. I was so positive I would run into someone that morning I didn't even react much when I saw her. I stood up, that was all. I told you, I had a feeling it would happen all morning, this viscera thing of mine. "How are you, cutie?" she said. She kissed me on the cheek and I got a wave of perfume in my face. "What in the world are you doing here on the Cape?"

I have to admit I was confused by all her friendliness. I found myself acting fairly shy at first. I couldn't remember whether or not we had been all that close at Briar but I didn't think we had. I hadn't seen her for about three years or something but she looked pretty much the same. She had these wide blue eyes and blonde hair that was slightly darker where it came out of her head and she had all these clothes on, you know, that layered look that people from prep schools like to affect sometimes, grey thermal socks over the bottoms of her jeans and hiking boots with bright red laces and a denim jacket and she was wearing about a thousand boys' shirts, one over another. She was about as pretty as you could get without being beautiful. "This is such a surprise," Sarah kept saying. "This is crazy. I never see anybody I know here. There's never anybody here in the winter except for old people and fishermen and drug dealers. You know, save the bales and so forth."

I heard myself explaining to her that I was up there visiting my aunt for the winter. I didn't think that was really a lie even though I hadn't quite made contact with my aunt yet. I was hoping Sarah wouldn't pursue the subject and she didn't. I asked her what she was doing on the Cape and she told me she was between semesters at Brown. "My parents have a place here. There's no heat on but there's a fireplace. It's pretty isolated I guess. Right on the water. Lots of geese quacking and herons and things." She brushed hair out of her face. Her cheeks were still pink from the cold outside.

We started talking about people we knew in common from Briar Hall. I don't want you to think that I'm one of those people who's hung up on his old school or his classmates, you know, someone who sits around all day counting the minutes until the next reunion but it was the only point of reference I had with Sarah. She was a couple of classes ahead of me so our conversation mostly centered around teachers we both remembered and then Arkie Cowan's name came up as I thought it probably would. She told me he was up at Bowdoin. "He's playing a lot of hockey," she said. "He even made the varsity in his freshman year. I guess that's some sort of honor if you're a freshman or a sophomore. I don't really keep up with him. He sent me a Christmas card but that's about all."

"I'll bet he didn't make it himself."

"What do you mean?"

I said, "I'll bet you it wasn't an original drawing or anything. Or I'll bet you it wasn't one of those biodegradable ones made out of old trees that have been axed or paper that you've revitalized all over the place, what's the word, reconstituted." That wasn't the word either but both of us knew the word I wanted even though I don't think I knew what I was trying to say in general. I always get nervous in front of people who knew both Arkie and me.

"Yeah, well, who has any time for that, right? Too much to do. Just buy the regular ones, it's easier." Sarah shrugged and then she looked down at the piece of paper I was holding. "Who are you sending a telegram to?"

I held the paper up against my chest. I said, "Oh, it's just a birthday thing, somebody's birthday."

"Me too. My father's fifty today. All day long he says." She was the kind of girl who had a very young athletic father with black hair, you know, very dynamic and philandering and all. I think he was Norwegian or something. "His girlfriend is taking him on a sleigh ride if you can stand it. For his birthday. She's bringing champagne and caviar and this quilt she made for him. Mom and I volunteered the horses. And we spent the other day chopping up the eggs and onions and all that other stuff. It sounds pretty romantic."

That's another thing I remembered about Sarah: She was one of those horse girls, the kind who when they're young spend all their time down at the stables volunteering to clean out the stalls and polish the horses' hooves and they're always letting the horses rip sugar cubes out from between their lips and slobber all over their faces. When they doodle they always come up with a horse's profile or a mane or a tail. It's all pretty sexual if you ask me, this horse love. You wouldn't go so far as to suspect those girls of having an actual messy full-fledged affair with any one of those horses but it came close. "That's pretty big of your mother," I said.

Sarah looked confused. "Is it?"

I said " Well, if my father were having an affair with some cocktail waitress I'd feel pretty weird chopping up onions and eggs so the two of them could go off and eat caviar on some sleigh. I mean, doesn't she care at all that they're going off together? Wouldn't she rather do something else for his birthday than hand him over?"

Sarah looked even more confused. "Why should she?"

"Oh, no reason." I can back down morally pretty fast.

"Oh, I see what you mean." She laughed. "They split up a couple of years ago. They're not together anymore. It's not a problem. Everybody's friends with everybody else. It all works out pretty well in fact. And she's not a cocktail waitress either, she's an artist. Bridget. She comes out to the house pretty lot, I mean quite a lot. My mouth is so cold I can't speak. She had a photo exhibit in New York about three months ago. All of us went up for the opening. It was all these pictures of my father rolling around in the snow without any clothes. It was pretty intense actually, both women being there. Dad was there too."

"Naked?" I said.

"No, he was wearing a suit. You know he's Finnish so he's used to snow against his skin, it's not as crazy as it all sounds."

That was it, her father was Finnish, not Norwegian, I knew it was one of those. I thought of my father rolling around in the snow naked while some girl said Hold It, Bob, Now Smile Now Turn Over. While Sarah was talking I kept remembering all these details about her family. First of all they were pretty loaded, affluent, whatever, and no one really knew how they got that way. I think they had quite a lot of family money stashed away in these archives somewhere and the Finnish father also managed to bring in quite a lot too. They lived on some big old farm out in the sticks where they kept all these different animals and they let the animals roam all over the place. I remember you used to ask Sarah what animals she had on the farm and she would be able to tell you exactly, you know, three roosters, two horses, four goats, one pig, eleven hundred kittens and so forth. People with a lot of animals have to keep track of everybody, I guess, because it could get out of control so easily. "Whose birthday?" Sarah asked.

I thought long and wildly and all I could come up with was "Girl."

"Girl? Where does she live?"

"L.A."

"Why don't you just call her up and say happy birthday?"

I said, "I thought it would be more fun for her to get a telegram."

"That's true. It would be, that's true. My brother's girlfriend lives out in L.A. She loves it out there. My brother goes out there and visits her every month." Sarah's brother was some surly hotshot photographer who lived in New York, in the East Village or someplace edgy like that. I think his name was Thor or Hans. He was a tall thin good-looking guy who wore his collars up and who was always going off to Africa or Asia with celebrities and taking pictures of them holding up mackerel and dead gazelles. You got the feeling Sarah worshipped the guy.

I said, "Maybe it's the same girl."

Sarah laughed again. "Oh, I don't think so. My brother has pretty particular taste in women." I said yeah, right, but I couldn't figure out what she meant by that and for some reason I took it as an insult. I don't know why, it was just a statement of fact, and this birthday girl of mine I was planning to send the telegram to was a complete invention but still I felt a little bit insulted.

Sarah said suddenly, "Look, you take down my number. You call me." She took off the cap of the pen she was holding with her teeth and then she took my hand and held it up with her fingers. "You don't mind if I write it here, do you?" Her blonde hair fell down around both sides of her face and I could feel the pen against my skin. "Does that hurt?" She started writing her phone number very slowly and roundly. "I don't want to hurt you. Tell me if it hurts." The tip of the pen felt very wet and warm against my knuckles. Her perfume rose up again and I looked down at the part in her hair and her ears. I breathed in her perfume, which made me feel like a dog or something, you know, smelling a girl like that.

Sarah wrote out the last four numbers. She drew the loop of the last number, which was a six, on my thumb so if I didn't keep my thumb pressed up against my other fingers the six looked like a one. I memorized it so I wouldn't forget it: six. She hadn't put a hyphen in the middle either, she had written the numbers straight across. Without the hyphen her number looked exotic and a little unfriendly. It looked like a number that might be issued to you on your first day of prison. Sarah straightened up and put the cap back on the pen. "Okay, you can't take a shower until you call me. You might as well, right? Okay, sweetheart?"

I watched her get into this little red BMW that looked as though it was about an hour old and then she drove off and on the way back to my motel I told myself that I was in love with her. I don't know if I was or wasn't, I just told myself I was. I've noticed that I fall in love fairly rapidly with people. I also fall out of love fast too so maybe it was never love in the first place. I didn't know. I liked to think it was, that I was normal, even if it was only a combination of things like perfume and hair and the weather or whatever. I kept looking down at the back of my hand and moving my thumb out so the six turned into a one and then back into a six. I mean, that sounded like love to me.

I was halfway up the stairs to my room when I stopped and read the bulletin board on the motel wall. There was this huge white sign that said Things Ta' Do and then beneath it were listings of everything that was happening on Cape Cod from January to June. Boy, I really hate spellings like that, you know, that "ta" business. I almost walked away from the bulletin board just to protest that spelling. "Ta" is a lot like "n'," which is just about the worst especially when it's followed by "stuff," you know, something "n' stuff." That makes you want to die when you read that. "N" made me think of "o'," like "cup o' plenty," which is another disaster. A lot of restaurants have *o*'s and *n*'s in their names and I refuse to eat in them, you know, I'd rather starve. I'd rather eat glass or fur or something. All the listings under Things Ta' Do sounded pretty depressing. There was a cat show in a gymnasium and a nonsmoking, nondrinking dance at some church up in Wellfleet but that didn't sound like very much fun, and then there was a flea market in the parking lot of some drive-in and a square dance sponsored by the Chowder Society. I wondered what it would be like to be a member of

the Chowder Society, you know, to stake your life around
chowder and chowder-related developments. There were announcements for the crazy whist club and the Boy Scouts'
car wash and for a combination bingo and boiled New
England dinner benefiting the Police League. There was a
list of the high and low tides for the week and a schedule of
lunches for the public school kids, macaroni and cheese
mostly and mashed potatoes and canned peas and those
cubes of red-and-green Jell-o. There was a picture of the first
baby born on the Cape in the New Year. The nurses had
sprinkled confetti on its head and wrapped three of its fingers
around a noisemaker. The parents had named it Eddie. You
knew that kid was probably going to be a barrel of fun when
it grew up, you know, in between killing sprees I mean. At
the bottom of the bulletin board was this enormous blowup of
a green-and-yellow parakeet standing in front of a Christmas
tree and a note that said, Lost, one parakeet, Answers to
Ribs, She Will Surely Die in this Cold Weather, and then it
gave a number to call if you saw her but you sort of knew you
never would. All this stuff on the bulletin board sounded
pretty dismal to me. It sounded like the kind of stuff you
might only consider doing if the world had ended and your
Saturday night was free and your date had died and you were
loaded, and crazy in addition to that. I mean, if those were
the highlights of the off-season you could just imagine what
didn't make the list.

I spent the rest of the day at a laundromat getting all the
pecan pie off my clothes. While my clothes were in the dryer
I went across the street to a car agency and tried to rent a
Datsun but the guy wouldn't let me since I didn't have a
credit card. The only things I had in my wallet were some old
school pictures and that California license I mentioned and a
photo ID that let me rent videos at this place in Santa Monica
and the guy wouldn't take any of them. I thought that was
pretty sickening, that you couldn't make a move without a
credit card. I went back to the laundromat to get my clothes

and then at around five I went out to this seafood restaurant called Bobby's Undersea Ballet and afterwards I walked back to my room and watched this shoddy TV movie. It opened up with a shot of an old beach and a subtitle at the bottom of the screen said Côte d'Azur 1947 but it was pretty obvious it was Venice Beach Last Year or something. All the characters were wearing khaki pants and striped blue-and-white jerseys like Picasso used to wear and drinking bottles labeled Vin Ordinaire but you could tell in a minute the whole thing was filmed in L.A. I wasn't fooled for a second. I switched the channel and I found an old movie that had a famous child actor in it who later drowned in real life. He was on some dock somewhere and his career was finished and he fell or jumped or something. Then it got too depressing watching this happy-looking kid in a suede cap running all over the place with his dog Pete when I knew he was going to end up in the water off some gamy southern California dock, so after a while I turned off the TV.

I got up pretty early the next day and I told myself that before I did anything else I was going to try and get in touch with my Aunt Ellis. I looked through the phone book under her maiden name and then I looked under the last names of her first two husbands but none of them were listed. I went downstairs to see if the front desk had any other Cape Cod phone books but they didn't and when I got back to my room there was a cart outside the door and some girl was in there vacuuming my rug. She barely looked up when I came in. She had short blonde hair and brown hairless arms and she looked like a gym teacher or something. Since I didn't want to get in her way I put on a couple of sweaters and went out onto the balcony and put newspaper under me and sat down on the lawn chair and watched people file in and out of the bloodmobile. There was a long line of people waiting to go in. The bloodmobile doors were open and people were coming out with Band-Aids on their arms, walking slowly, chewing or sipping from paper cups. After a while I heard a rapping on the glass behind me. I turned around. The girl was mouthing something at me. She slid open the door. She said, "I've only been standing here for a couple of eons, what are you, deaf? Would you please mind changing a light bulb in here for me?"

The burned-out light bulb was in the bathroom and I got up on a chair and changed it while the girl stood in the doorway playing with these packets of instant coffee. I had to take off a glass bowl. There were moths and bugs in it and she shook them into the toilet and handed the bowl back up to me. After I got down off the chair she said, "Now that I've got you in here you might as well help me make the bed." She got on one side of the mattress and told me to get on the other side and then she started stripping the sheets. "You're a real slobbola, you know that? Yesterday your sheets were all over the floor. You must kick them in your sleep. And you don't put the shower curtain inside the shower either so you get water all over the floor and I have to mop it up so my knees get all sopping. Then you leave the toilet seat up which is just plain disgusting."

"But I'm here all alone," I said.

She finished taking off the sheets and she threw them on the floor. "Well, it's not like I don't come here every day. I have better things to do but I still come here every day. Do you think this bed makes itself?"

She started unfolding the new sheets. "Okay, I can do the rest. You can go back to doing whatever it was you were doing. It looks pretty boring whatever it is." She went over to the dresser and sprayed the mirror with some sort of blue liquid and then she picked up a rag and began rubbing the glass. When the mirror was clean she opened the top dresser drawer. "There's a lot of motel stationery in here. You can take it if you want to. I'm not supposed to let people but you can. You changed the light bulb for me. If I see any missing anytime I'm supposed to report it and they add the price of it to your total bill but I'll be nice and let you go ahead and have it all if you want." The girl brought out a stack of cream-colored paper and about ten postcards with serrations down their sides. "There's a postcard of the swimming pool and one of the coffee shop. The coffee shop one is pretty nice. I mean, you could send it to someone and not be embarrassed." She flashed it at me. "Whoever took it is pretty talented. Look, he managed to get in most of the tables and a little bit of the street too. I guess all this small paper is for thank-you notes. Hey, you can write me a thank-you note for all this paper. That could be the first thing you write on this paper. To me." She looked pleased. "I love getting mail."

I told her I didn't think I was going to be writing anybody any letters and she put the paper and the postcards on top of the TV set. "I was only asking you. I think it was pretty nice of me to offer. Do you mind if I turn on the television?"

She didn't wait for an answer, she just turned it on and then she sat down on the floor. "The reason," she said, "is that usually I do this room last and I watch my soap opera in the room at the other end of the hall because for some reason it gets the best reception of all the sets in this place but I was doing my exercises yesterday and I yanked the cable out of the wall by accident." She stretched out her legs. "I was doing the ones where you're on your side and you bring the leg up, you have to keep it straight too. Let me show you." She snapped her leg up into the air and brought it slowly down. "You're supposed to do about thirty repetitions but I usually do fifty. It's a better number. I was on forty something or other and I put my foot down on the cable cord and it snapped right out of the wall. I could have been electrocuted but I wasn't. They'll kill me if they find out but I'll just tell them I found it that way." She looked at me. "If you say anything to them I won't clean your room anymore."

I walked over to the sliding glass door and looked out over the parking lot. I could see the start of a marsh and this old blue peeling rowboat tipped over on one side. The long sharp yellow marsh hairs were climbing around the oarlocks. "You

don't mind, do you?'' the girl said. She turned up the volume.
"That was pretty nice of me to offer you all that paper earlier.
What's your name anyhow?" I told her and since the program had started she just nodded and put her hand up. During the first commercial she pointed at herself and
whispered, "Ruth."

I personally dislike the name Ruth quite a lot. It sounds to
me like something being torn, or else stripped of all its good
leaves. It always makes me think of this TV interview with
Katharine Hepburn that I once saw. I'm pretty crazy for
Katharine Hepburn, everybody in my family is. My father
used to go out with Katharine Hepburn's sister or her second
cousin or something like that, some connection of hers. I
think he once took a ride in a third person's car with this second cousin after some losing tennis match at an enemy
campus or maybe he met her at a party. You can see I'm not
all that clear on the details, I'm actually fairly hazy. At the
end of this TV interview they had a final shot of Katharine
Hepburn striding across a wide field with a brown wicker
picnic basket under her arm. As she walked she kept bending down to yank up wildflowers from the ground and then
she would toss them in this wicker picnic basket until it was
practically overflowing. She was wearing blue jeans and she
had a red flannel shirt on that wasn't tucked in and the ass of
some small boy from a little Spanish country and a red-and-
black-checked lumberjack's coat. There was a glorious sunset spread out in the sky behind her, very East Coast–looking
and all by which I mean the colors were undramatic but
there was something attractive about them in a drained way.
The network had fitted her wrist with this long thin microphone, no bigger than a cigarette, and as she tore up the
wildflowers from the dry mud the sounds they made were
Ruth, Ruth, Ruth. As I said, I'm crazy for Katharine Hepburn but I could only stand listening to her rip up flowers for
a limited period of time. Ever since then I haven't been able
to bear the name Ruth.

Ruth lay on the floor watching her soap opera and now and

again lifting up her leg and after a while I sat down on the bed and tried to get interested but I didn't know what was going on and I didn't care all that much either. Everybody seemed to be the same person on that soap opera. Before long I started getting distracted and I was tapping my foot on the rug, not loudly or anything, lightly and sort of pleasantly, and all of a sudden Ruth whirled around and said, "Must you do that?"

"Do what?"

"Bang. Bang around like that. It makes the screen shaky when you do that."

That wasn't true. The screen wasn't even moving. "I'm not banging around," I said loudly and then I started to tell her that it was my room and she could leave if she wanted to but she held up her hand. "Be quiet," she said. "I can't hear what Matt's saying. I've waited all week for this part." When the show was over she went over to the dresser and picked up her duster and ran her fingers a couple of times through the fluff. On TV a woman was crumpling a dry brown leaf in her hand. "This is what can happen to your skin in the winter," the woman hissed.

"Dust, dust," Ruth said, looking at herself in the mirror. "I should go dust this mangy motel but I'm too tired."

"Why are you tired?" I said, just to make conversation.

She made a fencing move with her duster. "I was out late. I went to the movies. At the mall. They have eight theatres there. It's an octoplex. Not small ones. Sometimes when they expand like that they make the theatres narrow as anything. These are big ones though, regular-sized ones. Are you just visiting here or what?"

"Yeah," I said. "I'm just checking it out. For the winter. I have this aunt up in Provincetown."

"Well, that's really dumb. You shouldn't come up here unless you know a bunch of people. There's not that much going on otherwise. You either know some people or else you have a husband or a wife, kids, you know. Are you married?"

"Oh, yeah," I said. "My wife's taking a shower. My wife

Mimi. She's been in the shower since six this morning. She's vastly clean now. You can eat off her she's so clean." I was trying to be sarcastic. Anybody would have realized I didn't have a wife.

"Ha ha, very funny," Ruth said. "Are you always this nasty to people?" When I didn't answer she said, "Do you have a car here at least? Did you drive up here?"

Everybody always wanted to know whether I had a car. I told her I didn't.

"Well what good are you? Just kidding. You need a car. I think I'd go crazy without a car. To go up to Boston and so on. David and I drive to Providence sometimes. Go see a band, go eat something, go shopping. I shop and David stays in the van."

"Who's David?"

"My fiancé."

"Oh." I don't know why but even though I wasn't attracted to Ruth or anything it changed things to hear she had a fiancé.

"He's a developer. He has his own business down here. Four trucks. He owns three of them." She came over to where I was sitting. "Let me see your hands."

"Why?"

"Just let me see them."

"Tell me why first."

She looked exasperated. "It's not anything bad. I'm not going to do anything to you, I just want to see them."

I spread my hands with the palms up. I was smoking a cigarette, which was in my mouth at the time, so the smoke drifted up into my eyes and nose. "They're okay," Ruth said finally. She let go of my fingers. "But David's are bigger. David has hands they're so gargantuan he could balance babies on them. One baby to each hand. Like scales. You can't help it, that's David's job. He has to have huge hands so he does. You have a number on the back of your hand, did you know that?"

I turned my hand over. "Oh, my God," I said. "Jesus, when did that happen? Someone call an exorcist."

"You're a real card, Sam," Ruth said. "Has anybody ever told you that? You're a real comedian. You're just this hilarious guy. Is that your girlfriend's number? Does she think you're a hilarious guy too?"

I put my hand on my knee, suddenly embarrassed. "Sort of," I said. I thought of Sarah. "Not really."

Ruth pointed at the Magic Fingers box. "Why don't you turn that on?"

"It doesn't work," I said. "I tried."

"What do you mean, it doesn't work? Sure it works. Do you have a quarter? Never mind, I think I have one." She got out a quarter and put it in the slot. Nothing happened. "Sometimes you have to wait for these things to get warm."

"I put in about two bucks last night waiting for it to get warm," I said.

Ruth gave me this mysterious smile. "Wait here," she said. She went outside and returned a minute later with a nail file. She sat down on the bed and turned the box over and plunged the nail file into a hole and started unscrewing the bottom. "I'm fairly good at this," she said. "It saves you money. Sometimes when there's not all that much to do I go into an empty room and lie down and shake for thirty minutes. Afterwards you feel like you're walking underwater. You're a total blob." She was fiddling around with the motor. Ten minutes later the whole bed started to buzz. "I'm a genius," Ruth said. A bunch of quarters poured out of the machine onto her lap. "There are my quarters," I said.

"Yeah, you're really getting them back too," she said. "I fixed the thing. You can consider this my fee." She started screwing the bottom back on and when it was secure she replaced the box on the bedside table. The bed was still buzzing. It was a low even throb, like the noise an electric razor makes. It didn't really put you in mind of fingers. I suppose it was relaxing and all but I could see how after a while it could get you pretty wired. "Well, thanks," I said. "Thanks a lot. This'll calm me down I'm sure."

Ruth stood up. "What are you doing tomorrow night?"

I wasn't doing anything any night. "Why?"

"Do you like music?"

"Yes."

"There's this band I know playing tomorrow night. In the lounge downstairs. The Recreators. They're pretty fantastic musicians. They're all from around here too. The lead singer is a friend of mine. They just got back from Jamaica and Mexico, places like that. They were on tour." She went on to tell me that they had been playing aboard the Island Empress, which was a cruise ship that floated from island to island in the winter. "David and I are going. You're welcome to come if you want. David gets off work at around eight so we'll be there at eight-thirty."

"Isn't that a little early for a band?" I said.

"Oh, stop being so pretentious. Just because this isn't New York or Los Angeles or some city doesn't mean you have to be pretentious about the whole thing." She took her cart and when she left the room I lay on the bed for a while and then I got up and turned off the TV and put on some music. I had a couple of cheap black speakers that I'd bought off some Russian guy on Amarillo Beach in Malibu and my Walkman, and when I stuck the speakers into my Walkman it turned into a regular cassette player. I had six cassettes with me, one old Pretenders, Los Lobos, Talking Heads, *Elvis in Hawaii, Laurie Benoit at the Hollywood Bowl* and one classical tape, all this somber piano music, in case the weather turned bad. I like listening to classical music when it's raining or snowing. You can wander around inside and you feel as though you're wearing a black turtleneck even though you're only in a T-shirt or your underwear or something. I put on the Pretenders tape and lay down on the bed again and then the music stopped and when I went over to find out what was the matter I saw the machine had eaten the cassette. I tried to pry it loose from the gut of the machine and it snapped in my fingers. I put in the Los Lobos tape and ten minutes later the same thing happened. All in all my Walkman destroyed four out of my six tapes. I was left with Laurie Benoit and the Talking Heads, that was it.

I started getting a little bored and after lunch I decided I would go visit the Kennedy Compound in Hyannisport. There was this little blue pamphlet underneath my telephone that gave you some things to do in Hyannis and the Kennedy Compound seemed to be about the only thing worth visiting unless you wanted to go to the aquarium or something and watch the porpoises. When I went down the stairs I passed by the bulletin board again and under Things Ta' Do there was a new listing, a field trip to some beach led by a beach ranger. You followed this guy along the sand and when you saw a horseshoe crab in the water you seized it by the tail and the beach ranger stuck a rood of orange tape onto its shell right between the eyes and you threw the horseshoe crab back into the water and then you waited about nine months to see where it showed up. That was the whole point of the exercise. I kept thinking they had omitted something but that was it, nine months of waiting. I mean, you might as well have a kid in that time, to give you something to do in between the times you reach for your binoculars. The picture of Ribs the parakeet was gone and in its place was a note: We found Ribs near out back porchlight. Of course she was frozen solid. The child who didn't shut the screen door all the way—"You didn't tell me to, Mommy"—has been punished. Thanks to everyone who called us with sightings.

That really depressed me for some reason, that Ribs was gone. I'm not putting you on or pretending to have a heart or anything. I really did feel bad. I hadn't expected her to be alive but I didn't expect anybody to find her either, you know, to confirm the worst. I went over to the front desk and asked the pink-faced man how you got to the Kennedy Compound and he said, "You make friends with one of the daughters, that's how I'd go about it." He laughed for a long time at that. Then he gave me directions. It was too far to walk to so I called a cab. In about twenty minutes a red Maverick pulled up in front of the Tern Inn. Before I got in a tall beautiful woman with long reddish-blond hair got out. She was carrying a black purse and she smiled at me and held the rim of the door and smoothed her dress with her other hand. Then she started walking down the street in the direction of the marina. Her hips were going like crazy. "Come on in from the cold, Son," the cab driver called over the seat to me. He was an older man with a cigarette going in his hand. "Don't want to be staring too devotedly at that." I got in and shut the door behind me. The driver turned around and looked at me. "Where we going today?"

I felt embarrassed telling him but I did anyway.

"You an acquaintance of theirs?"

"Not really." One of them, a long-faced kid with freckles, had gone to Briar Hall with me but I didn't think that counted.

"Just want to be checking the place over, right?" The Maverick pulled out and we went past the tall beautiful woman again and she waved and the driver waved back. "Hello," he said. "That's a fellow, you know." He sighed.

"No," I said. "I didn't."

"Yep. Cape's only transvestite. That we know about, that is. Might be a few more up in Provincetown but not down this part of the Cape. That's Richie Tyson."

I looked back but the tall woman was too far back. All I could see was a figure that could be either male or female.

"Richie Tyson," the man went on. "I've know Richie all his life. Nice kid too. His dad put the fiberglass on my boat. Mom taught my kids tennis in the summers." He shook his head. "Good-looking kid too, dammit. Richie Tyson. Kennedys aren't up here by the way I don't think. FYI. They close it up for the winter and move out. Head for Florida the whole bunch of 'em, like a pack of birds. Except for the ones who have lives up here." We were driving through the center of Hyannis. Icicles with sun on them were dripping off eaves onto the sidewalks and the hard grass and there were soft patches of snow on the dirt path that ran in back of the jewelry store. "Yep, prettiest gal on the Cape just happens to be a fellow." He looked out his window and unrolled it an inch. "You have a nice Christmas?" We went over a bridge and the sound the tires made changed and then returned to normal.

"It was all right," I said.

"Just all right. What, you didn't get everything you wanted?" The cab driver was a pretty cheerful guy. He offered me a cigarette but I didn't take it because I knew I'd just end up adding the price of the cigarette to the tip and that really wasn't the point of his offer. Most of the time I give cab drivers enormous tips. It's a compulsion of mine. Even if the service is pretty terrible, you know, even if the guy crashed into a wall I'll overtip him. I'm pretty palliating that way. I guess I'm scared the driver will yell at me if I don't. I told the man no, I didn't get everything I wanted.

"No?"

"No."

"Well, that's too bad, Son," he said in this pleasant voice. We turned onto a side street and we went past a bay and a lumberyard and some new purple condominiums that were built to look like Spanish villas and a long white beach where this couple, a tall man and a short woman, was walking slowly. The beach was covered with black straw and the straw was turning white in the sun. There was foam on the edge of the water and it looked like fat. The water had triangles of light on it and they shivered whenever the wind blew. The triangles were so bright you couldn't look at them for long without your eyelids starting to shake. We passed a lake that was covered with a sheet of green scum but it wasn't the kind of lime green that made your tongue spring up, it was a dark thick green that made you feel worn out. On a bluff about a mile off I could see a patch of shingled houses and across the water a sour winter light coated the far islands. Even though it was only about two-thirty or something I could tell it would be dark soon. The cab driver said, "You from these parts, Son?"

"I'm from L.A." Then I added, stupidly, "Los Angeles."

"Oh, I know what L.A. stands for. El Lay, my father calls it. Ninety-four years young and he still refers to it as El Lay. That is when he's not calling it Sunny Sodom. My father's still got a lot of kick to him."

"Boy, sure sounds like it," I said, hating myself. I told you I was terrible at talking to people when I'm moving. I try and be polite and I can taste the words getting stiff in my mouth right as I'm saying them. I tried again. "Your father sounds like a real character." What does that mean? I said to myself, you never say things like that.

"Oh, he is, he is that. No, I been to San Francisco once in my life but never more southerly than that. Never really wanted to frankly, what with the smog and the people." He looked over his shoulder at me, then he looked back at the road. "Not in school?"

"I'm on a break," I said.

"Funny time for a break."

"There's a time difference."

"Ah," he said, nodding, "the time difference." We were in a quiet neighborhood now, lined with tall bare brown trees and large grey-and-white houses. The roads were wide and the pale yellow stripe down the middle looked shabby and the grass on all the lawns was short and white. It looked dead, everything did. There was smoke coming out of a lot of chimneys but otherwise the houses looked pretty vacant. Even though the driver's window was open only slightly and mine was shut I could smell the smoke in the car. At a point where the street seemed to come to an end I saw a series of tall dark thick hedges. "This is the place," the driver said, pulling the Maverick over to the side of the road. "This is what all the fuss is about. Hedges. You want me to wait while you look around?"

I told him no. I got out on the side closest the hedges and went around to his window. He rolled it all the way down and I held out the fare along with this monstrous tip. He took the fare but he wouldn't take the tip. "You might need it." He shifted the car into Drive. "You never know these things. You have to be prepared for life's emergencies, right? You give my regards to those wild Kennedy boys now. Tell 'em they're getting too old to be sowing their oats still." He was about to drive off but at the last minute he looked at me in this concerned way and said, "Everything all right, Son? You want to talk?" and I told him that everything was under control just so he'd go away. I hate it when they call you son, it sounds so biblical. The driver was a nice enough guy and all but I didn't really feel much like going into things. People usually leave you alone if you tell them everything's fine and the cab driver wasn't much different. I watched him drive off into the sharp grey afternoon and then I went over and stood in front of the hedges. There were all these cold plum-colored leaves lying in sloppy piles all over the place and I could hear a plane going over my head but I couldn't see it. I pressed my face up against the hedge but the leaves were so tightly curled I couldn't see much except for these flecks of gold light and twigs and dirt. The smell of wood burning in the air started putting me in the Christmas spirit. I usually get the Christmas spirit around that time of year, January or early February, when it's too late to buy another tree and everyone else is thinking of spring, which I think is just about the worst time of the year. I can't stand spring. In spring everything's thawing and leaking all over the place and you're supposed to be in love but you're not and everybody expects you to spend your whole life outside even if you don't feel like it. I stood in front of the hedges feeling nostalgic for Christmas Eve followed by Christmas morning and I kept on expecting to see some guard with a walkie-talkie come out of the bushes and tell me to get lost but there didn't seem to be anyone around except for me and a bunch of black crows barking like crazy in the trees and along the telephone wires.

The air was very quiet, just this lonely silence and the smell of fires and right before the road turned into a private drive-way I looked down and saw a grey chipmunk that had been run over by a wheel. The skin was flaking and the chipmunk was as flat as a piece of paper, flat as a drawing of a chipmunk done by someone who's very good, and I stepped over it and walked about a hundred yards until I was beyond the hedges. In the summer they had cops stationed at each driveway with coaches' whistles and nightsticks and they wouldn't let you go past a certain point but the only thing in my way was a baby blue sawhorse with chains running off either end of it into the bushes. I leapt it fairly easily and then I was inside one of the yards. The only thing I could see on the property were several pretty good-sized white houses facing the water. There were lots of lawns. An old green Plymouth was sitting in the driveway but I was pretty sure it belonged to one of the guys who worked there.

I just stood there, listening to crows. I had always thought that was where I wanted to be, you know, that it was a home, there in the salty predusk playing contact sports with the Kennedy kids as the sun went down. I don't know why I liked the sound of that so much: Kennedy kids. It had a nice sound. I liked to imagine myself playing game after game of touch football with them. I'd even play softball if that's what everybody wanted. I liked to imagine myself twisting through the soft mosquito-air air, past great tangles of gnats rising up from the bushes and singing, then having one of the big older freckled girls bring me down to the ground so I injured one of my legs and she'd pull me up to my feet and say, Play like a man, or something equally admonishing. The air would get gradually darker until you could scarcely make out the football anymore and after a while we'd quit because of the dark and the bugs and go in for dinner and all the children from all the various marriages would be there at this incredibly long mahogany table and they'd make me this honorary Kennedy and I'd stand up and make an amusing speech that was also strangely moving.

I started wondering whether or not I should do something. It occurred to me that I at least ought to take a picture or run up and touch the doorknob or something. You want to commemorate things after all, freeze them somehow, either by taking pictures of them or stealing their shirts or whatever. You want to remember things. I didn't know what to do though so I just stood there staring at the house. I started thinking that my touch-football fantasies pretty much belonged to the summer. I had a feeling that if I came back in August all the guards would be out in the early morning, sipping hot white coffee through slits in the plastic and I probably wouldn't be able to make it past the driveway. I got my cigarettes out of my shirt pocket and when I was about to strike a match I was shocked to see this red-and-blue picture of Jack Kennedy on the cover of my matchbook. His head and his neck were on the front flap and on the back flap there was an advertisement for a driving school or stamps or something. I thought that was a fairly amazing coincidence, you know, that there I was standing in the Kennedy Compound and I reach for a cigarette and my matches have Jack Kennedy on them. I started thinking it was an omen of some kind but then I realized I didn't know what kind of omen it was. I had no idea what it meant but I thought it was a pretty spectacular sign of something or other. When you think of all the other things my matches could have had on their covers you have to be a little impressed. Kennedy looked good on the matches too, handsome I mean. He had that sort of tired-eyed benevolent look he has in all those oil paintings that hang in the bedrooms of rich kids, you know, next to the encyclopedias and all the series guides to minerals and reptiles and volcanoes those kids are forced to read so they won't turn out to be the philistines their parents are. Rich kids always have oils of Kennedy around, done in kind of a bacon-colored pigment. You only see that color pigment in oil paintings of the Kennedys. There's Kennedy with the stripes of the flag behind him, Kennedy in one of those balloons that travels over vineyards, Kennedy handing some short-haired armed forces–type guy a medal for heroism, Kennedy and his kids waving at the floats in a parade. I put the Kennedy matches back in my pants pocket and then I walked over to the drive-way and dragged the toe of my sneaker around in a circle. I did it loudly so I could feel as though I was making contact with something. There were all these cracked blue and white shells, mussels and clams mostly, mixed in with the white pebbles and the dirt and sand of the driveway. I stared at the houses again. They were just plain old houses, that was the disappointing thing. I tried to force myself to look at them in some kind of historic context, you know, I tried to imagine all these decisions being shaped behind the windows but that didn't do anything. I expected the houses to change shape in front of me but they didn't. They stayed fairly untrans-formed. You always get to places like the Kennedy Com-pound and they never deliver. They don't change you any. You don't feel any different afterwards. There were lines of cold black oil around the roof shingles like wet icing and one of the second-floor windows had lost a pane. Someone had taped a brown cardboard square to the frame. I was about to go a little closer when I saw some guy with a wheelbarrow walking across the lawn toward the Plymouth. He saw me and he stopped. He started yelling at me. He told me I was on private property, which I sort of knew. It wasn't as though he was telling me anything I didn't know. Then he demanded to know who I was. Sometimes I can't stand people who work for famous people, they start acting like divas themselves. I think the most arrogant person I've ever met in my life is this guy, Monsieur Barry, who does my sister's hair for her. He actually has a chauffeur take him back and forth to the Col-ony, if you can stand it. There are a lot of maitre d's in the restaurants who are the same way too, you know, they figure that just because they have famous people in their restau-rants that makes them famous. Anyway, I recognized the type and when he started coming after me I ducked under one of the sawhorse chains and started off down the street.

I was about halfway to town when I started getting really cold. I had just read this article about frostbite and how you can get it and not realize you have it so I guess I was a little paranoid, but to be safe I went inside this bar called the Schooner and called a cab and then I ordered a beer and sat sipping it and looking out the window. There were four old Christmas trees lying in a puddle of needles on the sidewalk, with strands of old shriveled tinsel on them, waiting to be picked up and carted to the dump. You could see the dump far off, soft high crumbling hills crowded with sea gulls and yellow tractors and cranes. The hills looked like piles of brown sugar. I went back outside after a while and I could hear gulls crying and the crows and I smelled old fish and cigar smoke and burning brush. You knew about a hundred Christmas trees that had given their all were about to go up in flame. This time my cab driver turned out to be a young Chinese guy who didn't say a word to me the whole ride back. I asked him to drop me off a couple of blocks away from the Tern Inn and he stopped the cab in front of a combination candle shop and pizza parlor. I paid him and got out. I could see counter people in maroon caps waiting for customers and white candles with long wicks hanging down from the ceiling but I kept walking until I found a liquor store. I went in and bought about five bottles of champagne, four Great Western and one Dom Pérignon, and the old guy who worked there didn't even card me. I guess I must have looked pretty old that day, that was why. I hadn't slept all that well the night before and my face was cold and grey and the skin around my mouth and eyes probably held a couple of small straight lines that hadn't been there two weeks earlier. When I left the liquor store I went into this enormous supermarket next door.

I love supermarkets. They're practically my favorite places in the world. The best ones are really giant stores where you can go in and stop thinking. You can lose yourself. This one had about twelve different aisles and the floors were white and smooth and cool and there was music playing when I came in, an instrumental of "Don't Stand So Close to Me." I got a big basket and started wheeling it down the aisles. I began in the far left aisle and worked my way across. I picked up about five bags of Doritos and I also got some kind of bright orange cheese and then since I was worried that I wasn't eating a very balanced diet or whatever I pulled down this enormous jar of pink chewable vitamin C tablets and threw it into my basket too.

I guess the smoothness of the aisles put me in sort of a slick happy mood because after a while I noticed I was treating my basket as though it were some kind of wire skateboard. I would give it a big push, then tuck my feet under it and coast along until it started losing speed, then I'd give it another push. One of my rides took me to the very back of the supermarket, to the meat section. There was all the meat you could ever want back there, chicken, steak, turkey, veal, hamburger, and so forth, but that wasn't really the section that interested me. The dessert section did. When I saw all those desserts stacked almost up to the ceiling I brought my cart to a stop. I looked around to see if there was anybody watching me or anybody heading down the aisles. There wasn't. Then I checked to see if there were any of those security mirrors some stores have that reflect your hands but I didn't see any. The only other person I'd seen in the store besides myself was this single cashier, some guy who was standing at the front counter reading a pro wrestling magazine.

What happened is that when I saw no one was around I went over to the desserts and starting pulverizing them. I don't know if you've ever done anything like that but this is how you go about it roughly: You stand before some dessert you don't like for whatever private reason, a cake or a pie or a tray of fudge, especially one with a face or eyes, you know, any dessert that's staring up at you, and when there's no one around you pound it, using whatever tactics you care to. You can punch, jab, chop, pinch, pummel, squeeze or you can do all those things. The first thing I did was to pound three separate boxes of brownies, one after another, into total submission. It felt fantastic. It had been a pretty long time for me so I had a lot of energy stored up. Under the brownies was something called a Blueberry Crumb Lovers Cake and I punched it across the top, using small tight blows, my elbows in, and all this blue frosting squirted out of the sides of the box. I did the same thing to the Cream-Filled Blackout Cake and the Marshmallow Iced–Devils Food Scrumptious Cake and the Golden Honey Danish Pecan Ring. After a while I was attacking any dessert that had what I considered to be an unacceptable name. The final dessert I worked on was this sweet-looking orange cake and I think I got rid of it only because it was called the Orange Cream Pumpkin Honeymoon Valentine. It looked like some kid's pencil drawing of the sun, you know, it had big round eyes and chalky lips and it was smiling, and I grabbed the box and started squeezing it until the orange-and-green frosting exploded through the cellophane and onto the joints of my fingers. Afterwards I felt sorry and all for the desserts but also strangely exhilarated. I was flushed and everything and there was all this frosting glistening on my sleeves. Some people get a rush from lifting weights or rowing but I think my greatest rushes have come from punching out desserts in supermarkets. I know it's a waste of food and all and that if you want to get all psychoanalytic about it I was acting out some ancient anger toward someone I'm probably pretty friendly to, but that didn't detract from the fact it felt fantastic.

I got up to the front of the store and I was unloading my Doritos and my Vitamin C tablets onto the counter and all of a sudden I felt this hand on my shoulder and I turned around to see this short bald guy wearing a tight juice-streaked apron.

"Will you come with me please?" the guy said.

My stomach did a rolling motion as though everything in

my body had risen a couple of inches. The guy behind the counter let his wrestling magazine drop and it fell open to the centerfold. Some monstrous woman in black tights was bodyslamming a thin blonde. I could see staples up and down the blonde girl's spine. She was holding her hands over her breasts to protect them.

"What did I do?" I said to the bald guy. I think I said that only as a kind of formality.

"Just come back here with me." He led me back to the rear of the supermarket and when we were in front of the dessert section he held up one of the dessert boxes. It was a pineapple-cherry cake. "Look at this, just take a look in here and tell me what you see."

I peered inside the broken cellophane. The cake was mashed up into four parts. I didn't really have to look at it, I pretty much knew what it looked like.

"What am I supposed to do with this?"

I tried to think. "Well, if there are four of you guys at home you could feed four people with this. A family of four. The portions are sort of already decided. See." I traced the divided sections. "Two big ones here. That's maybe for you and your wife or maybe you have a son who wants a big piece."

"You want me to stuff this in your face?" the guy said. He was a very attractive guy and all, you know, a former Rhodes Scholar, extremely lucid and charming and gentle and everything. If you had a daughter you would have wanted to bring her around to the supermarket every day so she could learn about life with this guy and maybe dance with him. "You want to try eating some of this crap as well as paying for it?" He didn't wait for me to answer. He tossed the pineapple-cherry cake onto the floor. "That's three ninety-five for that one." He picked up one of the brownie boxes. "You really had some fun here, didn't you? What, you think nobody was around?"

He must have examined every dessert on that shelf. It took about half an hour or something. Whenever he found one that I had pulverized he would read off the price and add it to the general total and in the end he told me I owed him sixty-seven dollars. The only problem was that I didn't have that much money on me. I had spent about a hundred dollars at the liquor store and the rest of my money was back at the motel in my other pants pocket. All I had with me was a twenty-dollar bill and some change. I told the guy I would go back to my motel and come back with the money and when I said that he threatened to call the Hyannis police.

"Look," I said. I was really beginning to panic. "Don't call the cops. My motel is only a couple of blocks away." I didn't want cops in my life at that point.

"You think I'm going to let you leave this store? You think you'll come back? What do you think I am, stupid? You want to call someone have them bring the money down here, fine. Call Mom tell her to bail you out, fine. But you're not leaving the store."

I asked the guy where the telephone was and he pointed to a pay phone next to the magazine section. "Billy, watch this guy," he said as I walked over and picked up the receiver. Both of them were staring at me. The number on the back of my hand had gotten faint and I had to squint to make it out. I thought, please be at home. The phone rang three times and finally Sarah answered. I told her who it was and she said, "Isn't that funny, I was just talking to my father, he called to say he'd gotten my telegram and I mentioned to him that I ran into you at the Western—"

"Look," I said. "Do you have any money I could borrow? Until later on?"

Sarah sounded surprised. "Sure I do. Are you in trouble? What's the matter?"

I told her where I was and that I would explain things to her later. The cashier and the manager were still looking at me. She said, "Okay, it'll take me twenty minutes."

When I hung up I felt relieved. I said loudly, "I'll be able to pay for everything. It's not a problem." I was pretty angry that I had to pay for all those desserts but there was nothing I could really do about it. I told the bald guy that this friend of mine would be coming in twenty minutes and he said, "You're lucky." While I was waiting I wandered around the fruit and vegetable racks. Bags of onions and baked potatoes hung on hooks off the walls. Both guys, the cashier and the manager, followed me. I started getting pretty uncomfortable being tailed like that so I went back up to the front of the store. I leaned up against the express counter. The silence was driving me crazy. I finally said to the manager, "So what's it like managing a place this size?"

The guy didn't answer. There was a magazine next to the cash register called *Your Body* and my sister was on the cover wearing whites and holding a tennis racket. Sometimes I don't think Lucy has standards anymore. I said, "How long have you been at this line of work?"

"Fuck you," the manager said.

"Nice mouth," I said.

He hadn't heard me because I said it so softly. "I don't want to talk to you." He was looking at a point over my head now. "I just want the money you owe and then I want you to get out and never come in this store again."

"Nice mouth," I said again, even more softly. "Really nice lovely exceptional mouth."

Sarah's car pulled into the supermarket parking lot about ten minutes later and she immediately came over to me and pressed a hundred dollars into my hand. "Is that enough?" she whispered.

We sat in the front seat of her BMW afterwards not saying anything. I kept smelling the leather on the seats. I asked Sarah how old the car was and she said two months. The smell was pretty overpowering. It made you feel like a kid on the first day of the world. I wondered whether that was what the first man and woman on earth had smelled, leather from a new car. I was crazy about that smell. "This smell," I finally said and then I stopped in the middle.

Sarah had both hands on the wheel and she was leaning into them and looking ahead. "You could open your window if you want."

"No it's fine."

She turned on the heat. She looked at me. "I'm waiting for you to say something."

"Like what?"

"Like what in the world was going on back there. Why were those two guys looking at you like that?"

"I wrecked a little food," I said finally.

"What do you mean?"

"Punches. I punched it. Food." I punched the heat that was blowing out of the vent next to the radio. "Desserts and cakes."

"You mean devil dogs, garbage like that? Punch, you mean you hit them?"

"Yeah, but more major desserts. Desserts with names. Desserts they hire this team of people to sit around in a room thinking up names for. They just have that one job." I told her the names of a couple of desserts. While I was talking she started the car and drove slowly out of the parking lot. She turned left and in a little while we passed the Tern Inn but I didn't say anything.

"Why would you ever want to do that?" she said when I had finished talking.

"Have you ever done it?"

"Nope. I can't say I have."

We were at a stoplight. The red color looked very hard and bare in the cold. "So," Sarah said, "where's your aunt during this ordeal? Did you dump her someplace? Where do you want me to take you by the way? Where does your aunt live?"

I said, "I don't know."

"Well, describe the street. I've come down here all my life. I can probably tell you what street it is if you just describe it. I can close my eyes and tell you. What's it near?"

I said, "I don't know."

"Well, Sam." She laughed. "Help me out a little."

"I haven't really located her yet."

"Located her? What do you mean? I thought you were spending the winter with her?"

"I was," I said. "I mean, I am. I just have to locate her first."

Sarah stopped the car then. She pulled into the driveway of an old insurance office in the middle of nowhere. There were five parking spaces and she took the one in the center that was under the streetlamp. The insurance office was small and square with grey shingles and a yellow roof. She kept her headlights on so the white door and the brass knocker were lit. She turned on the heater. "Okay," she said, turning to me. "Can you tell me please what's going on?"

I didn't want to tell her at first. I guess I assumed she'd hate me or something. You don't want to go around telling people you like that you've been kicked out of another school but she was looking at me and so I told her just about everything. I told her about leaving California and how I was supposed to be in England but that I had come up to the Cape instead. I told her that I was planning to spend the winter at the Cape in a kind of handyman capacity. When I said that Sarah laughed.

"You mean sawing and refurbishing and so forth?"

"Right."

"And painting things? Sort of a general landscaper?"

"That's it," I said.

"I can't really see it," she said. "Sorry. I hope you don't take that the wrong way. I just can't see it. I don't think you're that type."

I felt terrible when she said that. It made me feel effete or something. I tried to act like a handyman but since I didn't know how they acted I ended up slumping and not smiling.

"Well, do you? See yourself as that? Honestly? Have you ever done anything like that before for anybody?"

"Well, no, not yet," I said.

"I have. Once only. In Hobe Sound for a summer. Me and about five guys. It was great. All of us wanted to get in shape that summer. We painted my grandmother's house and one other house. Then we'd swim or something the rest of the day." I wondered how many of those guys had been in love with her. She seemed like the sort of girl everybody would have to fall in love with at least once in a while. I moved my leg slightly over to the left and it accidentally touched Sarah's knee. Both of us moved our legs over in the opposite direction at the same time. I stared kind of sorrowfully at the space that had suddenly opened up. I guess both of us knew what had happened even though it was all done in the dark with the heat blowing. It changed things, I don't know why. All of a sudden Sarah asked me where I was staying and when I told her she turned the car around and began driving back in the direction of town. We got to the Tern Inn and she parked the car under my window and came up to my room with me since I wanted to pay her back the money I owed her. In front of my door I paused to get out my key and in the silence I could hear the Magic Fingers humming. It was a cold quiet night and the hum seemed to come right through the door. I half-expected my key to start trembling. Sarah was standing behind me and I suddenly got scared that she would think I was some kind of Las Vegas–type hustler who'd lured her back to my motel and who had the Magic Fingers already turned on. I mean, I imagined myself as this dark, obese gambler with sweat springing up all over my forehead and I'd be one of those guys who talk a lot during sex and who force the other person to by asking them direct questions that can't be answered yes or no, and in the morning I'd give her a chip to cash in or something depressing like that. I started whistling, both because I was nervous and also because I remembered it was something handymen did.

"What's that buzzing noise?" Sarah said as we entered the room. I turned on the overhead light as Sarah went over to the curtains and pulled them and said, "Do you have a view, no you don't." She rubbed the TV screen and it crackled. "Why is your bed jumping up and down?"

"It's Magic Fingers," I said. I went over and read the side of the box out loud. "Will provide hours of relaxing massage to tired joints and sore shoulders. Stimulates circulation, eases depression." I said, "This girl who cleans the rooms here turned it on and now you can't get it to stop."

Sarah banged the box against the table. "Do you suppose there's a master switch anyplace? Couldn't you just yank it out of the wall?"

"I don't know," I said. I didn't want to talk about Magic Fingers. I wished Sarah would take off her coat and stay. I thought, a good handyman would know how to shut off Magic Fingers. I wished I could just bend down over the box and fix it in front of her. I wished for a lot of things all of a sudden. Sarah sat down on the bed and crossed her legs. She was wearing small dirty white sneakers. I took the money I owed her out of my pants pocket and then I put on my Laurie Benoit tape. Laurie was singing a Spanish song with a backup group called Los Tres Caballeros. "Te Quiero, Te Quiero," she sang. "Here's your dough." I held it out.

Sarah waved her hand. "Oh, just throw it on the bed."

I held onto the money. I didn't want to just throw it on the bed.

"Does this really make you less depressed? Is that true what the box says?"

"I don't think so," I said. Then I said, "No. It just doesn't. That's a lie."

"It feels sort of nice." Sarah lay back and put her head down on the bed. Her shirt pulled up and I could see a couple of inches of her stomach. After a while she sat back up and her stomach disappeared. "I should get going or I'll stay here forever on this thing."

I tried to keep my voice level. "You can stay if you want." I added, stupidly. "It's not a problem."

The bed hummed. I stared at my cheap sneakers. "Stay here? You mean stay over?"

"Well, sure," I said. "If you want to."

"Oh." Then Sarah said, "I didn't mean just oh. I mean, that's very nice of you. Thanks." She was quiet. "It would be fun to stay, Sam, I think it would be fun, but I have a guest back at the house." She seemed embarrassed.

"A guest?"

She nodded. I said casually, "Anybody I know?"

"It's a friend of mine from school."

"Friend?"

"Friend. A guy. Beau."

"Beau?" I said. "You know somebody named Beau?" I tried to think whether or not I knew any Beaus and if I did what they were like. I said to myself that if I had known Beaus in the past I would know what kind of guy this one was. Did I have any good associations with the name? "Um, what does he do?" I said. "For fun?"

Sarah looked at me then. "He's a football player. He plays for Brown. He lives in New York too." She said that as though she wanted to be helpful.

"Fun," I said. "I said fun. That's not fun."

"He enjoys it. He's good at it."

"Do you go to all the games? Sit in the stadium?" I don't know why I was asking her all this. I suppose it was something I could picture, the girl and the football player meeting in front of gate eleven after a game. It was something I could get a grip on.

"Just about the whole sorority does."

"You're in a sorority too?" I said. God, she was moving farther and farther away from me. "What for?"

"It's a good way to meet people. I've made some good friends that way. Some really nice people. I know what you're thinking. I thought they sounded pretty queer once too."

The tape ended. I went over to the dresser and put on my Talking Heads tape. It was a live tape and the audience sounded drunk. They were clapping strangely. I turned around. "I'll bet he, Beau, is the captain of the whole team. I'll bet he's the captain of the entire Ivy League. I'll bet he's the captain of the entire Northeast Conference. I'll bet he's the captain of the entire spirit of football, past, present and future. I can't believe you're in a sorority."

"The thing is Beau *was* the captain this year. The Brown varsity. He has been for a couple of years. This year was his last."

I wished she hadn't used his name in a sentence that way. It was so casual. It made him sound more real. "You probably miss your girlfriend," Sarah said to me. "That's probably why you're feeling so depressed."

"Who said I was feeling depressed?"

"Well, maybe you're not. But you should call her up."

"She doesn't have a phone."

"Why, did she just move or something?"

"Yes," I said. "She just moved. She's just moved into the wilderness. She's just moved into the wild. No phones, no radio, no TV. No music. No tubular bells. It's an experiment for her. She'll see if she likes it and then she may or may not come back. Personally I don't think she will. I think the wilderness will claim her as its own spawn." My syntax can get pretty crazed when I'm tired and right then I felt suddenly exhausted.

"Where did you send the telegram to then?"

"General delivery." I shook my head. "Care of some trees." I felt as though I had no life left inside me. I stared at Sarah and I knew she would never be my girlfriend and that I'd never be a realistic handyman. Even though I was younger than she was I felt about a hundred years old. After a long silence I said, "You seem like the sort of girl who would go out with the captain of the football team."

"Well, we haven't been going out all that long," Sarah said. After a minute she said, "I don't think that was a very flattering thing to say. Was it? I mean, I'm not the sort of girl

who would do anything in particular. Or not do anything. I'm
not the kind of girl who you would say she's the kind of girl
who does this or that about." She stood up then and she
looked confused. I stood up too. The tape said, "We're going
boom boom boom and that's the way we live." Sarah nodded
at the Magic Fingers box. "I hope you manage to get that
fixed sometime. That shaking."

I said stiffly, "I'm sure I will. I didn't mean that," I went
on. "Sorry, I didn't mean to insult you. I just meant you were
pretty and all and nice and so on. Vivacious. Blah, blah,
blah." I was making her sound like a little red ball. I remembered I hadn't given her the money yet so I handed it to her
and she took it and then she put her hands in her pockets.

"I feel like I'm made out of foam," she said. She reached
over and kissed me on the lips. "Good-bye, cutie." I could
smell her perfume again. "You can come back to the house if
you want. If you want to get away from all this. We have a fire
going and everything. Food, records. Beau is a really nice
guy."

"I'm sure he is." I wasn't lying. Beau was probably a terrific guy. Then I thought, I could never get along with someone named Beau. There was something I wanted to ask her
before she left. She was at the door and she had her hand on
the knob and I said, "How did you manage to do what you're
doing?"

Sarah said, "What are you talking about, Sam?"

"Wearing perfume and things," I said. "Calling people by
names that aren't their first names?"

"What, this perfume?" Sarah sniffed the bones in her
wrist. "This isn't anything. This is just my mother's perfume.
I stole it from my mother."

"No, seriously," I said. I was perfectly serious myself but
Sarah was acting as though she thought I was putting her
on. "You wear all this perfume and then you call me things
like sweetheart and cutie. I just wanted to know how you get
to a point like that, that's all."

"I call a lot of people sweetheart and cutie. It doesn't mean anything. Sam—"

"That's not the point," I told her. "It's just that you say it as though you've said it about a million and a half times before. You say it like this veteran. You say it with this authority. Well, where did you learn that? How to do that? When do you turn into someone like you, who's all formed? Is it from watching movies or TV? Is that it? Am I just watching the wrong shows? Or is it from hearing your parents talking? Or just you getting older or what? Reaching some point where you use words like *cutie* and *sweetheart* and probably don't even think twice about it?" I was practically shouting. "Just let words like *cutie* that you've always heard other older people say just slip into your voice as though they were born there. I mean, when are you going to start calling people honey?"

"Look, Sam—" she started to say.

"Seriously, Sarah," I said. "Seriously. Get serious. When did all that start going on with you? When did you turn into this person, this normal person who uses all the old words that you grow up hearing other people use?"

"Oh, I don't think I necessarily turned into a normal person." She opened the door and cold air came in. She looked pretty angry. "I have to go. Maybe I'll see you in New York sometime."

"You're just not worried about anything," I called behind her. "You're never going to be worried about anything."

She was halfway down the corridor and she turned around. "I'm worried about a hell of a lot of things," she yelled at me. "I'm worried about more things than you'd ever look at me and expect me to be worried about. It's not so easy." She sounded as though she was about to cry. "You think it's easy being me. You think it's easy for everybody but you. That's why you don't trust anybody," and then she was gone.

I went back inside my room and cranked up the music. I

felt very weak for some reason. I opened up one of the champagne bottles and drank about half of it. I used the red cap of
my shaving cream can as a cup. I brought the champagne
bottle over to my bedside and then I lay down on the bed,
right where Sarah had lain, and I shook. I went back and
forth from feeling I didn't understand anything to thinking I
understood everything. After a while the bed started to make
me feel sick. My spine felt as though it were turning to
string. I turned over onto my stomach because I thought that
would make me feel better but it didn't. It seemed like the
whole room was vibrating. It was like one of those soft general tremors you get in L.A. right before you get a bigger one,
when everything you know is shivering a little. I got up and
turned the music up as loud as I could make it, so loud I
couldn't hear any individual voices or instruments, just
noise. Then I picked up the Magic Fingers box and threw it
against the wall as hard as I could. "Cut it out," I yelled. I
threw it again but nothing happened. All I managed to do
was disengage the silencer. The box began making a loud
ticking noise.

I spent the night on the floor. I stripped the bed of sheets,
blankets and the pillows and brought them down onto the
floor and covered myself up and lay there as the bed chugged
and ticked. The next day I didn't leave my room at all. I just
sat there on the floor and listened to the hard buzzers of
game shows and the screaming winners and ate Doritos and
vitamin C tablets. A rerun of my sister's show came on at
four and I watched it even though I'd seen that particular
episode before. It's the one where the aging wine merchant
begs Sister Kate to find his missing daughter Cindy so Kate
takes the case and at the end of the show she finds the
daughter who's been running some little sporting goods shop
in Santa Barbara, which is what she's always wanted to do
but felt her father wouldn't allow her to, blah, blah, blah.
Kate reunites them and makes this long speech about expectations and then she coasts back to the convent on her moped

to grapple anew with the problems of simultaneously being a woman and a nun. It wasn't one of the best episodes of all time but I have to admit it was pretty nice when that father and daughter got back together.

I stayed in my room until about seven-thirty watching the news and then I took a shower and around eight I went on downstairs to the Littleneck Lounge. I wasn't really looking all that much forward to seeing Ruth again, or seeing anybody for that matter, but for some reason I was feeling a little bit lonely. I was also pretty nervous. I had started having all these fantasies that the headmaster of the school in England hadn't gotten my telex and that he had called up my father asking him where I was and my father had said, What do you mean? I thought he was with you. I was also getting worried that I was going to run out of money pretty soon. I had already spent about half of the money I had brought with me and I didn't have all that many traveler's checks left and I hadn't even come close to finding my aunt yet. I tried to make myself feel better about everything by putting on these bright green corduroy pants that used to belong to Bob and this navy blue jacket and a battered old red-and-black tie and these old brown topsiders I've had forever that are splitting across the toes. You can see the skin of my feet right through the leather. I looked pretty nautical that night. I looked as though I should be drinking a Bloody Mary aboard some yawl or something while my wife desperately tried to reach the ship-to-shore operator so she could leave the boat.

The Littleneck Lounge was small and dark and grubby and the dance floor looked as though it could hold maybe four dancers at the most. There was one of those huge silent glittering globes on the ceiling, you know, the ones that spin and throw off beads of yellow-and-red light. When I got there the globe was spinning but there was no one dancing. Beads of light were swimming over the floorboards and the ceiling and the walls and the tables. Not only was there no one dancing but there was hardly anybody in the whole place. A couple of raw-faced fishermen types were sitting at the end of the bar but they looked as though they'd been sitting there since the place opened, you know, a hundred years ago. It wasn't as though they'd made a special trip that night or anything.

I looked around for Ruth but I was early and she hadn't arrived yet. There was a sign by the door that said to please wait for the management to seat you but I went ahead and sat down at a corner table near the kitchen and lit a cigarette. I'd been smoking like crazy that day, ever since Sarah left actually. I'd finished the cartons Bob bought for me at the airport and I was already halfway through a third. I don't know why but it seemed I was getting progressively agitated the longer I stayed at the Tern Inn. After a while the waitress came over and asked me what I wanted. She was a tall blonde-haired girl with a sharp chin and she had a red rubber band stretched around her wrist which she kept rolling up and down her forearm snapping as she was waiting for me to order. I told her I'd like a frozen margarita. "Give me a break," she said as though I'd asked her to transfer ownership of her child to me or something. I said that if they didn't have margaritas I would have a Cape Codder instead. It seemed like the drink I deserved but the girl said she would have to go see if there was any cranberry juice at the bar, she didn't think there was. She came back a minute later and told me there wasn't so I told her to just bring me a glass of wine.

She disappeared and I watched the band set up. There were four band members and all of them were deeply tanned. The lead singer was a very small woman with blonde bangs and white shorts and high white leather boots. She was holding a tambourine. You knew she must have thought she was still in Kingston or Aruba or wherever. Behind her a couple of guys were setting up this big white drum on the stage. The drum said on one side, The Recreators, Just Like the Real Thing. The two guys got into place on the stage. One of them picked up an acoustic guitar and the other one sat down behind the drum and the room got dark and then this old Leslie Gore song came over the speakers. The woman in the white shorts and boots starting lip-synching the words. "It's my party," her mouth said, "and I'll cry if I want to." As she pretended to sing she smacked this tambourine against her hip. I guess she had wanted to contribute something musically so the band had stuck her with this tambourine. You can't do all that much major damage with a tambourine even if you want to.

Ruth came in about twenty minutes later followed by this enormous guy with black curly hair and a square face. She introduced him to me as David. "Sorry we're late," she said when both of them were sitting. "David's father was giving an exhibition up at the high school and we stayed to see the start of it."

I asked her what kind of exhibition. "Knives," she said. "He's a butcher. He sharpens peoples' knives. He'll do scissors too. Everybody came and brought their knives along with them, not all the knives they owned or everything, just the blunt ones. When we left he had two at a time going."

"Dad was going crazy tonight," David said. "Maniac." His hand was resting on the table and it covered one of the scallops. The table was glass with all these pink-and-white shells suspended in a kind of clear gelatin and David had all this black hair pouring out of his knuckles. I looked over at his other hand and it was the same story. All that black hair was pretty depressing to me. It's not just because my chest is bare or that I want to have a bunch of black hair coming out all over me either. You knew David was one of those guys who had black hair coming out of his toes and all over his shoulders and his neck and sticking to his ribs and clinging to his spine and continuing down over his ass and even worse, that he'd probably had a beard as a child, you know, very masculine and all but I have to admit all that hair makes me just a little sick to my stomach. He was about thirty, I'd say, and he had enormous shoulders and an enormous neck. He looked a little like the guys at Briar Hall who were big deals on campus but as soon as they graduated they were through. You had to feel a little sorry for those guys actually. They were popular and all in high school but then the school forced them to graduate so they went to college and lived off-campus with their old Briar teammates who were the same size as they were and after college they entered these training programs at banks in Hartford or Montpelier, places like that. Then one by one they got married to girls named Kathleen or Denise, these little girls, you know, very petite and all, with thin black hairs on their arms you knew they spent all their waking hours thinking up ways to eliminate. All these guys go to their high school reunions and you can see their stomachs welling out against the bottom buttons of their shirts since they've quit exercising what with their increased responsibilities at the bank and they have mustaches and they try and act pretty nice to you, forgetting what ungovernable assholes they were at Briar.

The blonde waitress came back with my white wine and Ruth said, "Hi, Jessica."

"You all know each other?" I said.

"Hey, Eleanor," David said.

"That's Jessica," Ruth said to me. "Sure we know each other. Why wouldn't we know each other?"

"No reason."

"I told you he was weird as anything," Ruth said to David. She turned to the waitress. "So what's up, Jessie?"

"Not too much," the blonde girl said.

"Wait," I said. "Is it Eleanor or Jessica?"

"Eleanor," she said. She moved her feet but stayed in place.

"Don't you think she looks a lot like Jessica Lange though? The mouth? And they have the same eyes and the same hair. I'm always asking her how Sam is. You're Sam too so this could get confusing. Uh-oh." Ruth turned to Eleanor. "So what's going on with you, J-girl?"

"Oh, you know. Slow night. Not much happening. So

what else is new, right?" Eleanor dropped her arms down to her sides and then lifted them and let them fall again. She was a pretty drab girl, I decided. "Charlie and Dee were by here earlier."

"What's Dee up to?"

Eleanor shrugged. "Not too much. So," she said, "you guys just hanging out or what?"

"That's about it," Ruth said. "How's Misha's baby?"

Eleanor smiled. "She's fine. Beautiful baby. She's dancing all over the place. She misses her father though."

"Who's her father?" I said to Ruth.

"Mikhail Baryshnikov," she said.

"Do you guys talk this way to each other all the time?" I said. Nobody seemed to have heard me. I thought wildly, maybe I didn't say it. Maybe I didn't say anything at all.

Ruth said, "Might head over to the Jib later on. There's a pretty good band up there. All the drinks are half price too."

I was feeling pretty left out. I said in a strong voice, so I could be sure I'd said it. "What are you all talking about?"

Ruth stared at me. "Friends. People you don't know."

"What are you drinking?" David said to me. "What did you say your name was again?"

"Sam."

He pointed at himself. "You call me David."

You knew he expected me to say something binding like, "All right David, I will," you know, use his name immediately in some kind of context, to seal the transaction. I refuse to do stuff like that, I just flat out refuse to play. I can't bear that kind of mediocre stuff. It makes people think you're co-operating with their mediocrity.

"What are you drinking?" David asked me.

"Wine." He made a face.

"Charlie works for David," Ruth said to me. "Dee's his wife. They just got married. My brother James videotaped the wedding but one of the cameras broke down at the reception.

They got married on Christmas morning, in front of the fire-place. Dee's brother used to go out with Jessica. Before Sam that is."

"Dee does color analysis at Skintastic," Eleanor said to me. "It's all based on your skin undertones. I'm a peach. She gave me a peach scarf. On your first visit there she gives you a scarf that's the color of your best color."

"You are a peach," David said. "Ha ha ha. I could have told you you were a peach. A real Georgia peach." He looked at me. "Why don't you just have a beer?"

"It's a science," Eleanor went on. "She's really excellent at it."

"Boy, it really sounds like a science," I said. "For a second there I thought you were describing physics or biology. It sounded just like physics." I was trying to be sarcastic but no one noticed. When I said that they all nodded. I really hate it when no one notices when you're trying to be sarcastic. It's such a waste. You make all this effort to say something using sarcastic inflections and when no one reacts you're left feeling like an asshole.

The band started doing "Brown Sugar." Since the vocal was male the guy with the acoustic guitar took the blonde woman's place in the center of the stage. She sat on the drums. I mean, it didn't really matter where any of them went since none of them were playing.

"These guys are great," David said after the song was over. Ruth and Eleanor were still talking and I could tell he thought it was right that we should have a conversation. I couldn't hear what he had said so I asked him to say it again but in the meantime I realized what it was so when he leaned over I was already nodding my head up and down. "They're authentic," he said loudly, pumping his thumb at the stage. "The band. They're really a good band."

I screamed, "Well, of course they're fucking authentic. It's somebody else's music playing. It's the fucking Rolling Stones who are playing. You'd probably be authentic too if you could pipe in the Rolling Stones every time you had to go on the line."

David took his face away from mine. He said, "Why do you want to go around saying something like that? Why do you, man? Why do you have to be so critical? They're a lot better than anything you have in L.A., that's for sure." He reached for his drink and drank some of it and then he looked at my wine glass. "Sitting there with your pussy drink saying things about friends of mine."

Eleanor asked me if I wanted another wine and David rapped the side of his beer bottle. "Get him one of these. Get him a real drink. Wine's a pussy drink. Get me one too while you're up." He said to Ruth, "What are you guys doing?"

Eleanor went to get the drinks. "Talking about Bobby," Ruth said.

"Who's that?" I said.

"He's a friend of ours," Ruth said. "Was a friend of ours. He disappeared. We think he's dead."

"Terrible stuff is always going on with great guys," David said. "That's like a rule."

I tried to look sympathetic but I really wasn't feeling all that sympathetic. I didn't even know the guy.

"Bobby gave us this amazing gram of coke," Ruth said. "It was a prewedding present. Ninety percent pure. It was like parmesan cheese, that pure I mean. It was all I could do not to do it all the morning he gave it to us." She shook her head. "I could have done it all that morning and not told anybody I had it. See, he gave it to me. David was at work, nobody would have known a thing. I guess I'm too honest." She laughed hysterically.

Eleanor had come back with the drinks. She put a beer in a green bottle in front of me. I just stared at it. I didn't want beer. She stood listening to Ruth talk and then she said, "I went to this seance a couple of months ago. It was to try and communicate with the spirits of people who've died. Ruth knows this story. I just went ahead and assumed Bobby was dead, you know, that he was not coming back. I assumed all that. But the guy in charge of the seance, this guy Wilbur, wouldn't let me stay at the table. He told me I was vulnerable to that stuff. He said I was too sensitive." She smiled apologetically. "He kicked me out of the room. So I went and watched TV in his bedroom. There were all these green posters on the wall. I used to go out with Bobby," she said to me.

"Bobby went out with my younger sister for a while," Ruth said. "We all know what happened there."

I said, "All you guys do is sleep with each other."

"Yeah, what do you do?" David said. He burped loudly and said Excuse me. He burped again. "Excuse me," he said afterwards both times. Ruth said, "You're excused." She patted his hand. "When I was growing up I wanted to die in some really violent way. You know? Something exciting."

"Oh, I couldn't do that," Eleanor said. She was sitting down now. "I'd take pills if I had to die. About two bottles worth."

"How did you want to die?" Ruth said to me.

"I didn't say I did."

Ruth looked at David. "How about you? If you had to die how would you die?"

When David didn't say anything Eleanor said, "I'd wash the pills down with something too." She looked thoughtful. "Like bourbon on the rocks. I'd have to be sure I took enough pills though. I wouldn't want to have to live after I'd tried to kill myself. Can you imagine anything more embarrassing? To jump off a building and survive? Or to try and kill yourself and just end up wounded? I think I'd end up making up some story."

David said, "I guess I'd shoot myself in the throat." He shrugged. "I don't know."

"Come on," Ruth said to me. "Everybody wants to die every now and again. Everybody makes up things like that."

"Nope," I said.

"Say you had to then." She was pretty persistent. I told her

I'd probably shoot myself just so she'd stop asking me. The only reason I said that was because David was at the table and I wanted to die as roughly as possible in front of another guy. Actually, I had always imagined dying of some silent wasting disease and not telling anybody about it, particularly my family. Then with about a day or a half-day left before I was scheduled to die Bob would invite me out to an evening of classical music at someplace like Lincoln Center and I'd have to tell him, I'm sorry, I can't, I'll be dead by then but thanks anyway for thinking of me. Then I'd die and about a month later Bob would be cleaning out my closets. Someone would have told him that life was for the living, to quit moping around and so forth, and he would discover this remarkable series of oil paintings that I'd been working on in private and which I kept in a tall stack in the back of my closet. And Bob would take them to this big art dealer we know on Seventy-first Street, this guy named Peterson, and Peterson would take one look at these paintings of mine, and say, Why, why, these are brilliant, extraordinary works of genius. I must meet the old Flemish master who painted these. My father would say, The artist is my son Sam, who died roughly a month ago. Peterson would say, carefully, Bob, sit down, and when my father was sitting Peterson would say, Bob, Sam was the greatest natural painter I've ever seen in all my years in the art world. Why weren't you nicer to him while he was alive? I don't even know why I have that particular fantasy, I really don't. I don't even like to paint. I'm a terrible painter. What I do is I keep adding colors onto colors so in the end everything is grey. I don't even like museums all that much.

After a while Ruth asked David if he wanted to dance. The Recreators were taking a break and the bartender had turned on the jukebox and Eleanor was over at the bar talking to the woman in the white boots. This great old song was playing on the jukebox, this old Frankie Valli and the Four Seasons song that has to do with seeing someone in September. I think that's even the name of it, "See You in September." I was

watching Ruth and David dance and all of a sudden I started
thinking of summers in Southampton when I was a kid, sitting in the backseat of Lucy's dirty little red car buzzing
around to the beaches. I could remember being on some
beach once and hearing "See You in September" coming out
of somebody's transistor radio. It was hard to hear since the
radio was wrapped in a little plastic baggie to keep sand from
going into the speaker holes but you could still make out
most of the words. I figured that once I walked down the
beach that would be the last I heard that song but as I was
picking my way across the sand I realized that everybody on
that beach had their radios turned to the same station and
that "See You in September" was blasting at me every few
feet. I remember walking along the brown boards that were
spread out across the sand and getting into the car and putting my head back against the broiled leather and eating
those onion rings that looked like Shirley Temple's hair and
then Lucy turned on the engine and I heard the final chorus
of the song over and over again.

On the dance floor Ruth was doing a lot of slinky things
with her hands and she twisted down to the floor and then
rose up while David just kind of rocked from side to side and
snapped his fingers when he remembered to. The dance floor
was so small they kept dancing out of it and into the shadows.
After a while I went over to the bar and got another glass of
wine and then I walked over to the jukebox and crouched
down on my knees to see what kind of a selection they had.
The jukebox was framed by a long skinny tube of purple light
and whenever you put a quarter into the slot the tube ripped
around the sides a couple of times just to show it was capable
of a rampage or two and then it reversed itself and dribbled
back down to nothing. They had songs by Bing Crosby and
Ed Ames and the Temptations and Tommy James and the
Shondells as well as some guy singing "Happy Birthday." I
don't think they'd changed the songs in about a hundred
years. I had both hands on the frame of the jukebox and I was

going down song by song looking for the name Valli or the Four Seasons so I could see what was on the flip side and I was holding onto the machine so tightly the song jerked ahead to the chorus, 'Bye, baby, good-bye. Since I wasn't able to find the song anywhere I started looking under "September" and finally in the bottom left-hand corner I saw in someone's writing "See You in September" and the group listed was Brian Hyland and the Happenings.

I don't know why that upset me so much but it did. I must have stared at the name Brian Hyland and the Happenings for about fifteen minutes or at least it felt that way. My first thought was that they had gotten mixed up somehow and attached the wrong group to the right song and that a strip of paper with Frankie Valli's name on it was lying on the floor of some jukebox factory in New Bedford or someplace and no one had realized the mistake. Then I thought that maybe they had simply attached Frankie's name to another song title and that it could easily be switched back so I went down the songs again and I still couldn't find his name or any mention of the Four Seasons. I don't know why it was so crucial to me that "See You in September" be sung by Frankie Valli and the Four Seasons but it was. For twenty minutes there it was the most important issue in my life. Ruth yelled at me to put on another song so I put in a couple of quarters and pressed a Springsteen song and a couple of others and then I put on "Happy Birthday" by accident. I almost went over to the bartender to ask him where the strip of paper with Frankie Valli's name on it was but he was drinking beers with the fishermen and I didn't know what I would say to him anyway. He didn't look as though he had ever cared about anything anyhow.

I felt like I was going crazy. I simply couldn't accept the fact that "See You in September" was sung by Brian Hyland. I had never even heard of Brian Hyland and the Happenings. It changed everything. I'd gone along for years thinking it was sung by Frankie Valli and now it wasn't.

Whenever "See You in September" came on over the radio
and people said, Who's singing this? I would always tell them
it was Frankie, or if they knew Frankie's name but didn't
know any of his songs right off I'd mention "See You in September." The fact it was sung by the Happenings destroyed
the song for me. It changed all the good things I remembered. It changed the day on the beach when I had stood
there on the sand and heard "See You in September" coming
out of a hundred different transistor radios. I stood in front of
the jukebox, not knowing what to do. I drank my wine and
got another. Ruth and David were still dancing and I felt
miserable so I went back over to the table and sat there gulp-
ing my wine. Eleanor had stopped talking to the lead singer
and she was sitting down in Ruth's chair drinking a Diet
Pepsi and smoking one of David's Marlboros, taking fast
careful inhales and blowing them out just as quickly. I got up
to go to the bathroom and when I got back I stood behind
Eleanor's chair and looked down at the back of her neck. The
hair on her neck was blonder and thinner than the hair on
her head and it curled and the curls touched the white collar
of her shirt. I could see skin underneath the curls, and sad
ears. As I was standing there I realized her neck looked exactly like the neck of someone else I'd liked a lot once, but I
couldn't remember who that person was. The necks were
practically identical and the ears were small and before I
knew what I was doing, as if I were in the middle of a dream,
I had leaned down and kissed the back of Eleanor's neck. I
was thinking about this other person's ears and neck and
how it would have been normal to kiss them but Eleanor
jumped about a foot and dropped her cigarette on the floor.
She whirled around. "Jesus Christ," she yelled. "You scared
the shit out of me. Don't ever do that to someone."

I tried to apologize to her and she kept saying over and
over again, "Jesus Christ, I can't believe you actually snuck
up behind someone and did that," and I told her I had
thought her neck was someone else's neck and she said,

"Oh, right, tell me about it. How could it have been someone else's neck? I'm the only person here. Do you see other people here? No. I'm the only person here." I told her I didn't know how it could have been someone else's neck and that I was sorry and she seemed to calm down a little bit then. Finally she held up her hand. "Listen, I don't want to know your reasons. I don't think they're all that much different from any other horny guy's in the middle of winter. I'm sorry but I don't. I mean, let's be honest, right? Just don't come up behind someone like that and scare them like that. Ever."

I tried to change the subject entirely, you know, ask her about the Cape and what it was like to work as a waitress but she kept rubbing the skin on the back of her neck and saying, "Jesus, I can't believe anybody would ever do anything like that to someone." Then Ruth and David came back over to the table and Ruth asked me if I wanted to dance. I think she felt a little sorry for me but I jumped at the chance to get away from Eleanor and we went out onto the dance floor and started dancing to an old Bob Seger song. I'm not a particularly good dancer, in fact I'm sort of mesmerizingly bad. I remember I was once dancing at this club at the Imperial Gardens in L.A. and I caught sight of myself in the mirrors across the room and I wanted to kill myself on the spot. My arms were pumping in this idiotic, pretentious way and my eyes were all squinted up and I remember Lucy once tried giving me dance lessons on the beach in front of her house but the wind kept blowing me over and the whole thing was pretty pointless. When the song was over Ruth and I went back to the table. I was sweating like crazy and my collar was sticking to me and my hair was damp. David asked Ruth whether she felt like going to the Jib. I guess that was another bar.

"Sure." Ruth looked at me. "You feel like coming with us?"

I told her no, I was tired. "Well, the least you can do is take a walk with us out to the van," she said.

"I think I'll just stay here," I said.

Ruth hesitated. "We have a surprise for you. It's your Cape Cod good-bye present."

I didn't want any surprises and I told her no, thanks and then she sniffed long and loudly and raised her eyebrows. I guess all that meant she had cocaine. Sometimes I'm pretty slow about these things, you know, these codes various people have. When the bill came Ruth stared at it for a long time and her mouth made the shape of the numbers she was reading. "You owe six dollars and forty, no fifty-five cents," she said to me. She was one of those miserly people who made you pay exactly what you had spent and you knew she wouldn't pay a dime over what she was supposed to. I can't stand people like that. They suddenly turn into strangers, people with secret sides that turn out to be pretty defining. They're like those people at movie theatres who clap when they're amused by something. I mean, you're watching a movie with some girl and everybody in the audience laughs and that's all but the girl you're with takes it upon herself to start applauding. She starts acting like the spokesman for the audience, you know, as though she's been planted by the movie studio to rouse things up, and when you stare at her again she's become unrecognizable. You want to say, Who are you? Everybody put in money and Ruth went over to the bar and paid the bartender and outside the kitchen I could see Eleanor stacking ashtrays and emptying bowls of peanuts into a plastic yellow sack. Ruth went over and said something to her and I stood at the door with David who didn't speak to me and then Ruth joined us and we went outside into the parking lot. It was very cold out and the white paint of the bloodmobile shone under the moon. "Van's over there," David said, pointing.

Ruth was walking beside me. "You do do coke, right?"

"Constantly," I said. "I'm like this drug kingpin. My name is Johnny something."

"Well, do you or don't you?"

You couldn't say anything remotely unclear around those two. I stopped and turned to her and said in a very clear voice, "Yes, I like cocaine. Yes. I like it fine."

Ruth looked at me as though I weren't from earth. "Don't be so weird," she said. "Really. Just don't. It just makes everybody uncomfortable."

"Both of you shut the hell up," David said.

I could hear our heels clicking on the cement. It was the only sound in the night, heels and an occasional car going past and faint jukebox music soaking out from the Littleneck. The cold air froze my bangs and I started to shiver. We passed by the green Dumpster. Its lid was raised on two rusted arms and behind it was the flat yellow marsh and then, back in the woods, the yellow living room lights of someone's house. "Back there," I started to say, "there was this song on the jukebox, 'See You in September.' "

"Yeah, I know," Ruth said. "We danced to that song."

"Good tune," David said. He stopped in front of a brown van and slid open the door and we got in.

"Too bad Eleanor has to work," Ruth said. It was dark inside the van and it smelled like sweat and cheap incense. There was a long uncomfortable bench in the backseat and I sat down on it next to Ruth. David climbed into the front seat. I touched the twisted frozen front pieces of my hair and tried to snap them off in my fingers. It was like touching glass. David put the key in the ignition and turned it a notch to the right so there was power but no noise and then he inserted a white cassette into the tape deck and pressed the rewind button. Rewinding made a high singing sound.

"Anyway, did either of you have any idea it was sung by Brian Hyland? That he was the singer on it?"

"No," Ruth said. "I didn't know who sang it period."

David said, "Ruthie, you got a bill?"

Ruth started digging through her purse. "What does it really matter anyway? That's such an old song. It doesn't even count anymore." She took a five-dollar bill out and handed it to David, who unrolled his window and bent the outside mirror toward him and unclipped something behind the glass. The round mirror plate came off in his hand and he put it on the seat next to him. "I have that song on a WRKO sixties album," Ruth said. "At least I think it's that song. It's four sides, all sixties songs. I'm really broke," she said to David. "Don't forget to give that back to me."

I tried to explain that I'd gone on all my life thinking that "See You in September" was by Frankie Valli and the Four Seasons and David looked back at me and said, "Who gives a shit who sings it?" He held the tightly rolled five-dollar bill up to his eye.

"Hey, pirate," Ruth said. "Hey, Mr. Pirate."

He started measuring out lines on the mirror. "It's the words that count. It's not who sings the song that counts."

Ruth watched his fingers scrape and bulldoze. "Remember, ladies first," she said at one point. She laughed.

I could barely make out her face in the dark. After a minute David handed her the mirror and I could see her eyes coming forward. She gave the mirror back to David when she was done and David turned it so the two largest lines were facing him. I stared down at the glass. Its sides were rough and there were chalky letters across the top that said Objects in Mirror Are Closer Than They Appear. I could see my fingers reflecting in the glass and I did the lines and then handed the mirror back to David who did the last two. The tape had stopped rewinding but no one did anything.

After a while Ruth shook me on the knee. "So do you like Eleanor?"

David put his arm across the top of the seat. "The guy kissed Eleanor," he said. "Sucker kiss. Right from behind. Sneak attack. That's what she told me. Right on the neck. Like a vampire."

"You did?"

"It was a mistake," I said to her. "I didn't mean to kiss her."

"Right," David said. "Mistake. You're the mistake, man."
He laughed.

"How can a kiss be a mistake?" Ruth said.

"I thought she was someone else."

"She's Jessica Lange," Ruth said. "See?"

"Eleanor's a good kid." David put his arm on Ruth's shoulder and started stroking it. Ruth raised her knee like a cat. "Eleanor is a totally unaffected human being."

"I like Eleanor," Ruth said, sort of unnecessarily I thought. "Don't you think she looks like Jessica Lange?" she said to me.

"Yeah," I said. "Eleanor's a wonderful human being. And a great conversationalist. You get Eleanor on any subject imaginable and get prepared for fireworks. She's a real raconteur, that one, a master raconteur in fact. Really." I don't know why I was acting so unfriendly. I guess I was still pretty upset about the song. I got up to go. "Thanks for everything."

"Are you leaving?" Ruth said. "What were you talking about just now?"

"The guy's a fucking lunatic," David said. He squinted at me. "You are a fucking lunatic."

"Go find Eleanor," Ruth said.

"She's got Sam," I said. I started trying to pry the van door open but I couldn't find the handle.

"Well, will you?"

"Will I what?" I couldn't get out.

"You know what I mean. Look Eleanor up. She likes you." She leaned over and slid the latch downward with the heel of her hand. The door opened out to cold and quiet. I could hear a dog barking across the marsh. "See you guys around," I said. I hoped I wouldn't have to see either of them again but when you say something like See you around it makes your good-bye a lot less dramatic, you don't have to be so serious. I turned and started walking across the parking lot. My head hurt from the coke and the cold and the wine and the cigarettes and the music and probably the company. I heard the van start up behind me and out of the sides of my eyes I saw the headlights flash on and then David switched to the higher beams and back a couple of times. He raced the engine in place. I was practically at the entrance to the Littleneck Lounge and I turned to wave. The van was heading toward me. I figured they had something to tell me or else I had left something in the backseat. I could see David's shoulders shaking through the tinted windshield glass but I couldn't see Ruth and when I realized the van wasn't going to stop I started running in the direction of the marsh. The van's two headlights pinned the ground on either side of me, still flicking from dim to strong, dim to strong, and I went straight past the Dumpster and down a hard hairy bank of marshgrass until my shoes touched a sheet of ice, loosened it and then the coldest water I'd felt in a long time came rushing in through the split leather of my topsiders.

*   *   *

When I got back inside the Littleneck Lounge I was pretty shaken up. My shoes were soaked and there was mud and water caked between my toes and my green pants were all slicked with dirt and leaves and my heart was beating like crazy. I looked around for Eleanor but she wasn't there and then I went over to the side of the stage and sat down on a bunch of thick black cables. The jukebox was playing some old Fleetwood Mac song and all the lights were on in the bar. As soon as I heard that song I started feeling pretty anonymous. I mean, in L.A. we sort of know Fleetwood Mac and all, personally I mean. I don't want to make a huge deal out of it or anything but the lead singer, or the one who used to be their lead singer, the one who wears all those spacey clothes and who had all those nodes scraped off her throat a while back, Stevie Nicks, that's her name, is a pretty good friend of my sister's. They have the same exercise instructor or at least they used to, this giant guy named Ned who makes house calls and who stands over Lucy while she kicks and rocks and does sit-ups. I'm not trying to say that I'm some friend to the stars or anything but Stevie's been out to my sister's house quite a lot. She once told me, Stevie did, that I had nice eyes in fact. I don't want to pretend that Stevie and I are married or that Stevie keeps a piece of my sweaty clothing in a wall safe guarded by Dobermans and electric wire or anything but I think if she were passing me on the street, and not just some L.A. street either, that she'd probably wave at me or at least she'd nod her head a couple of times, you know, the greeting would be unmistakable. She'd acknowledge me somehow is my point here. As I said, it's not as though when Stevie dies she's going to leave me her estate or anything but I guess what I'm trying to say is that out there we know people who perform and so forth for other people. I was sitting on the side of that stage with all those oily black cables running under me and all of a sudden I felt terrifyingly distant from people like that, you know, from actors and singers and so forth. I listened to the end of that song and I began thinking that I was nothing more than a listener, a consumer, you know, one of those wonderful people in the dark. I felt like one of the masses. I felt like someone at a movie theatre who had a ticket off a roll of tickets and that all the tickets looked the same. I hated that feeling. I didn't want to live with that feeling. I wasn't sure whether I could even. It was as though Stevie Nicks had never told me I had nice eyes in my life.

After a while I stood up and went over to the drumset. My feet were warming up, in fact they were so warm they were beating. I climbed up onto the drumset and picked up one of the long brown sticks. It had a pad of white cotton knotted around its tip so it wouldn't make any noise when it touched the drum skin. I put my foot on one of the pedals but no matter how hard I pumped it I couldn't make a sound. At least I started feeling better. Being on that drumset, being on a stage, at least put me on the side of the performers rather than on the side of the people who are being performed to.

The drummer came over about ten minutes later and told me he had to dismantle the drums so I got off and watched him take the set apart. The back door of the Littleneck Lounge was open and outside I could see an orange station wagon with its trunk raised and running along the border of the marsh a line of wooden posts with blue peeling tips and I could hear the dead unlit silence of the night. I suddenly decided I would leave Hyannis in the morning and head up to Provincetown. The prospect of that cheered me up quite a lot. I went over to the bar. The bartender was still talking to the fishermen but when he saw me he came over.

I said, "This is my last night here and I want to buy everybody a round of drinks." There weren't that many people left so it wasn't all that magnanimous a thing to do but I wanted to anyway.

The bartender stared at me. He was pretty drunk. His eyes were blue and red. "Forget it," he said after a moment. "You're not the type."

I didn't understand. "What?"

"The type," he repeated. "You're not the type to say something like that. You're not the type to make that sort of gesture. To make it work. It doesn't sound right coming from you. Save your money." He turned back to the fishermen.

I was so hurt when he said that I almost started to cry. I felt like I wasn't the right type for anybody. I saw Eleanor at the entrance to the kitchen. She had her coat on and she was wearing thick white mittens. All of a sudden I remembered that I had walked off without leaving her any tip. I went over to her and when she saw me I think she tried to pretend she hadn't. I told her again that I was sorry about kissing her earlier. Then I gave her a twenty-dollar bill. It was the smallest bill I had.

"Don't you want any change?"

She said it sort of halfheartedly. "It's all right," I said. "Buy the baby something. Buy the baby some borscht." She was all right, Eleanor, Jessica, whatever. She wasn't the greatest or the most interesting girl in the world but at least she wasn't the sort who held a grudge. Plus, it was pretty doubtful I'd ever find the greatest girl in the world on Cape Cod in the off-season anyhow.

When I got back to my room the Magic Fingers was still going. I flopped down on my bed and I proceeded to have the worst dream I'd had in a long time. I won't tell you about it since I told you, I think other people's dreams are pretty boring but just say that in my dream were the following things and people: Ribs, the frozen parakeet, my father, my mother, the headmaster, Mac Davis (I guess I got the Mac from Fleetwood Mac) and the back of Sarah's neck. There were a bunch of hand puppets, which I hate, and a lot of children screaming for me to jump, jump from somewhere. I woke up at around four and I couldn't get back to sleep.

* Chapter 6 *

THE next morning I felt like hell. The Tern Inn Coffee
Shop was closed for some reason so I walked down the
street about a quarter of a mile and went into this
place called the Hollywood Diner. I ordered coffee and some
scrambled eggs but when it came I just glared at it. There
were large sharp yellow stars on all the plates and across the
center of each star was the name of an actor or an actress,
just like the stars on the pavement outside Mann's theatre in
L.A. I scraped my eggs over to one side and saw that I had
gotten Fred Astaire. My butter plate said Sal Mineo. The
waitress kept circling me with a pot of coffee. The second I
was off guard she would pour more into my cup. I drank
about five cups to be polite but as she was pouring the sixth I
told her to go away and leave me alone. She looked injured so
I apologized to her. I felt as though I was apologizing to a lot
of people that week. I sat at the table as my eggs cooled and I
looked out onto the Main Street, the barber shop, the small
white funeral parlor, the row of fast-food shacks, a glassed-in
tunnel where white and purple flowers were growing, a
sporting goods and bait shop and Thelma's Souvenir Barn,
which was dripping with mobiles and lamps made out of life

preservers and lawn animals and hats and tackle and red lobster floats and postcards that said Greetings from Cape Cod.
An oil tanker had gotten stuck on some flats not far from
Provincetown and someone had taken a lot of pictures of it
and made postcards out of them, glossed them and put a date
on the bottoms. They sold three for five dollars. A sign offered
poinsettias and Christmas trees at half price. Across the
street was a movie theatre that was showing something
called "Sensuous Teenagers." I started wondering whether I
was a sensuous teenager. I didn't think I was. My mouth was
dry and my eyes hurt and I was jittery from caffeine. I wasn't
sensuous, I was a disaster. The marquee said there were two
shows a day, three if it rained. It didn't look as though it was
going to rain, though. The air was soft and the sky was
slightly orange, the way it gets when it's about to snow.

I was feeling good enough after a while to smoke a cigarette and then I paid the bill and when I got back to the Tern
Inn I went upstairs to my room and packed up all my clothes.
I thought that if I was ever going to find this aunt of mine I
had better get serious. Provincetown wasn't all that big a
place so I thought the chances of someone knowing her were
pretty good, that is, if she still lived there. Plus, I was fairly
anxious to leave before Ruth came in that day so I brought
my bags downstairs and settled my bill and then I went upstairs a final time to see if I had forgotten anything but I
hadn't.

I stood on the road with my bags and then I started walking away from the center of town. I know a lot of people make
these big signs for themselves, you know, black letters on
brown cardboard that say New York or Newport or Big Sur,
wherever they're going, but I've always thought there was
something slick about that, something overly professional. It
takes away from a hitchhiker's innocence. I walked past a
Sunoco station and a water tower and when I reached the
entrance to the dump I put my bags down on the side of the
road and held out my thumb. A lot of cars went past me but
none of them stopped. There aren't that many more lonely

sounds than the sound a car makes when it doesn't pick you up. There's the whoosh as it first goes past you and your eyes follow it to see if it'll slow down but it doesn't. You stop hearing it and then you stop seeing it and after a while you look down at the nail-grey pavement again and you see sand and old white paint and sticky needles and wrappers and grease. That's the stuff you remember, what's on the side of the roads, the stuff that nobody ever talks about.

About twenty minutes later I finally got a ride. This old yellow Cadillac drove past me and as I watched it came to a stop about thirty yards away from me and it waited. Then the driver honked a couple of times. I grabbed my duffel and my suitcase and ran up to it and before I got in I looked through the window. The driver was an old man and he was wearing a bright red blazer and a battered painter's cap that said Frank's Diner on the brim. In the backseat there was a big fat old black dog with its mouth hanging open. There was a black dot at the end of its tongue and I could see a lot of pink inside its mouth and then teeth and then complete darkness.

"Come in, friend, come in," the old man said. He leaned across the seat and pushed open the door. "Fit your bags right there in back, that's the way. Just tell Tom there to move, he won't mind."

When I got in and shut the door behind me I almost fell through this enormous hole in the floor on the passenger side. It was about a foot across and you could see the road underneath it. The old man pulled slowly out of the breakdown lane. "Don't look down," he said. "You'll want to jump. It does that to you. My name's Sidney by the way, what's yours?"

"Sam," I said.

"I don't ordinarily do this, this stopping for strangers. Too dangerous. People these days are hiding all sorts of things on them. Bazookas, knives, corkscrews, rifles. Ice picks. All kinds of artillery. I hope you don't have anything under that coat." He looked at me and I shook my head. "Do you?"

"No guns," I said.

"Where you going?"

"Provincetown."

"What do you want to do in Provincetown? Terrible place to find yourself. Not Cape Cod. It's what people may think of when they think Cape Cod but it's as far from the real Cape Cod as the planet Jupiter. Farther."

I told him he could take me as far as he was going and Sidney said, "Oh, I wasn't going anyplace in particular. That's the problem. Just out for a little spin with Tom back there. See if anything's gone up overnight. See what's risen, that's the only purpose to being on the road anymore. We'll take you as far as Provincetown if you'd like."

"You don't have to." I was thinking about how slowly the guy drove, actually, that it would probably take about a year to get there.

"No, no, you're perfectly right. We don't have to, that's right we don't. We barely know you. You could have a weapon on you. But I see it as an adventure on a poor dark devil of a day. They say there might be snow later on, that has a little to do with it."

We drove for about half an hour on the main road and then we crossed over some old railroad tracks and then Sidney put on his blinker and we turned left. We followed that road for a while and then we turned onto the highway. The car didn't turn sharply enough so the blinker kept ticking. Sidney seemed oblivious to it and after a while it started to drive me crazy so I reached over and moved it back into place. When we got onto the highway the dog in the backseat lifted its head and panted for a while and then its mouth slumped shut. I heard jangling and I looked back and saw that the dog had all these metal objects hanging off its collar. There was a small gold clog and a mussel and a miniature Golden Gate Bridge and a tulip and a bee with striped wings. I asked Sidney what they were for. "Mementos," he said. "Tom and I go everywhere together. And Tom collects lovely things. Mementos from the places he's seen and liked the best. We've traveled so much, you know, that on Sunday when I go around the house looking for money to do my laundry with, when I look in all the compartments and the glass bowls and the pockets what I come up with are pesos and francs and pence. I find brown paper bills with queens on them. Not presidents but old queens. Unfamiliar women hiding in my house, shocking the dog. It's quarters you need for a wash and it's dimes you need for a dryer. They won't accept foreign coins at my laundromat." Sidney was silent. "And what do you do?"

He hadn't taken his eyes off the road. "Not all that much," I said.

"You're between answers. Ah. Well, you're not under any obligations to tell me anything. So long as you don't have a gun in that suitcase of yours. I think if you did you would have let me have it by now. Of course the opportunity might not have shown itself. If an animal ran out from the bushes and I put on my brakes suddenly you could take the wheel from me then. Tom wouldn't do anything. His reflexes are so dull. Too much sleep and too much food, not enough exercise. Sometimes I think I spoil him. I think Tom might sit there and watch and not do anything. I don't think I'd be able to do anything either." Sidney looked at me sadly. "I'd try and talk you out of it, sure. Sure I would. But when there's force around you know words are just politeness. Words are just props."

I thought, I can't deal with any more crazy people. We didn't say much for the rest of the ride. Sidney occasionally said something about the scenery and I mostly looked out the window or down at the road unraveling between my shoes. After a while I started seeing signs for Truro and Provincetown. The land seemed to be getting flatter and wilder. There were fewer houses and a lot of brown woods. To the left and right of the highway were high white dunes and I started seeing piles of sand sprinkled on the sides of the road. "You have friends up in Provincetown, is that it?"

I explained to him that I had this aunt I was planning to visit. "What's the name of your aunt?" he said. "Maybe I know her."

"Ellis."

"That's an unusual name. Whereabouts does she live?"

"I don't know," I said. "Somewhere in Provincetown."

"You don't know."

I shook my head. I was starting to feel very pessimistic. To the left an expanse of pines and grey water and marsh opened up suddenly. It was as though we were leaving solid land. The marsh looked pretty desolate. A long row of grey shacks crowded the beach for as far as I could see. All the shacks were the same size and I began thinking that if my aunt lived in one of those shacks then I'd never be able to find her in a million years. Fog was drifting down off the tops of the dunes and onto the highway. In the sand you could see the heads of boats sticking up like fists. We passed by a pond and a bird sanctuary. Sidney had been turning on the wipers every few minutes so they gave the windshield a single wipe and then he would wait until the glass misted up before turning them on again. Now he left them on. There seemed something depressingly final about that. Sidney said, "Looks like we might get flakes any minute. Usually we get the rain up here. The city gets all the snow."

"Boston?"

"Hyannis. Hyannis gets socked with snow, well, of course Boston does too, and up here we get a mist or else we get rain. Rain and high tides that cover over your marshes practically. You go swimming and the water is like a consommé. Nothing like the rain to warm up an ocean." We drove along a quiet narrow road and we passed a church and a couple of motels and then I saw a sign that said Parking Lot Full lying on its side and Sidney steered the Cadillac past a green booth and into an empty beach parking lot. He turned the engine off. I could hear him breathing and I could hear the sound of waves through the hole in the car floor. Tom got up and shook himself.

"There's an information booth someplace around here. Somewhere along that beach. Little cupolated thing with a green roof. They used it in a famous movie once so it's a very well-known thing. They ought to be able to help you out there. Find your aunt. Just keep walking, it'll be on your right. Look for the stills from the movie tacked to a bulletin board out front. They were proud of that day when the cameras were here. You can't miss it."

"Well, thanks," I said. "Thanks a lot for the ride." Suddenly I didn't want to get out of the car.

"Not at all, not at all. Gave Tom and me something to do with ourselves on a dark day like today. There's a high tide out there, it looks like." He looked at me. "You know, don't you, if there's a high tide and you leave your footprints in the sand you have approximately twelve hours and fifteen minutes before they cave in, wash away, before the water fills them up and cleans out any reference to you. Before they disappear. Low tide you have barely a minute before the newer tide sweeps them away. So this is a propitious time for me to be dropping you off, during a high tide. You'll last a little while. Half a day, longer than the entire lives of some things." Sidney put out his hand and we shook and then I got out of the car and pulled my bags from the backseat. The strap of my duffel caught on the seat belt and I had to pull and I almost fell backward. The dog was staring at me. I slammed the door and waved. "Good-bye, Sam," Sidney called. The windows were shut but I could hear his voice clearly through the hole in the floor. He pressed the horn twice and I watched the Cadillac pull away in the fog, the headlights sweeping across the beach briefly before the car left the parking lot. I stared at the back lights until I couldn't see them anymore and all I could see were the trees and the whittle of orange sparks out of a chimney. There was an old green cabin in the middle of the parking lot that sold hamburgers and suntan lotion and beach umbrellas and I walked over to it and peered through its windows. Inside was an old gleaming fryer and a rectangular net to lower the french fries in and a glass coffeepot with a charred bottom and a black register with its drawer open. I went down some wood stairs and onto the sand and as I started walking I noticed three radio towers in the distance. They were tall and gaunt and they stood next to each other like the prongs of a fork and they looked to be about a mile from where I was standing. Each tower had five red blinking lights on it. Even though it was getting dark you could see those red lights throbbing across the water. I tried to keep them ahead of me. It was getting so foggy I needed a compass point of some kind, something to aim toward, and those three radio towers did just fine.

I walked along the beach for a pretty long time but I didn't seem to be getting all that much closer to the towers and there was no sign of any information booth. I hadn't passed anything on my right except for dunes and cowlicks of old seagrass and signs saying Keep Off and Erosion and at one point I saw about half a dozen polaroid pictures spilled on the sand. In one of them a Portuguese family was sitting down to dinner and in another a young black-haired girl was trying hard to smile. All the other pictures were black and shiny. I don't know what those pictures were doing on the beach but they scared me for some reason. I left them where I'd found them and I kept going. After a while I dropped my bags on the sand. I guess I had started to feel incredibly sorry for myself. I was sorry that I hadn't told Sidney to drop me off at some motel before I tried to go about finding my aunt. I still felt pretty bad that the bartender wouldn't let me buy everybody in the bar a drink. I kept thinking about Sarah and whenever I did I'd get terrifically sad. I looked down at my hand and her number had completely washed off except for a very faint curve, like a small light vein, on my thumb. I started thinking about being inside my aunt's house with this huge fire going. I would be drinking coffee and smoking and maybe there would be some kind of passive animal on my lap, a big old drugged cat or something. The fog on the beach was getting thicker. The waves were pretty boisterous by then and I realized I must be closer than I had thought to the shoreline. I could barely see ahead of me so I had to go by hearing mostly. It had started snowing very lightly. The sky looked dark and burnt. The flakes were very raw and they landed inside my clavicle, where they melted. All that fog made me think of the weather conditions in one of those greeting cards that you're supposed to give your girlfriend, you know, the ones that show this light-skinned black couple strolling arm in arm along a beach joking lightly and all these muscular white ponies are rearing up in the surf, nipping and fighting and everything is in soft focus and there's writing at the bottom of the card like that thing from Corinthians about love and clanging that everybody wants to have read at their funerals. Somebody buys those cards, I don't know who, though. I think if I gave a card like that to anybody I liked it would just drive them away.

Just then this huge white sloppy wave washed over my shoes. I ran up the beach away from the water and as I ran I could hear gulls crying in the fog over my head. There was a tall, bright orange lifeguard's chair about twenty yards up the beach from me and I went over to it and started climbing the stairs. When I got to the top I maneuvered my body so I was still facing the radio towers. I rested my shoes on a ledge. The heels were soaked and the leather was turning orange and sticking to the sides of my feet. A few feet away from the chair was a sign that said End of Protected Beach. The lifeguard's chair was a pretty agreeable place to sit actually. On clear days you knew the view was probably pretty spectacular. I sat up there for a while and then I realized I was pretty hungry so I climbed down and got my duffel and brought it back up with me. When I was sitting again I undid the zipper and took out the last bag of Doritos and the bottle of Dom Pérignon. I had gone through all the domestic stuff but I had held onto the good French bottle in case there was a special occasion in my life like a triumph or something. It didn't seem as though there was going to be one so I popped the cork and it flew out over the sand somewhere. Since I didn't have a glass I drank straight from the mouth. I drank most of the bottle. It was excellent. I mean, the French may be small, vicious people and all the men wear those small stretchy bathing suits that make you want to get sick all over the place but their champagne is usually sensational. Most of their wine is, in fact. The champagne started making me feel a lot warmer. It made the ocean softer at the same time. Midbottle I could barely hear the waves. It sounded as though they were made out of wool. I left about four inches at the bottom of the bottle and since you can't really save it I poured it out onto the sand. When the bottle was empty I looked down and saw a black shape. I thought it was a cat or something at first. Out in L.A. there are a lot of skinny homeless cats roaming the beaches digging for fish and chasing mice into the water. Some mornings you wake up and they are on your doorstep, hot and coiled and chewing on rope and buds and insects.

I was staring at this black shape and then I saw another shape that was also black, and a third and a fourth. One of the shapes was curled around one of the legs of the life-guard's chair and I looked down at its markings more closely and saw that it was a skunk. All the black shapes were skunks. There must have been about fifty skunks on that beach, big ones and little ones. I waited up there until they had thinned out and then I very slowly climbed down off the chair and went over to my suitcase, which was lying in the sand, and when I looked out again I saw that the beach had ended and that there was nothing ahead but more water and that the radio towers weren't even attached to land. They were screwed to the deck of some big boat and the boat was moving across the waves in the snow and the fog and since I wasn't moving at all the towers were gaining ground on me. The whole time I had been using them as my compass point they had been moving aboard some enormous boat. They weren't even radio towers. I might as well have used a bird.

I had pretty much given up trying to find the information booth. I think Sidney had been thinking of another beach, another movie. The snow was coming down fairly thickly by then. I looked back at my footprints and they were deep and cold and wild. They were filling up with snow. I felt sorry for them. I felt sorry for everybody who had ever made footprints and then had them wiped out. The sand seemed to be made up entirely of footprints except for the parts the cold water rubbed flat. I walked a little while longer until I saw street-lights. I went up a slope of sanded pavement and then I cut through the middle of a wood fence. I was a little bit too smashed to leap the thing, plus I was carrying my two bags, and when I got onto the other side of the fence I found myself in a rotary of some kind. I think it was one of those places you go with a girl to kiss and watch the sun redden and die. You're kissing her but out of the corner of your eye you see the red sun collapsing and you kiss more weakly without realizing it. In the driveway of this rotary I saw a black VW and it had a Briar Hall sticker pasted across its back window. I wasn't imagining it, there really was one. In blue letters it said Briar Hall and then right beneath that was the school motto, which is in Latin and which has something to do with keeping the faith. Underneath the Briar sticker was an enormous dark red one that said Harvard in this curly, ludicrous script. That didn't surprise me in the slightest. As a matter of fact it was pretty typical. If you went to one school you usually went to the other. You weren't even supposed to think about it. It was supposed to be one fluid, economical gesture on your part across the Charles River. No one was inside the car and snow was piling up on the windshield and along the edges of the black rubber wipers and I considered writing something on the hood but I was pretty sure the letters would get buried. About fifty feet away from the rotary was a Dairy Queen, a square yellow stucco building connected to a miniature golf course. The Dairy Queen was open but the golf course was closed for the season. There was a sign on the gate that said See You in April. The little white barns and the pendulums were still in place but the greens were dark and covered with canvas.

There was a pay phone next to the Dairy Queen and I don't know why exactly but I suddenly had this impulse to call my sister out in L.A. If anybody knew where my aunt was hiding out it would probably be Lucy. Plus, when I get a little smashed I like calling people up. Sometimes I don't say anything, I just listen to them saying Hello? Hello? and I feel fond before I hang up but usually I end up saying something, having a conversation. I was feeling pretty nostalgic that night. Snow always makes me nostalgic, so does the water, especially the Atlantic. I guess the water is just melted snow, that it's all the same thing. It's only the Atlantic that does anything for me, though, the Pacific doesn't really stir up anything in me. It's colorful and vast and all but it's just not all that suggestive.

I went over to the pay phone and put in a quarter and dialed Lucy's number. I got a recording that said it would cost around five dollars to talk to L.A. for three minutes. It was the East Coast operator again and as she was repeating the message I said to her out loud, "Sure, I'm really carrying around five dollars in change." I hung up and called Lucy collect. The phone rang and I could hear the West Coast operator and it began to snow upwards and finally my sister answered. The operator asked whether she would accept the call and Lucy said she would.

"Boy, if you hadn't," I said, "I'd drive you out of this family."

Lucy sounded pretty happy to hear from me. "So what's going on?" she said after a minute. "Everything's all right?"

"All right where?"

"Has it all started?"

I was confused for a second. "Has what started?"

"Your school. The school part of it."

"Oh," I said. "No, I'm still waiting around. Getting oriented."

"What's Bob's friend like?"

I didn't know what Lucy was talking about. "What?" I said.

"Why don't we start this all over again. Hello? Sam? Everything okay?"

"Everything's under control," I said.

"I can barely hear you."

"Well, that's the U.K., Lucy," I said as jocularly as I could. "Everything barely works, it's all breaking down but we love it here."

"Right," my sister said. Then she said, "You didn't hear about my house, Sam. That's the big news. Actually, how could you have heard about it. Have you gotten my letter yet?"

I knew I would never get her letter. "No."

"Well, I mailed it on Monday. I'm staying at the Marmont. In town. The cool dispossessed people's hotel. I get all my calls forwarded in here."

I said, "Lucy, what happened to the house?"

"Oh." She sounded calm. "Well, it went down. I wrote you all about it. It buckled. It collapsed. There was a storm and some slides and one of the legs just did a pathetic curtsy forward. A curtsy motion and then the balcony fell down."

I said, "Jesus."

"This was all last week sometime. Around New Year's Day. It was a total mess. I was pretty lucky actually. The Nichols' house was knocked down completely. And I wasn't even at home at the time. So here I am spending a fortune with all these one-shot writers out of Albany and Amherst and Bard creative writing class, you know, hoping to make the big bucks. Hoping to cash in. But we leave each other alone."

"Is your house all gone?" I couldn't believe my sister's house wasn't there anymore.

"Pretty much. I wrote you all about it, Sam. It really doesn't matter all that much, you know. It really doesn't. I have some things with me. I mean, there's no such thing as home probably anyhow. It's always just the things you know. It's all the things you're familiar with. That's what you think of when you think of home, the things you know, that's all. In my letter I went on about it. How terrific the air smells now. There's this fantastic ashy smell all over the city. Do you remember the fires a couple of weeks ago? How we could see them? How utterly beautiful they were? That smell is very evocative. It makes you want something." She paused. "Don't ask me what but it's something. I got up the other day and I drove up to Trancas and I could smell it all up and down the PCH, just this essence of pure ash, that's all, everybody losing their lives and their houses and mailboxes getting torched and I found myself not caring, you know, my immediate concern was that the smell was reminding me of something so strong it made me want to laugh. It was crazy. It made me feel like a monster. Monster woman. Have you heard anything from Bob?"

"Not yet," I said.

"Well, he's fine. He called on my birthday and left a Happy Birthday Sweetie message. He said to call him back collect but please to remember the time difference, which he claims I never do. The thing is, I always do. It's just I can't believe anyone goes to bed that early."

I had completely forgotten. "Happy birthday," I said.

"I thought that was why you were calling."

"Well, it was one of the reasons," I said. I felt terrible.

"I'm thirty. A real thirty-year-old."

"Happy birthday," I said again. I thought if I kept saying it it would make up for the fact I had forgotten Lucy was turning thirty.

"Yeah, I get the message, Sam. I started smoking again. At this party somewhere on Coldwater some dumb guy gave. I got so depressed about turning thirty I said to someone, Excuse me, could I have a drag of that Camel and then ten minutes later I actually left the party to buy a pack. Then I came back and some oily guy from Brazil came over to me and said he'd take care of me for the rest of my life, you know, pay for everything, watch over me, so long as I stayed pretty for him. Those were his exact words. Stayed pretty for him. Can you believe someone actually said that to me? You know, I can look in the mirror and actually see my face starting to change? No one told me that."

"What?"

"Your face. It moves around. It looks different. But I guess when you're thirty you're supposed to have gotten so mature about things you don't complain. You don't even mention it to anybody."

"You're not so old, Lucy," I said.

"Yes, I am. On my birthday there was no one older than I was. No one in this state. Trust me. Oh, and you know something?"

I waited.

"I don't know why I was thinking of this the other day but I was. Out of the blue. I was having lunch and I suddenly thought of something I used to do to you when you were little. When you were about two. You know what I used to do to you, Sam? I used to trip you. Isn't that a terrible thing to admit?"

"What do you mean, trip me?"

"You know, trip you. Push you down. Sneak up behind you and push. So you'd cry."

"Lucy," I said, feeling a little desperate for some reason, "you don't have to tell me that. It's not so big a deal. I mean, I forgive you and everything. You didn't injure me or anything like that. I'm okay, you don't have to tell me this now."

"Wait," she said. "It gets better."

"I don't want to hear about it." For some reason I wanted to get off the phone. I didn't think Lucy was talking about the right things. If you had asked me what the right things were I wouldn't have been able to tell you but I just knew they weren't being addressed.

"You'd cry and then I'd console you. Isn't that sick? Isn't

that the sickest thing you've ever heard? That's why I'd push you down in the first place, so you'd cry and then I could console you."

"That was ages ago," I said. "Ages and ages."

"I know it was. Thirty years ago, right? Remind me, why don't you. But you're all right now, aren't you? You didn't hit your head or anything during one of those times I tripped you, did you?"

"I'm fine," I said. I found myself touching my head.

"All I've been doing is talking," she said. "I'm sorry. Tell me what's going on with you."

I said, "What's the name of Mom's sister?"

"Um, Ellis. Why, do you have amnesia?"

"I know her name is Ellis," I said. "I know that. What's her last name?"

"Why do you want to know?"

"I'm just curious. I couldn't think of it. Her name's been going through my head and I couldn't think of her last name."

"Her last name this month, you mean," Lucy said. "Well, just a second. Hold on. Hold your horses, bud." She went away for a minute. Across the country between us I could hear faint voices, busy signals, rings and then my sister got back on the phone. She gave me a last name. "Do you have her address?" She read that off too. "I didn't know you two were such good pals."

"Well, we're not exactly," I said. "I'm just trying to touch base with people. That's all I really want to do this year is touch base with people like that. It's my New Year's resolution. I figure I'll never get any mail unless I write people occasionally."

We said good-bye pretty soon after that. I told her I'd write her in care of the Marmont and she said, "The Marmont doesn't care," and I told myself to remember to write her in a week. Then I started worrying about the postmark and that Lucy would see the letter came from Provincetown. I began thinking I should have told her where I was. The snow was coming down crazily now, flakes flying upwards and sideways. The roads were very wet. I had written my aunt's last name on my wrist and I got her number from information and then I put in the same quarter, which had been sitting in the dish all that time, and I dialed and waited. A woman answered and I said, "This is Sam Grace."

There was a short pause. "Sam, Sam Grace, Sam Grace." Then my Aunt Ellis said, "Well, hello there, Sam Grace! I had you confused with your father for a second. Dear, how are you? Where are you, which is more relevant? Manhattan? Dear God, I haven't clapped eyes on you for how long now? Four years? Five years?"

My aunt has this emphatic way of speaking that I had forgotten all about. "I know," I said. "I know, it's been a while. I'm in Provincetown."

"My Provincetown? Tip of Cape Cod Provincetown? Not Providence, Rhode Island, you mean, which sounds so much like it?"

"No," I said. "I'm definitely in Provincetown."

"Where, though, sweetheart? Where in Provincetown? You're as vague as your wonderful father is."

I looked around me but I couldn't really see anything that I felt qualified as a landmark. "Well, there's a Dairy Queen near where I am. And a miniature golf course that looks pretty inactive. I think it's closed for a while, for the season. And I'm near some water."

"You poor baby," my aunt said. "Poor baby. Are you all alone?"

I told her I was and she said, "Are you staying with anybody? Friends?"

I said, "I'm staying in a phone booth."

"A phone booth? Do you even have an umbrella with you?"

"Listen," I said to her all of a sudden. "You know my mother?"

There was another silence. I thought, I probably could have phrased that better. A black Camaro passed and then it stopped in front of the Dairy Queen. It had orange flames painted on its sides. A woman was sitting in the front seat and a man with a brown beard was driving and in the back-seat I could see this huge lemon-colored dog with its nose sticking out the window, pointed and two-chambered like a rifle, breathing in the freezing air. Everybody on Cape Cod seemed to have a dog for company. The radio was on in the car and Casey Kasem was counting down the top ten songs in the country. He was on three. I could feel snow lying on my eyelids. The Diary Queen man shook his head and waved the Camaro away and then he slapped a board across the drive-in window.

My aunt said, "Sweetheart, of course I remember your wonderful, thoughtful, beautiful, funny mother. She was my sister too, don't forget. Of course I remember her. How could I ever forget my own sister?"

I said, "Did she ever tell you anything to tell me?"

"Tell me anything?"

"Like some sort of communication of some kind," I said. "I mean, if she told you and you forgot all this time that's all right. I wouldn't be mad at you or anything."

"Sweetheart, I'm afraid I'm not absolutely sure I know what you mean—"

I said, "A message. You know, a message. Sometimes people leave messages with third parties or else maybe they write them down inside old spiral notebooks and they stuff the notebooks in antique desks and then you discover the notebook during a custody battle for the desk. You know, the divorce is going amicably enough, the money part, but then it comes down to who gets what piece of furniture and there's yelling and during the yelling this notebook turns up. Or else people maybe tape something on a cassette late at night when they're feeling emotional or whatever and then they bury the cassette someplace private." I slowed down when she didn't say anything. "Does any of what I'm saying sound familiar? That kind of message, you know, someone telling you whatever, what to do. She wouldn't have had to blurt the thing out, she could have, say, come up quietly behind you and said Ellis, and you'd say what, and then she'd give you this message and tell you to pass it on to me at some point. And then you see, you could have forgotten it. You might have easily forgotten to tell me."

When I finished talking my aunt was quiet. Then she said, "I can't remember anything like that, Sam. Why, did someone tell you that my sister had done that? Is that why you're asking?"

"Nobody told me anything," I said.

"Sweetheart, I'm pretty sure there was nothing like that."

"Are you positive?"

"Baby, I'm as positive as I can be. I think maybe very possibly these things, these things that you're describing, happen only in the movies, the secret messages in desks, cassettes, all that. It sounds like a spy thing to me. It sounds like one of those James Bond spy movies. Is there maybe a movie you saw recently that had something like that in it maybe? I mean, it's certainly misleading of the movies, movies really shouldn't do that to us, mislead us in that way, our expectations of things, but the fact is they do and I think there's nothing we can really do about it frankly except keep our heads on, don't you think? Anyway, enough of this, where are you, Sam? Don't you want to come over for some hot cider with a little applejack in it or some hot tea? Do you like Celestial Seasonings? We could talk about all this and if you're in trouble in any way—"

"So she didn't say anything." I felt something turning off inside me, I don't know why, it was just the accumulation of everything. The lights turned off too in the Dairy Queen and in time the man behind the drive-in window would come out, lock up, rub the snow off the windows of his car and drive home. I thought about staying on Cape Cod for three more months and I realized that now I had actually arrived in Provincetown I wanted to leave. I wanted to get off the phone and leave that night. I wanted to leave a couple of hours ago. I wanted to go anywhere, be any place but in Provincetown. "She didn't say anything," I said again. Oh, I said to myself.

"Sweetheart, as I said I think you must have been weaned on some motion picture or another. These sorts of things, these spy things, just don't happen all that often outside the movies. Now tell me where you are, baby, find a street name, and I'll go warm up my old tomato soup–colored Falcon in the garage and I'll come over and scoop you up and bring you back here and we can stay up and have a great time talking. We can talk all night if you want. No one talks to anybody any more these days, have you noticed that too? Really talks, I mean, families especially. I haven't spoken to anyone in your family in it seems like a century, although of course I watch your sister whenever she's on and she's marvelous. I hope your father got the case of chocolate twigs I sent to New York for Christmas. Now, there's a Humphrey Bogart retrospective, Sam, right here in town this week at our little local theatre. The Nickelodeon. Isn't that a great old name for a movie theatre? Something for us film fan people to do with ourselves in the snow and the cold. Do you like Bogie at all, Sam? I remember my sister used to say he was the ugliest, most attractive man she'd ever laid eyes on. This is when we were growing up. She went to every single one of his movies, too, he made her swoon. There's one at nine-fifteen, *Dark* something with Bogie and Bette Davis and Betty Bacall, which I hear is awfully good—"

I laid the receiver down softly on the hook so she couldn't hear me doing it. All of a sudden I didn't feel like going through with anything I had planned. I think I just knew all of a sudden that the film she was talking about was *Dark Passage* and that my aunt probably thought it was *Dark Victory,* which is this Bette Davis film where Bette loses her eyesight at the end and can't even see well enough to plant bulbs even though she's dug all these perfect little vaults in the earth. Humphrey Bogart plays a stableboy in that one and he has about two lines or something. It hardly counted as a Humphrey Bogart movie. I knew *Dark Victory* wasn't the film they were showing. Lauren Bacall isn't even in *Dark Victory*, although I bet she wished she had been, but she is in *Dark Passage*, which is a terrible movie, just terrible. It wasn't my aunt's fault, a lot of people confused the two, thinking one was the other. It was just that I didn't want to be around when my aunt discovered her mistake and laughed and then said something like, "Oh, darn, well, you can see why I made the mix-up, Sam, blame it all on the word *dark*. But maybe this one is just as good." I would have to laugh too and tell her it didn't matter when the truth was it did matter and then I'd have to sit through *Dark Passage*, which as I told you is a real botch-up of a movie. There was nothing wrong with confusing the two movies, it's just that it had happened to me before with other people. They had all reacted the same way. There were only about three ways you could react when you found out you had mixed up *Dark Victory* and *Dark Passage* and none of the three were all that interesting. I'd heard all of them before. I just didn't feel like going through it all again, you know, hearing one of those three. I felt sorry that I'd hung up for about a minute but when the phone was back on the hook I got my quarter back and then I heard a second noise and I put my hand in the dish and discovered this strange bright dime I'd never seen before. I think it had come down with my quarter. It was hardly a fortune or anything but it gave me a good feeling. It left me with about four hundred dollars and thirty-five cents. It made me feel pretty good actually.

I left the phone booth and then I stood for a while by the side of the road and let myself get snowed on. There was something black on the side of my nose, some black speck. Whenever I looked straight ahead at something my eye

would see this black speck on the way out. The object would
have a black speck on its side. I tried rubbing my nose but
the speck wouldn't go away. I went back over to the phone
booth and tried using the metal as a mirror but it was
clouded up with steam, a blush almost, so I couldn't see anything. Then I put my quarter back in the slot and called information and got the number of the bus company. It was an
eight-hundred number and I called it. The guy I spoke to was
practically the most obtuse person in the world. I know it was
late and snowing and all but that's not really an excuse for
obtuseness. I told him I wanted to go to New York and he
started reading off all the bus times for New Haven until I
realized what he was doing and the only reason I realized it
was because he kept saying I could get this connecting bus
to Yale. Finally he got it straight that it was New York I
wanted. He told me there was a bus, the Night Rider it was
called, that left Provincetown at midnight and got into New
York at six twenty-six. I said, "You're positive it'll get in at
precisely six twenty-six because if it doesn't I'll have to shift
all my plans," and the guy said, "Yes, I'm sure." He was a
very literal guy. He told me to show up at the Provincetown
bus terminal an hour before the Night Rider left to buy my
ticket.

All the trains and buses out of New England have these idiotic American Revolutionary names, I've noticed: the Night
Rider, the Patriot, the Nathan Hale Limited, the Colonial, the
Minuteman, the Paul Revere and so forth. It makes you embarrassed to get aboard them. The thing is if you boycott
them no one notices and you don't get anywhere. They'll just
leave without you. New England is full of that stuff, though,
but they can't make you say those names. It's like when you
go into a restaurant and you have to order something like
"the Old King Cole Burger" but to order it you have to say
those words. When I see something like the "Old King Cole
Burger" I refuse to deal with it. I end up pointing at it or else
I act it out. Sometimes I think there's a general conspiracy

afoot to embarrass people in the country by making them say things like that, to see how far they'll go before they start shooting, especially people from New England. Bringing a New Englander close to the breaking point is an attractive thing, it really is.

* Chapter 7 *

I	T didn't happen the way it was supposed to. Nothing was happening the way it was supposed to. When I got to the Provincetown bus station the man at the ticket counter told me that the Night Rider had been canceled because of snow conditions on the road. I couldn't believe it. I just stood there and stared at the guy. He said it was snowing all over the Northeast and there had been seven accidents reported on Cape Cod already. It was only the third time, he said, that a bus from his company had been pulled off the road. I think he expected me to feel honored or something, you know, to be a part of bus history. I told the guy that was a brilliant transportation record and all but that I had to get back to New York that night.

"Have to get back to New York?" He was a middle-aged guy with a yellow pencil behind his ear and he brought the telephone around in front of him so it was resting on the desk. I think he must have been expecting a swell of media attention to surround the canceled bus. He was in kind of a jokey mood, too. Snow puts a lot of people in a jokey mood, I've noticed. "Why do you have to get back to New York? What's the big hurry? What's in New York? What does New York have that we don't have up here?"

I wasn't about to start in on that. "I just have to," I said. I don't know why I was feeling so fanatic about getting back to New York. I think mainly I just wanted to get away from the Cape. "It's sort of an emergency."

"I'm sorry," the man said. "It wasn't my decision. They decide all this road stuff in New York. That's where they make the decisions. We just carry them out on this end."

I said, pretty desperately, "Isn't there some route the bus could take that gets around the snow? A southerly route? Or planes? Or a train? Isn't there any other way to leave here?"

"Airport's shut down, I'm afraid. Last flight out was at seven, the eight o'clock was canceled. First bus we got is out of here four o'clock tomorrow afternoon." He hesitated. "What's the matter with it here? Lovers' quarrel? You been fighting with your girl? Another night here won't hurt you. Give you a chance to patch things up."

I said, "Another night in this joint will kill me." I kept glancing out the window into the parking lot. I was sure my aunt's grubby red Falcon was going to pull in any minute and that she would get out holding a gun and order me to go see *Dark Passage* with her.

The ticket man looked at me kindly. "Don't leave here without making up with Susie. You don't want to be leaving Cape Cod with bad feelings. You don't make up with Susie you'll always be associating Cape Cod with friction, bad times."

"You don't understand," I said and I went over to one of the chairs and sat down. There was nothing I could do if the bus wasn't running. I tried to think if there were other ways to get off the Cape. I wondered whether I could maybe hire a limousine or charter a ferry or something. I wished all of a sudden I had a guitar. I wished I were one of those people who dragged out a guitar and sang "Edelweiss" or "Hey, Look Me Over" when they were troubled. I looked around the waiting room. I was the only person there except for a couple of gay guys with brown beards and scarves who were

sitting next to each other scowling. About ten minutes later
the ticket guy said, "Hey" and all three of us, the two gay
guys and me, looked up. It was me he was gesturing to.

I went over to the counter. The man said in a very low
voice, "Okay, you, there's a bus leaving for New York tomorrow morning. One bus. It leaves here at five sharp. Five in
the morning. It's still dark out when the bus leaves. I
shouldn't even be telling you this. I should make you go back
to your girl, make you tell her you love her to pieces. But then
I say to myself that's another person's business. Five in the
morning, in back of the K-Mart across the street. It gets into
New York at about nine-thirty, ten."

"What line is it?" I whispered back.

"Not a line. It's an independent. It's a no-name."

"Who's on this bus?" I expected him to tell me it carried
drugs or dissidents.

"Elderly women," he said. "The Duse Society. That's the
Cape Cod theatre group. They bus them into the city for a
Friday night show and a Saturday matinee and some sort of
Italian buffet afterwards and they're bussed back here Saturday night. I'm pretty sure you could get a ride with them. My
mother's a member. Let me call my mother if she's not
asleep." He looked at me. "Sure you don't want to patch it up
with Susie first?"

I was getting pretty used to dealing with crazy people. I
tried to look as sad as I could. "I'm sure," I said. "I've had it
with that bitch."

The ticket guy had his mother on the phone and I think he
must have woken her up because he was talking very softly
and slowly, the way I guess he imagined people talk in
dreams. He called her "Ma." It made me think of Ma Barker.
I remembered Ma Barker had sons too. When the ticket guy
hung up he said to me, "It's fine. It's all clear. She'll be glad
for the company she says. They'll only let you aboard though
if you're a family member so you have to say you're her
nephew. Nephew or her grandson, whichever one you feel

comfortable with." He put out his hand. "I sure hope everything turns out all right in New York for you," he said.

I spent most of that night lying across four chairs that I'd
pushed together. The station seats were lemon-colored and
sponge, covered with a tough shiny plastic that was tearing
on the sides. I arranged the chairs in front of the radiator,
under a window. It was a fairly warm place to be but for some
reason when I lay down and spread my duffel out and put my
head on it I started shivering. After a while one of the gay
guys came over. He stood above me so I could see the bottom
of his beard, which was growing in red. "Here, take this," he
said. He was holding out a blanket. "We have an extra one.
You look pretty freezing."

I took the blanket and said thank you. I thought that was a
pretty nice thing for someone to do. I draped the blanket over
my chest and stomach. The guy went back over to where his
friend was sitting and said something and they both looked
over at me. I must have fallen asleep after that because when
I woke up again it was ten of four. The station was dark and I
could see the backs of chairs and dark doors and knobs. The
light in the bathroom was on and it pushed out an inch into
the room. Outside snow was still coming down, filing across
the outside lights. The ticket guy was gone and so were the
two gay guys. I looked to see if they had taken back their
blanket and they hadn't. I got up and went over to one of the
big vending machines and found change and got a pack of
cigarettes and a white cup of hot watery coffee. I sat back on
the radiator with the strange blanket hooded over my head
and smoked and watched it snow and felt the hot radiator air
push up the back of my shirt and blow the hairs on my neck.
The snowflakes were huge and eerie. Each one looked as
though it weighed about a pound and a half. The snow covered the ground and rose on the railings and the windshields
of the cars parked across the street. The steam from my coffee was making the paper on my cigarette damp. I could see
the K-Mart from where I was sitting and I stayed on the ra-

diator staring out at the snow and the advertisement for shovels in the K-Mart window until the bus arrived and it was time to leave.

That's how I ended up going back to New York, on this old theatre bus. The sides of the bus had a drawing of two theatrical masks on them, the pinched, smiling one for comedy and the downturned one for tragedy. Those masks really frighten the hell out of me for some reason. I thought it was a pretty great idea, though, you know, all these old women pulling out of Cape Cod in the dark in this weird painted-up bus. At the start of the trip the leader of the Duse Society, whose name was Mrs. Dennis, handed out two sets of tickets to everyone on the bus but me. The society was planning to go see two musicals, *Cats* and some new show about women and diets called *Tab!* which I thought sounded fairly awful. All the old women were pretty excited, you could tell, and none of them seemed in the least bit sleepy even though it was five in the morning. I sat next to the ticket guy's mother and she kept trying to give me her tickets, saying she'd rather shop than sit in some stuffy theatre, but I kept saying no. After a while I attempted to fall asleep but there was a stick or something lodged in one of the bus wheels and whenever the bus went over forty that stick started racing around and clacking. The wheel was right under my seat too, which really didn't help, so by the time we got into Port Authority I was exhausted. I also had this enormous bruise on my left leg from climbing out the window of the Provincetown bus station. The ticket guy had locked all the doors when he left for the night so there was no way out except through one of the ground-floor windows. First I threw my bags out onto the snow and then I put my upper body and one leg through but I slipped and the window slapped shut on my other leg, right below the knee. It stung like crazy. I didn't even want to see what it looked like.

In the terminal a lot of things were starting up for the day. Some guy was wheeling out a stainless-steel juice cart from a closet and setting up a tall cylinder that pummeled the hell out of oranges and another guy, a chocolate store owner, was pulling up the black metal sheet of diamonds that protected the front of his store. This incredibly well-dressed man who looked like your girlfriend's father or something was lying on the floor at the base of the down escalator so you had to step over his head if you wanted to get anyplace. The station smelled of piss and frying onions and smoke and I went over to a pay phone and tried calling my father. I was pretty scared to speak to him but I figured I had to do it at some point. I couldn't hang around New York for four months on four hundred and fifty dollars. There was no answer at his apartment so I tried it again and after ten rings I hung up. I considered calling my sister just to tell her where I was but it was about six-thirty in the morning out in L.A. and I didn't want to get her up so I just took my bags and wandered through Port Authority for a while. There were a couple of dark, sleepy-looking whores with blue on their lids standing around in front of a bookstore drinking coffee and waiting for it to get dark again and some dirty, good-looking black-haired kid who looked like a runaway was trying to bum menthol cigarettes off the cleaning crew. There are always runaways hanging around bus stations not taking buses. I'm not really sure why but runaways seem to adore buses and bus stations, it's a thing with them, that is when they're not hitch-hiking around the southern states, which is another thing they adore doing. One of the whores saw me looking at her and she did something snaky with her lips, formed some word and tried to make contact with her eyes but I wouldn't let my eyes do anything back. I kept them staring at the dirt streaks on the floor. It was pretty early for that kind of thing.

I got this idea that I should probably stow my bags until I was sure Bob would be at the apartment, you know, so I wouldn't have to lug them around town with me. On the second floor there was a wall of lockers, each about the size of a pet coffin, and I shoved my duffel and my suitcase inside one of them and put in fifty cents and turned the key. I unlaced

my sneaker lace and inched it through the hole at the head of
the key, then relaced my sneaker so that when I walked the
key walked along with me, shining like a half moon, and I
could see it whenever I looked down. I felt a lot lighter without my bags and to celebrate all this new lightness I went
into a pharmacy inside the station and bought a *New York
Times* and a pair of dark glasses with navy blue lenses that
cost me about sixty dollars. I figured I might as well spend all
the money I had left over from my trip, the money I would
have spent if I'd stayed on at the Cape. I bought Lucy an
ounce of perfume and for my father I bought one of those little weather radios that gives you the forecast twenty-four
hours a day. My father likes expensive gadgets like that, plus
I thought maybe he'd scream at me less if I gave him a present. Then I put on my dark glasses and tried to find my way
out of the station. They were terrific glasses. It was a very
good investment on my part. The lenses gave everyone in the
station dark blue skin and the shadows of teeth and they softened the sharp light outside on Fortieth Street. My nose has
this very small bump in it and these glasses fit in back of that
bump pretty perfectly.

On the way out of the station I passed by this woman who
was sitting at a flat white card table about ten feet inside the
station doors. She was pretty glamorous-looking in kind of a
cheap way. Everybody's always saying glamour is dead, glamour is dead, but I thought this woman had some, not that
much but some. She was wearing a gold-beaded bandanna
and a black leather tie and a madras jacket and black pants
and her legs were crossed. A hand-lettered sign was leaning
up against one of the legs of the card table and it read: Madame Judy, Past, Present, Future, Love, Work, Play.

I'm crazy for that occult stuff. In L.A. I used to go to this
woman named Katrina who would read my tea leaves and go
into these frenzies where she'd start speaking no language
you've ever heard. I love all that stuff. I asked the woman if
she was Madame Judy and she smiled and said, "Indeed I
am." She had all these sharp little white teeth in her mouth.

She must have had about a hundred of them, all the same size, in a row. She was pretty young too. I mean, you always have to admire someone that young doing what they want to be doing. I asked her how much she charged for a reading and she said fifteen dollars, more if I wanted my tarots read. She had a strange accent, Middle Eastern European Spanish, I think. It kept coming and going like a station you hear on the radio at night.

I sat down opposite her and Madame Judy told me I had to pay her first so I gave her three fives which she stuffed under her gold bandanna. She took a battered deck of cards out of a black metal box and sort of smeared them across the surface of the table. "Pick ten cards," she said. "Quickly. Hurry."

When I'd done that she turned the cards up and shut her eyes once very tightly. She opened them again. "Your wish will come true."

I said, "What wish?"

She arched her shoulders. "Your wish."

I told her I hadn't made a wish and that she hadn't asked me to make a wish and she didn't say anything for a minute. "That's not my fault," she said finally. "I see in the eight of hearts you plan a trip to New York City." She smiled. "The Big Apple, very vital. I see music, museums, movies, theatre. I see theatrical numbers that stop the show, you know? This is a vital center. But of course you're already in New York City, the Big Apple. Here you are at Judy's table so there's your trip already a fact of fate, already resolved." She seemed awfully pleased with her prescience or whatever. "See the power of Judy's cards," she said after a minute. "It's a gift you see." She fell silent and then she gathered up her cards. "Good luck to you."

"Could you maybe be a little more specific?" I said.

"No, I can't."

"Is this smoke maybe bothering you?" I was holding a cigarette in my hand. I thought it might be clouding her vision or something.

"I smoke myself. Bad habit, very dirty." She smiled sadly and started putting the cards back inside the black box. "Unless you have questions." She leaned down and straightened the sign. "Careful of my sign. You shake my sign and it falls and breaks you buy it. You buy me a new sign." She smiled again.

"Well, yes, I do have some questions." I was starting to get annoyed. "Of course I have questions. I have lots of questions. You haven't told me a damn thing so far. I mean, what my life's going to be like."

She said, "You don't want to know something like that. You don't. Makes you always live self-consciously. That's no good for anyone." She shook her head, violently. "I can't go answering so big a question as that."

"Well, try," I said. "Give it a shot."

She shut her eyes and then she opened them. "Fine," she said at last.

"What is?"

"Your life."

"Could you explain maybe a little?" I said. "Please? Maybe some specifics?"

"I told you, your life will be just fine." More than anything she sounded bored. She started shuffling and reshuffling the cards and then she cut the deck with one hand. That impressed me a little, the fact she could do that. Her hands were pretty immense and she held the deck against the hard sunken part of her hand and let half the deck drop into her palm. Her middle finger with its dark red nail pushed the fallen half over onto its side and then the cards she was still gripping between her fingers fell into place and the deck was cut. She rested the cut pack on the edge of the table and licked her lips.

"Can you see anything more in there for me?" I said. "In the cards or just in general?" I was trying to give her the benefit of the doubt, I really was.

She said, "The reading is over."

I stood up then. "You should be ashamed of yourself," I said. "You really should. Jesus Christ, that was a terrible reading. That wasn't even a real reading for God's sakes. That was the worst reading I've ever had from anybody."

"Oh, go fuck yourself," she said, not looking up.

I couldn't believe she had given me a reading like that and it had cost me fifteen dollars. I felt like kicking over her sign. I almost did actually but then I thought she was telling the truth and I would have to pay for it. In the end I just gave her card table a little shake, more a perturbation really, enough to make the lid of the black box fall shut. Madame Judy froze when I did that but she didn't even look up then, that was the worst part. She was totally ignoring me.

The encounter with Madame Judy put me in a pretty foul mood. When I got out to Fortieth Street I realized I was starving and I walked a couple of blocks north. I had about two hundred and fifty dollars left over in my wallet and I looked around for an expensive restaurant so I could blow it all at once but there didn't seem to be any in that part of town. Instead I went into a diner in the middle of the block called Tippy's Acropolis and sat down at a corner table overlooking Forty-third Street. Someone had just finished eating at my table and there were small white plates stacked on large plates and a tip of seventy-five cents in three quarters spilled beside a box of pink sugar packets. I stared out the window for a little while. An enormous truck was backing up onto Eighth Avenue and everyone was honking like crazy. In one corner of the street a man had his back to me and he was pissing into a doorway. Behind him a long stream of urine was rolling down the street. It was about twenty-five feet long and steaming in the cold. I couldn't get over that, the fact the guy had his back to me, you know, guarding his privacy like crazy, and this long tail was trailing him. On the corner of Forty-second Street this kid who looked like he was about a week old or something spread out a rug that looked Indian and turned on a long silver radio and prepared to dance.

Across the street a group of five or six Latin men were gathered around an old Plymouth Fury changing a tire. A fire set inside a garbage can kept their hands warm and it sent up clear thick vacillating fumes. The neon on all the marquees was lit and shaking in a listless way even though it was the morning and no one was thinking all that much about sex except maybe about sexual theory or something like that.

I really don't care for that kind of weather, I really don't. That kind of weather more often than not makes me pretty crazy. It was very cold inside Tippy's Acropolis. The door kept opening and these blasts of freezing air would come in and the glass windows would steam up and bead with moisture and all these sad-faced people on the counter stools would huddle inside their coats. Tippy's had an old space heater glowing in the corner but it didn't seem to be generating all that much heat. I started getting a little depressed sitting there actually. There were all these old thick pieces of yellow pie under globes of scratched-up plastic that looked as though they'd been born there, you know, that the plastic had served as a kind of incubator. The floors were dirty white and all over the walls there were pictures of that long-faced Greek woman singer, I can't remember her name, Nana something or other, the one who wears huge black glasses that look as though some kid charcoaled them on her. She was staring out at all the diners through her gigantic black frames even though she was probably a million miles away at the time on some beach in Athens or wherever sunbathing, trying to get her skin the same color as those glasses so she wouldn't look so jarring all the time. I think those frames are all wrong for her face, I really do. I'm surprised nobody has ever said anything to her about them all these years, you know, she's been around forever. I think a face like that needs some gold in it, or else nothing—just not those eighty-pound black barbells.

I waited around for someone to take my order but no one did. I tried to read the *Times* but it was too boring and after a while I put it under my chair. All these tall bald waiters were rushing all over the place mumbling to themselves and at one point they took the dirty plates and the tip away from my table but they didn't bother to replace them or give me a placement or a napkin or anything. Watching that man piss had sort of wrecked my appetite so I just sat there at the table for about half an hour in a stupor and then I got up and started walking toward the door. No one stopped me. I felt sure that the woman behind the cash register up front would at least look to see if I was leaving without paying my check but she was talking on the telephone. Right before I reached the door I turned around. I wanted to give the management one more chance to acknowledge me, you know, I wanted to accept their apologies but nobody noticed me leaving. I walked right out onto Eighth Avenue. No one noticed a thing.

Outside on the street I tried hailing a cab. The air was cold and there was all this purple pushing up into the sky and the clouds were small and flat. I stood there with my arm out for a while but all the cabs I saw were either off duty or pretending to be. I walked out a little ways into Eighth Avenue traffic and started waving my hand but then I noticed a lot of guys on the street were staring at me. I thought I must have been doing something effeminate as hell so I stopped waving and brought my hand up and over my head so it looked like an unbroken scratching motion. There were five little black kids on the other side of the street in front of a gay porno theatre and they were laughing like crazy. I don't know why but whenever I'm in New York little black kids always seem to be laughing at me. I think they're ridiculing something about the way I move or something. I can go away for the longest time and then when I get back to New York there they all are waiting for me. Sometimes they're even at the airport when I get off the plane. When I see them laughing I usually pretend to be chewing on something or looking for a place to spit or else I light up a cigarette or take a deep inhale of the one I'm already smoking and then blow out through the nose. I throw my match down as though it disgusts me. You make yourself look a lot less vulnerable that way, if you chew or send out smoke. You do anything that looks as though it hurts.

I started working my jaws up and down and then I jammed a couple of fingers into my mouth as though I were adjusting a piece of soft gum and after a while the kids stopped laughing at me but they wouldn't stop staring. I gave up trying to get a cab and started walking uptown. At Forty-seventh Street I went into a deli and bought some Cheez Doodles and tore them open with my side teeth and ate them as I walked. I had to stop pretending to chew in order to eat. I kept passing these old bombed-out, boarded-up theatres and I went by the street where my sister used to live but her building had gone co-op and they were turning the ground-floor apartments into a health club. At Columbus Circle, in front of the fountain, a guy in a black hat muttered sense, sense to me, which I knew was short for sensemilla but for some reason it didn't register with me when he said it. I guess I'd been away from New York too long. I thought he was saying sex, sex. I mean, it didn't really matter what he was talking about, sense, sex, senna, cells, sines, zones, zens, whatever, I would never buy anything I needed from one of those guys on the street, certainly nothing in bulk, you know, nothing in cartons. From Columbus Circle I walked over to Fifth Avenue and when I was in front of the Plaza Hotel I saw a group of mean-looking girls heading my way so I started chewing like crazy, almost as though I were struggling to get a word out, and I kept chewing until they had passed.

All the while I was walking up the sidewalk that runs parallel to Fifth I kept seeing all these blonde models, at least I pretty much assumed they were models. All of them were attractive as hell and quite a few of them wore glasses but you quickly did a subtraction in your mind so these girls' faces were the same as the faces of people with brilliant eyesight, except their pants and shirts were baggy and their features were small and sharp and perfect. I know that type of

girl fairly well, actually. They usually live in one of those incredibly ugly East Side buildings that have supermarkets or
banks or dry cleaners built into their ground floors. Those
buildings may be ugly but you sort of knew the parents of
these girls told them that safety was the greatest asset of an
apartment complex, or something. That was probably one of
the conditions of moving to New York and modeling in the
first place, that these girls had to move into a safe ugly building. Anyway, models only seem to come out after about nine
in the morning when they know everyone is at work and
can't bother them or yell things like Hey, Baby or Sweetheart, I Like It, I Like It. That's just about the only time you
see really good-looking people in New York, when everybody
is working or else really late at night dancing and drinking
and falling. They like to wait until the coast is clear and then
they come out and jog and bicycle and go to the movies and
the grocery store and the card shop, you know, boring things
like that.

    I kept tripping over pigeons as I made my way up Fifth Av-
enue. I'd be walking along and a couple of purple pigeons
would suddenly walk out in front of me and get to the curb
and then turn around and walk back. I can't stand pigeons,
especially the ones in New York, which are fat and vicious.
They hide under park benches and under the bumpers of
cars and surprise you as you walk by. Plus, they're so used to
living in a city that they refuse to fly anymore. I think there's
something pretty pathetic about that. What they do instead
of flying is start walking very quickly, never breaking into a
run, just speed-walking like people late at night who think
they're being followed. You could kick those pigeons and
they wouldn't leave earth. You could drop them off a sky-
scraper and they wouldn't fly, they would fall heavily and hit
the sidewalk and probably kill someone, they were that kind
of nonbird. I think they had forgotten how to fly actually. I
think that was the basic problem.

    I had to go to the bathroom pretty badly by then. I know a

lot of people would say, Go in Central Park, there are lots of bushes and so on, but I felt bad about doing that. Also, there are always so many people around you get embarrassed, at least I do, I shouldn't speak for everybody. I ended up going into the Frick Museum and paying the four bucks or however much it was and using the bathroom there. It was a pretty expensive way to handle the situation but it felt better than pissing in the park. The Frick had a nice bathroom too, not nice enough to necessitate having one of those strange attendants in there staring at your back or anything but nice enough, and warm. I tried calling my father again on the pay phone outside the bathroom but there was no answer. I had just hung up the phone when it rang again. The first thing I thought was that Bob had traced my number, that he knew I was at the Frick somehow and wanted to scream at me. I was all prepared to hear his voice when I picked up the phone on the third ring. It wasn't him. It was a soft male voice that sounded slightly out of breath and it asked to speak to Flora.

I thought that was a pretty strange name. I had never known anybody named that. I said, "There's no Flora here."

"Do you know when she'll be coming back?"

I was confused. "Well, never. There's no Flora period. This is a pay phone. This is a public phone. This is the Frick Collection," I added stupidly as though I were the head of Frick P. R. or something.

"Can I talk to you then?"

What was I going to say to the guy, No? I didn't know what to say. I was silent and then I said, "Sure."

"What's your name?" The voice sounded more out of breath than ever.

I said, "Sam."

"Sam, I'd like to suck—"

"No, you wouldn't," I said quickly, cutting him off. I held the receiver away from me. "No, you just wouldn't. I promise you. That's not what you want. You don't know what you want but that is not it. Happy New Year." I hung up. The guy was a pervert, I should have figured that out ages ago. Anybody who calls up a pay phone in a museum has got to be a pervert. The phone started ringing again but I backed away from it, shaking my head. I was still shaking my head when I got back onto the street. I circled back down to Sixty-fifth Street and went into Central Park right at the entrance to the zoo. In front of the monkey house I walked over an outline of a sleeping body that someone had drawn on the cobblestones in blue and white chalk. The arms and the hands were up close to the mouth and the legs were bent as though they were running away from something. There was a small puddle of rainwater over the mouth all filled with brown leaves and cigarette butts and ticket stubs and when I passed it I started shivering. It was about seventeen degrees out and all I had on were these grubby white socks with red bands around the top, you know, the kind campers and milers wear, and this ratty old pair of blue sweatpants and my coat and my sneakers. I was feeling pretty dizzy too. I think it was the combination of staying up most of the night and not eating anything except for the Cheez Doodles.

Just before I ducked under a footbridge I stopped because I felt like I was going to fall. I breathed in and out, deeply, for about five minutes. I noticed they were doing a lot of construction at the zoo, in fact they were doing a lot of construction all over the city. The city seemed to have come apart while I was out west and now they were occupied with the repairs. There was spiky scaffolding all over the place, gashes in the sidewalks, detours, lanterns and peanut-colored boards nailed up in front of the zoo cages. Some of the boards had murals of beaches and water and sky and fish on them so people walking by would think they were inside another season. The animal cages were empty. There was a stiff green board stationed in front of the polar bear's cage. It had a hole chopped out of it and I looked through it but there was nothing in the cage except for a couple of old drink straws and a sopping black denim jacket with wet sand on the sleeves and a crayon, I couldn't tell what color since all I could make out was the orange wrap. I had no idea what they'd done with the polar bear. When I was at Lane I remember reading some-place that it had attacked some old guy who'd been feeding it spoonfuls of hummus through the bars. The polar bear had just reached out and swiped this guy across the head and I remember somehow the guy got inside the cage with the bear and the bear stomped him to death inside the wading pool. Everybody found out later that the guy was some old drifter who was stoned on Thunderbird but even in cases like that people are always favored over white zoo bears. The guy didn't have any immediate family but then some uncle in Arizona suddenly came on the scene and demanded some ac-tion be taken against the bear. I don't know what happened after that, I don't really want to know.

My face was hot and my head was pounding and when I looked up I saw this brown elephant playing an accordion. The elephant was standing next to a brown bear who was playing a tambourine and a brown kangaroo with a couple of strange skinny flutes resting on its lip. Beside it was a brown penguin bearing down on a small drum and a brown goat with a horn and then far up, almost so you couldn't see it, a brown hippo with a violin wedged under its chin. All these animals stood in a ring on top of a dark gleaming gateway that led into the zoo and beneath them was a clock and the hands said seven-thirty, which was all wrong. I walked past the animals and under a bridge with green curling letters sprayed on its walls and I rounded a corner and all of a sud-den I saw this huge old dog standing on top of a pedestal of grey rock. It was a sled dog, a husky, and its coat was matted and green and its mouth was open and it had a kind of rough saddle rigged up on its back. It was just standing there star-ing in the direction of Fifth Avenue and the models and its tail was all curled up like a scorpion's and its soft cold tongue was out and its eyes were wide and dull. Behind it was an old black lamppost and a silvery wastepaper basket and bits of yellow grass on the tar and a bunch of ant-swamped pizza crusts and napkins. The inscription on the rock said that the dog's name was Balto and then underneath that it said in Latin, Endurance, Fidelity, Intelligence, just like something you'd see written on the gymnasium of some prep school or on a bookplate you'd never want to own. You can't get away from people trying to cram Latin down your throat.

I climbed up onto the rock and sat down on the dog's back. From where I was sitting I could see nurses in soft white stockings and down jackets walking carriages slumping with rich babies and people asleep on the hard muddy ground using their sneakers and soft laces for pillows and joggers running along the paths, running as though someone had told them all at once to scatter, and I could hear firetrucks and people yelling at each other on Fifth Avenue. I took off my sneakers and emptied out all the rocks and dust that were in the heels. There must have been about ten pounds of sand in there from the beach in Provincetown and after I'd emptied out each sneaker I climbed down off the saddle and lay down on my back across the rock so I was facing the dog's stomach. The rock was cold and hard but my hair warmed it up after a while and I actually started getting pretty relaxed.

I got so relaxed there I fell asleep. I guess I must have been a lot more tired than I let on to myself. It occurred to me later that maybe I was one of those people who fall asleep in the middle of things, like driving or shopping or eating. It's a verifiable medical condition, falling asleep like that, but I can't remember the name. It's a long name that's fun to say, that's all I know. Anyway, for a while I was convinced I had that sleep disease, whatever it's called, since I fell right asleep like that in public and under the stomach of a dog and I didn't wake up until it was almost four in the afternoon. When I woke up I didn't know where I was exactly. I felt as if I were trapped beneath the arch of a small green bridge somewhere in central France but then I realized where I was and my first thought was that I had to call up my father. I could smell pretzels burning, coals. I seemed to be the only person in the whole park. I mean, you're never totally alone in New York, there's always someone sleeping behind a rock that looks bare or else staring at you through your window but what I'm saying is that at that particular moment I couldn't see or hear anybody, just white birds and olive-skinned squirrels making furious tracks across the lawns and along the thin grey branches of the trees. Most of the squirrels had lost the full brush off their tails. Sometime during the winter I guess the brush had beaded up, frozen and then come away in jags, leaving grey-blue wire and maybe a bristle or two like the hair on an arrow.

I got out from under the sled dog and when I stood up I realized I was still wearing just my white socks but when I looked around for my sneakers they weren't there. I remembered putting them on the ground, not more than two feet away from the inscription, and they weren't there anymore. I climbed down off the rock and started combing the joggers' paths in my socks, stepping lightly so I wouldn't cut myself on all the yellow and green glass. I went back under the bridge to see if anybody had thrown them there but I couldn't find anything except for old wine bottles split into pieces and a wrench and some candy wrappers. About half a mile away I could see the Sheep's Meadow, covered with white birds. It's this huge patch of green lawn that used to hold sheep, at least that's what they say, back when New York was someone's farm and there were weathervanes and wheat fields all over the place. If you squint you can imagine the birds are small sheep but that's stretching it a little. If you've lost your sneakers you can imagine the white birds are a flock of Keds or something but that's stretching it too so I concentrated on sifting through the dirt and the bushes on the hill that ran up the side of the bridge. After thirty minutes or so I gave up and went back over to the dog. I couldn't find my sneakers anywhere. The only thing I could think of was that someone had stolen them while I was sleeping and then I reached for my wallet and I nearly had a seizure because my wallet wasn't in my coat pocket where I'd left it either. I looked to see whether it had fallen onto the grass behind the rock but it was gone too. Someone had obviously wandered over and seen me sleeping and reached into my pocket and taken my wallet, two hundred bucks or however much I had left over and my driver's license and a bunch of sentimental things I kept for various reasons including these pictures of people, and then they had said, Oh, sneakers too, and gone and taken my sneakers. I thought the whole thing was pretty low. The only money they left me with was a dollar and thirty-eight cents, which had slid out the back pocket of my sweatpants while I slept and which was now lying on top of the rock. I gathered it up and when I went back over to the bridge once more to look for my sneakers I saw that the brown animals were twirling around now in a slow wordless circle and the clock said twelve forty-five, which was still wrong. I sat down at the end of one of the benches and then I saw this Hispanic couple making out in the bushes about fifteen feet behind me. The guy was standing up and so was the girl and she had her legs wrapped around his waist and her long arms around his neck and I think his fly may have been down and when the guy saw me he started to laugh quietly and the girl whipped her head around and the look she gave me had so much hatred in it that I got off the bench pretty quickly and went back over to the dog.

One of my problems was that no one I know goes around New York in their socks. You just don't. You can't get anywhere. I saw this immigrant guy in a dirty white apron pushing a shiny cart underneath the bridge and I realized all of a sudden I was ravenous. The guy was selling pretzels and Cokes and hot dogs and all this thin grey smoke rose up from his charcoal fire. Everything about the guy looked illegal as hell. I think he was probably in this country illegally and you just knew he had about a zillion children he'd left behind in some country ending -ivia or -izia. I stared at him as he pushed his cart up the hill toward Seventy-second Street. Even though I was starving I couldn't very well go over to the guy and get something to eat because then I'd have to go past the Hispanic couple with their legs mashed around each other and I didn't have shoes on and I didn't even have any money in the first place. All I had was that dollar and thirty-eight cents. I could smell hot dogs on the grill and even though I really can't stand hot dogs they smelled that moment like the best things in the world. I kept hoping the illegal guy would come over and offer me some free food, you know, that I would turn out to be his millionth customer or something and be entitled to a five-minute raid on his cart but I just watched as he wheeled it uphill and then he turned onto Fifth Avenue and I couldn't see him anymore.

I stayed on that rock for another half-hour trying to decide what to do with myself next. I decided the best thing would be for me to go to my father's apartment even if he wasn't at home. I still had the keys he'd given me on the way out to the airport and unless he'd had all the locks changed I thought I could probably let myself in without any trouble. It was also getting pretty dark inside the park and I really didn't want to be wandering around New York at night in just my white socks, if you know what I mean. I walked up the hill on the sides of my feet until I reached the road that runs in a loop shape through Central Park. Ahead of me was a stretch of sidewalk that was all potholes and bottle glass and beer tabs so I took off my jacket and wadded it up into this little ball and threw it out a couple of feet in front of me. When I'd done that I sort of leapt onto it and then I lifted it out from under my feet and tossed it out again and leapt on it again. That way my feet barely touched the pavement at all. As soon as I got past the ratty stretch of pavement I put my coat back on and walked along the grass on the side of the road for about half a mile. There was smoke in the air, and black birds. The birds were flying in a formation that looked like tonsils. I went past the boat pond and past a woman who was walking about fifteen dogs at the same time. Each dog was on a different length of rope and each was a different breed and this woman was stomping along in yellow boots behind them and the dogs were dividing up and taking sides and trying to confuse the hell out of this woman. She kept yelling at them but they refused to look at her.

At Eighty-sixth Street I saw this huge guy standing in the baseball field under a tree. He was wearing a red T-shirt and playing a black clarinet and this old yellow-and-black coffee can was sitting in front of him and there were all these coins and crushed bills at the bottom that you sort of knew he had put there himself so you would think that right before you came along a huge crowd had broken up and this guy had been the toast of New York or something but that you'd missed all the excitement. The only song the guy seemed to know was "My Favorite Things" from *The Sound of Music*. He must have played it about five times in a row. I can't stand that song. I can't stand those kids, actually, is who I can't stand. Out in L.A. they have this TV show called "Where Are They Now?" and I remember once they had on all the kids who played the Von Trapp children in *The Sound of Music*. All of them had grown up to be insurance salesmen or dental assistants or something, the women had a million kids and the guys said they kept physically active and played with their daughters, Kimberly. All of them had these daughters named Kimberly. Only a couple of them were still actors. None of them had grown up to be what you wanted them to be. None of them lived anywhere near the Alps. All of them looked like old children.

After a while I started feeling guilty just standing there listening to the guy play, even if he was playing a song I couldn't stand, so I dug into my pocket and dropped all my change, thirty-eight cents, into the can. I would have given the guy more if I had had it. If my wallet hadn't been ripped off I think I probably would have gone on giving out large sums of money to undeserving people all day long, until I ran out. Sometimes when I see musicians on the street I have this fantasy of going up to them and giving them five hundred dollars or something and telling them to please stop playing and leave people alone, you know, to try and retire them on the spot. When I dropped the change into the can the guy didn't stop playing, he just nodded his head and finished the song and then he took the clarinet out from between his lips. The reed was all chewed up and glistening. "Now," he said. His voice was very deep. "What would you like to hear for that kind of capital?"

I thought about it and I came up with "New York, New York." That's another song I can't stand but I wasn't feeling all that imaginative at that point. The guy said he didn't know the song and would I sing some of it for him but I wasn't about to sing anything in front of someone I'd never met. I hummed the chorus and after a minute the guy licked his reed and played what I'd just hummed. Then he violently broke back into "My Favorite Things." I think he had missed playing it, actually. I had a feeling maybe it cheered him up, you know, the raindrops and the little kittens and the kettles, blah, blah, blah. You get yourself consoled however you're able to maybe.

I kept edging my way along the grass until I reached hard mud on the bridle path. I stepped lightly over the frozen hoofprints. There were tire marks in the dirt and the cold had frozen them and the treads were flecked with pieces of old snow. There was ice and dirt and garbage inside the hoofprints. I climbed the steps up to the reservoir. My left foot was starting to sting like crazy. A couple of hundred yards back I had stepped on an old red jump-rope grip that was lying coiled in the high grass around the boat pond and this long slim splinter had gone straight up through my sock and into my heel. The jogging path along the reservoir crunched under my socks. I was so cold I couldn't feel my toes anymore. There was a water fountain in front of the pump house. I tried to drink from it, but it wasn't working. Just then this bum, this really handsome young guy, came out from behind one of the benches. He stood in back of me while I was bent over and I could feel his eyes on me. He was holding an old blue coffee cup with a picture of the Parthenon on it. I moved away from the fountain because I felt bad that he would think I was keeping water from him, a bum with a coffee cup with the Parthenon on it. Seeing the Parthenon reminded me of my own laziness. I remembered not being able to answer the Parthenon questions that were asked on an architecture exam I took at Lane. I don't want to go into the whole thing but I assumed wrongly on this test that they'd concentrate on the second half of the semester, the more modern buildings, and leave the old ones alone, but they didn't. Practically the entire exam had to do with the Parthenon. I watched the bum fill up his cup with nothing. Even though he was handsome and young and bearded and all I still felt pretty bad for him.

I walked along the jogger's path for about sixty yards or so. At the Fifth Avenue entrance to the park, at about Ninetieth Street, a rat suddenly ran out from the rocks along the bank of the grey water and started pacing me. As I walked it walked along with me and then I paused and it ran on, traveling over the dark sloping rocks light as a dancer. I thought, if I ever get married and have a daughter that's how I'd want her to move: light, airy as all hell, like a kid in a nursery rhyme or a rat. Finally the rat pushed its head between two long stones and its body followed and I didn't see it again. Across the water I could see a row of buildings on Central Park West. New York looked pretty old that day, the buildings looked shabby and they made me think of old brown cardboard boxes. The trees around the reservoir had lost their leaves and their buds and most of their best branches. The trunks looked thinner and there seemed to be more of them. The light leftover branches filled the air like smoke.

Farther down I could see the brown-and-green gambrels of
the Dakota. A lot of the buildings to the south had their high
floors covered with fog. Parts of the reservoir were frozen
over but there were crooked breaks in the ice and red tin
signs nailed to the wire that said *Veneno de Rata* and No
Dogs Allowed. Even though the water was reservoir water it
was acting just like real water out of an ocean. The air blew
it, made it slap the reeds, and at the north end there were
whitecaps and hundreds of loose feathers, long grey-and-
white pins shed by ducks and gulls, washing up against the
rocks. Hundreds more were trapped under the ice in
bunches. There were graffiti on the trees, white lines and
crosses and names of girls you'd probably never get to know.
Even if you met one of those girls you'd probably never know
it was the same one and you wouldn't say anything anyway if
you suspected it. I don't think you're really meant to interact
with people whose names are sprayed on trees and rocks. I
think you're just supposed to note them or something. I was
about to cross over to Fifth Avenue when I saw what looked
like an animal thrashing around in the water and I stopped
and squinted. At the same time it began to rain and the frozen dirt under my socks started to speck. I put the perfume
and the weather box underneath one of the flaps of my coat
and as I stared out through the dark wire fence I saw that it
was a large squirrel.

That old squirrel was struggling like mad. It was large and
reddish and I guess it had been walking along the ice and it
had slipped and fallen into the water. It was trying to get a
decent hold on the border of the ice but the ice was moldy
and it kept slipping back into the water. I stared out at that
squirrel for ages. The trees around me were turning dark in
the rain and they were creaking. I got kind of mesmerized
watching that squirrel. I got so mesmerized I forgot I
couldn't feel my feet and my ankles anymore. I had my fingers squeezed around the wire and I made myself flat against
the fence and watched this big squirrel rise and then fall

back. It looked as though it was having a fistfight with itself.
There was this strange little grey bird sitting on the rim of
the fence watching too, just about as mesmerized as I was,
and then it flew away and I took off my dark glasses to wipe
them and when I did I realized the squirrel had a much
lighter coat than I had thought. After a couple of minutes it
sank down into the reservoir water and I could see rain needles stinging down over the spot where it had gone down. It
seemed as though the rain was packing the spot so the squirrel would have a difficult time coming up again, and it didn't.
I stared at that point in the reservoir where it had sunk and
told myself I would remember that exact place for as long as I
lived. I turned around then because a jogger was going past
me, sweating off beer, and I watched the jogger's ass until it
rounded the corner and when I looked back at the reservoir I
couldn't remember the spot anymore. All the water looked
the same. I knew the general area where the squirrel had
drowned but I couldn't be all that specific about it. It could
have been six or seven places actually. Clear drops dangled
from the wire and a couple of them went down my face. The
rain had started to hurt and even though it was the middle of
winter and cold the reservoir started releasing some of its
smells, leather, moss, salt and mud and the beer lingering off
the runner and the smell was so bad I crossed back over to
the bridle path and walked along in the stiff, empty hoofprints of a horse for a while until it broke into a gallop and I
couldn't keep up any longer. I went past an old playground
on my right. There were five rusted swings hanging from a
bar and a jungle gym and a guy was sitting at the bottom of
the slide with his head tipped back and his eyes staring. For a
minute I thought the guy was dead but as I went past the
gate he looked at me and a minute later he waved. I was so
surprised I waved back. I had a feeling that the only reason
he was acting friendly was because I was wet and shivering
and my hair was in my eyes and I looked like a disaster, not
because I was likable or anything, if you know what I mean.

Other guys are sometimes pretty strange that way. They like you and act decent to you when you're wet or bloody or wounded but when you dry off they won't even talk to you.

As soon as I got onto Fifth Avenue and started walking south it started to snow. By that time my clothes and my socks were completely soaked through and the brown paper bag which held Lucy's perfume and my father's weather box was starting to separate at the bottom. I turned on the weather box just to see how accurate it was but all I got was static. Thinking about my socks made me think of my sneakers and I remembered for the first time that the key to the Port Authority locker was hooked around my shoelace, which meant I wouldn't be able to get my bags out of storage. The thought of that made me so depressed I stopped walking and just stood there on the sidewalk for a long while before going on. It was all right walking in socks along Fifth Avenue because the doormen kept the sidewalks pretty clean. Cars were parked along the side of the street and brown-and-yellow buds and needles stuck to the moist hoods and the rain made all the paint jobs look like new. At Eighty-fifth Street I went inside a phone booth on the corner and dialed my father's number again. Even though I could see his building from where I was standing, the grey branches of the old tree on his terrace, I had to call collect since I didn't have any more change. It was pretty embarrassing to have to call collect when I was only a block away. I guess I just wanted to know if Bob would be there when I went up, so I could be prepared. There was still no answer. I have to admit that made me feel a little relieved. I hung up and crossed the street in front of the Metropolitan Museum and went under my father's dark green awning. There was snow caught in the bushes on either side of the two heavy front doors, an inch of it on top of the air conditioner belonging to the ground floor apartment. A little Spanish doorman I'd never seen before opened up one of the doors. "Yes, sir?" he said.

The guy sounded fairly rude. I suppose he had every right

to talk to me like that but still it annoyed me just a little bit. They're snobbish as hell in my father's building to begin with and when they don't know you they can make you feel incredibly unwanted. My skin was red and soaked and my head hurt and the splinter was pushing through my heel into my heart almost and all I wanted to do was get upstairs and under the shower. The doorman, whose nametag said Dario, was staring at my wet clothes, especially my socks. I moved past him. "My father lives here."

"What's the name, please, sir?"

I took this incredibly wet bang out of my eye. "C. The penthouse. Robert Grace."

"And your name, please, sir?"

"El Lobo," I said. "El Lobo de la Noche." I don't know why I said that, just to be an asshole I guess. I was just getting irritated at having to stand there in my father's lobby, that was all. While Dario went over to the house phone and started dialing I pushed my way over to the mailboxes. "He's not up there," I said. "Save yourself the trouble. I just called."

Dario had the phone pressed against his ear and he kept looking down at my socks in this incredibly disdainful way. Boy, if you ever want to make someone feel like a jerk just look down at his or her feet. It's effective as hell. It makes you feel as though your entire foundation is faulty. I could tell that Dario didn't want me to mess up his lobby with my socks. I probably forgot to mention that the lobby of my father's building is set up just like someone's living room. It's ornate as hell, all this old dark muted furniture and chandeliers and sconces and a pile of *Architectural Digests* on a chest that have been around for so long they're probably collector's items by now. At the entrance, opposite the elevators, there's this big fake fireplace where an orange-and-yellow heatless fire flickers like crazy all year round, even during the summer. The whole living room looks so well preserved you feel like tossing a couple of grenades at it.

"I just called," I said again. "It's empty."

Dario put the phone back on the cradle. "Does Mr. Grace expect you?"

"Yes." That wasn't really a lie. My father expected me at some point.

"You said the penthouse, right? The Penthouse C, right? There's no one answering now in the penthouse. You come back later."

"I just told you," I said. "It's twice I told you. He's not up there. I have keys," and then I began walking toward the elevators but Dario called out for me to stop. "I can't let you go any further," he said.

I shrugged and kept on walking.

"Don't go any more," he said. "I call the police."

"Look, Dario," I said, turning around to face him. "I live here. My father lives here. I can tell you who lives in practically every apartment here." I started listing off everybody I could think of who owned an apartment in the building. I began with the Thorntons and I went on to the Thomases, the Williams, the Thornes, Mrs. Henry, the Crows, the Jennings and the Hales. After about fifteen names I stopped. I felt like some kind of informer. "All right?" I said. I started walking toward the elevators again but before I could get very far Dario was blocking my way. "I'm sorry," he said. "I can't let you go up there."

I started stuttering. That always happens to me when I get agitated. I tried to say, "I'm his son," but I couldn't get past the ess so it came out, "I'm his-s-s-s."

Dario spread his hands, which were small and square and red. "I'm Mr.'s doorman."

I tried going more slowly. That's supposed to help you if you feel like stuttering, that and taking long breaths of air. I said, "I have a fucking key. It's not as though I'm going to go up there and trash the place. I just want to take a shower. I want to eat something. I want to get my clothes. I have clothes up there. I want to get my clothes and eat something." It happened again. I couldn't get past the ess in "something" so it sounded as though I said, "I want to get my clothes and eats." It made sense and all but *eats* isn't a word I ever use for food. You'd never hear me say, "Hey, good eats" or something idiotic and ingratiating like that after a meal. I don't know why I was worried that Dario would think I used the word *eats* a lot, you know, casually, but I was. It didn't really matter all that much. My forehead was sweating by then and I had chills along my spine and I couldn't tell the rain from my own sweat. Dario shook his head. "Please leave the building, sir," he said. "Please don't make this a complicated thing for me."

When I didn't move he crossed back over to his little table where the telephone was sitting. The guy had an entire telecommunications center over there practically. I didn't pay much attention to him, I just started walking again and when my back was turned he came up behind me fast and hit me across the shoulders. At the last second I heard him but I didn't turn in time and when he hit me I went forward but I managed to keep my balance. It didn't hurt that much, I was just surprised. Then one of the elevator doors slid open and Dario said something to the guy who was standing there and this guy, who was pretty well built and had white eyebrows and all this blond-white Princeton University hair, sprang out of the elevator and the next thing I knew he had me in a headlock. I mean, I was standing around wondering why Dario had hit me and all of a sudden this guy from Princeton had his forearm wrapped around my throat. My face was pressed up against the gold freezing buttons of his uniform and I couldn't swallow since my Adam's apple was caught under his watch strap and it couldn't lift. Lucy's perfume fell from beneath my coat and the bottle smashed on the floor and the perfume started soaking up in the dark red rug. The weather radio fell too and tripped on. I heard static and then something about the snow. I could smell the perspiration on Princeton's skin and the gold-red hair on his arm was touching my teeth. My socks skidded into the perfume. I was struggling like crazy by then but the guy was strong as hell, probably from rowing for the Princeton crew on that little sham lake they had built out there for all the assholes, and then I saw that Dario had a blade in his hand. I guess the sight of a blade excited Princeton because all of a sudden he decided that having me in a headlock wasn't forceful enough or something. He kind of worked me over to the fireplace and started banging my forehead off the edge of the mantle.

I can't remember what happened next. Dario was on the telephone and the edge of the mantle was hard and sharp and I kept yelling for Princeton to cut it out. I remembered the word for "stop" in Spanish, which is *basta,* so I shouted *Basta, basta* at him a couple of times but he kept whacking my head against the edge of that mantle so rhythmically I wondered if he were doing it in time to a song in his head. Dario came back over and he was passing his knife back and forth from palm to palm as though it were very hot. Out the corner of one eye I remember seeing snow coming down lightly and the sky slightly burnished-looking and then as my head butted dully again into the wood I saw the flames slithering in the fireplace and my scalp felt very warm and wet as though after all these years the fire was finally giving off some real heat. I remember looking at the mantle and seeing that my head was taking paint off it, that my head was restoring it to its original red coat, and then Princeton stopped banging me and there was a police car in front of the building with its siren going like mad and its light twisting and a white ambulance pulled up behind it and I must have blacked out.

What I guess happened is that someone carried me out into the ambulance. I woke up and I was lying on a long white sectioned table that felt hard and soft at the same time. A black guy wearing a white shirt and a bright green baseball cap was leaning over me and I think he was humming "Lullaby of Birdland." I remember screaming something about revenge. I think I must have been thinking of some movie I'd seen or something. The cop was looking at me with real sorrow in his eyes and he said something like "Good-looking boy" and then he said, to no one in particular, "Saturday night, *que lástima,* right?" I think it was about the only Spanish expression he knew because he kept saying it to Dario and then Dario would shrug and say it back.

As the ambulance waited on the curb with me in it I remember a couple of interesting things. One was seeing a boy and a girl standing at the corner of Eighty-first and Fifth. It was pretty obvious they were boyfriend and girlfriend. They were waiting to cross the street in the snow and whenever a car would drive past the girl would take a couple of steps toward it and then all of a sudden she'd go limp and fall backwards into the arms of the boy. He was always fast enough to catch her, too. He had these very honed reflexes. Everytime she'd fall back toward him his arms would slip right up around her middle, under her breasts, so you sort of knew they were sleeping together since she didn't act startled or offended or anything. What she would do was look down at her breasts and his hands as if to say, "Oh, are these mine?" and then she would open up her mouth just like Balto the sled dog and start laughing. She was really attractive, too, that girl, and the guy was good-looking, plus he had those reflexes. They were the perfect couple, just about. She kept falling, it was her job to fall, and the guy was always there to grab her. Both of them were getting pretty snowed-on and even when the light said Walk they stayed where they were. Then I saw this old woman who lives in my father's building and who had just come back from walking her dog. The dog was a collie and it was enormous. Its fur looked as though it were in bloom. The woman was holding the collie by the collar and even though the collie didn't give a damn about whether it was wet or dry Dario was holding his black umbrella out over the dog's head. I remember thinking that not only did that dog look a hell of a lot like Lassie—all collies

look like Lassie I guess to some extent—but that it actually
was Lassie and that she'd grab me up in her jaws and take
me to where there were a lot of lakes, like Scotland. I looked
back at the boyfriend and girlfriend and they had had about
three opportunities to cross the street by then and they still
hadn't done it. They really looked like nice people. You knew
she was a graphic artist or something and that she probably
wore all these great old white smocks at home and that he
was a yacht broker but he also had a fairly generous trust
fund and that they went to inns on the weekends. I started
imagining what those two would be like to have as friends
but then I heard a siren and I realized it was coming from the
inside of the ambulance. The girl put her hands over her
ears, which made me hate her, so did the boy, to imitate her,
then both of them stared at the ambulance and the girl stood
on her toes. You knew she wanted to see a little blood. I hated
both of them. I hated the fact they both wanted to see blood
and that I was the blood. That siren put a huge wedge in our
friendship. Behind them the red Don't Walk sign was flashing about a hundred times and I knew it would keep flashing
like that, as though it were rigged up to a person's heart, all
night long, even when there wasn't any traffic and the streets
rose up with snow it would still keep up that pointless old
gesture of telling you when to walk and when to keep still.

∗ Chapter 8 ∗

T HE next thing I remember I was in a small, yellow-walled room with a couple of other people I had never seen before in my life. There was this big black woman sitting in the chair next to me and across from us was a very thin, grey-skinned guy who was saying something in a language I didn't really recognize. He would start talking low and then his voice would get progressively louder so in the end he was practically screaming and then he'd bring his voice back down to a whisper. I asked him whether he would please keep his voice down but the guy acted as though he hadn't heard me. Then the woman next to me told him to shut his goddamn mouth or she'd slap it shut. After that he was quiet. Five minutes later the guy asked me if I had a cigarette I could spare. I said no. He pointed to the pack that was sticking out of my jacket pocket. "What are those?"

"Those are the boy's own cigarettes," the black woman told him in a sharp voice. "That's what those are." She pointed at me though she really didn't have to since I was sitting right there. "You understand that? I don't know what tongue you're getting around in but I hope English is your second because I'm saying to you now if you don't mind your

299

voice and your pleading I'm going to push you down onto this floor.''

I had a bandage around my forehead, tightly wrapped and taped in the back. I could feel the short rough strips when I touched the back of my head, four of them in all and a hard flimsy brooch. Down the hall I could hear someone yelling something about vegetarian menus and I heard a radio. The deejay said, You're tuned to one hundred point seven and it's the Million-Dollar Weekend. The seventeenth caller, he said, would get two free tickets to see Rush or Foreigner or Journey, you know, one of those groups you can never tell apart, and the black woman leaned over to me. "Hold on to your cigarettes. They fly off like birds around here. Magic. It's the magic of flight. If you've never seen cigarettes fly off it's an awesome thing. They have legs and they have wings, they lift off under their own sway and before you know it the nest is empty.''

I asked her where I was. "Sandstone,'' she said. Then she smiled. "You don't remember it?''

When she said that I have to admit I was pretty shocked. In case you've never heard of it Sandstone is a hospital on the West Side, about as far west as you can get actually and still be in Manhattan. It looks out onto the Hudson River and it's named after this guy Alfred Sandstone who was some sort of robber baron in the late eighteen-hundreds. He was always going around having breakdowns so he built his own hospital. The reason I knew all that was because my father went out for a little while with his great-great-granddaughter Pamela, who was about half Bob's age and who dressed in a black leather zoot suit half the year. It would be a hundred degrees out and Pamela would come over and moan about the heat and you'd want to scream, "Well, take off all that fucking leather, you lunatic,'' but you never did because Pamela was one of those people who dissolved easily. You used to read about her all the time in the social columns donating checks to this or that group or hosting dinner-dances with Mambo themes and she was always being described as "wispy" or "gaminelike." My father had a pretty long gamine period a couple of years ago. Every time you'd see him he'd have some consumptive type on his arm, someone whose features had all shrunken away—I mean, even I looked robust compared to some of those women. Anyway, Sandstone was a fairly well known place. A lot of famous people went there suffering from nervous exhaustion, whatever that is. Whatever it is a lot of people get it. People are getting it all the time actually. You try and picture someone with it but the two words cancel each other out. I think nervous exhaustion can cover a lot of things actually.

"You were yelling your head off earlier," the woman said to me. "What was the big deal? I said to myself, we have a live one, finally a live one. Strong too. Lashing out at the doctor, oh, baby, it was beautiful. I'm Anne, by the way." She put out her hand.

I couldn't remember lashing out at anybody. I had no recollection of anything except the ambulance in front of my father's building. They must have shot me up with something, that was the only thing I could think of. I shook hands with Anne. She had a big warm palm. The grey-skinned guy opposite us started sighing very loudly.

"Will you just quit it please?" Anne said to him. She looked at me. "Never been here before? A place like this before?"

"No, never," I said. My head was rocking inside.

"You were bleeding. And shivering. It kept coming through the bandage. They kept changing the bandage and it would come on through again, charge, and they would have to take that one off and put on another. I tried giving you my sweater but they told me they could manage themselves. Sons of bitches all of them. What's your name?"

I told her. "If I were you," she said after a minute, "and I'm not you, I'd keep my mouth quiet. You can tell me to shut up now sure but otherwise I'd keep silent. You were saying some things over there I certainly wouldn't say if I had my very own best interests in mind."

I couldn't remember any of that earlier. I felt mystified.

"Oh, sweetheart," she said sadly, "you can't see too many things at the same time for it makes you crazy, so crazy. By one time I mean between two blinks of your eyes. You're walking along and you see a man with a baby girl on his shoulder, balanced that is. You see there the looks of those two. You see the particular, that the baby is bald, that the man has a big chin. You see the general things. That's that they're specific people. That they're human. That they're here to carry on a race. The baby's got pebbles sticking to her heel, so where'd they come from? From a driveway sure, but it's also the top of the earth sticking to that baby's foot and the earth is just a planet whizzing along among the other planets in the middle of a big black sky you can't even see. And that baby girl's holding onto the man just the way a woman should. You see she'll grow to be a woman. You hear the language they speak and it's a foreign one to so many people and you had to learn it yourself once just as the baby did, just as you had to learn to handle your money. Things like that, that silence you, are what other people keep talking through. And you see too much in one image, just like that, one man with his one baby girl perched on a shoulder and you realize there's too much to realize at one time and if you try it your mind explodes into a million bits. You hear me?"

While she was still talking a very tall dark-haired woman in a grey-and-black kilt came out of a small office and nodded at me. "Will you come with me please?"

I stood up and when I did I almost fell backward I was so dizzy. I realized for the first time that I was wearing a pair of light blue rubber sandals, the loud flabby kind that you wear on the beach in the summer, and that other than these sandals I was barefoot. I think they had probably burned my socks. The grey-skinned guy tried to eat the cigarette he was holding but when he realized the tall woman wasn't looking at him he spat wet paper and tobacco out onto his palm. I followed the tall woman into her office and she sat down behind a desk and told me to take a seat. I sat down in a chair opposite her. There was a policeman outside the door.

"How is your head?" the woman said when I was seated.

"What am I doing here?" I said.

"Your head. The wrapping, is it too light for you? Is it cutting off blood? We can loosen it, you know, the bandage, if it's too tight."

I told her it was fine. "What am I doing here?" I said again.

She smiled. "I don't know. You'd probably be the best judge of that, wouldn't you? What do you think you're doing here? In your opinion what do you think you're doing here?"

"I don't know."

"What's your name?"

"Sam Grace."

"The reason I ask is that you had no identification on you. When they brought you in."

"My wallet was stolen," I said. "And my sneakers were stolen."

"Of course they were," she said. "Do you know where you are?"

I nodded. She said, "Where?"

"Pamela's great-great-grandfather's place."

She looked a little concerned when I said that. "No," she said. "No, you're not."

"Like hell I'm not," I said.

"This is Sandstone," she said.

"I know."

She looked up. "Who's Pamela?"

"Pamela Sandstone," I said. "She's this loon friend of my father's."

"More to the point," she said, "more to the point, this is a psychiatric hospital. And we're here to see everybody get better."

"Boy, I'm stoked for that," I said.

"What does that mean? What you just said?"

"Stoked," I said. "Amped. You know, excited. All roused up. I'm an enthusiast that means. That's a California expression. Anyway, that's what I just said. Sandstone."

"No," she said, "you did not, Sam. Or rather what you said was expressed in such an indirect roundabout way as to suggest something else entirely."

"Well, sorry," I said. "I won't do it again. From now on I'll be direct. It'll be boring as hell but I'll do it anyway."

She took this long yellow legal pad out of one of the desk drawers and then she pulled a pencil from a cup. "How is it you know of Pamela Sandstone?" she said, casual as all hell.

I said, "I know Pamela socially." I know that was a pretty snotty thing to say.

"Socially?"

"She went out with my father. Then he dumped her. He was tired of the fact she never ate any meat. I mean, they'd go to these dinner parties and everybody would be eating steak and Pamela would stand in the middle of the room in her dominatrix outfit and say in this incredibly loud voice, 'Are you enjoying the flesh of the helpless dead?' or something like that. I mean, she's the type of girl who should probably have permanent guest quarters here."

I stopped talking all of a sudden because I noticed the woman was looking at me in this incredibly intent, interested way. She wrote something down on the top of her pad.

"Is that your diary?" I said.

She shook her head. She kept her pencil straight and her eyes on the paper. "Why would you think that, Sam? That this is my diary?"

"No reason."

She was silent for a minute. Then she said, "I'm going to ask you some questions, Sam, and I want you to give me the answers as best you can. All right? And if you don't know the answer to a given question don't pretend to know. Just say, I don't know the answer. Is that fair? All right?"

I nodded and she asked me who the president was and I told her. She asked me who the vice-president was and since you don't hear all that much about the vice-president I didn't answer immediately. I had to think back to when the president was campaigning and his name was linked with the vice-president's and I was able to picture an ugly red-and-blue button with both their names on it and then I was able to tell her.

"Who is the author of *As You Like It?*' "

"Shakespeare."

"What is Hadrian's Wall?"

I said, "It's a defense thing. A defense wall. It's between Solway Firth and the start of the Tyne." I don't know how I know things like that. My mind is crowded with useless pieces of information like that. The woman asked me to count backward from a hundred by sevens so I started to do that and I stopped at fifty-eight. I'd been counting backward and thinking of the subway stations in New York which more often than not went by sevens but when I got to fifty-eight my system collapsed. The subway stations were on Fifty-ninth Street. I thought by that point I had made it fairly clear that I could count by sevens but the woman told me to go on until she said stop. When I was at twenty-three she said suddenly, "What does the proverb 'People in glass houses shouldn't throw stones' mean?"

"It's not something I say," I told her.

"Well, even if you don't ever say it what do you think it means?"

"I don't use it," I said. "I just wouldn't. I don't know anybody who says that."

"What do you think it means though?"

"It could mean whatever the hell you wanted it to mean."

"Well," she said, "that's why I'm asking you. I'm interested in your opinion of what it all means. What does it mean to you?"

I said, "I guess in Pamela's case you shouldn't go around telling other people not to wear leather zoot suits. I mean, you shouldn't criticize when you're going to leave yourself open to massive retaliation is my point."

She was writing on her pad again. She turned the page and looked up. "Is that your answer?"

"Is that right?"

"Is it your answer?"

"Well, it's one of them."

"Do you want to add anything to that? Please feel free to go farther with it."

"That's all."

She made another note on her pad.

"Well," I said, "is that right or wrong?"

She looked up. She looked at that moment very kind and very tired. "There's no right answer here and there's no wrong answer here either."

"There has to be."

She shook her head. "I don't think there has to be."

I said, "Well, there has to be. There just does." I could feel myself starting to tense up a little bit. "Isn't there someone you could ask? If you don't know the answer yourself?" I was scared that if I'd given the wrong answer she'd commit me for a hundred years or something. "I mean, don't these things usually have teachers' manuals to go along with them? Who made the thing up in the first place? Couldn't we ask the person who made it up? Didn't whoever it was leave an answer book of some kind around?"

"Don't get excited," she said. "And the answer to your question is no, he didn't. I don't have an answer book."

"Well if there's no answer why the hell did you ask me it?"

"To see what your interpretation would be. That's all."

"But what's the point?"

"Point? No point. There's not a point."

"Well, I'd like to know if I was right," I said. "I don't really think that's a hell of a lot to ask, to find out what your results were."

"I wish I could help," she said.

I said, "We have nothing in common."

She laughed. "That could be true," she said. "That could very well be." She was always saying these tentative, insubstantial things and then smiling like crazy. She closed her pad and put it on the desk. "Now, why don't you give me your version of things?"

I didn't tell her all that much about anything. I guess I was too scared I would incriminate myself in some way. I told her I'd been on Cape Cod for a while but that I'd come back to New York and then I told her about my wallet and my shoes again and how I'd tried to get into my father's apartment. When I told her I'd felt dizzy in the park she looked really interested.

"This dizziness you were feeling," she said, "during it, did you ever hear anything?"

"Like what?"

"Oh, I don't know," and then she made this slow, flirtatious gesture with her pencil. "I don't know. Voices for example. Did you ever hear any voices? During the dizziness?"

I shook my head.

"Directing you to do various things? Carry out certain tasks? They needn't even have been loud voices, they could have been whispers. Or they could have been shouts."

"No."

"Are you positive?"

"You mean like telling me to kill someone or whip them or something?"

Boy, she really brightened up when I said that. That made her the most excited I'd ever seen her. She took her yellow pad back and then she put away her pencil and got out a blue pen and scribbled with it to make sure it wrote. I guess the subject of voices deserved a pen. She was all set to bear down on her pad and she looked so hopeful it killed me to have to tell her no.

She looked confused. "Then why did you use that particular example of what the voices told you to do?"

"There were no voices," I said. "I promise. No voices. I think I would have known if there were voices."

She wasn't going to give up. "That was a very specific example you drew, though. You said whip someone. Earlier you mentioned someone appearing in a dominatrix outfit I think." She paused. "You can see why the two seem to complement each other and suggest something specific."

She was staring at me now. "Okay," I said finally, "I admit it. I really like it when women march all over me in their heels and break my ribs and use the bullwhip on me. I mean, I have lots of orgasms when that happens. I like their heels in my face and I like it when they call me dog or Mr. Nothing."

She ignored me. "Can you tell me what day Veterans Day is?"

I thought for a while. "February."

"February," she repeated. "Early February, late February? In the middle of the month?"

"Late February." I was guessing.

"So Veterans Day occurs in late February, right?"

"Right." Then I said, "I think that's when it is."

"It's November," she said. She wasn't looking at me.

"November," I repeated.

"November eleventh."

"I never got the day off." That was true. At Lane and Briar Hall they never gave you Veterans Day off. There was a ceremony around the flagpole where no one talked but that was the extent of it.

"Well, that's odd," she said. "Most people do."

"I didn't."

"It's curious that you know who wrote *As You Like It* but you don't know what day Veterans Day falls on. Don't you think that's curious? Or not?" She picked up the phone and dialed a number and she told whoever it was she was talking to to come to her office. She hung up. "We'd like to keep you here, Sam, for a couple of days' observation."

"Forget it." I stood up and nearly fell.

"Please stay where you are." She pulled a long sheet of paper out of her drawer and then she stood up and came around to where I was standing. She told me to sign the bottom and I said I wouldn't.

"Sam, all that this piece of paper says is that you are here willingly and that your stay is covered by medical insurance. It's on a purely voluntary basis." She looked at me. "Purely voluntary. Let me stress that. We'd simply like to observe you for a little while in a patient atmosphere and then you leave when you want to leave. Fair enough? You leave when you feel like leaving."

I asked her if I could call my father first and she gestured toward the telephone and said Of course, call your father. I dialed the number and I must have let it ring about thirty times or something. I didn't want to admit to myself Bob wasn't there. I started thinking that if my father wasn't at home I had no place to go and then I thought about what the woman said about how you could check out whenever you wanted to, which made it sound like a hotel of some kind. I didn't have any money or anyplace to go, that's why in the end I signed the thing. I signed once in the middle of the page and once at the bottom and the woman asked me if there was anybody in New York she could contact and I told her no and then in a few minutes a young guy in a white shirt came into the office. He was wearing blue jeans and sneakers and he had a red whistle hanging from a striped shoelace around his neck. The guy was good-looking in kind of an unctuous way. He reminded me a little of all the groovy young interns in nineteen-fifties TV shows, you know, maverick as all hell, who bent the rules of the hospital and broke into song a lot too, singing the beautiful dying girls to sleep with soft jazzy versions of "Stewball" or "Michael, Row the Boat Ashore" or something. I hate those movies and I hated this guy on sight. He introduced himself as Dr. Brian Pace and gave me this incredibly punishing handshake and then he told me to follow him.

When we were in front of the elevators he said, "So how are you doing today, Sam, my man?" you know, all friendly and patronizing but I didn't say anything back. The elevator door opened and we got in and I moved to the back. The walls were brown and there was a mirror up high in one corner that made your face long and curved like a moon. Someone had stuck a green Mountain Dew can behind it. Dr. Pace stared at the doors. We were the only people on the elevator except for a woman with headphones over her ears. I could hear muffled music coming out her ears. She had it cranked up pretty loudly. I couldn't tell who she was listening to but I could hear the heavy bass. I stared at a white elevator certificate posted inside a black frame. It said Do Not Overload. Do Not Leave the Car without Assistance If the Elevator Should Stop More Than Nine Inches from the Landing Floor. I didn't know where they got off calling an elevator a car but they kept referring to it on the certificate as car, car. Hoistway and Car Must Close before Activating. Please Face Car Doors. This Car Holds Nine Hundred Pounds and Six People. Six people into nine hundred pounds divided up exactly, which cheered me up a little. I like it when things, people, numbers, turn out evenly. That meant the Sandstone elevator could hold six people who weighed a hundred and fifty pounds apiece. I tried to imagine the six and I decided they would all have to be pretty thin, joggers probably with the huge staring foreheads and pointed chins marathoners have, all rising to heaven on the Sandstone elevator. I noticed that the guy who had inspected the elevator, car, whatever, was the same guy who inspected the elevators in my father's building. The guy went by his initials and he was Italian: J. P. Thomasino was his name. I can't tell you how good that made me feel, seeing Thomasino's name in a strange place. I sort of pictured an older, kindly, greyish guy, a little bit overweight maybe, who doctored the elevator weight allowance to accommodate heavy guys like himself. On the glass over the certificate, next to Thomasino's name, someone had written Clouseau.

"All out," Dr. Pace said when we reached the fourth floor. "After you, Sam." I got out onto a long hallway. "How are you feeling, Sam?"

I said, "You mean in general?"

He looked at me. His eyes were very blue and damp. Behind us the elevator door rolled shut. "I mean right now, Sam, right this second. Right now, as I'm asking the question."

I looked down at the floor. The carpet was brown and shabby and the walls were drab and the ceilings were high and slightly yellow. The place looked like a college dormitory or something. I made a note to myself that if I ever saw Pamela again to tell her to lay in a new rug, that the old one was just too depressing for words. There were all these gloomy paintings on the walls too, oils of waterwheels and marshes and streams and mountains and rock formations, you know, no people in them. It was all terrifically undistinguished art. You would never in a million years want to have those paintings in your house. I turned to Pace, who was waiting for me to say something. I told him I was getting the hell out of there.

He was blocking the elevator door before I could do anything and then he took my hand. He didn't twist it or anything, he just caught it as it was flying past. "Whoa," he said as though I were his pony or something. He held my knuckles tightly. "Give us a chance here, Sam."

"Stop calling me that," I screamed.

He looked surprised. He dropped my hand. "That's your name, isn't it?"

I kept screaming. "Sure it's my name. Sure it is. But that doesn't mean you have to keep calling me by it after everything you say or in the middle of everything you say. I know who the hell you're talking to and so do you. I mean, I'm the only one around. It's not as though you're talking to some June bug buzzing around my head or anything. It's just so fucking distracting being called by your name all the time. It's all your fake sincerity too. I mean, you're trying to pretend you've internalized me to such an extent my name just comes out of your mouth naturally. You might as well call somebody Tom or Larry or something for all the identification you get when someone is calling you by your name every other minute. Do you understand that, how unreal it is? It's so unreal."

"That's a pretty disturbing metaphor," Pace said when I had finished talking. "The bug, I mean. The June bug." A blond-haired guy in a faded blue polo shirt came over to us. There was a white horse's head insignia stitched over his nipple. I thought of Sarah. "What's up?" he said to Pace.

Pace was looking at me the whole time he was talking. "Kevin, if you would get our friend here out of his street clothes and into some regulation, then bring him around to the nurses' station."

"Sure." The blond guy turned to me. "I'm Kevin. What's your name?"

Everyone there was treating me as though I were four years old. I mumbled something about not having a name. I know that was pretty immature of me but I really didn't feel like dealing with the guy. He looked like the sort of guy who would get cute on you, you know, start calling you "Mr. No Name" or something.

"Well, there's nothing the matter with not having a name," is what Kevin actually said as he led me down the corridor. "You don't have to have a name if you don't want to." We stopped in front of a small room at the end of the hallway and went inside. There was a window on the right. It swung out a couple of inches and I could see white wild flakes coming down, some landing on the sill but burning up immediately since there was an old brown radiator under the window. The tile on the floor was grey-and-black squares. Inside the room was a sink and a shower. The shower didn't have a curtain and the cold water faucet was dripping. The drips fell about five seconds apart and they sounded like thuds. I stood there dumbly. Kevin stared at me. "You probably want to rinse off, don't you? Shower probably make you feel a whole lot better. Make you feel like a whole new person."

I stared back at him. "No thanks."

"Well, sorry to have to tell you my friend, it's the rules here." He leaned into the shower and turned on the hot water. He kept one hand under the spray and with the other hand he twisted the two faucets. "That ought to be the right temp," he said finally. He wiped his hands on his thighs. "Any time you're ready."

"Are you just going to stand there and watch me?" I said.

"Yes." He didn't seem particularly concerned. "Do you want to give me your watch for safekeeping?"

"It's okay," I said. "It's waterproof. You can go under the ocean with this watch." I don't know why I said that. The truth of the matter was that my watch wasn't in the least bit waterproof. I just didn't want him to have it. I turned away from him so I was facing the wall and unclasped my pants and unzipped my zipper and then I pulled my shirt over my head and I was in my scraggly old underwear. I stepped out of it. It looked like a patch of old snow. Kevin didn't take his eyes off me once. All I was wearing was my white bandage and my hair. I got so embarrassed I tried putting my hands in my pockets before I realized my pockets were on the floor. I went into the shower. The soap was small and hard and yellow like hotel soap and I tried to make a lot of lather on myself. A couple of times Kevin looked out the window at the snow falling and at the pattern of the tiles but otherwise he stared at me the whole time. I was under the hot spray and I had my head jerked over to one side so my bandage wouldn't get soaked and I tried keeping my watch away from the water too but once I forgot and when I looked down again at the face there was steam and bubbles under the dial and the minute hand had quit at twenty-three.

When I got out of the shower Kevin pressed a skinny white towel against my chest. I grabbed it from him and told him I could do it myself. He shrugged. "Just trying to be of some use." I wrapped the towel around my middle and Kevin handed me a pair of soft light blue pajamas and watched as I put them on. The bottoms had no back and there was a thick white drawstring around the waist. "Do I have to wear these things?" I said.

"It's for your own good," Kevin said. He walked me down the corridor. He was holding all the clothes I'd come in with, my sweatpants and my Briar Hall sweatshirt and my coat. "We want to make you feel at home here."

"I don't wear pajamas at home," I said. "I hate pajamas."

"Pajamas are great. How can you hate pajamas?"

"My keys are in my coat," I said. I was walking slightly behind him and when he slowed down every few feet so I could catch up I slowed down too. "Don't lose my keys."

"We're going to put everything you came in here with in a special box. For safekeeping. A box with your name on it. That is if you tell us your name. You can get all your stuff in a couple of days."

I told him I wasn't going to be there in a couple of days and he didn't say anything. He led me inside an office and told me to wait there for Dr. Pace. I gave him back the white towel and he shut the door behind him. Alone in the office I started getting pretty sad for some reason. The office had no windows and the radiator had no cap so pure steam was chugging out the hole and it smelled like wet wool. Pace arrived about twenty minutes later and the first thing he made me do was get on this weighing machine. He took my measurements and then he wrapped this black thing around my arm and squeezed it full of air and when he was finished he asked me whether I had ever heard any voices. I told him he was the second person to ask me that already.

"Who was the first?"

"Oh, some voice asked me." Then I said, "That was a joke. I was just kidding."

Pace was sitting on the edge of his desk with his legs

crossed and he didn't laugh. He had a whole bunch of pencils sticking out of his shirt pocket. He asked me to tell him everything I had done in the last two weeks so I had to go over everything again. After I was done he said, "You watched a squirrel drown?"

"Well, yes."

"And what went through your mind as you were watching?"

"Nothing."

"Nothing at all?" He shifted his legs. "The chances of that happening are fairly slight, Sam, don't you think? Didn't you feel at all inclined to intervene in some way? Help out the squirrel?"

"No."

"Call firemen?"

I shook my head.

"Something must have gone through your mind."

"Nothing," I said.

"Did you feel at all sorry for the squirrel?"

"No."

"Were you jealous of the squirrel perhaps?"

"I've always been jealous of the squirrel," I said. "Always."

"Have you ever had pets of your own?"

I said, "Uh-huh."

"Do you still have pets?"

"Dead," I said. "All of them were squished."

Pace put both his feet on the floor. "You're not making this at all easy for me, Sam, you know that? Don't you want to get to the bottom of this at all?" I think he was starting to get pretty pissed off at me because all of a sudden he began asking me all these sex questions. He asked if I ever masturbated and I said no just to see if he would believe me. Then I told him Sometimes and he asked me how often was sometimes and I said I didn't know. He smiled this big fellowship-of-man smile at me then and said that if I didn't know who

316 HIGHLIGHTS OF THE OFF-SEASON

did know? I told him that was an excellent point, very inci-
sive. After that he started asking me a lot of questions about
my mother and I didn't feel like answering any of them. That
line of questioning really clams me up. "You seem unwilling
to answer questions about your family," he said.

"Right."

"Why is that?"

"I don't know."

He made this little gesture with his hand. "How did your
mother, uh, pass away?"

"She was scalded to death."

He nodded. "How did you feel about that?"

"Pretty bummed," I said. "I went to the movies. I saw two
movies in a row. Four and a half hours of movies. Nobody
should die that way."

He said softly, "You know, you're not really addressing the
way you felt."

I didn't say anything for a minute. Then I said, "Okay, she
wasn't scalded to death at all."

"She wasn't. What was she, then?"

"What do you mean what was she."

"How did she pass away?"

"She just died," I said.

"So how did you feel when she died."

I said, "Aren't you even going to say I'm sorry she died?"

Boy, he really leapt on that one. "Do you want me to say
I'm sorry? Do you need my sympathy?"

"Well, not if it's a big deal for you," I said. "Forget I said
anything."

He raised his eyebrows. "Can you tell me the circumstances of your mother's death then, Sam? Give it to me
straight this time too?"

I told him my mother wasn't really dead at all, that I had
been making it all up. I told him everyone thought she had
died but instead she had gone to this retreat in the Virginia
countryside, horse country, country where passenger planes

crashed, and that she was living in a commune-type situation with a bunch of other people who for various reasons wanted the public to think they were dead. I don't know why I told him that, just to see how he'd react, I guess.

"Commune-type situation," he repeated. "Who else is in this retreat?"

"Dean," I said.

"Dean?"

"James Dean. Jimmy. Jimmy's up there. Playing the bongos."

"James Dean the actor?" I nodded. He said, "Who else?"

"Janis is up there. Janis and Elvis. Jimi. A lot of musicians. In fact it's musicians mostly. They're always trying to get my mother to jam with them, you know, she used to play fairly decent stride piano once but she always says no, no. She says if you're not the absolute best at something you should leave it alone, not do it." After I said that I didn't feel like making things up anymore so I tried to get out of my lie in sort of a quiet way. "She's not up there anymore though. She took off. And then after she left she died. Without musicians around her. That was a while ago. No music though."

"I'm sure we'll discuss all this later on," Pace said. He stood up and we went out into the corridor and into a huge smoke-filled room. He told me he would see me later on and he left me there. The room divided up the two wings of the hallway. There were card tables and chairs set up in an incoherent order and an old green Ping-Pong table in one corner next to a large window. A color television was blaring. A lot of people were sitting on an old red sofa smoking cigarettes and watching TV. Everybody looked pretty bored.

I felt pretty embarrassed wearing those pajamas. The back flap kept falling away so I was kind of moving around sideways and backward. I saw Anne sitting in an armchair and she was wearing the exact same kind of pajamas I had on. When she saw me she waved me over. "Come on white boy, you got a beautiful ass, don't be ashamed to flick it around.

Remind people of it." She peered into my face. "The one downstairs, remember him? The cigarette pleader? They turned him down."

"I didn't know they could do that."

"Oh, sure. Sure. All the time. Didn't want what he had particularly, so go away with him. Oh, they reject many wanting emergency houses for the night. Especially in a snow like this snow. This is a famous joint, you know that."

"But he was crazy."

"Oh, sweetie, I doubt it. Probably just had a brouhaha with his girl and wanted to prove her a point. Else she locked the door behind him, told him to go sleep in one of those twenty-four-hour banks. He'd be better off at the Hilton for the night."

One of the nurses came out of the nurses' station then and while she was writing something down on a pad I went over to her and asked if I could use the telephone. The nurse was a small woman with short dark hair. She looked Lebanese. "I'll have to check with Dr. Pace first," she said, "and he's on another floor." I told her it was an emergency and she hesitated and then she said it would be all right provided I didn't take too long. She pointed me to a phone booth. I asked her if I could borrow a quarter and she sighed and disappeared into the nurses' station for a long time and then she came back out with a Styrofoam cup full of dimes and nickels. "Here," she said. "In case you go overlong."

I slid the door of the phone booth shut and a pale yellow bulb came on above my head. The walls had words and drawings on them. Someone had painted white over the words but the ink had soaked through. I dialed my father's apartment and there was no answer so I tried the number out in Southampton. There was no answer there either. I was pretty desperate at that point. I couldn't think where my father could be. I had no inspiration. I tried to think of people he might be staying with but I couldn't think of anybody he knew. I realized I knew practically nothing about his life, where he ate, what he did on the weekends, who his friends were, what he talked about with them. Then I had this idea that my godfather might know where he was. I dialed Massachusetts information and got Louis's number in Cambridge. He picked up the phone on the third ring. "It's Sam," I said.

"Sammy, where the hell you calling from? The continent? Why didn't you reverse the charges? What's it doing over there? We got nine inches of snow up here."

"Do you know where my father is?" I said.

"Do I know where Bob Grace is? No I don't, Sammy. Should I?"

"I don't know." I suddenly felt very depleted.

"Where the hell are you, boy?" Louis sounded a little drunk.

"I'm in some ward somewhere."

"In Britain?"

"New York," I said. "Sandstone."

He was quiet for a while. "Well," he said finally, "place has a damn fine reputation, Sammy, I'll say that much for it. Among my doctor friends that is. For those kinds of places. None of them is precisely Edenic of course." He said it slowly, E-den-ic. "You can't expect luxury. It's dear too, isn't it? Costs you an arm and a leg, that's what I remember. Old friend of your father's and mine, Nicky Whiteside, used to go there every year just about to get his lithium level or some effing thing either raised or lowered, played with, but that was a long time ago, before you were born. I imagine the place has changed a little since then. Hell of a nice guy, Nick Whiteside, once he had all the drugs working inside him. You all alone there?"

"Me and about twenty other people."

"Listen, Sammy, and I'll tell you this only once. Any kid worth his salt is in a place like where you are by his twenty-first birthday. Twenty-one's the cutoff."

Somehow that didn't help my mood any. "But you haven't heard anything from my father recently?"

"Bob Grace you mean?"

I was getting impatient. "Yes."

"Well, you've got me on that particular one, Sammy. You've really stumped me. If this were a riddle of some kind you can just bet the answer would involve some play on the name Grace. I've always envied you and your pa a last name you could have a little play with. Have you tried him out on the island?"

"I tried already."

"How was England by the way? You're back awfully early aren't you?"

"It was just great," I said. I stared at the blue writing struggling to come through the white paint. "I didn't think it was possible to have so much fun and not fall. Not fall down. Stay standing up. The way you're taught."

"Well, that's quite a testament. That crazy old coat of mine manage to keep you warm at all?"

"Very warm," I said. "Warm, warm." I couldn't think of what else to say.

My godfather said, "One thing that concerns me here just slightly, Sam, and I'd be lying if I said it didn't, is how this hospital business might sit with someone like Wheatie Enright over at the college. What I mean is that I understand what this is all about but I'm no officer in admissions, right? I'm just your godfather. You get what I'm trying to say? You have to understand Wheatie's straight as an arrow, family money, the whole route straight through. And he comes out of a place where all this psychiatric analysis therapy business means you can't do it by yourself. Means you've had to go out of the family, engage a total stranger. Not only engage him, Sam, but pay the guy. You have to understand the generation here. Now your generation—"

"I don't think I have one," I said.

"What do you mean you don't have one?"

"A generation," I said. "I don't think I have one. I think I just came in between two others. I don't think I have one of my own."

"Sammy, sure you do. Everybody's got one. You're just not aware of it yet. You never know anything while you're in the middle of it, while you're doing it. Where are all your buddies now?"

I didn't know. I didn't have any idea. We weren't what you'd call a united front. I'd heard a couple of them were in rehabs. Three of them were living together in Hanover, New Hampshire, and making musical instruments, harps and flutes. Four of them had hanged themselves. One of the guys used to be road manager for Lice, this dance band from Hollywood. One of them had died of cancer but no one knew her very well. Most of them were in college, about to finish, about to move to a city and start something else. Half of them would probably get married soon if they hadn't done it already. The math and computer jerks would marry the first girl who slept with them in college. The jocks would start writing poetry and the next time you saw them you'd be shocked. They were all over the place, the Northeast, Texas, Canada. A few of them were studying abroad, always living with older people. There would be an organized reunion at some point but all the best people would stay away. The ones who showed up would have nothing in common except they all knew the words to a couple of TV show theme songs and at the party before the class split again they'd get smashed and sing along. When I hung up with Louis five minutes later I tried to think of someone in my class to call but everybody was strewn all over the place. There was no one to call. I tried calling Lucy out in L.A. but I got her answering service. I told them to have her call me the minute she got in. When I stood up I had cane lines across my ass from the seat of the chair.

That night I sat on the couch with everybody watching situation comedies. They came on one after another. It was a retrospective almost: "Gilligan's Island," "The Addams Family," "I Dream of Jeannie," "The Andy Griffith Show," "Bewitched" with the second Darren, "The Brady Bunch." A tall thin wild-looking girl with bandages on both arms wanted to watch a movie on another channel about some girl who gives birth to quintuplets in a woman's prison but the nurse told her she couldn't, so she was sulking. I kept getting up and going over to the windows and looking out onto the Hudson and onto the highway that stretches all the way up and down the highway and whenever I got up Kevin's eyes would follow me. I could see a lot of bridges but the snow was coming down heavily so their light was indistinct. They looked like chains. I put my hand out through the bars and it took me about two minutes to get it back in. The Hudson's always been a fairly grimy river to look at but when you're trapped indoors it looks pretty brilliant. I could see night joggers in Riverside Park and the black water slowly moving and the snow sinking into it and the reflections of color from the buildings on the other side of the river. Someone was lobbing a flashlight beam down from a balcony and onto the sidewalk. People were walking around the light, staring at it, trying to step on it. You can tell no one knew where it came from.

I stared at the people on the couch. There were a lot of women there on account of men. On the floor beside the TV set a little Chinese kid who must have been about ten was prying apart Ping-Pong balls with his fingernails and when they were open he'd bring the two halves up to his nose and breathe in the trapped gas and say, "Ahhh." After a while Kevin told him to stop and in the same sentence he asked me if I wanted to play crazy eights. I was pretty bored so I told him I would and he came over to the window where I was sitting. The Chinese kid took his place on the couch. He looked pretty dazed. The Brady kids were screaming for some reason, all six of them at the same time. They had lost their dog, I think they were on vacation in Hawaii. The parents seemed to think the dog would turn up or else they could get another. Right before dealing the cards Kevin said in a low voice, "Don't worry, pal, I've seen people come in here in much worse shape than you walk out of here a whole lot better."

"Boy, thanks, Kev," I said. "That's great news. That's great to know. Fuck you. I'm really glad you told me that." We played for about thirty minutes. At one point Kevin said, "Hey" and I looked up from my cards. "We play volleyball tomorrow morning. At eleven. Upstairs in the gym. Recreational therapy. In case nobody's mentioned it to you yet. I'm captain on one of the sides." He put a card down, an eight. He made the suit spades. "You want to play for my side?"

"No." I didn't want to play volleyball, period.

"We're the better team. Cast keeps changing but we still win all the time. Got our own dressing room, our own showers. This time you could watch *me* take a shower." He laughed.

I said, "I'm probably not even going to be here tomorrow."

"Oh, really?"

"Yes." I threw my cards down. I had two eights but I didn't feel I'd been given a good hand, I just felt that someone had shuffled badly.

Kevin yawned. "For your information you're here at least, at least seventy-two hours. That's three days. Three days' worth of me and Dr. Pace and yourself. Anybody under observation is here at least that long. So you play volleyball with us and we'll play volleyball with you. That's just the way it works."

When Lucy called me the next morning the first thing she said was, "Where the hell are you? What number is this? Why are you at a New York area code?"

I told her.

"Sam, then where were you calling me from two nights ago or whenever it was? When you called?"

I told her that too even though I really didn't want to that much.

"You mean you've been on Cape Cod all this time? Does Bob know? Have you told him?"

"I can't find Bob," I said. I felt totally miserable.

"Oh, Jesus," my sister said. "Jesus, and now you're in

some asylum for the stars." She was silent for a minute. "Well, did you at least stay with Aunt Ellis?"

"I was going to," I said. "I was all set to. I was planning to spend the whole winter up there. I really was. I was going to do a lot of handyman work and read a lot. I really was. I called her when I got to Provincetown. That's why I got her address from you."

"And then what?"

"Well, I talked to her," I said. "And she mentioned something about going to see a movie in town. And I'd seen it before."

"You'd seen it. So you left the Cape."

"It was *Dark Passage* and she, Ellis, thought it was *Dark Victory*. And the way she described it, she said Betty Bacall was in it, Lucy, that just drove me up the fucking wall. It drove me crazy. I wanted to wince when she said that. I couldn't stand her, I couldn't stand anything. I mean it's Lauren Bacall or else you don't say it. You don't go saying Betty Bacall. Only her friends call her Betty. I don't know where the hell Aunt Ellis gets off referring to her as Betty as though they're very close friends or something, you know, confidantes. And then she called him Bogie. It was all so pretentious. It's like calling Hemingway Papa. I thought, why doesn't she just quit pretending all three of them are best friends and just rest it?"

My sister bawled me out for about ten minutes. I was sort of half-listening to her. I don't think she was really all that angry but sometimes you can't tell with her. When she was done she asked me how long I thought I was going to be at Sandstone.

"Probably until tomorrow. Until tomorrow afternoon. That's all though. I'm leaving after that." Dr. Pace was walking by when I said that and he came over and stood outside the phone booth. "I wouldn't count on that, Sam."

I put my hand over the receiver. "Count on what?"

"Who are you talking to?" Lucy said.

Dr. Pace said, "Where did you ever get the impression you'd be leaving tomorrow? Certainly not from me."

"It's seventy-two hours," I said. "That's what the woman downstairs told me. I signed myself in. That's all the time you have to be here."

"If we decide you're ready to leave then, yes." He gestured at the receiver. "Who's that?"

"My sister Lucy."

"May I speak to your sister Lucy?"

I handed the phone over. "This is Dr. Brian Pace," he said. "Who is this?"

I could hear my sister's voice very faintly in the background but I couldn't make out what she was saying. Pace said, "Well, I'm very honored. I didn't know there was a connection. This is very exciting." They talked for a while. My sister's voice got louder. At one point Pace gave the name of some medical college or another and he looked embarrassed. "On the contrary it has an excellent academic reputation, it is not, as you say, four years of fucking and water-skiing—" and then I guess she cut him off. After a while he handed the phone back to me and he didn't say anything.

"Listen," Lucy said to me when I got back on. "I'm going to see what I can do from this side of things, okay? Who was that asshole? Don't worry about things. Just stay put and don't worry. Are you going to be at this number? Is this the general hospital number?"

We hung up and Pace, who was still standing there, said, "Your sister seems to be a hugely angry young woman."

"She is," I said. "I think she could do with some counseling."

"You put 'counseling,' the word, in italics. When you said that."

"Italics run in the family," I said. "I can't help it. It's like being born with a set of flippers."

"You're acting very hostile to me right this minute, Sam." We walked in the direction of his office since I had a ten o'clock appointment with him. Inside his office he went behind his desk and sat down and loosened his tie and then he put his hands on the desk. "Why are you so anxious to get out of here, Sam?"

I sat down, not on the chair but on the arm and I didn't say anything.

"So Veterans Day is in February?"

"Who cares when Veterans Day is?" I said.

"What I want to tell you first of all, Sam, is that we want to keep you here a little longer." He was watching my face very closely. "Do you have any feelings about that?"

"Yes."

"Well, can you share some of those feelings with me?"

"I'm sorry, no."

"Why won't you share?"

"Because," I said, "I do not like you."

"Hating your therapist is actually quite normal," Pace said. "You expect it sometimes. Did you know that?"

"Well, this hate I feel for you is definitely not normal," I said. "It's a giant decathlon hate. It has no bounds. It's epic. It's the Dr. Zhivago of hates. I mean, I could trudge across that ice field in the middle of winter just to hate you."

"See, it's when you say things like that that I get worried," he said. "Why can't you just say you hate me? Why can't you share some of this hate with me?"

"I don't like to share."

He took his hands off the desk and joined them and then put them behind his neck. "Why is it you don't like me, Sam?"

"Because you're an asshole," I said.

"Oh." That quieted him. He said, "I know you don't want to stay here, Sam. I frankly expected you to get more angry with me."

"If I got angry with you you'd just tell me I was being hostile."

"You look very unhappy," he said suddenly.

"I'm not."

"But you looked sad, though, a moment ago."

"It's a trick," I said. I pointed out the office door past the TV to the window. "It's a trick of the light. It's all this winter off-season East Coast light, it makes everything sour. It makes the brick look yellow even."

"You look like you want to cry."

I stared at him. "I don't."

"Now you seem angry."

"I am."

"Why?"

"Because you're an asshole," I said. "I told you that."

He didn't seem to hear me. "I think you might be angry for another reason, Sam. Does my asking you whether you're angry make you angry?" He came around behind me and shut the office door. "If you're angry why don't you show me?" He looked kind of amused. "Come on. No one can hear us in here. The walls are solid. Come on, get angry. This is a hospital, Sam. It's not as though someone's going to pick you up and put you away for disturbing the peace. You're already in a hospital and it's one of the best. You have nothing to lose by screaming your head off."

I was staring at him so hard my eyes hurt. He stared back at me. Neither of us said anything for a long time and I could hear wet steam rushing out of the radiator.

*   *   *

After dinner that night Anne intercepted me in the hall-way. "You come along with me," she said and we walked down the hallway until we reached this old Ping-Pong table. Its boards looked greasy and the net was slack. Anne went behind one side and she told me to get on the other side. She picked up the red sandpaper paddle. "Where's a ball? Or did that child inhale them all? Go, there's one under there."

I picked up the ball and served it to her. She hit it back and we rallied for a while in silence. "The reason we're playing this straight-man's game," she said after a while, "is that I want to help you out some."

We rallied for about ten minutes. Then Anne hit the ball into the net and when she came around to the side of the table to get it she didn't return to her side. "You shouldn't be here, Pie," she said at last. "You're taking the place of someone who could be sleeping deep in the bed they made up for you. Someone who could be eating off the place set they laid for you, someone who could take all those baby's tests they're going to make you take. People who belong in camisoles. Can you believe this place sometimes? Everything's so laundered they call a straightjacket a camisole and everyone just nods as though a straightjacket's always been called that all right. They'd call me cocoa or café au lait if I let them do it probably." Anne laughed. "Like a guy downstairs in the waiting room the other day. After you left I was alone with him. You know what he did to get in here? He told he'd lined up all the old stuffed animals from his childhood, put rags in their mouths and then guess what he did? He shot them. Gangland, he said, that was the word he used, like the Mafia. Said it was because there was nothing more to do with them. Your children and your grandchildren like fresh ones of their own and you've grown up, or at least grown taller, you don't want them anymore. You feel bad they're all worn out and sitting in a box. You're just guilty and it's not a good important guilty either. So this man, this gentleman, shot from down, all of them, the pig and the duck and the little bear family, sprayed cotton all over the room, and in my opinion a person like that ought to be up here playing Scrabble with the Jesuses. And any pale rich girl cuts her wrists over a man belongs here too because that's one thing you don't do for a man is cut yourself in his honor." She shrugged. "Downstairs they turned Mr. Stuffed Animals man right around. And you have a New Year's disagreement with a doorman because he's never seen you before and he knocks your mind into a mantel and here you are."

"Do you want to have a game?" I suddenly felt scared. Anne went back over to her end of the table and picked up her paddle.

"The point here is not this game," she said. "The point is loosening you. Otherwise they'll keep you around until it's you showing the new ones the rules. You don't want that. You don't want to be a guide. They'll keep you on until you have no more insurance, that's how it all works out. Then they tell you to relocate. The truth, my baby, is it's people such as yourself they like keeping here the longest. It's not the kill-'em-Jesus-types they keep long anymore. They can stun those people up, dope 'em. With people like you they just have to take your word you'll go out and stay with yourself whatever happens."

"Well, what am I supposed to do?" I said. "I can't go any-place."

"There's places you can go to. Always. Don't let that be your reason. I know places you can go to. Stay as long as you like too, long as you pitch in just a little if they ask you to. If they ask, there's no guarantee of that even. You do your share for people and you got beds all over the place. Hard beds too, nothing that'll turn the spine into potatoes."

She leaned over and served the ball. She had a high-bouncing serve with topspin on it. I hit it back but she wasn't paying attention to the ball. "Now, you signed yourself in, you can go sign yourself out too. I accept you know that. But you got to give them some notice." She picked up the ball behind her and served it again. It went past me and under the bookcase and I ended up moving one end to reach the ball. There were spit-out pills and dust in back of the book-case. I tossed the ball back to Anne.

"But you may know all that notice business takes some time. They don't go out of their way to let you know the right procedures either. They won't give you ink for your pen around here."

"Well, how about you?" I said.

"Third time I've been here," she said. "I tell you that?"
I shook my head.

"Third time. My old man put me here."

"Why?"

"So you see," Anne said, "I can attempt to sign my own
self out and this place is sure to challenge me so they'll deliver me to court. They rush you out of here you see with
their ambulance lights all lit up and people will think, Who's
the dying woman? and it'll just be me in the backseat dreaming up how you make peach-plum jelly or dye a shirt the new
color you want. And see if I lose my trial and they send me up
to a state hospital then my children won't be able to see me
ever. And I'd say I wouldn't want them to see their mother
ended up like that. And if I win and I'm free there's not a
chance I go back to the man who put me in here with his
pencil, there's not a chance. But I got to see my kids. My
older kid gave me a week before all this happened some sad
little pointless called something rhyming like 'From Sad Go
Get Yourself Glad.' She shook her head and rolled the ball
against the table with her palm. "Can you believe that, what
a sweet thing. To be able to push from one to the other, like
that." She looked at me. "This isn't a locked place, Pie. Seven
and eight are the locked places. You don't want to fuck with
people up there even for fun. Not only do they hear the stuff
going on inside their heads but they repeat it out loud.
Fourth floor is for the rich and the foolish and the love-
unlucky and people like me who are here because the fifth
floor was too crowded. So they put me down here with all the
thin wounded girls with their rickety fingers and it's an education for me, being around some of them. Unbelievable to
see the ways in which a beautiful girl can chop herself into
pieces for a boy. You take the steps, white boy, is what you
do. Four flights." Anne didn't have the ball anymore, it was
sitting on the rug. She carved a serve into the air anyway and
it made her sleeves tug against the veins in her wrist.

✳ Chapter 9 ✳

W HEN I got up in the morning I called my father's apartment. I wanted to make sure he wasn't there and when I was sure I went in for breakfast. I had coffee and some kind of orange fruit that was all cut up. At ten o'clock Kevin asked me again if I wanted to play for his volleyball team again the next day. I think I surprised him when I told him I would. I told him I'd be his co-captain. At eleven I had the bandages on my forehead changed and thrown away and the little Lebanese nurse put on a new one. She told me my forehead was looking better. After lunch I saw Dr. Pace outside his office and he told me that the Lebanese nurse had told me she had a cold and that I had replied that there was an agency in Los Angeles that obtained money for your pain and suffering, and that I would try and get the address for her. Those were my exact words, Pace said, and then he asked me just what I meant by those words. When I didn't say anything he told me we would discuss it during my appointment. Before he left he said he wanted to put me on a combination of drugs beginning in three days. At four o'clock I called up the Southampton house and let it ring and ring and then I stuffed my pajamas up the back of my Briar

sweatshirt. I thought the bottoms would be fun to wear sometime. I felt for my father's keys and they were still in the top
left pocket of my coat. At six I ate dinner. It was somebody's
birthday so there was a cake with frosting. I gave my slice to
Anne. I thought it was the least I could do. After dinner
everybody went into the TV room and people started playing
cards and smoking. A couple of kids, this brother-and-sister
team who had tried to kill their parents with chairs, were
playing a word game where you try and see how many words
you can create out of a limited set of letters. Kevin was trying
to organize a Ping-Pong tournament but no one looked all
that interested.

Sometime after eight a whole bunch of people were arguing about what TV show they were going to watch at nine.
Anne was sitting on the windowsill with her legs crossed
drinking tea and I was standing in front of the nurses' station. Anne suddenly threw her tea down onto the rug. It
spilled and the saucer broke and she started screaming. She
had one of the loudest screams I'd ever heard. Even I be-
lieved it. As the tea stain spread she kept screaming. Kevin
stood up and said, "Easy, Annie, easy." I could tell he didn't
know what to do. Everybody in the room looked scared except for the two little murdering kids who went on trying to
see what words came out of the word *solace*. Kevin went over
to the windowsill but before he could reach Anne she fell
forward onto the rug. Her eyes went white and her mouth
started to shake. Three nurses came out of the nurses' station then and one of them tried to turn her over but I guess
she was too heavy so four of them, the three nurses and
Kevin, turned her onto her stomach and when I looked away
Kevin was shooting her with something wet and gold-
colored. Anne's lips fluttered and she stopped moving. I almost didn't move myself, I forgot to. I stared at Anne. She
was lying next to the couch on her back. On TV the kind of
teenagers who are all named Tex were terrorizing Dennis
Weaver on some sand dunes while his family hid in the

camper. Anne's shoulder was over the tea stain and all of a sudden I thought of wrestling rules and what constituted a pin. I didn't think Anne's shoulders were quite touching the floor.

I didn't stay around. I walked very quickly and lightly down the hall. The stairway door was beside the elevator and when I pushed it open I found myself on a grey landing. There was a fire extinguisher on the wall and a thick canvas hose. I took the stairs three at a time and when I got to the ground floor landing I opened the fire door and I was looking out into the hospital lobby. The door to the outside was about thirty feet away and nothing stood in my way except for a small glass office where an old woman sat, checking in guests and doctors. I could hear classical music coming out of the office and I considered crawling along the floor but I was scared someone would see me and I wouldn't be able to get on my feet fast enough. In the end I made a run for it. I ran straight through the lobby and past her office and out the doors and I don't know if she saw me or not and I didn't look behind me. It was pouring rain. I ran past taxis and past the unlit fountains that were filling up with rain water. It was hard running in blue rubber sandals. Sandstone was part of this whole huge medical complex and there were all these tall dark buildings surrounding it and a lawn that was roped off to pedestrians and a bunch of pavilions named for donors and I ran like crazy across the grounds until I was some-where in the vicinity of Eightieth Street. There were large cold puddles on the sidewalk and they looked like puddles of coffee. I waded through them and the shock of four inches of freezing dirty water on my bare feet made me run even faster and I didn't slow down until I had reached Broadway.

On Seventy-sixth Street a play was just letting out for in-termission and a crowd of smokers was standing under the marquee, women, families, single men in long coats. Practi-cally everybody had an umbrella and a cigarette and they were watching the rain beat against the crates stacked up in front of a liquor store. The crates were old boxes that used to hold salt and beer and fruit and they had wax flaps and the wax gleamed in the rain. All these abandoned umbrellas were sticking up out of the cartons and the garbage cans, looking like stars that had crashed to earth and gone dark. Most of them were bent or else slit across the top and some of them had turned completely inside out. I felt sorry as hell for all of them. I don't even like umbrellas all that much to begin with but I can't stand the fact that people abandon them so quickly the minute they don't do what they're supposed to do. I think it's a pretty fickle thing. I tried to break through the crowd of people standing under the marquee but the umbrellas were so thick that at first I couldn't make any progress. There must have been about fifty umbrellas right at eye level blocking my way. It was like a harbor of masts. I saw black umbrellas and white ones and little red ones and striped ones and designer ones and all their ribs were dripping with rain and the spikes shone under the streetlamps.

I pushed past the largest umbrella I'd ever seen in my life, an enormous black one, and the man holding it said something to me but he lifted it anyway and I ducked under. I could see a hundred different-shaped hands in front of me, rings, cigarettes smoked down to nothing or else just begun, fingernail polish, sharp knuckles and round ones. Ahead of me was a pink-and-blue-plaid umbrella and a dull brown one with the name of a television network on it. I pushed between them and a spike from the plain umbrella caught the bandage that was strapped around my forehead and took it off my head. I looked up and the spike had pierced it. It swung off the spike and finally it fell. The dry paste underneath the gauze began dripping into my eyes. I got a cigarette punched out in my cheek, under my eye. Some old woman yelled at me for walking in front of her and someone else offered to sell me his ticket stub so I could see the second half of the show. My forehead started to sting. When I saw an opening between two white umbrellas, tall soft high ones, I bent at the knees slightly and charged through them and at the very last second the white one on my left side dropped, the woman holding it hadn't seen me coming, and the long cold pin tore across my forehead. It split my stitches. I could feel the skin open back up and my face got very hot all of a sudden. The woman looked as though she wanted to put her hand over her mouth but she couldn't since she was holding an umbrella and a cigarette.

In the middle of the street a woman was sitting crouched on a wooden door and cars were veering around its bright glass knob and the woman had a skillet on her head. She was staring across the street at a video of a hot yellow fire in a fireplace through the diamond grate of a closed VCR store. I ran through a long narrow puddle and when I brought my hand down from my forehead I saw it had blood all over it. I held it out in front of me as though it were someone else's hand and I were only a messenger. The rain made my blood light, red drops splashed up in my palm and came back down a different color. I looked at my fingers fascinated. I smelled them. They smelled like dirt and onions. My forehead was screaming but my mouth was locked and I realized I hadn't swallowed in about a year and a half or something. At the entrance to Central Park at Seventy-ninth Street I swam my hand across the surface of a puddle and swallowed, I forget what it finally tasted like. I ran through the underpass. There were cars stalled both ways. Except for the headlights and brakelights it was black in the underpass and there was about a foot of water on the ground. The water came up practically to my knees and there were things floating in it, branches and leaves and whole bushes. I felt like a clammer. Under the bridge, about halfway across the park, the wheels of the cars would lock and the cars would have to back up. The water rose almost as high as the headlights. It was about half a mile over to the East Side and when I finally reached Fifth Avenue my sweatpants were soaked up to my waist and I had stopped running because it made my forehead hurt.

I suddenly got this idea of going down to Katharine Hepburn's place in the East Forties. I wasn't exactly sure where Katharine lived or anything but I thought I could probably ask someone. Someone would know, her florist maybe or the head of the block association. I had this fantasy that I would knock on her door and tell her who I was and ask her to take me in until things calmed down. My steadiness and my New England appearance would impress her and remind her of men she had loved when she was younger and she would say, Sure, come in, what's mine is yours. Katharine Hepburn has always seemed to me the type who would know instinctively how to handle these things, you know, where to get a duplicate key to a Port Authority locker, how to go about finding my father and so forth. Besides, as I think I may have mentioned, Bob knows Katharine Hepburn's sister or her second cousin or something, he had an affair with her or at least he kissed her once on the lips on a boat or a jumbo jet or during some campus mixer, I'm hazy on the specifics but it did happen unless my father is making it all up and why would he have. That was all a pretty long time ago and I was pretty sure Katharine would slam the door in my face and call me a maniac but on the other hand I had a small strong vision that she and I would drag this heavy comfortable couch I know she'd have in her possession out into her garden and we'd sit out there drinking beers and she'd be reminiscing nonstop and then after a while she'd get up and call Port Authority and she'd know exactly who to talk to there. She'd probably turn out to be best friends or something with the man who had all the keys to the lockers. After she made the phone call she would come back out to the garden and say, "Well that's solved. That's one thing out of our way." Then I started thinking that what would probably happen would be that Katharine Hepburn would tell me to get off her street, that her sister or second cousin had never even heard of my father, that it was actually June Allyson's stepsister my father had been mixed up with, and she'd call another ambulance and I'd have to go back to Sandstone.

•

I decided not to bother Katharine Hepburn that night. In retrospect I think that was probably a good decision. I think it was sort of an off-the-wall idea to begin with. I'm not sure why in the end I went back to my father's apartment but it was mainly because there was no other place for me to go. What I did after I reached Fifth Avenue was to walk one block over to Madison so I could work my way back over to my father's building on a cross street. That way if Dario was on duty I could see him from one of the side entrances and run. There was nobody on Madison Avenue. The only place in the neighborhood that was open was this little Korean grocery that we've gone to for as long as I can remember. They have no real food there, just fruit and vegetables and bran muffins so I pulled down about ten baggies and started stuffing them full of random vegetables and fruit. My father has an account there so when I had everything I went up to the counter and charged it all and signed my name. The Korean woman at the register pointed at my forehead and made a sad face. She offered me a handful of cherries, free. "Not in season," she said. "Hard to find." The cherries looked like pink marbles and they didn't taste like much but I thought that was pretty nice of her. She gave me a pile of napkins and then she pointed at my forehead again.

I left the market and walked along Eighty-first Street back toward Fifth. There was a dark green truck parked in front of the building next to my father's and two men in foul-weather gear and black boots were trying to lift a large oak that had fallen out of Central Park across Fifth Avenue. The truck's hazard lights were blinking. From where I was standing I could see the rain dripping off the canopy of my father's building onto the gold railings. The men were trying to get a rope under the tree. Traffic was being routed onto Park. I looked into the lobby of my father's building and I could see a figure sitting on a stool but I couldn't see whether or not it was Dario. My head was bleeding pretty badly by then. It was coming into my eyes and onto my lashes. Whenever I blinked I felt this resistance as though I were blinking underwater,

in slow motion. I heard one of the men say there was substantial limb damage all over the city. A couple of broken
branches were lying on the sidewalk and I picked up the
smaller one and held it in my arms like a doll. It was torn in a
couple of places and you could see the wood inside, which
looked a lot like white chicken meat. I set it on its end to see
if it could be used for a cane but it was too short.

Inside my father's building I was relieved to see that the
tall strange doorman was on duty, the same guy who had
been working the door on New Year's Eve. I think he was
French-Canadian or something. If Dario had been there I
don't know what I would have done. When the guy saw me
he hopped down off his stool. "How are you, my friend?" he
said. "Long time."

He was looking at me pretty strangely. "You're bleeding,"
he said. His voice was incredibly soft. The French aren't bad
for some things, certain pronunciations like "bleeding" for
example sound grim and heartbreaking in a French accent.
"You want a doctor?"

I told him I could bandage it up myself. The doorman nodded but he looked pretty worried. I kept taking napkins out of
my bag and wiping my eyebrows and since I didn't know
what to do with the sticky napkins I held them in my fist
along with my stick. Since the elevator man wasn't anywhere
around the doorman said he'd take me up himself. I stood in
the back of the elevator and he stood to one side and as we
were riding up I looked at the white certificate behind glass
and saw that the elevator had been inspected on the ninth of
January and then I saw J. P. Thomasino's name in blue ink
on the fourth line. That made me relieved. For some reason
seeing Thomasino's name there in my father's elevator was
the most consoling thing in the world.

"What's the date today?" I said to the doorman.

He checked his watch and told me it was the tenth. That
meant Thomasino had come in to inspect the building's elevators the day before. I had missed seeing the guy and his

entourage by only one day, twenty-four hours. "Excuse me,"
I went on, "but were you around here any time yesterday? In
the building I mean?"

"From three o'clock to seven o'clock," he said.

"By any chance you didn't see this guy Thomasino hanging around the building, did you? Inspecting the elevators?
Sort of a heavy-set grey-haired guy, burly kind of? Cliché
Italian-looking man, very powerful hands, missing a thumb
on one of them, holding a blue pen?" I pointed at the signature. I started thinking, whenever Thomasino signs something it means he also approves of it at the same time. It
meant that Thomasino thought things were going all right
these days. He couldn't help it, that was the nature of his job,
approving. Whatever the guy signed he had to approve. He
couldn't not approve of something he signed.

The doorman stared at the certificate as the elevator
opened onto my father's floor and then he looked at me and
shook his head. "Can't even read the name there without my
glasses."

I got out of the elevator. "It's Thomasino," I said. "J. P.
Thomasino, American. I guess you never saw the guy."

"Sorry." The doorman peered at me. "You should go
change your forehead now."

"Yeah," I said. "I know." As the door closed I waved my
stick at him and screamed, "Remember Thomasino's name."
I was pretty disappointed that I had missed Thomasino. In
my mind Thomasino had a stature that none of the people I'd
met anytime recently had. The guy was there for you year
after year, in the heat and the snow, with handwriting that
stayed the same except for a slight progressive slant to the
left. I began thinking that maybe Thomasino had missed
something during his inspection or that he'd spent a restless
night regretting something he'd approved and that he'd be
back in a couple of days to straighten it all out, but I was
pretty much dreaming, I think.

The first thing I did when I got inside my father's apartment was to go from room to room searching for signs of life. The rooms smelled old and hot and brown. I went into the bathroom after a while and stared at myself in the mirror. My forehead looked disastrous. I held my heart and pretended to stumble. I soaked a towel and pressed it against my eyes and my hair. I thought, everytime I come home I'm bleeding for one reason or another. The phone rang in the kitchen and I froze and it rang sixteen more times and then it went dead. It stopped in the middle of the seventeenth ring which meant the next time the phone rang the first ring would be a half-ring, not really a ring at all. I thought, this is what the phone ringing must have sounded like when I was calling here every hour, and this is what the apartment must have looked like when there was no one there. I went into the kitchen where there was a radio and I turned it to one hundred point seven and I heard a couple of commercials and then the dee-jay said it was the end of the Million-Dollar Weekend. He apologized for the rain as though he were the host of the city or something, you know, as though the weather was all his fault. He said that for the next few hours he was going to play only songs associated with bad weather: "Singin' in the Rain," "Rainy Days and Mondays," "I Can't Stand the Rain," "Come Rain or Come Shine" and so forth. I thought that was a fairly bad idea so I turned off the radio and let the water in the sink run for a while. The water was very cold and you knew the water company would take credit for its coldness even though it was the middle of winter and every-thing. I picked up a lemon seed from the floor and examined it. I brought it up under my nose but it was a pretty ancient seed and all the smell had dried off it. I threw it toward the window and it spat against the glass.

I went out into the terrace and looked up and down Fifth Avenue, toward the museums and Harlem and then across the park at the trees and the water and the West Side. I could see the huge red RCA letters sharp in the drizzle and the tall bright silent buildings on Fifty-ninth Street. On the terrace, leaning against one of the railings, I saw this large metal sign that Lucy dragged back from Memphis right after Elvis Presley died. It said Graceland in big gold letters. It was electric, you could plug it in, the letters lit up. My sister took a special trip down to Tennessee to get the thing, not because she was at all crazy for Elvis Presley but because she knew they would be selling a lot of good souvenirs with the word *Grace* in them.

Down the street the men had managed to lift the oak onto the sidewalk, in front of the museum fountains. Its muddy roots stuck up helplessly. There wasn't all that much traffic on the street except for this one yellow Checker cab that was driving slowly down Fifth Avenue. The driver had managed to hit the lights exactly so that whenever he coasted to within six feet of one it turned green and his car rolled on through. Those green lights seemed to be timed exactly to the approach of that Checker cab. I would have loved to be a passenger in that cab, it would have felt like surfing. I stared down at it with awe. I was holding onto my stick and my fist was closed around the break in the wood and I started wondering whether I should put it into a couple of inches of cold water or something. I felt pretty sorry for it. It was already drying off, getting grey, and it looked just terrible, like one of those wet young beautiful rocks you bring back with you from the beach which turn so old in your house. I cradled that stick in my arms for a long, long time. I kept looking down at it and thinking poor stick, poor stupid stick.

* Chapter 10 *

M y father came home about a week later and in all
that time I didn't leave the apartment once, I lay
there eating fruit and vegetables and reading all
these old children's books I found in a carton. It turned out
Bob had been with Susan the druggie at one of the houses
her husband left her down in Nassau, in Lyford Cay, but in
the meantime Lucy had flown in from L.A. and rushed over
to Sandstone and of course I wasn't there. She found me
later on at the apartment and I had to go to Lenox Hill Hospital for a couple of days since my forehead had gotten pretty
infected. I was left with a beautiful little scar over my eyebrows so now I always look concerned about things even if I
couldn't care less about them. When my father walked into
the apartment I was all ready for him. I had the Beatles'
White Album on the record player and the needle poised over
"Honey Pie," which is one of their songs I know he likes a
lot. Bob likes any Beatles' song that's slightly jazzy or that has
good timing in it or that's very British. I thought "Honey Pie"
would palliate him but it didn't. He practically wouldn't
speak to me for about two weeks but then he calmed down
and on Valentine's Day in February I started going to this

prep school in a brownstone on East Seventy-fifth Street that my father had to bribe about fifty people to get me into. It was me and about twelve child actors who didn't want to go to a school where they would be forced to talk to nonperforming types so it was a fairly affected educational experience. I had to come home directly after classes were over, which was a drag, but somehow I got credit and then I went to summer school in New Hampshire and after that I went out to California for a long visit.

Thomasino never showed up. Six months later when the elevators in my father's building were inspected again there was a new guy doing it, someone named Alvarez, Luis Z. Alvarez. Alvarez had the worst handwriting in the world, plus, I don't think the Z stood for anything, I think it was just to give the guy distinction. This girl from Paraguay who I know slightly said that the whole name sounded made-up, that Alvarez in Puerto Rico is like Jones or Williams in English. I wasn't around when it was time for the guy to inspect so I never found out what the real story was. I have a theory that it was Thomasino gone undercover, Thomasino in disguise. If it wasn't Thomasino you have to wonder what happened to the guy, whether it was booze or drugs, did his wife leave him, was he fired or did he retire to Florida or was he just rerouted to the lofts down in Soho and Chelsea or what exactly happened. There are people who know the answers to things like that but you don't know who they are and even if you did you can't get in touch with them, no one's ever shown you how.

About the Author

Peter J. Smith, 27, lives in New York City.
This is his first novel.